# THE GREAT HARPAZO DECEPTION

## *the real story of UFOs*

BY

# STEPHEN M. YULISH

AmErica House
Baltimore

Scripture taken from the New American Standard Bible®
Copyright © THE LOCKMAN FOUNDATION 1960,1962,1968, 1971, 1972, 1973, 1975,1977. Used with permission.

First printing

ISBN: 1-893162-58-3
PUBLISHED BY AMERICA HOUSE BOOK PUBLISHERS
www.publishamerica.com
Baltimore

Printed in the United States of America

*To my three sons Joshua, Avi, and Noah*
*who I now hope will not be deceived.*


*In loving memory of Geneva Labenske and Louis Kaplan who both*
*were a source of great inspiration to me.*

# Acknowledgments

I would like to express my sincere gratitude to a number of people who assisted me in the writing of this book. I am most thankful for my dear wife Paula Dawn who was there right from the beginning. Not only did she offer me constant encouragement and insightful suggestions, but she also was the inspiration for the character of Dawn. To her I am forever grateful as usual. What a blessing she is.

I would also like to thank my close friend Don Garrett for his support, encouragement and most of all for his technical expertise. Being a West Point Grad and a University Engineering Professor, I often came to him for advise on some of my outlandish aerodynamic plot themes only to be set straight. I listened to his wise counsel on most occasions. Chuck and Darla Lassen, James and Ruth McCord, Marge Garrett, Larry Hale, my daughters Andrea and Kendra, Walter, John and Edee were also always there with an encouraging word.

I am grateful to publisher Willem Meiners and Senior Editor Christen Beckmann for having the courage to take a chance on me and publish this provocative book.

First and foremost, however, I am most thankful for a loving, merciful God who gave me the strength and the inspiration to do this book in spite of my battle with Multiple Sclerosis. His amazing grace was sufficient for me. Thank you, Yeshua!

# PART I

*"For our struggle is not against flesh and blood,
but against the rulers, against the powers,
against the world forces of this darkness,
against the spiritual forces of wickedness
in the heavenly places."*
Paul's Epistle to the Ephesians 6:12

*"The battle with UFOs is not for the planet of
man but for the soul of man."*
Trevor James Constable-
Military Aviation Historian

# I

Judah's computer flashed that he had an E-mail. As he opened the mail, he jumped back in astonishment.

*I will instruct you and teach you in the way that you should go. I will counsel you with My eye upon you.*

It was signed *Maskil*.

Judah knew of nobody by that name. He could not find a return email address either and became increasingly agitated. Who was this person that had contacted him? Who was this Maskil? Judah just sat bewildered at his computer and stared at the screen. All around him were the symbols of his prowess. There was the certificate on the wall from West Point as well as the insignia of the Israel Defense Force. There was even a photograph of him with Prime Minister Netanyahu.

Judah had dual citizenship. He was raised in Israel and served in the army, but his mother was American so he maintained an American citizenship as well. While in the IDF he had been in the Special Forces. Work that he had been doing for the Mossad in Syria had been unsuccessful and because of the increasing pressure and scrutiny, he had decided to come to America.

On this night, outside his window, the sky was churning. Huge black, thick clouds boiled in a caldron of seething lightning flashes and deafening thunderclaps. Judah decided to shut off his computer to prevent any short circuiting. He got up and lay down on the bed. It was only midday, but he suddenly felt very sleepy. His mind wandered to the increasing plight of his Israeli friends and family. They lived right on the edge every day of their lives.

As he drifted off to sleep, he found himself in his living room. While he was asleep, or at least it had felt that way, he also felt awake and aware of his surroundings. It was a waking dream state just under the threshold of consciousness yet oddly enough even more aware than a waking state.

All of a sudden it began to rain; yes, rain inside his living room. It did not rain water, but small particles of light. Judah sank to his knees as the light rained upon him. Tears welled up in his eyes and he began to sob. These tears poured out of him from an unknown fountain of deep-seeded emotion. He wailed like a newborn child as he felt the presence of the Ruach Hakodesh *(Hebrew for Holy Spirit-see glossary at end of book)*.

Then in an instant he was awake again. He was still in his bed. He jumped up and ran into the living room. It was of course dry. On his way back to the bedroom,

8

he happened to look into the large hallway mirror. His face was red and there were tears all over his face and shirt.

A loud clap of thunder sounded and the lights went out. He heard a large tree limb crash against his roof. Judah scrambled for a flashlight. He felt a twinge of fear and panic. He reached down for his Uzi pistol, but of course it was not there. Suddenly, he thought that he heard Arabic voices rattling through his head. He looked all around and slouched in a corner with his flashlight. He even considered going back to the bedroom to get his automatic pistol, which he kept on his dresser.

Judah took several long deep breaths. He felt chilled and grabbed an afghan. This feeling of fear permeated him like a cold wet blanket. Intuitively, he knew that something really evil was going on, and he scampered over to the hallway table and found his Bible.

Since graduating from West Point, Judah had worked for several months for the CIA's Remote Viewing program. Initially, he could not get the necessary security clearances. It finally took the insistence of a total stranger, a member of the Senate Select Intelligence Oversight Committee. This Senator had waived his past with the IDF and Mossad for no apparent reason, other than he said that he liked Judah, and thought that he would be an asset to the program. There was much dissension from the intelligence community, but Judah soon earned their cautious respect.

The Remote Viewing program had utilized the efforts and talents of psychics to enhance the military's ability to know what the enemy was doing without ever having to leave the CIA. These persons with telepathic sensibilities could zero in on a specified target without any danger to themselves. It had proved successful enough that Congress had granted them millions of dollars.

"Honey, are you home?" sounded a small, sweet voice from the garage. It was his wife Dawn.

"Yes, I am, I'm in here," he answered.

When he saw his petite, beautiful wife he ran over to her and embraced her tightly.

"What's the matter, Judah? Are you all right?"

"Yes, yes. I think so. I just got the strangest email."

She watched him clutch his Bible tightly. It was only a short time ago that he would have nothing to do with her religious sensitivities. Dawn had been a secretary at the Pentagon when they first met. He was this brash Lieutenant Colonel with the world by the tail, and she was a sweet Christian lady - the antithesis of him.

"Come on, honey, calm down. Relax. You are shivering like a baby," Dawn consoled as she held him tight.

"I knew that this day would come sooner or later," he whispered.

"What day? What are you talking about, Judah?"

"It's nothing. I cannot talk about it."

"Why not?"

"You know, security reasons and all that. It will be all right. I just need a cup of coffee."

Judah and Dawn headed towards the kitchen.

Unexpectedly out of the shadows, a figure scampered in front of them. Dawn screamed and ran her wheelchair into the wall, and it knocked her out the chair and onto the floor. Judah stared at it with the eyes of a man who had seen it before. He reached out to grab it, but it was as elusive as smoke. One minute it was there and the next it was gone. He bent down to pick up his wife, all the while wondering how he was going to explain it to her.

"What was that, Judah? You know, don't you? I saw you staring at it," Dawn stammered as she tried to regain her composure. Her long black hair was flying in all directions, and her steely blue eyes were glazed over.

"It wasn't anything, honey. I think it was just a shadow or something," Judah replied rather unconvincingly.

"Come on, Judah. Level with me. You have been so distant lately. I know something is bothering you. Don't give me that National Security garbage. This is bigger than all of that, isn't it? I feel in my spirit that something is going on with you. I have never seen you clutch your Bible like that, and that was no shadow that I just saw! Trust me!"

Judah helped Dawn back into her chair. She fought him all of the way. She tried so hard to be independent, and she had for the most part succeeded, ever since being stricken with Multiple Sclerosis a year ago. She had tried to maintain herself as she had before. The constant misfiring of her neurons, however, had made that a hit or miss proposition. She kept her job at the Pentagon and even learned how to drive a car without using her legs. Her mind, though, was as sharp as ever, and she knew that Judah was not telling her all that he knew.

"Come on, Judah, level with me. What is going on?" Dawn cried out with a burst of anxiety. "I know it has something to do with your work at the Institute, doesn't it? Ever since you went to work with Dr. Lazant you have not been yourself."

Judah paced the floor. He did not want to have this discussion. Not now and not here. He clutched his Bible ever so tightly.

"Something is happening, Judah. What is it? I have never seen you hold your Bible before, and certainly not like that, for sure. Please, honey talk to me."

Over the past year Judah's life had changed dramatically. He had been a Lieutenant Colonel assigned to the CIA's Department of Remote Viewing. He had worked with psychics who were used to spy on Foreign Nationals. He never before had bought that ESP hocus pocus, but he had been impressed by what he saw that these people could do. In the midst of that, he had fallen in love with Dawn, one of the Pentagon's administrative secretaries. Initially, she had wanted nothing to do with this egotistical, prideful, self-assured, cocky military man. All she had heard about him was that he was brash, sharp as a tack and Jewish. She was a born again Christian. What could they have in common?

Judah stopped pacing and sat down next to Dawn. He placed his arms over her

10

wheels and bowed his head. He began to moan.

"Sweetheart, I am so sorry for the way that I have treated you lately. It is just that I have found myself in the midst of such strange, confusing goings on. Remember when we lost our Congressional funding for the Remote Viewing program late last year, and I went to work for the Lazant Institute? Ever since, all Hell has broken loose. I have not wanted to share it with you because you will probably tell me to get out, and I don't want to hear that. We need the money right now."

"What is going on?" Dawn asked as she reached out to hold his hand. Here was the tough no nonsense man whom she had fallen in love with, despite all warnings. In the midst of their courtship, she had been stricken with this debilitating condition, but Judah had stayed right with her. They were married shortly afterwards in spite of her wheelchair. She would always love him for that.

Judah softly continued, "Dr. Lazant has changed the object of remote viewing techniques. Instead of looking across the world, he has directed the psychics to scan the heavens. He says that they have talked to Jesus and to God. They have also contacted extraterrestrials."

"Oh, my God, Judah," Dawn responded in extreme anguish. "That sounds really malevolent to me."

"I know, honey. In fact he said that Jesus told them that his name was not above all other names, but was just another name. I know that it is a false gospel. They all think that it is so great. He has even added a new member of the staff. A Reverend Shea, who is a member of the Faculty of Harvard Divinity School. Shea believes that there are profound religious implications to this work. Profound, yeah right! It is all so bizarre, but I honestly believe that I need to stay there for the time being."

Judah opened his Bible and read to Dawn, "For our struggle is not against flesh and blood, but against the rulers, against the powers, against the world forces of this darkness, against the spiritual forces of wickedness in the heavenly places."

The two of them just grabbed each other and held on tight. They stayed that way until morning.

The next morning they each got ready for work. Dawn was unable to use her legs, so she was happy to have her husband lift her into the shower. They laughed and joked like only two lovebirds could. They truly loved each other. Each was a blessing to the other. It was hard to believe that Dawn used to be a downhill skier. Now her legs were shriveled and useless. Likewise it was hard to imaging this brash no nonsense military man was down on his knees washing her feet. It was truly a match made in Heaven.

Before they each left for work, they decided to pray. Something very sinister was going on, and they felt that they needed Divine protection. They held hands and quietly bowed their heads. It had only lasted a few minutes but both then felt refreshed and ready to go.

Dawn wheeled into her big blue Chevy Van and prepared to start her engine. She had a sticker across her dashboard that read, *My boss is a Jewish carpenter.* As she started the engine it immediately began steaming profusely, and it blew up, sending the hood nearly through the windshield. She just sat there in shock. Judah had already left. She got out of her car and wheeled over to the nearby walk. She then began to cry hysterically. After a few seemingly endless minutes, she composed herself and began to pray for Judah. She feared that he was in harm's way and needed protection.

Judah screeched up to the tree-lined entrance of the Institute in his MG. It looked so cold with its dull metallic architecture and dim lighting. He did not know what he was going to say to Dr. Lazant and the others about what had happened last night. He was not ready to tell them that something had been in his house. That was going to have to be somewhere down the line.

"Good morning, Colonel Meire," the receptionist said as she buzzed him in through security.

"Hey, Judah, I've been looking for you," a voice sounded from the shadows. It was the new Harvard Divinity Guru Reverend Shea. He was a short man with glasses and a beard. He looked almost comical, as he scampered to and fro with a white lab coat and an Episcopal collar. "We had some very interesting communications last night. The remote viewing protocol seems to be working fine with the heavenly targets. Did you hear that Endora communicated with Jesus? What a fabulous find! We can actually talk with him. I'm so excited!"

Judah knew that Reverend Shea was telling him this because he knew that Judah was Jewish and that it would not affect him as it might some Christians.

"I heard, Reverend Shea. Seems like he said that his name was not above all names, but was just a name."

"Boy, Judah, you remembered that all right. We theologians have been saying for years that Jesus was just a man. It was the Christ consciousness within him that was special. It is what makes all ordinary men like Jesus or Buddha or Lao-tsu or Krishna, avatars, god-centered men. You Jews knew all the time that he was just a nice Jewish boy from Bethlehem whose mother thought that he was god, didn't you?" he laughed as he slapped Judah on the back.

Judah, once again, did not want to tell him about the strange unknown email, or the dream of raining light, or the encounter with the dark entity. Judah felt somewhere down deep that he should not.

"Look, Judah, what Stephen drew from his remote viewing exercises."

Dr. Lazant showed Judah a drawing of a dark angelic like being with wings. Its face was totally black except for two white eyes. It had dark black foreboding wings. Judah could not help but shudder. "What is that?"

"It is the being that he has been communicating with," Dr. Lazant stated with an air of displeasure.

"Did it have a name?" Judah asked, fearing the answer.

"Yes, it called itself AZAZEL."

Judah felt faint and smiled as he ran for the bathroom. Once inside, he splashed cold water on his face but still had to sit down lest he keel over. He remained there for twenty minutes or so. His neatly pressed uniform was disheveled and sweaty. His forehead was covered with large drops of perspiration. Finally he staggered out of the bathroom to his desk. People stared at him, but he explained that he was not feeling very good.

When he turned on his Institute computer and entered his password, he saw that he had an email message. Judah suddenly remembered the email message from yesterday. It had started this emotional rollercoaster.

*Thou art my hiding place; Thou does preserve me from trouble. --Maskil*

Judah became agitated. He put his head down on the desk and closed his eyes. Things were happening over which he had no control, and it was getting to him. The Institute computer was very secure. It was tied in to the CIA, NSA and other intelligence networks. How did this Maskil override the security programs? He needed to tell Dr. Lazant about this, but he just could not make himself do it. He was losing control of the situation and that was something that he never liked to happen. It was antithetical to his military and intelligence training.

This all began eight months ago when he started talking to Dawn. She was so at peace in her life while his was running at full speed in all directions at once. She wanted to pray with him but he would have nothing to do with that. He ran from Christians who had a Bible in one hand and an agenda in the other. Probably just as his ancestors had from Christians who wanted to convert, save, or kill them. Jews knew to be wary of Christians bearing good tidings. You just never knew. Judah's grandparents had perished in the Holocaust. Dawn was such a sweet lady though, and they had even gone to a company skiing get together once, but this religious stuff was out of the question. Judah ran from God but God obviously had a plan for his life. Judah had not found God, God had found Judah. He had fought it all of the way.

Suddenly the phone rang, waking Judah from his stupor. It was Dawn

"Are you all right, Judah?" she questioned emotionally. "The car just blew up on me. I feel that you are not safe either."

Knowing that the phones were monitored, Judah chose his words wisely. "Are you Okay Dawn, what happened?"

"The engine blew up and the hood almost hit the windshield."

"Well that doesn't seem too bad. Call the garage to pick it up." Judah answered matter of factly.

"Not too bad? It could have killed me!"

"Calm down, Dawn."

"Are you all right, Judah?"

"I'm fine, honey. I've got to go now. Bye."

Judah hung the phone up without waiting for her reply. He was too upset to wait. It seemed as though the whole world were coming crashing down around them, and he suddenly felt that this AZAZEL or whatever had something to do with it. The thought of that drawing still sent shivers up his spine. It scared him to the core of his being. He felt intuitively that he was embarking on the battle of his life.

Judah sat at his desk and stared at the floor. He shook his head in disbelief at the course of events. Dawn's safety suddenly grabbed his attention. He got up from his desk and scurried out of the door.

"Dawn's been in an accident," he shouted at the receptionist as he ran past her. "I've got to go home!"

Judah raced his MG around the streets in a reckless abandon and arrived home in a few minutes. He found Dawn in the living room with her head in her hands.

"Judah, oh thank God you've come home," she cried out as she saw him. She threw her strong arms around him.

"What is going on!" she cried out.

"Nothing, honey, it probably was just a coincidence. I'm sure that there is no connection with what happened earlier. What could it possibly be?"

Once again they sat there in each other's arms and held tight. Neither of them knew why, but each felt really scared. There was something going on that was beyond their control and neither of them liked it. Each of them was an independent person who liked to be in control of the situation and each of them felt that control slipping away.

Dawn wheeled into the kitchen and made them some hot chocolate. Judah followed her like some lost puppy. As they sat at the table, they just stared at each other.

"What really happened last night, Judah?" Dawn began very earnestly.

"Nothing much."

"Come on, Judah, STOP! Be straight with me. We are in this together, remember?"

Judah fidgeted around. He gulped his hot chocolate in nearly one swallow and scorched his throat. Gagging, he ran over to the sink to get a drink of water. Judah was very tense. He dropped to the floor and did fifty pushups. He needed to release some tension. When that did not work, he tried fifty situps, but he was still taut as a spring.

"Judah... Judah... Stop it!" Dawn yelled. "Come over here."

Judah ignored her.

"Judah, stop!"

She wheeled over to him and grabbed him. He fought her initially, but finally collapsed in her arms.

"It's all right, sweetheart," she consoled him. "Remember what you read to me yesterday from your Bible?"

He shook his head no.

"You don't? Why did you read it to me then?" Dawn continued, wondering how he knew it in the first place.

14

"It was from the Book of Ephesians, remember? It said that our struggle is not against flesh and blood, but against the rulers, against the powers, against the world forces of this darkness, against the spiritual forces of wickedness in the heavenly places. This struggle, Judah, is not against flesh and blood. The work at the Institute seems to be with these powers of darkness in Heavenly places."

Judah just sat there and listened. His breath was labored and his eyes scanned back and forth across the room.

"There is something that you did not read, though. Wait here a minute. Actually, please get me my Bible."

Judah got up and walked over to the desk and got her Bible.

"Look here, honey. Right before the passage that you read to me it says, *be strong in the Lord and in the strength of His might. Put on the full armor of God that you may be able to stand firm against the schemes of the devil.*"

Judah stood and began pacing the floor again.

"The Lord chose a soldier, Judah, to fight this battle. I think that it is you, Judah. Praise God. We need to pray about it constantly. You need to put on the full armor of God to protect you. Your flesh cannot do it. It says in Second Corinthians 10:4 that *though we walk in the flesh we do not war according to the flesh. For the weapons of our warfare are not of the flesh but divinely powerful for the destruction of fortresses.* That is why you are so tense, Judah!"

"Dawn, you know, yesterday I had a dream. I fell asleep during the day, and I was in the living room and it started to rain. But it rained light particles all over me. I began to cry. What does that mean? I felt closer to the Lord than I ever had before!"

Dawn felt tears welling up in her eyes. She put her head down and began to praise the Lord. Her husband, the Lieutenant Colonel; her husband the brash know it all no nonsense military man had felt the presence of the Holy Spirit. Everything had happened so quickly, so unexpectedly for Judah over the past several months. She had never seen anyone change so much so fast. At first she had thought that he was just faking it to please her, but that soon changed. Things were happening so quickly that even Dawn was unable to explain them. Now everything began to make some sense at last. The Lord had a mission for Judah.

"Judah listen here," she read from her Bible, "*the Lord will come to us like the rain. like the spring rain watering the earth.* God is using you, Judah, to fight this battle against the powers of darkness."

Suddenly a peace came over Judah. It was a peace that surpasses human understanding. He fell to his knees and began to cry. He also began to praise God and thank Him for having confidence in him. Judah had been in many life and death battles during his lifetime, but he felt that this one would supersede all the rest.

Without warning, the house began to shake. It was night by now, and the sky was dark and foreboding. The vibrations knocked the china off of the shelves. There was no sound however as there would be in a tornado or storm. Suddenly a bright light

15

shone in the skylights. It blinded Judah and Dawn. Judah thought that it might be an aircraft, but it was eerily quiet.

"What is it, Judah?"

"I don't know. Stay here, I'm going to check it out."

Judah raced to the back door. It was difficult to open it. The pressure was so great on it. He struggled with it for a while and then broke it down in frustration. When he stepped outside he was further blinded by the light. It was a beam coming from up in the sky, but he could not see from where. He attempted to shield his eyes but it was difficult to do. He heard Dawn scream, and he ran back into the house.

"What happened?"

"I saw that dark creature again," Dawn babbled.

"What dark creature?"

"You know, the one I saw yesterday in the hallway. What do you mean what creature? Come on Judah, level with me. I know that you know more than you are telling me."

Judah raced back outside and raised his fist to the heavens.

"Leave my family alone!"

Nothing happened.

He raced back inside and got his Bible and raced back outside. Holding it to the heavens, he yelled, "I rebuke you in the name of Jesus!"

The light went out and the vibrations stopped.

Judah sank to his knees. He remembered how Endora had told them that Jesus was just a name. Nothing special. He remembered how Dr. Lazant and Reverend Shea had been thrilled by that supposed revelation. Judah now knew for a fact that it was blatantly false. The mere calling out of the name of Jesus had caused the blinding light to disappear. He had tapped into a power source beyond his wildest imagination.

When he went back into the house, Dawn was upside down on the floor with the wheelchair on top of her. Judah raced over to help her. She was unconscious.

After taking the wheelchair off of her, he carried her over to the bed. She had a nasty bruise on her forehead. He went to get the first aid kit. By the time that he returned, she was waking up.

"What happened, Judah?" she moaned, half awake.

"Don't talk, honey. It's all right. You must have fallen out of your wheelchair."

"How could I fall out of my..."

Dawn slipped back into unconsciousness. Judah was concerned and lifted her up and took her into his MG. He decided that a visit to the emergency room was in order, but his car would not start. The van was parked next to him with the blown-out engine. Both of their vehicles were out of commission. He had to call 911. Dawn was slipping away from him. Her pulse was barely present, and her breathing was shallow. Judah began to give her CPR. The ambulance was not coming. Dawn began to turn blue. Judah tried all that he knew to revive her, but it was to no avail.

When all else had failed, he remembered his wife's words to trust in the Lord. He began to pray.

Judah was frantic by the time that the ambulance finally arrived. Dawn was barely breathing.

"Where were you!" he screamed at the woman EMT.

Her partner moved to restrain Judah, who was losing control. That was no easy task. Judah's large muscular frame was no match for the smaller man.

"Take it easy, buddy," the male EMT cautioned. "We cannot take care of the lady if you don't calm down, and I mean right now!"

Judah backed off. They hurriedly worked on Dawn. He could tell that she was slipping away. Finally they loaded her into the ambulance with all the IV's flying. Judah convinced them to let him ride along since his car wouldn't start. He tried to calm himself down through prayer but it was very difficult. Whenever he looked at his wife's face, tears came to his eyes. He put his head in his hands and sought the peace of the Lord.

Dawn was whisked off to intensive care as soon as they reached the hospital. Judah was stopped from going with her. He paced the floors of the hospital for what seemed like hours but in actuality was only a few minutes or so. Finally, a Dr. Levin arrived. He was accompanied by a lady with a clipboard full of papers. Judah knew that she was probably the one who was to see who was financially responsible for all of this. Judah completely ignored her and focused his attention directly upon the Doctor.

"How is she, Doc?" Judah asked expectantly.

"She has sustained a concussion. She is still unconscious at the present time, but we have stabilized her breathing." answered Dr. Levin, a small man with glasses and a shiny almost bald head.

"When will she regain consciousness?"

"It is hard to tell. It could be hours or days. By the way, how did she sustain the injury? She appears to be disabled from the waist down."

"Yeah, Doc, she has Multiple Sclerosis and is wheelchair bound. I don't know how this happened. One minute she was in her wheelchair, the next minute she was on the floor with it on top of her. I know that sounds weird, but it is the truth. I was outside and heard her scream and came back to find her like that."

The Doctor looked askance at Judah. He felt something suspicious might be going on, so when he left Judah he called the police. Judah did not want to bother with the lady, so he gave her his insurance card and shooed her away. She initially refused to leave, but finally did as Judah's eyes became inflamed.

The time that he spent with Dawn was only broken by the persistent questions of the two police detectives.

"Come on, Judah, tell us what the hell is going on would ya! You got into an argument with your wife and flipped over her wheelchair, right?" rattled Holmes, the tall skinny black detective. "We know you are a Special Forces type. High strung and all that. Come on Jude, tell us the truth."

"Watch it Sherlock! My name is Judah. I'm not in the mood for your shenanigans. I did not hurt my wife. Now why would I do that?"

"Okay, you want us to believe that her wheelchair just flipped over by itself? You must think that us cops are really stupid. Not smart like you Rambo types," said the other detective, a middle aged man with a potbelly by the name of O'Malley. "Hey buddy, I once was a Green Beret in Vietnam. Maybe you've got that Post Traumatic Stress Syndrome?"

"Look fellas, I am telling you the truth. I went outside, and when I returned I found her upside down on the floor. I know it sounds crazy, but it is the truth. Maybe she flipped it over on herself somehow. I really don't know."

The two detectives finished taking down Judah's account of the incident and left. They told him that they would be in touch and not to leave town.

"Why would I leave town, you idiots?" Judah shouted. "My wife is here in a coma, and I am not going anywhere."

They could not help but notice that he did seem to care for his wife. They wondered what would drive a loving husband to do such a thing to his crippled wife. It was now up to the DA to decide whether to file formal charges or not. It would probably depend upon the story that his wife would tell when and if she regained consciousness.

Judah remained in the hospital at Dawn's side.

Days went by but there was no change. The doctor visited regularly and repeatedly told Judah that only time would tell. Dawn was breathing as a result of the machines that surrounded her. When the Doctor tried to bring up the subject of at least considering the possibility of having to unplug Dawn from life support, Judah would have no part of it.

"Judah, I know that it is early to be discussing this but you might begin to consider taking her off of life support if this persists. We don't know if she has any brain activity left. The time without oxygen was critical."

"Forget it Doc! She has more brain activity than most people around here. I know she is going to make it. She is a fighter and has survived all adversities against all odds. She even learned to drive a car without using her legs."

"You need to go home, Judah. You need to go back to work and get on with your life. I'll notify you if any change occurs."

"But you don't really expect any, do you Doc?"

"I really do not know, Judah but the longer this goes on the less optimistic I can be."

Judah remained at Dawn's side. It had been nearly a week now, and he had begun to smell. The nurses had brought him food, and he had washed up in the bathroom, but he finally realized that he needed to go home and clean up. He was fearful, however, that once he left that they might pull the life support.

"Look, Betty, I am going home to freshen up. Please keep an eye on Dawn.

18

Don't let anybody pull the plug! Okay?"

Betty was the intensive care nurse who had been there with Judah. She smiled and assured him that everything would be all right.

"Go get some rest and get cleaned up, Judah. This place is beginning to smell," she laughed causing her rotund body to shake.

Just as Judah was saying goodbye to Dawn, the two detectives returned.

"Judah, can we have a word with you?" O'Malley whispered.

"Speaking of lack of brain activity here is frick and frack again," Judah moaned pushing past them. "I'm going home to take a shower. Want to join me?"

The two detectives followed him down the hall.

"Actually guys, would you give me a ride home?"

They did and on the way they began to interrogate him after they rolled the windows down.

"How long has your wife had M.S.?" Holmes interjected.

"How long have you been so ugly?" Judah countered "What difference does that make?"

"Well we thought that you might have become frustrated with your wife when it happened. One could understand that. It must have been difficult."

"Listen, guys, my wife got M.S. before I married her. Haven't you got anything better to do than harass me. Aren't there some criminals out there?"

The three of them went to Judah's home. The detectives asked if they could look around inside.

Judah told them to beat it. He needed to rest and get into the shower. They produced a search warrant. Judah reluctantly let them in. He showed them the hallway where Dawn had the accident. Her wheelchair was still upside down. They prepared to take it back to the lab for testing.

"Now what happened again, Judah," Detective Holmes inquired as he stared at Judah with a funny look on his face.

"Like I told you before, I went outside and when I returned she was upside down."

"Why did you go outside?"

"I heard a noise," Judah answered, knowing full well that he could not tell them the truth.

The detectives walked the route that Judah had described and came to the back door which had been broken down. They stared at the door and at each other.

"What happened here?" O'Malley asked, shaking his head back and forth. "Don't tell me that it broke itself down!"

"The door was stuck, and I got frustrated and kicked it."

"You got frustrated and kicked down a solid oak door, but you want us to believe that you did not become frustrated with your disabled wife and throw her down?" Holmes countered angrily. "You must think that we are really stupid, man."

Holmes and O'Malley conferred privately and took copious notes. O'Malley called the crime lab to send out a team to dust and take pictures of the site. Judah was becoming agitated. He was upset about Dawn and now he had to deal with all these questions which he could not answer honestly. Suddenly, he had an idea that might just work. It just popped into his head.

"Sherlock, come here!" he yelled to Detective Holmes. "There was an intruder in the house last night. In fact, it had happened a few days before also. My wife saw this shadowy figure running down the hall. She screamed, and I chased after it. I thought that it had gone outside, and when I could not open the back door I broke it down. When I got outside, I heard my wife scream so I raced back inside. He must have flipped her over to cover his escape."

"Why didn't you say that before?" Holmes asked, shaking his head in disbelief.

"I work for an Institute that does top secret espionage work. It was probably someone looking for sensitive information. I did not want to bring it up for security reasons, but this has gotten so far out of hand that I need to tell the truth."

The Detectives had Judah sit down and tell the entire story into a small tape recorder. When he had finished, they looked over the rest of the house. They scanned his desk and his computer. It was flashing that there was an email message. They asked if he would retrieve it. Judah was hesitant but finally conceded.

"This could be classified material, gentlemen," Judah said seriously. "Are you sure that you want to see it?"

"What happens if it is?"

"I'll have to kill you!" Judah quipped, trying to keep a straight face.

"Just open it." Holmes yelled.

*Do not be as the horse or as the mule which have no understanding, whose trappings include bit and bridle to hold them in check. Otherwise they will not come near to you. Many are the sorrows of the wicked, but he who trusts in the Lord, lovingkindness shall surround him.   --Maskil*

"What does that mean? Who is Maskil? Are you some religious nut, Judah?" Holmes quipped.

"Leave him alone, Holmes," O'Malley interjected. "Sounds like what the sisters told us at St. Mary's. His religious beliefs are not our business."

"Oh yes, they are when a crime has been committed," Holmes replied sternly. "What is this, Judah!"

"I really don't know. I've gotten several messages from this Maskil, whoever he is, over the past few days. Probably just some internet prankster. He does seem to be talking about you two guys. You know the horse and the mule? Ha!"

Holmes was not amused. This entire affair was becoming more convoluted by the minute. Maybe he needed to call in the FBI. He asked Judah to print out the email messages from Maskil and he took then with him as he finally left. "The lab boys will be here soon," Holmes said as he went out the door. "We'll be in touch. Don't leave town, Judah."

As soon as they left, he jumped into the shower and cleaned up. He did not want to be there when the lab boys arrived. When he tried to start his MG it surprisingly started right up. The only place to go was the Institute. At least there he would have some privacy.

# II

Judah decided to stop at the Athletic Club on the way to the Institute. At least there, he could try and work off some tension. He tried for an hour, but he still felt tense. Sitting at the juice bar sipping some hot Chai, he thought about Dawn. She meant everything in the world to him. He had never thought that he could ever love another woman again, but Dawn's sweet demeanor and loving heart had grabbed him unlike anything that he had ever felt before. Tears came to his eyes and he nearly spilled his Chai. Dawn had loved that Himalayan tea mixture so much that she had gotten Judah to like it as well. He had been a black coffee man all of his life. Finally he got up and left, all the while thinking and praying about Dawn.

On the way to the Institute, he decided at the last minute to veer off to the left and stop in at the military shooting range. He barely said a word to his acquaintances there before pumping three clips of rounds from his Uzi revolver into the target in front of him. All were a millimeter from dead center. Once again, Judah left the range as tense as ever.

On the final approach to the Institute, he pulled off the access and stopped under some beautiful shade trees. He shut the car off and bowed his head.

"Oh Lord, please heal Dawn. I love her so. It breaks my heart to see her lying there unconscious. Please Lord, you are the great physician, the great healer. Bring her back to me," Judah prayed intently.

He felt a peace wash over him. A peace that he did not get from the club or the shooting range. It was a peace that surpasses human understanding. He sighed loudly and smiled.

"And by the way, Lord, please give me the words to say to the people at the Institute," he continued. "I am not sure what is going on, but I know that you will give me discernment."

Judah finally wheeled into the Institute lot and parked his MG. He entered the Institute knowing that he had called them to notify them what had happened to Dawn. There would be no surprises.

"How is Dawn, Judah?" spoke up the receptionist as soon as he walked into the Institute.

"She is stable but still in a coma."

"I'm so sorry to hear that."

"Judah, how are you doing?" piped in Dr. Lazant. "We have really missed you around here. We all hope that Dawn regains consciousness soon. Could you come

22

into my office, Judah?"

Judah followed Dr. Lazant into his office. Judah was a bit perplexed over his rather lackadaisical attitude about Dawn. It seemed as though he was more concerned about Judah. Judah fought the urge to confront him. That was his former style, but he had tried to mellow recently.

When they entered his office, he called in Reverend Shea as well. The three of them sat together around the table.

"Judah, Reverend Shea did some research into the possible identity of the AZAZEL entity," Dr. Lazant began rather quietly.

"What is the AZAZEL entity?" Judah countered, knowing full well what it was.

"Remember the angelic being that Stephen contacted by remote viewing? Here is a sketch of what he saw."

Judah cringed inside, but answered, "Oh yeah, now I remember. It has been a crazy week, sorry."

"That is all right, Judah," Reverend Shea intoned with a smile. "Listen, Judah, I found a reference to this entity in the Apocalypse of Abraham."

"The what?"

"The Apocalypse of Abraham. It is a pseudopigraphal work. Sort of like a midrash, Judah. You know, a fable or myth based upon the Bible."

"If you say so, Reverend!" Judah answered, knowing full well what he was talking about. After all, Judah's late father was a Biblical scholar at Hebrew University.

"It says that AZAZEL scattered over the earth the secrets of heaven and has rebelled against the mighty one."

"Sounds like Satan or Lucifer to me by that definition," Judah laughed nervously.

"Judah, let's please be objective. You seem to have been influenced by your Christian wife. We need you to be unbiased in your perceptions. Am I making myself clear?" Dr. Lazant scolded.

"Sure guys, relax. What is all the fuss?" Judah replied trying to make light of their concerns.

Dr. Lazant and Reverend Shea confided amongst themselves for a few minutes. Judah squirmed around in his seat. All of a sudden, Dr. Lazant spoke up in a serious tone.

"Judah. Did some entity enter your home? It has come to our attention that you told the police that a dark stranger entered your house and frightened Dawn causing her to fall. Is this true?"

Judah did not know what to do. He didn't know if he should tell them the truth or not. How could he tell them the truth, however, when he did not even know what it really was. Better to be evasive at this point," he decided.

"Dawn said that she saw something, but I'm not so sure. Maybe it was a hallucination or something. I told the police that it was an intruder because they

23

want to blame me for the accident. They thought that I threw her down."

"Did you?"

"Of course not!"

"Then what about the broken door?"

"I got frustrated over Dawn's ranting, and I could not open the door so I kicked it in," Judah said with an air of frustration. "Come on , guys, don't you believe me? I am our head of security. You've got to trust me."

"We want to Judah, but this AZAZEL finding might put a new spin on what happened. Maybe Dawn did see something?"

"No foolin?!"

"When Stephen communicated with AZAZEL, it told him that *there are many worlds that intersect your own reality of normal waking consciousness. You may encounter these worlds for brief moments of time while asleep or in altered states of awareness, but then you spend a great deal of time denying either their existence or their validity. Of course, they do not need your acceptance to exist, and they are there no matter what you choose to believe.*"

"That happened the very night of the incident, Judah. Quite a coincidence isn't it?"

"Let me see that drawing again, Doc," Judah asked, trying to stall for time.

When he looked upon that "angelic being" with black wings lifted up and covered with strange symbols, he cringed once again. Its head was black with white eyes and was also covered with strange symbols.

"I don't know, guys. The thing in the house moved too fast."

"Ah ha, Judah. You do admit that something was there after all?" Reverend Shea jumped in.

"I don't know anymore. Things happened so fast. I can't say for sure about anything."

Dr. Lazant called in Stephen and Endora, the principal operatives in the Remote Viewing project. Stephen was a former Doctoral student at Harvard who had heard of the Institute's work at a lecture by Reverend Shea. He had dropped everything including his dissertation research to join the team. He was a short East Indian man sporting a definite professorial look with his sportcoat with elbow patches and his meerschaum pipe. His work on the Taoism of physics was nothing compared to this adventure where he could make use of his other abilities. His strong Hindu and meditative background had enabled him to see things that others could not.

Endora was a middle aged heavy set woman with salt and pepper hair and nearly black eyes. Judah could not look at her straight on for very long without feeling uneasy. Endora had no formal college education, but had worked as a medium and a psychic channeler until running into Dr. Lazant. Her extrasensory abilities had proven to be very significant and replicable.

"Stephen, what do you make of this AZAZEL entity?" Dr. Lazant asked as he stared intently at him.

24

"That is a very interesting question, Dr. Lazant. I feel as though it is far wiser than we are. It seems to know what I am going to ask before I even ask it," Stephen answered with a half-hearted smile.

"Do you think that this entity is extraterrestrial in origin?" Dr. Lazant asked.

"As I told you last week, it told me that there are many worlds that intersect our normal waking reality. It seems to me that it is interdimensional, not extraterrestrial. In fact, just his morning it told me that they are the *Watchers*."

"The Watchers? What does that mean?" Dr. Lazant said looking at Reverend Shea.

Reverend Shea took out his handy Bible pocket computer and punched in the word *Watchers*.

"I don't believe it. The term *Watchers* is found in the Book of Daniel. *As Daniel lay on his bed an angelic watcher, a holy one descended from heaven.* These beings that we have contacted may be angels."

"But then, why did that AZAZEL, rebel against the mighty one as you found, Reverend Shea, in that pseudopigwhatever story?" Judah interjected, realizing too late that it was not what they wanted to hear.

"Judah!... Judah!" Dr. Lazant consoled, "Remember our earlier discussion. Try and be objective, man. Maybe these angels are rebelling against Satan himself. They want to share the secrets of heaven with us against the wishes of the mighty one, Satan. Could be, you know!"

"When I communicated with Jesus," Endora piped in smiling, "he told me that there is a great tribulation coming upon the earth. Many will perish but it will lead to an evolution of the planetary consciousness. The so-called Christians with their narrow minded judgmental bigotry were hampering this development, and they would have to be removed before this change could take place."

"Removed? What are you trying to say, Endora?" Reverend Shea asked curiously.

"I don't know yet, exactly," she answered, "but I will sure ask Jesus next time."

Judah was feeling sick. His insides were churning and his head was pounding. He asked to be excused, telling them that he needed to go and check on Dawn.

"Remember, Judah, stick with the program,"Dr. Lazant remarked as he stood up to show Judah out the door. "We need you to be a part of the team. That is why I hired you. You have an excellent reputation with intelligence gathering, and you are not one of those fanatical Christians. Don't let your wife's dogma hamper your objectivity. And watch your back!"

Judah left all the while trying to digest Dr. Lazant's words. Stick with the program...part of the team...fanatical Christians...watch your back. What was going on here? He knew as he raced his MG out of the parking lot that he had found himself in the midst of a hornet's nest of deception.

Lazant, Shea, and their remote viewing mediums were actually convinced that they were communicating with angels who would tell them the secrets of the universe. Judah felt that these so-called angels were not of God, especially when they talked of removing the Christians. It sounded like what the Nazis said about the Jews. Were they talking of genocide? That is what happened to his grandparents. What was he to do? What could he do?

When he arrived at the hospital, Judah found Dawn the same. He sat next to her bed and cupped his hands in prayer.

"Oh Lord, please heal my precious wife Dawn. Bring her back to me. I need her advice and support in this present situation, Lord. Please, Lord, what am I to do?"

Dawn heard Judah's words. She was concerned about his situation whatever it was, but she could not move or communicate at all. She was aware of Judah's words, but she was trapped in a useless body.

At first she thought that she was just dreaming, but while she was aware of her dreamstate, she could not wake up. Then she thought that she was dead, but that could not be because she knew that she would be with the Lord. Her faith never wavered, not even for a minute. She finally realized that she must be unconscious. The last thing that she remembered was being thrown upside down in her wheelchair by the dark thing. She screamed out to Judah but he could not hear her. She called out to the Lord to ease Judah's grief and to help him with whatever situation that he was facing.

Judah suddenly lifted his head as he thought that he heard Dawn's voice, but she was still out.

All of a sudden there was gunfire all around him. The sound was deafening as the walls were torn apart, and the lights were shattered. Judah dove under the bed and drew his Uzi. He spotted two figures darting into the room, and he emptied his clip into them. They went sprawling over the floor right at his eye level. Judah scampered out from under the bed with his pistol drawn. He quickly put in another clip and ran down the hall. People were screaming and running in all directions. He glanced in several rooms and all he saw was blood and dead bodies. Judah spotted several more dark figures running, and he chased them down the hallway. He cornered them in the stairway and shot them in the back. He remembered his wife and raced back down the hallway. As he entered the room, he saw her laying across the bed all covered in blood. He screamed for a doctor, but it was to no avail. She was already dead. Judah threw himself across her body and screamed. Other soldiers entered the room. they saw him in all his anguish and left him to his grief. Alarms began blaring and emergency personnel began arriving from all directions.

"What happened?" Judah screamed to them.

"It was a terrorist attack by Hamas," one young soldier yelled.

"Oh my God," Judah sobbed. "They have killed my wife and son!"

Judah emptied his revolver into the ceiling, all the while screaming for revenge against the murder of his wife and son. He drew his revolver and pointed it at the two men who just happened to come into the room. Judah had his Uzi up against the man's forehead. The other man attempted to stop him, but Judah pushed him up

26

against the wall also and moved the pistol back and forth between their heads. They saw that he was acting in a stupor.

"What is the matter with you, Col. Meire?" Detective Holmes screamed.

Judah suddenly awoke from his nightmare. He looked around slowly, and then at the Detectives, and then back at Dawn.

"Oh my God, guys, I'm sorry," he blurted out as he put down his gun and ran back to Dawn's side.

"What is going on, guy?" O'Malley asked quietly. "I told you that it was Post Traumatic Stress Syndrome!"

Judah comforted Dawn. He did not really want to talk, but the two Detectives were mighty upset with him.

"Judah, we can bust you for assaulting a police officer. You better talk and talk now, and it better be good, or you will be leaving Dawn for a long time!" Holmes yelled into his ear.

"Ten years ago, I was visiting my wife, Ronit at the hospital in Israel. She was preparing to give birth to our son. The hospital was attacked by a terrorist splinter group of Hamas. My wife and son were killed," Judah spoke in a monotone. "Now are you happy? I don't know what triggered that memory, but I relived it all over again. I guess it was seeing Dawn in a hospital bed."

"Man, you do have that Post Traumatic Syndrome. You are messed up, man. Maybe you did flashback when you flipped Dawn's wheelchair over?" Holmes answered.

Judah jumped up and grabbed him by the collar. O'Malley restrained him the best that he could, but Judah was stronger than both of them.

"Don't ever say that again, Sherlock!" Judah demanded, "Or I'll break your ugly face!"

Judah let go of Detective Holmes' collar and stepped back. He sat down next to Dawn and bowed his head.

"He is really messed up, O'Malley. You were right on with your post traumatic stuff. Do you think that he could have flipped out with his wife?" Holmes queried as he straightened his collar. "This is one tough dude. I wouldn't want to make him too angry."

"It could have happened," O'Malley responded, "But I don't think he would attack his wife... But I am no shrink!"

They just watched Judah quietly as he rubbed his wife's arms and kissed her on the forehead.

"I need you, baby, "Judah whispered. "I need you real bad right now, Dawn. Please, God, make her well."

Judah left the room followed once again by the Detectives.

"Judah! Slow down a minute!" Holmes yelled.

"We found only your fingerprints on the wheelchair," Holmes spoke as he put his hand on Judah's shoulder. "Yours and your wife's, of course."

Judah stared at Holmes but did not respond. As he walked past the floor desk, Betty the I.C. Nurse handed him a folded note.

"Someone left this for you, Col. Meire," Betty spoke quietly as she watched the Detectives hang all over Judah.

Judah opened the note. It read, *As the deer pants for the water brooks, so my soul pants for thee, O God. Why are you in despair, O my soul? And why have you become disturbed within me? Hope in God, for I shall again praise Him for the help of His presence. --Maskil.*

Judah looked all around. He went back and asked the nurse who had left the note, but all she could recall was that it was a young man.

"Let me see that, Judah," O'Malley demanded with a smile. He really did not want to make Judah upset all over again.

When he and Holmes had read it, they both looked at each other, puzzled. They wanted to know who this Maskil character was but Judah was of no help. Holmes crumbled it up and put it into his pocket.

Judah left the hospital, got into his MG, and raced away leaving the detectives standing there without him. After the day's excitement, they were just glad to be out of his sight. He was, they decided, a troubled man just waiting to really explode, and they wanted to be there when it happened. They wondered if these messages were coming from a right wing fanatical extremist organization that Judah might belong to. They decided to share what they knew with the FBI in the hopes of learning more about Judah.

When Judah got home, he jumped in the shower and let the water beat down on him for nearly an hour. He felt so dirty after what had happened at the Institute. He wanted to be away from the people that were there, but he knew that he could not. After showering, Judah walked through the empty house. He went over to the piano and sat down. Across the top was a portrait gallery of the dead. There was a picture of Ronit, and one of Bob and little Caroline. Dawn's first husband and daughter had been killed in an automobile accident. The counseling sessions that they attended had told them to put up these pictures of their loved ones, to never forget them. Judah wondered if Dawn's picture would be next. This caused him great anxiety, and he knocked off all the pictures with a sweep of his powerful forearm. He put his head down and sobbed.

His mind wandered off to the time that he had first met Dawn. She had been a secretary at the Pentagon, and he was working with the Remote Viewing program that was then situated at the CIA. He often found himself at the Pentagon commissary, and he could not help but notice this petite pretty lady. He asked his friends who she was, but they warned him that she was a born again Christian, and that he should stay away from her. Interestingly, Dawn had noticed the tall broad shouldered Lieutenant Colonel with short cropped blond hair and green eyes as well. She also had been informed by friends that he was Jewish and that she should probably stay away from him as well.

28

In spite of these warnings, the two of them felt drawn to each other and often ate lunch together. Dawn used the opportunity to tell Judah about the Lord. Judah listened on one level but was more content to gaze into her beautiful blue eyes.

"Judah, Jesus died for your sins. He is the Jewish Messiah," Dawn would say seriously.

"Sure, he lived at home and his mother thought that he was god," Judah replied with a laugh. "All Jewish mothers think that their sons are god!"

"Judah, be serious!" Dawn countered with an air of frustration. "Haven't you ever read the Bible?"

"Bible, schmible! You Christians often have a Bible in one hand and a gun or noose in the other. My people are very wary of Christians bearing so-called gifts. Remember the Crusades and the Inquisition and the Holocaust?!"

"Judah, those were not real Christians. Real Bible believing Christians love the Jewish people."

"Yeah, right. You could have fooled me. What do we need, a scorecard?" Judah answered with a tone of frustration.

Judah and Dawn met like this for months over lunch. Judah did not really understand why he kept coming back for such abuse. Dawn even invited some of his old friends on occasion like General Desporte. The General had always been more direct and beat up Judah often with his words and challenges.

"Judah, you stiff-necked Jew! Read the Bible! It is the story of your people. You Jews are so secular now that you don't even know the covenants that God made with you. Boy, I get so frustrated with you sometimes, Judah, that I feel like smacking you around a little," General Desporte would say with a Texan drawl.

"Oh that's Christian, General!" Judah would reply with a big smile.

The Christians kept waving the Bible in his face and telling him that God loved him and that they would die for him. Judah would often reply that all he wanted was a little peace.

Finally, Judah said to them that he wanted to see the burning bush like Moses did. If God revealed Himself to him, then he would believe. Judah was convinced that this would cause them to back off at least for a while.

"Do you really mean that, Judah?" asked Dawn, "for if you really do, and only God knows your heart, then He will show you."

"Don't be foolin' around, Jewboy," the General piped in. "Be careful what you pray for, it might come true!"

The Christians were going up to the mountains for a skiing weekend with their families and they invited Judah to go along. While at first he was hesitant, he decided to go to be with Dawn. They had never been together outside of the commissary at the Pentagon. Dawn, he discovered rather quickly, was an excellent skier. He was average and relied too heavily on his brute strength rather than style or finesse.

The group all held hands and prayed once they arrived. Judah closed his eyes and was immediately troubled by what he saw. He was afraid to open his eyes, lest the image disappear. He cocked his head back and forth trying to see what it was. The others had obviously finished praying when he finally opened his eyes.

"What did you see, Judah?" General Desporte asked as he shifted his tall lanky frame back and forth.

"Nothing," Judah replied.

"Yes you did. I saw your head moving!"

"No I did not, General."

"Listen you stiff-necked Jew, tell me right now what you saw or I'll throw you off of this mountain!" the General bellowed as his large brown eyes twinkled.

"Oh, that's Christian, General. I thought that you people are supposed to love all us sinners?"

"What did you see, Judah?" Dawn asked quietly.

"It was nothing. It was stupid," Judah said as he looked rather sheepishly at Dawn.

"Just tell us, please." Dawn replied soothingly.

"I saw a man in a suit of armor waving a sword at a being in a hooded robe with no face. It was just black." Judah slowly spoke, waiting for the laughter.

A gasp went up from the group. They all began whispering to each other. Judah felt very uneasy and vulnerable. He didn't know what he had said, but it was certainly not the reaction that he had feared.

"Someone get me a Bible!" General Desporte yelled and several men went running.

Several minutes later one haggard soldier returned with a frayed King James. The General began reading, "*Be strong in the Lord and in the strength of His might. Put on the full armor of God that you may be able to stand firm against the schemes of the enemy.*

"That is from the Book Of Ephesians. Have you ever read the Book of Ephesians, Judah?" the General questioned firmly.

"No," Judah replied. "Is it a part of the Bible?'

Again a gasp went up from the group, along with a dozen choruses of "Praise God." Dawn reminded Judah that he had stated that he wanted to see the burning bush, and God was answering his request. She told him that Jews often required signs from the Lord to believe especially considering their treatment by so-called Christians throughout history.

"You got that right, Dawn. My people have often been accosted, persecuted, expelled, annihilated by Christians with a Bible in their hand. We probably do need to experience it firsthand. But that was just a coincidence."

This began Judah's direct encounter with the Lord. Things began happening on a regular, almost daily basis. One day Judah was sitting at his desk when he saw an image hovering in front of him. He had blinked his eyes but it remained. It was Jesus on the cross. Not the image that a Jewish person would normally see. His head was down and it was night and lightning raced across the heavens. Suddenly, it was day and Jesus lifted up His head and light beamed from His eyes skyward. He broke the bonds holding Him and got off the cross and walked all over the earth with this light beaming. Judah had immediately known in his heart that Jesus was the Jewish Messiah. He was the light of the world. He had come to earth to die for our sins, and so that we would not perish but have eternal life. It was not an intellectual or head thing, it was a thing of the heart. Judah just knew that he knew. It was like Paul's experience on the road to Damascus. God had chosen him, he had not chosen God.

That evening Judah dreamed that he had to die for all his friends to live. He did not want to be crucified, but he knew that if he did not allow it to happen, then all his friends would perish. Judah could feel the floggings on his back and the nails being driven through his hands. He awoke in a cold sweat looking at his hands. He instantly knew what sacrifice Jesus had made for him, for all of us.

The next morning when he had called General Desporte and Dawn, and told them about his vision and dream, they both had rushed over to his office. Judah had been just staring at the non-existent marks on his hands. They closed the door, and Judah got down on his knees and confessed his sins and asked Jesus Christ into his life as his Lord and Savior. Judah had sobbed as had Dawn and the General.

"Why do I keep looking at my hands?" Judah asked as he stared constantly at them.

"Judah, it says in Galatians 6:17 that *from now on let no one cause trouble for me for I bear on my body the brandmarks of Jesus.* You had a powerful religious experience, Judah. I never had anything like that. You Jews always seem to have a dramatic born again experience," General Desporte said joyfully as he embraced Judah.

Judah awoke from his daydreaming. He remembered that he had told General Desporte not to say anything to anyone about this because he was fearful of losing his job. The General had told him not to be ashamed of Jesus. While he needed to come clean and trust that God would protect him, the General kept quiet.. A couple of months later General Desporte had succumbed to a brain clot on the brain. His secret was safe.

Judah was despondent over the fact that all those persons who were important to him, whom he needed and trusted had been taken from him. First his wife Ronit had been killed by terrorists. Then around five years ago his father Moshe had died of cancer. It was then that his mother Bertha and he had decided to come to America. Judah's escapades in Syria for Mossad had dramatically failed, and they were anxious for him to leave the country as well. General Ben Shlomo had given him a good contact at West Point where he had gone despite the fact that he was too old and needed a special dispensation. His mother was content to return to her roots in Highland Park, Illinois.

After his father's death, Judah needed a positive father figure. His Dad, Moshe, was a Polish freedom fighter during the War and later joined the Hagganah. Only later did he make use of his Doctorate in Biblical Studies from the University of Warsaw. Judah spoke frequently with his Dad about life. He missed the little old man with the Yiddish accent. General Desporte became a sort of father figure for him. He was about the same age, but that is about the only similarity between the two men. Desporte was about six and half feet tall and had a thick Texas drawl. He found himself relying on the General for advice as he had his Dad. After his salvation experience, the General had bought him a Bible and began discipling him everyday on the Word of God. The General had Judah over to his Virginia ranch for barbecue beef ribs many times to discuss the Word. The General also knew the best place inside the beltway to get a good thick, juicy steak.

Now the General was gone and his dear wife Dawn was in a coma. Judah shook his head in anguish. That woman had been through Hell. Shortly before they were to have been married, which was several months after his born again experience, Dawn had begun to experience numbness in her hands and feet. Her balance was off, and she was losing bladder control. When she began to slur her words and lose sight in one eye, she decided to see a Doctor. It could have been a brain tumor.

The doctor set her up for some tests at Bethesda Naval Hospital. The MRI had revealed that she had severe brain lesions. That coupled with the results of the other tests had left no doubt that the diagnosis was Multiple Sclerosis. The prognosis was not good, and she would probably not ever ski again. Within a few short weeks she was unable to walk, and had been in a wheelchair ever since. Judah went ahead with the wedding even though Dawn's physical condition had suddenly and dramatically deteriorated. He truly loved her and wanted to spend the rest of his life with her, even if that meant that she would be in a wheelchair. The only thing that changed was that they were married in the Pastor's study instead of in the Sanctuary

Judah lamented these losses of those so close to him. His mother was way off in Chicago and he had not spoken to her in weeks. He had not told her of his religious experience. She would not understand and would put a real guilt trip on him about how Jews were assimilating into the mainstream American Christian culture without regard for the struggles and deaths of their ancestors who had resisted this move.

She knew that he had wed a Christian woman and that was difficult enough, but to tell her that he too had become a Believer was something that would happen sometime down the road, if ever. His mother was concerned also that he had wed a woman in a wheelchair. She felt that he might of done it because he pitied her or felt sorry for her.

"That was no reason to get married, Judah!" she had cautioned him, but Judah had gone on with it because he loved Dawn, not her body. Theirs was a spiritual relationship from the beginning not a physical relationship.

Judah went to the refrigerator to find something to eat. He found some Humus and Tahini that Dawn had made, but it had mold growing on it. He found some Hebrew National hotdogs which he threw into a pot of boiling water. Along with some dill pickles and some pretzels, he had his first meal in days. That is, if you didn't count the hospital food which was white bread, jello, and meatloaf.

Judah walked over to his computer and flipped it on. There was an email message waiting for him. He gulped down the last half of the hotdog and opened the message.

*The struggle with UFOs is not for the planet of man but for the soul of man.*
*--Maskil*

Judah instantly began to choke on his hotdog and ran to the bathroom for a drink of water.

In the midst of his gulping a glass full of water, the phone rang. It had not rung in what seemed like an eternity.

"Uh, Uh, Heello?" Judah managed to say as he still could not swallow very easily.

"Judah, it is your mother. Are you all right?"

"Sure Ma, I'm fine. I just choked on a hotdog," Judah replied with a chuckle and a cough.

"Hotdog? What kind of dinner is that? Isn't that woman feeding you?"

"Yeah Mom, she is. It is just that she is in the hospital,"Judah said very matter of factly, not wanting to upset his mother.

"In the hospital? What happened?"

"She fell out of her wheelchair and is unconscious."

"Oh my God. Is she going to be all right?"

"I don't know, Ma, it has been over a week already."

"Oy *(Yiddish exclamation)*, tatalleh *(Y.little boy)*. I told you not to marry an invalid," his mother responded as her tone changed. "Maybe God is punishing you for marrying a shiksa *(Y.Gentile woman)*!"

"Ma, I don't want to hear that. That is cruel!"

"Well, your father probably is turning over in his grave over this marriage. He saw his whole family killed by these Christians!" Bertha began her assault on Dawn.

"Ma, stop it!" Judah yelled into the receiver.

"You didn't even invite me to the wedding. Can you imagine at 65 years of age, I am still treated like a stranger. What would have hurt to invite me. It's all right, though, I stayed home by myself. It's all right, I suffered alone. That's the thanks I get for sacrificing all these years for my only son."

"Ma, give up the Jewish guilt trip routine," Judah countered.

"Actually though, I heard that you were married in the Church. No thank you, feh *(Y.yuck!)*! I am too old to accept such things."

"Ma, we held the ceremony in the Pastor's study. I did it for Dawn," Judah replied as he tried not to lose his cool.

"You know, Judah, they are going to get you. Those Christians are going to get you to convert to their religion and their yeshu pandeira *(derogatory name for*

*Jesus)*."

"Ma, stop it. First you attack Dawn and now you slander Christians and Jesus. It is enough already. My poor wife is in a coma in the hospital and you are acting like a jerk!"

"Call your mother a jerk! Oy vey ist mir. Oh woe is me! I never thought that my sweet boy would ever talk to his mother like that," Bertha countered with tears in her voice. "And you are defending that yeshu. Do you know how many Jews have died because of him?"

Judah sat at his desk and stared at the computer screen as he listened to the queen of the Jewish guilt trip. It was 10:30pm. He read once again, *The struggle with UFOS is not for the planet of man but for the soul of man.* What did that mean? He held the phone away from his ear as his mother ranted on and on.

"Do you want me to come out there, tatalleh? I can cook for you while Dawn is in the hospital."

"Why don't you show a little more compassion, Ma, for your daughter in law?" Judah quipped.

"I do care for her, son. She is no Ronit, but I have come to accept her."

"Oh, that is mighty Jewish of you. Geez, Ma, she is my wife for better or worse. Why don't you pray for her recovery. That would be a nice gesture."

"Pray, shmay, Judah," Bertha answered indignantly. "Is that what the Christians have taught you? They have always prayed to their God and then gone out and killed some of us Jews!"

"That's enough, Ma. I've got to go now. I'll be in touch. Love ya, "Judah finished as he put down the receiver in disgust.

He stared at the computer screen and shook his head at his Mom's attitude. Imagine if he did tell her that he had accepted Jesus. She would probably have a heart attack. *The struggle with UFOS is not for the planet of man but for the soul of man.* What did that mean?

Suddenly, Judah saw a large black shadow cast itself over the study as something moved over the skylight and blocked out the full moon. Judah looked up and saw a large saucer shaped object. He raced to the back door. It was still fastened shut with the police tape. He tried to unravel it but it was impossible. Once again he kicked it open . As soon as he got outside, he saw a huge saucer shaped object hovering over his house. It did not make a sound.

As Judah stared at it, a bright beam of light appeared from the bottom of the craft and shot down to the ground right onto him. He felt frozen and unable to move as the beam lifted him up into the sky. He screamed as he moved past his rooftop, but no sound came forth. He looked at the huge approaching craft and noticed flashing lights all underneath it. He marveled at how quiet it was.

His wonder, however, was quickly tempered by abject horror and fear.
Once inside the craft, he found himself on a table. There were small dark entities scurrying all around him. They were hairless with big black eyes. They seemed to

communicate telepathically because he saw no mouth organs. Then out of the shadows appeared a large angelic like being. It was black with wings and small white eyes. It looked at Judah and lifted up its wings to the ceiling and cried out some monstrous call. All the other beings scurried away. Judah recognized this thing as the AZAZEL entity from the Institute's Remote Viewing project. The one that Stephen had been communicating with.

The next instant Judah was bombarded by flaming missiles to his entire body. They pummeled him mercilessly. He tried to scream out in pain but no sounds came forth. He felt himself being consumed by this bombardment of blazing projectiles. Judah thought of Dawn and of his mother. His entire life raced before his eyes as he prepared to meet his Maker.

# III

Judah found himself staring at his hands once again. He remembered what General Desporte had told him about that; 'let no one cause trouble for you, for you bear on your body the brandmarks of Christ!' Judah remembered also the vision that he had at the skiing outing about putting on the full Armor of God that he would be able to stand firm against the schemes of the Enemy. Judah prayed fervently and pleaded the shed blood of Messiah over himself because this struggle was not against flesh and blood but against the rulers, against the world powers of this darkness, against the spiritual forces of wickedness in heavenly places. He felt the presence of the Holy Spirit as he put on the full Armor of God and stood firm against AZAZEL. His loins were girded with Truth, and he put on the Breastplate of Righteousness and shod his feet with the Gospel of peace. As it says in Paul's letter to the Ephesians, Judah took up the Shield of Faith with which he was able to extinguish all the flaming missiles of the evil one, AZAZEL. The Helmet of Salvation was upon his head and the Sword of Truth which is the word of God was in his hand.

AZAZEL jumped back as his flaming missiles bounced off Judah's Shield and the Sword of Truth waved in its face. The bombardment stopped, and Judah found himself back at his desk. Maybe it had only been a dream, a bad dream, a nightmare? When he looked at the clock on the computer it read 2am. He had just looked at it what seemed like only a minute ago and it had read 10:30pm. When Judah went out to look at the back door, he found it broken open again. He stared at his hands and fell to his knees on the lawn and thanked God for His merciful assistance. In spite of Dawn's condition and in spite of his dear mother's nasty attitude, Judah knew that God was in control. He still could not understand why God had chosen a man like him?

Judah remembered a talk that General Desporte had with him a while ago when Judah asked him why God had called him, because Judah knew that he was not worthy. The General had responded that, "You are in good company, Judah! Moses stuttered. David's armor didn't fit. John/Mark was rejected by Paul. Timothy had ulcers. Hosea's wife was a prostitute. Jacob was a liar. David had an affair. Solomon was too rich and practiced witchcraft. Jesus was too poor. Abraham was too old. David was too young. Peter was afraid of death. Lazarus was dead. John was self righteous. Paul was a murderer as was Moses. Jonah ran from God. Gideon and Thomas both doubted. Jeremiah was depressed and suicidal. Elijah was burned out. John the Baptist was a loudmouth. Moses had a short fuse as did Peter and Paul and lots of folks, especially you, Judah."

"What's your point, General?" Judah had asked.

"It means that God's gifts are free and are not based upon our deeds. We have all sinned and fallen short of the Lord. God will use us in spite of who we are, if we put our lives in His hands. God even spoke through a jackass once, Judah."

Judah missed the General, especially during times like this. The General had become such a powerful teacher for Judah. He mentored Judah about the word of God on an almost weekly basis. Then of course there was Dawn. The Lord had definitely put her into his life not only to witness to him but to also give him the love of a Godly woman. Without the General and Dawn, Judah felt alone and insecure.

The next several weeks at the Institute were very interesting to say the least. The minute he had returned he was cornered by Reverend Shea, that strange looking Divinity Professor with the white lab coat, a beard and glasses. He looked like the caricature of a mad scientist.

"Judah, can I talk to you for a minute?" Reverend Shea asked, putting his arm around Judah.

"Sure, Reverend," Judah replied.

When they entered the Reverend's new office, a place that Judah had not seen since furnished, Judah looked at the walls and smiled. He saw a huge mural commemorating John Paul II's gathering at Assisi, Italy in 1986 of 130 leaders of the world's 12 major Religions to pray for peace. Praying together were snake worshipers, fire worshipers, spiritists, animists, North American witch doctors, Buddhists, Muslims, and Hindus. Across the bottom of the large colorful mural was a quote by the Pope that, "We are all praying to the same God." Next to the mural was another smaller picture of the Dalai Lama replacing the Cross on the altar of St. Peters Church in Assisi with the Buddha as Pope John II looked on approvingly. On the opposite wall, Judah found a framed picture of the Louvain Declaration of 1974 which was made at the Second World Conference on Religion and Peace in Louvain, Belgium which was blessed by Pope Paul VI. Judah walked over and read what it said.

"Buddhists, Christians, Confucianists, Hindus, Jains, Jews, Muslims, Shintoists, Sikhs, Zoroastrians and still others, we have sought here to listen to the spirit within our varied and venerable religious traditions... we have grappled with the towering issues that our societies must resolve in order to bring about peace... We rejoice that...the long era of prideful and even prejudiced isolation of the religions of humanity is, we hope, now gone forever."

"Hey Reverend, you have quite a collection here," Judah said facetiously. "But I cannot believe that my people would associated with these idol worshippers!"

"You Jews always say that, Judah. The whole world does not revolve around your people," Reverend Shea countered sarcastically.

37

"God said that we were the chosen people, didn't he?" Judah snapped back.

"Sit down, Judah. You know, I really feel that we are at a crossroads spiritually in the world. I sincerely believe that we have the potential to jump to a new level of spiritual consciousness on the planet, and I know that you are aware of this. I just feel it. You have been put here for a reason, Judah. You are part of the plan for the greatest spiritual renaissance in history."

Judah just sat there and listened to the Reverend's thesis, knowing all to well that it was just idle talk to cover a more sinister undertaking. "But how can you say, Reverend, that this spiritual consciousness raising will involve the removal of the Christians?" Judah spoke quietly, yet forcefully.

"I never said that, Judah," Reverend Shea answered quickly. "It was the Jesus entity that Endora communicated with that said that. I do tend to agree, however, that the narrowmindedness of some Christians is preventing the move for world unity. All of the people that you see here on the walls have shown us that there are many paths to god not just one. We need to celebrate the diversity of religious expression not penalize or judge people because of them."

"Then why do you not have a picture of Rabbis or the Temple or of Jerusalem? The Jews have sought God for thousands of years and have spawned the other two great monotheistic religions, Christianity and Islam." Judah asked again.

"Judah, we embrace all the expressions of world spirituality," Reverend Shea said as he avoided answering the question. "We need to celebrate the Christ consciousness within all great religious leaders whether they be Jesus or Buddha, or Lao-Tzu or Krishna. This god centeredness makes them more than just men-it makes them like gods. We all have the potential to be like them if we let the Christ consciousness enter us as they did. Meditation is a way to open the chakras and let it in."

"My wife says that the representatives of the World Council of Churches and the Vatican do not represent real Christianity?" Judah spoke up, knowing full well what would happen.

"That is the problem, Judah. Some Christians are so narrow minded that they think that everything that speaks of world unity is of Satan," Reverend Shea said shaking his head back and forth. "We are on the threshold of a quantum leap in the potential of our spiritual growth and all these people can say is Satan or Lucifer. Lucifer was the angel of light that brought knowledge to mankind. He is the torch bearer for humanity not some fool with a red suit and a tail and a pitchfork. They just want us all to remain ignorant. There is so much knowledge out there, Judah, that we have access to but we refuse to examine it because it might shake up our beliefs."

Judah decided to keep quiet and let the Reverend speak. It was of no use to argue with him. He felt that he knew the truth and everything else was just ignorance. Of course, Judah knew that what he was saying was plainly against the word of God. His one world religion was spoken of in John's Book of The Revelation as a sign

38

of the end of the age. Judah tried to figure out why he was telling him all of this.

Shortly after this encounter, Dr. Lazant also called Judah into his office. "Judah," he asked very directly, "what do think about our remote viewing findings?"

"What do you mean?"

"You know what I mean, Judah! Don't give me that standard Jewish response of trying to answer a question with a question. What about AZAZEL?"

"I really don't know, Doc. It appears that Stephen has established communication with some entity in the heavens. As to if it is extraterrestrial or interdimensional, I really cannot say. What do you think?" Judah attempted to answer him as objectively as sounded feasible.

"You are doing it again! It doesn't matter what I think, Judah. It matters to me what you think since you are apart of this team. We are all on the same page. At least that I hope that we are, but you have given me reason to question that of late."

"What do you mean, Dr. Lazant?'

"I think that you are not telling me all that you know about this phenomena, about AZAZEL."

"What could I possibly know that you do not know?"

"Well, I think that it has something to do with Dawn's accident. It is awfully coincidental that her accident or whatever it was, happened the same night that Stephen established communication with AZAZEL. According to your Police Report, you said that a dark intruder entered your house and scared Dawn and turned her wheelchair over. The Police Report also said that you broke down your door chasing it."

"Dr. Lazant, did they tell you what I said about it later?" Judah answered as he grasped for a reasonable diversion.

"No, what?"

"I flipped out at the hospital and had a flashback of my first wife and son being killed by terrorists. When they walked into the room, I held a gun to their heads. They called it Post Traumatic Stress Syndrome. They think that is what happened that night with Dawn."

"Are they saying that you might have done that to Dawn?" Dr. Lazant replied. "Maybe you should take some time off, Judah. I wouldn't want you to flip out around here."

Judah shook his head affirmatively. He had shifted Dr. Lazants concerns from AZAZEL to his own safety. He had managed, he thought, to keep his role with AZAZEL a secret.

"Judah, take some time off," Dr. Lazant spoke up. "Oh, by the way, who is Maskil? I see that you have received some email messages from him?"

"I have no idea. I cannot understand how he got access to our secure system at the Institute," Judah answered, seemingly concerned.

"Judah, Stephen also said that AZAZEL mentioned your name?" Dr. Lazant said with a smile on his face.

Judah was glad to be off for a few days. Things had been going so fast lately that he needed some R& R. When he drove up into his driveway, he felt his stomach jump into his throat. His mother was inside washing the windows.

"When did you get here, Ma?" Judah asked as he gave her a big hug.

"Oh, I arrived this morning. I flew all night," she answered. "Good thing I remembered where you hid your house key. Anyway, somebody has to cook for you. Look, you are so thin, Judah."

"Ma!"

"By the way, what is this?" Bertha asked, pointing to the pictures on the piano.

"These are pictures of Dawn's first husband and daughter and of Ronit of course," Judah spoke, waiting for the coming diatribe.

"It is so depressing, Judah. You need to move forward, not dwell on the past. They are dead and gone. You have got to forget about them. Listen, I need to discuss some things with you."

Judah sat down at the table with his Mom. She was a little old Jewish lady with white hair and glasses. His Dad had been only about five and a half feet tall. Why had he grown to over six feet?

"Ma, why I am so tall when you and Abba were so short?" Judah asked nonchalantly.

"That is the great Jewish mystery, "Bertha answered lifting her right hand up. "It must have been those farchadat (*Y.dopey*) Cossacks!"

"Seriously, though, Judah, I am worried about you. You hook up with a shiksa, a Gentile, who is in a wheelchair. She is bad luck. Look, her previous husband and daughter are dead. She cannot be a real wife to you with her condition. You are still a young virile man. What kind of life is this for you? You have needs and desires like all other men, don't you?"

"Ma, stop it," Judah jumped in. "I love Dawn. She is my wife for better or worse. Married life doesn't revolve around sex. You and Abba certainly knew that!"

"Oy, don't talk to your mother like that, "Bertha screamed. "Your father and I had a normal relationship early on but..."

"I really do not want to know . All I know is that you slept in separate bedrooms for as long as I can remember."

"Judah, what does this have to do with you and Dawn. I really wanted grandchildren. There are no more Meires after you. All were killed in the Holocaust by Dawn's Christian ancestors!"

"Ma!"

"Why couldn't you find a another nice Jewish girl like Ronit?"

"That was over 10 years ago, Ma. Talk about letting it go."

"And why did you have to fall in love with a shiksa? You really know to tear a mother's heart!" Bertha lamented as she grabbed a kleenex.

"You don't choose who you fall in love with, Ma."

40

"Jews have been falling in love with Jews for thousands of years. There have always been pretty shiksas around, but Jewish men never married them. There are girls that you have relations with and girls that you marry."

"Well excuse me!"Judah interjected as he got up and got some water.

"By the way, son, two Detectives were here today. One was a shvartzsa *(Y.black man)* and one was an Irishman. They said that they felt that you might have done that to Dawn."

"Ma, he is called an African American. Will you ever enter the modern world?" Judah blasted.

"He said that you might have some stress thing as a result of Ronit's death. You might just fly off the handle for no reason. It's alright, Judah. I could see how living with a paraplegic could cause you such stress," Bertha said as she got up and put her arm around her son.

"Ma, forget it! I did not hurt Dawn, and I am not frustrated living with her!"

"See you are overreacting right now. Why then did you break down the back door, twice?"

Judah stopped talking. His mother and he slipped into a quiet battle of staring. He could not reason with her. Here he was, a 38 year old man, and he was fighting with his mother about his women like he had done twenty years ago except for the fact that his mother had gotten much more rigid in her views. They agreed to disagree about Dawn. Bertha sent Judah to the store and he brought back sacks of groceries as she had requested. That evening they ate brisket and farfel.

"Ma, would you like to go and see Dawn tomorrow?" Judah asked as he gulped his food.

"Don't eat so fast, tatallah, you will get sick. Sure, I would love to meet Dawn in person. Then I can finally put a face with a phone voice," Judah's mother replied. "But I am not going to promise you anything."

The next day they went together to Bethesda Naval Hospital. Judah's mother was impressed by the facilities and the staff.

"You should have been a doctor, Judah."

"Ma!"

They went up to the intensive care wing where Dawn had been for weeks. They met Betty the nurse who had been taking care of Dawn.

"How is she doing, Betty?" Judah asked.

"She is the same, Col. Meire. Still no change," Betty replied with a smile.

They entered Dawn's room and there she was still hooked up to a lot of machines and tubes. Judah went up to her and kissed her on the forehead. His mother stayed her distance as if she were contagious.

"Ma, come over here," Judah pleaded, but she would not budge.

Then Dr. Levin came into the room.

"Hello Doc," Judah perked up. "Well, how is she doing?"

"She is the same, Judah. It has been nearly 5 weeks now, "Dr. Levin answered.

41

"Have you given any more thought to what we talked about?"

"Forget it, Doc! I am not going to unhook her and let her die!" Judah said quietly yet firmly.

"Excuse me, Doctor, but I am Judah's mother from Chicago," Bertha piped in. "What were you talking about?"

"I had just mentioned to your son that he should consider unhooking his wife if this coma persists. She may be only a vegetable in there."

"Vegetable, that's enough, Doc. See you next time," Judah yelled, motioning for him to leave.

"Judah, don't talk like that to the good Doctor. He is only trying to get you to face reality," Bertha scolded. "Doctor, I was thinking the same thing myself. Judah needs to move on with his life."

"Ma!"

"Mrs. Meire, try and talk some sense into your son. He is very hotheaded," Dr. Levin said as he left the room, keeping an eye on Judah all of the time.

Judah spent the next several days with his mother. He took her to the Holocaust Museum in D.C. and to the Smithsonian. She walked arm and arm with her son, and you could tell that she was so proud of him. He wore his military uniform which she had insisted on pressing again. They talked about a lot of things. They finally landed in a small cafe in Georgetown. Judah had ordered some hot Chai and convinced his mother to try it also.

"What is this stuff?" Bertha grimaced as she first tasted it.

"It is Himalayan spiced tea, Ma, " Judah replied as he eagerly sipped it. "Dawn put me on to it."

"You are a different man, Judah. You seem to have changed in many ways. Sometimes, I do not know who you are," Bertha answered with a quizzical look on her face.

"That is for the better, I hope?" Judah laughed.

"Son, I am really concerned about you, "Bertha began quietly. "You seem to be under a lot of pressure. I know that this incident with Dawn has brought back bad memories about what happened to Ronit. Every time you start getting your life back on track, something like this always happens. That is our family's luck. If it weren't for bad luck, we would have no luck at all!"

"Ma, everything is going fine," Judah replied as he patted her on the hand. "I've got a fascinating job at the Institute, and I know that Dawn will recover."

"How can you know that?"

"I have been praying for her, as have lots of her friends."

"What do you know about praying?" Bertha questioned as she shook her head. "You never prayed a day in your life. That is what I mean about you changing. You seem to have adopted your wife's Christian thing. We Jews have given up on praying to a God that has stopped listening to us. Look at what we saw today at the Holocaust Museum. It makes me so angry. This Dawn of yours with all her

42

Christian praying is in a coma. Did her a lot of good, didn't it?"

"Ma, you don't understand!"

"Well then, explain it to me, big shot prayerman!"

"Ma, there is evil in this world. It is a fallen, sinful place," Judah began trying to move slowly. "But God gave us all free will. We can choose either good or evil."

"So what?" Bertha answered, not really listening.

"Ronit was killed by evil people as were Abba's family in the Holocaust. Dawn suffered a bad accident. That does not mean that God is not listening to us. He is there at our side if we really take the time to look for Him. He is not there to prevent the bad things from happening to us but to help us through them."

"Who needs Him then?" Bertha spouted forth as she shook her head.

"We all do, Ma. That is what has gotten me through this ordeal with Dawn. I know God has a purpose in all of it."

"Purpose, schmurpose! Why does this God always have to put our people through the fire for His purpose?"

"Because He loves us, Ma," Judah pleaded. "He wants to bring us back to Him."

"Judah, you sound different than I can ever remember you talking before. You look the same but your words are different," Bertha remarked as she looked deep into her son's eyes. "You seem to be a different person although I know that it is you. I cannot put my finger on it. What is it, Judah?"

"I have learned the love of God, Ma."

"Did you learn it from Dawn?"

"Well Dawn definitely had a part in all of this, but I learned it directly from Him," Judah said with a big smile on his face.

"You did what? She is not into some sort of cult, is she?"

"Oh, no, Ma. She..."

"I don't want to know, Judah. I am too old for these things," Bertha quickly shut off the conversation. She insisted that they order some food at the beautiful Georgetown cafe that they had been sitting at for an hour. When Judah ordered a steak, she felt somewhat assured that not everything had changed. She ordered her usual Chicken Caesar salad.

Judah returned the next day to the hospital to spend it with Dawn. His mother had decided to stay at his house and do some cleaning. She also was preparing his favorite Chicken Paprikash dish which she had not made him in years.

Judah sat at Dawn's bedside. He bowed his head and prayed for her recovery. He honestly felt as though she were all right in there. He never felt any fear or anxiety over her condition which was not normal considering her prognosis. He told Dawn what his mother and he had discussed yesterday. He chuckled as he relayed his mother's reluctance to go too far with the discussion.

Dr. Levin entered the room and saw Judah and turned around.

"No, stop, Doc!" Judah spoke up motioning for him to return.

"I do not want to fight with you, Colonel," Dr. Levin responded.

"No I'll behave, Doc. Come on back in."

When the doctor reluctantly reentered the room, Judah offered him a seat next to the bed.

"Doc, what do you think is going on with Dawn?" Judah asked seriously. "Do you think that she is aware of what we are saying right now?"

"Of course not, Judah. She is in a deep coma. Her brain functions are at a minimum. Only enough to maintain her heart. Even her breathing is done by our machines!" Dr. Levin said very coldly as he scratched his balding head.

"I just cannot believe that, Doc. I know that she is functioning on a higher level than that. She must be."

"Well, there is no scientific basis for that kind of thinking. It is wishful thinking not reality thinking. She is in a deep sleep from which she may never wake up and she knows nothing of what is going on. I am certain of it!"

"Honey, are you aware of what we are talking about?" Judah asked his comatose wife.

Dr. Levin got up and shook his head and prepared to leave. He checked over Dawn's readings on the machines supporting her and started out of the door.

"Doc, Doc, look at this!" Judah yelled.

The Doctor came back into the room and saw that Judah was pointing at Dawn's hand. She had her thumb up.

"Look Doc, she is acknowledging us!" Judah screamed.

"Judah, Judah it is probably just a nerve or muscle spasm. Nothing special," Dr. Levin responded. "You are hallucinating, Judah. Relax. Go home and get some sleep!"

Judah looked down and her thumb was down. Maybe it was just a muscle reaction. He did, however, feel confident that the Lord was not finished with her yet. He continued to pray for her recovery. He really needed her in his battle with AZAZEL as well as with his mother. She was his best friend, his wife, his confidant, his spiritual soulmate. Without her, his life felt so empty. He needed her at his side at this critical juncture in his life. Every time he drank that Chai, he thought of her. It was a sweet, warm soft feeling.

Judah and his mother settled into a routine. Judah would go the Athletic Club and to the Hospital in Bethesda every day and his mother would stay home and clean and cook. This went on for nearly a week. By that time, Judah was anxious for his mother to go back to Highland Park and she was feeling the same. She and Judah had very little in common to talk about anymore.

"Judah, I think that it is best if I return home," Bertha said one night at the dinner table. "I have prepared some meals and put them in the freezer for you. You should be able to manage for a while. If you need me please call me and I'll return."

"What is the rush, Ma?" Judah replied, not really meaning what he said. He loved his mother , but she was very difficult to live with for any length of time. She still treated him like her little boy, her tatalleh.

44

"You don't need me, tatalleh. You are a grown man now, and I am just a burden to you."

"No you are not, Ma."

Suddenly the phone rang. Judah jumped up to answer to it. His faced beamed as he listened to the voice on the other end of the line.

"Ma, it was the hospital!" Judah shouted. "Dawn has begun to breathe on her own and they have taken her off of life support."

"That is good, Judah. Promise me though, son, that you will not put her back on life support again. Let her sink or swim on her own. Promise?" Bertha asked, as she held her son.

"Ma!"

Judah raced out to the hospital. His mother did not want to go. His heart raced as he thought that Dawn might be coming back to him. When he arrived at the hospital, he was greeted by Dr. Levin who was at Dawn's bedside.

"See, Doc, I told you that she was coming back to me!" Judah said happily.

"Judah, this does not mean anything," Dr. Levin burst in to break Judah's bubble. "She is still comatose. While her body has decided to resume some autonomic functions, it does not mean that she will necessarily recover. I want you to sign a release that you do not want her put back on life support if she regresses. That will put a definite line in the sand for all of us to go by."

"Forget it, Dr. Kevorkian!" Judah responded angrily. "I will not sign my wife's death warrant!"

Judah sat there at Dawn's side. Without all the tubes she looked almost normal as her chest moved up and down naturally. Dr. Levin left the room. Judah held Dawn's hand and prayed for her. He thanked the Lord for what only He could have done.

"Thank you, Lord, for enabling Dawn to breathe on her own," Judah said with tears in his eyes. "Please, Lord, bring her back to me. I need her so desperately now."

As Judah sped home to Potomac, the sky was dark and lightning flashed all around. Thunder bellowed from unseen cannons in the sky. The road became a mass of hailstones and his car swerved from side to side. He had to slow down to a crawl. He put on his lights and pulled off the road. After a few harrowing minutes, he could move again although it had to be very cautiously.

When he neared his beautiful Tudor-style home, he groaned in terror. Above his house in the midst of the black thunderclouds was a huge saucer. From its base emanated a narrow beam of light. Judah raced into the driveway just as he saw his mother being taken up in the beam. He struggled to get out of his seatbelt, but it became all tangled. His mother was now above the roofline and all the while was in an apparent trance. She looked almost asleep.

As he finally cut the seatbelt with his pocketknife, Judah sprang from the car. He raced up to the beam but it had already deposited his mother inside the ship Judah

45

jumped up, but the beam was out of his grasp. He could not reach it. He lay on the ground amidst the hailstones and the pelting rain and yelled out in extreme anguish.

"Bring my mother back, you beings from the pits of hell," Judah screamed shaking his fist at the heavens. "She has done nothing to you. Leave her alone. I am who you want!"

Judah then emptied his revolver into the hovering craft but nothing happened. The craft suddenly disappeared from the Maryland sky with his mother on board. Judah scrambled all around to try and figure out what he should do. He could not call the police . He could not go after them. What could he do? He thought of calling the Institute and speaking with Stephen. Maybe he could put him in touch with AZAZEL. He tried but everyone had gone home. He went over to his computer and saw that there was another message. Nervously, he called it up.

*God is our refuge and strength. A very present help in trouble. Therefore we will not fear, though the earth should change and though the mountains slip into the heart of the sea. The Lord of Hosts is with us. The God of Jacob is our stronghold --Maskil*

Judah shut off the computer and got onto his knees. Who was this Maskil? He seemed to know everything that was happening to Judah. He had access to his home as well as his office computer. That was highly unusual because both were on rigid security access. Without the proper passwords, it was next to impossible to access them. Who had that kind of access?

Judah asked God for strength. He put on the full armor of God, as he was bathed once again in the rain of righteousness. He prepared himself to meet the enemy once again on his turf to save his mother, but he needed to be prayed up or else AZAZEL would devour him with flaming missiles. He also needed to bathe himself in the shed blood of Christ to ward off all the wiles of the great deceiver.

He did not know if he could save his mother. She was not a Believer and thus was open to the attacks of the Prince of the air as was everyone, but she did not have the weapons of the Holy Spirit to defend herself.

Judah pleaded with the Lord to let him rescue his mother. She was old and frail. He did not know how much of this that she could take. He could only imagine her waking up in a strange craft and being interrogated by those hideous creatures of the night. It was almost morning now but Bertha had not returned. He knew that AZAZEL was doing this to get at him. First Dawn and now his mother. They would stop at nothing to continue to pursue their ends.

Suddenly, Bertha's body fell right through the skylight without breaking it onto the floor in front of Judah. He screamed and ran up to her lifeless body.

# IV

Bertha was barely breathing. There was a look of absolute fright on her face that scared even Judah. Her eyes were wide open as was her mouth. Her pupils were fully dilated. Her hair stood out like she had put her finger in the light socket. Judah gave her CPR, but she barely responded. He did not want to leave her, but finally had to go and call the paramedics. As he dialed, he abruptly thought of their probable reaction. Here was another family member of his unconscious without any apparent cause.

When they arrived, the EMTs quickly loaded his mother into the ambulance. Ironically, it was the same team as before with Dawn. They gave him strange looks.

"What happened to her?" one of them asked, shaking his head.

"I don't know," Judah answered. "I heard a noise and came out and found her this way. What could have happened to her? Look at her face. It looks like she saw a ghost."

"I don't know for sure, but it looks as if she is in shock. Something or someone scared her real bad," answered the other attendant as she stared right through Judah.

Bertha was transported to Bethesda Naval Hospital as was Dawn. In fact, they put her into the same room as Dawn. Judah spent the rest of the night with the two beloved women in his life. When he woke up the next morning, he was greeted by Detectives Holmes and O'Malley.

"What happened this time, big guy?" Detective Holmes asked with a scowl on his face.

"I don't know. I really do not know," Judah replied with his head in his hands.

"Did you go into another flashback and freak out and scare your mother half to death?" O'Malley piped in. "This is becoming all too predictable, Colonel. Why don't you just come clean, and we will try and get you some help. That Post Traumatic Stress Syndrome is a bummer. You need professional help, partner."

"I did not do anything, honest," Judah said, gritting his teeth.

"Oh I guess your mother just scared herself, right?" O'Malley replied with a laugh.

"Don't tell me that it was that mysterious intruder again," Holmes sarcastically quipped.

"Well, actually..." Judah began.

"Don't give me that trash, man! You are a strange dude. I checked the FBI and Military files on you and found zero, zilch, nada," Detective Holmes said as he stood an inch before Judah's face and looked him up and down. "Are you one of those black bag boys? Maybe you work for the NSA. I heard that they are some bad dudes. I cannot figure you out. Your files are too clean. They are as white as you are!"

"What did want them to be, as black as you are!" Judah snapped back at Holmes.

"That's not funny, man!" Holmes reacted as he threw down his hat.

"Who's laughing?"

"Colonel, you cannot really believe that your mother scared herself?" Detective O'Malley entered the fray and separated the two men. "And you cannot really believe that we will buy that nonsense. It is just too coincidental that both your wife and now your mother has been rendered unconscious by some unknown intruder."

"I don't care what you believe," Judah replied as he jumped up. "Either indict me or get out of my hair. I have important work to do. Let me just tell you that all of this is a matter of National Security. If I were you, I'd stay out of this. I'm warning you. I cannot vouch for your safety."

Judah walked right past the two detectives. He decided that things were beginning to unfold and he needed to keep abreast of them. Frick and frack could do what they needed to do, but he could not waste his time any longer with them. He got into his MG and headed for the Institute.

It was a beautiful spring day and the flowers were beginning to bloom. This area became a wondrous scented garden as the cherry blossoms bloomed. Judah raced along with the top down and breathed in the heady fragrances. For an instant, just an instant, he felt that the world was a beautiful place. Then his mind shifted to the sinister goings on of AZAZEL and the Watchers and a shiver went up his spine and there was a check in his spirit.

When he entered the Institute, he found everyone waiting for him.

"How is your mother, Judah?" Dr. Lazant asked. There were Dr.Lazant and Reverend Shea and Stephen and Endora. They all had smiles on their faces that made Judah shiver. This quartet of his sinister grinning colleagues made him feel very uneasy.

"She is doing fine considering," Judah replied looking at all the smiling faces. "What is everybody grinning about?"

"AZAZEL told me what happened," Stephen began slowly as he played with his pipe. "We all think that it is so wonderful that He is interacting with you and your family. These Watchers have been guarding over humankind since the beginning, but He has chosen you and your family to interact with at this time. Maybe it is because you are Jewish."

"What are you talking about?" Judah replied as he shook his head.

"We think that these Watchers have been watching humankind ever since the beginning," Reverend Shea said beaming as his eyes shot upward. "They have often even tried to mate with humans as described in Genesis 6. You know when the sons of God took the daughters of men as wives. The sons of God were these angels, the

Watchers."

"What?" Judah again quipped. "You have lost me."

"These angels are what we have called extraterrestrials, Judah," Dr. Lazant interjected. "They have been trying to assist the growth of mankind for millennia. In today's paradigm we have called them aliens or ETs, but they are not from another planet or galaxy but they are from another dimension of the air surrounding the Earth. They have often abducted humans in an effort to mate with us or to alter our DNA so we could evolve into a higher race like them. The government has known about them since Roswell and Project Blue Book and the Condon Report, but has kept it from the public for fear of widespread panic. The real irony is that even the government does not know the truth. They sincerely believe that the Watchers are aliens from another galaxy. Even they do not know that they are angelic beings! That is why our discovery is so earthshaking, Judah. We have stumbled upon the workings of the heavenly Watchers. And for some reason, they have zeroed in on you, Judah."

"As I said before, Judah," Reverend Shea continued, "maybe it is because you are Jewish. Angels have always appeared before your people. Remember Jacob wrestling all night with the angel?"

"Then why has it attacked my wife and mother?" Judah questioned bluntly.

"We don't know. Maybe it was because they were seen to be hampering the evolution of the human race?" Stephen said, shaking his head.

"Or maybe they just got caught up in the divine machinery," Endora interjected with a wicked smile.

"Divine machinery. What kind of nonsense is that?" Judah yelled.

"Relax, Judah, she doesn't mean anything by that," Dr. Lazant attempted to reassure Judah.

"When did you figure all of this out?" Judah questioned.

"Judah, it began when I lost the Federal contract to do Remote Viewing for the CIA," Dr. Lazant began. "I wanted so badly to continue my work in parapsychology. I sincerely believed that it would benefit mankind in the long run. In the meantime, I had established a correspondence with Reverend Shea after I had attended one of his lectures on the spiritual concept of world unity. We both believed in the coming together of all world religions and people. When I founded this Institute and instructed Endora to look upwards instead of across the globe, things began to happen."

"I know all that, Doc," Judah interjected, "Remember I was with you all of the way?"

"I know Judah, but listen. When Endora communicated with Jesus and the protocols were confirmed to be as accurate as they were when she saw into the Kremlin, I called Reverend Shea. I felt that we were on the verge of something monumental here. He took a leave of absence and came to me with Stephen."

"I understand all that," Judah again said emphatically, "but what does all of that have to do with alien abductions and the Bible? I am totally confused."

"When Stephen began looking to the Heavens with the same remote viewing protocol, he found AZAZEL," Dr. Lazant continued. "Reverend Shea began doing some research and he came up with the concept that it was a Watcher, an angelic being. Think about it, Judah, we have made contact with angels and with Jesus. They both tell us that we are entering a critical phase in our evolution."

"But what about the abductions and all that breeding shtik *(Y. nonsense)*?"

"As Reverend Shea pointed out, it is mentioned in the Book of Genesis that the sons of God mated with the daughters of men. He scoured the Scriptures and has found additional material of angels from heaven. They have always wanted to mate with humans to improve our DNA. It has been characterized for the last fifty years or so as alien abductions. It is a long story, Judah, but that should suffice for the time being."

"Sounds weird to me, Doc. You are mixing religion and aliens and only God knows what else together," Judah stood up and paced the floor. "Even if I can accept that, now you tell me that I am at the center of all of this? I thought that I was in charge of security not the center of the project?"

Judah heard a small, quiet voice within tell him to calm down. It reminded him of the email message from Maskil which said that the struggle with UFOs is not for the planet of man but for the soul of man. It told him to go along with them for the sake of mankind. Judah had never heard that voice before. It caught him totally off guard. He stopped pacing and sat down. The words that next came out of his mouth were not his.

"What do you want from me?" the voice said in a calm manner. "I know that I have been put here for a purpose. I really don't fully understand what is going on, but I want to participate in this project no matter what the consequences to me or my family. It is a big sacrifice, but we are in a battle, a battle for the soul of mankind. I really don't know what AZAZEL wants with me or my family, but I ready, willing and able to help you find out. Whatever you want me to do, I will do. I am a soldier after all and you are the commander."

Dr. Lazant smiled. He saw the air of reconciliation in Judah's eyes, and he welcomed it. He went up to Judah and embraced him as did all the others. They shook his hand and Endora even kissed him on the forehead. They all committed to work together on this grand project. Each felt that they were participating in the evolutionary development of the human race.

"Like the serpent told Eve in the Garden," Endora laughed an irreverent cackle, "eat from the tree and your eyes will be opened, and you will be like god. This remote viewing communication is our eating from the forbidden tree. Our eyes are being opened, and we will become like gods. Hallelujah!"

Judah just sat there and faked a smile. He was being asked by whoever that small inner voice was to pretend that he was one of them. Who were the good guys? Who was Maskil? Someone else obviously knew the great charade that was being played out here at the Institute, but who were they? Judah did not mind doing what he had to do, but he did not like the fact that his wife and mother had been caught up in the "divine machinery". What a blasphemous statement from that witch Endora. Everytime he looked at her his blood curdled.

"You know, guys," Endora spoke up , "my most recent communications with Jesus have been right along these same lines. He tells me that the world as we know it is coming to an end. There will be much tribulation and discord. He will have to bring unity out of the chaos."

"That is why the work of the Pope and other world religious leaders is so critical," Reverend Shea chimed in. "We will be at the nucleus of this unity. We will be Jesus' allies in this fight against discord and disunity."

"Yeah, and that is why he also told me that the fundamentalist right wing fanatical so-called Christians will have to be removed. They want nothing to do with this concept of unity or a one world religion," Endora lectured as she turned beet red.

"Enough. enough," Dr. Lazant said as he broke them up. "Let's get back to work. Stephen, you try and contact AZAZEL. Endora, you try to bring up Jesus. Judah, come here. I need to talk with you."

Judah followed Dr. Lazant into his office. As founder of the Institute, it was needless to say the most spacious and most lavishly decorated. Dr. Lazant had studied parapsychology under the famed J.B. Rhine at Duke University. He was an average sized man about five foot eight inches tall with a crewcut and long sideburns. His small beady brown eyes were annoying to look at.

Judah found himself looking at the surrealistic works of Salvador Dalí and Magritte hanging on the wall. Dr. Lazant also loved the Art Deco period and had various beautiful lamps and art glass pieces scattered around the room. The floor was covered by a beautiful silk Isfahan Persian rug.

"Judah, I changed all of the security codes while you were gone. Here are the new ones," Dr. Lazant said matter of factly, and Judah took them without comment. "I don't know who this Maskil character is but this should hold him up for at least a while. He must be somebody in the intelligence community. NSA worked these out for me. As I said they should be impenetrable. Let me know if he gets through, will you?"

"Of course, boss," Judah replied. "You know I almost forgot how nice your office was. It is like a museum."

"Well, I have been fortunate to have been collecting for years, Judah."

"I love your rug!"

"I know. It is beautiful. I got it an auction for peanuts. You really have to know your Isfahans, however. Imitations are everywhere."

"How about a drink, Judah? Some Chivas as usual?"

"No thanks, Doc, just some seltzer if you have it. I am frazzled enough already," Judah countered.

"It will relax you, son," Dr. Lazant insisted.

"It will put me to sleep!"Judah replied, shaking it off once and for all. This was not going to be easy. He would need all the help that he could get.

Judah went back to his office. He punched in the new security codes and lo and behold there was an email message.

*Why do they boast in evil, Judah? The loving kindness of God endures all day long. They love evil more than good, falsehood more than speaking what is right. They love all words that devour, O deceitful tongue. But as for you, you are a green olive tree in the house of God. You will trust in the loving kindness of God forever and ever. You shall wait on His name, for it is good, in the presence of thy godly ones. --Maskil*

Judah quickly erased the message in the hopes that no one else had seen it. He tidied up his office a little and headed for the hospital. The two most important people in his life were there. When he walked into the room, he was elated to find his mother conscious and sitting up in her bed.

"Ma," he yelled, running up to her. "You are all right! I was so worried about you."

"No thanks to you," she responded, looking away. "Where have you been? I awake in a strange place all alone. After all that I have done for you. I sat by your bedside while you had the measles. I sat by you when you had your tonsils out. I sat by you when you were hurt in that car wreck chasing terrorists. Remember those days at Hadassah Hospital. I even changed your bedpans. And now you abandon your poor mother. Its all right, I'll survive. I'll manage alone. I've done just fine since your Abba *(H.Father)* passed on. God rest his soul."

"Ma, I sat with you all night," Judah answered holding her hand as she looked away. "I had to go to work. But I have been praying for you all along just as I have for Dawn."

"Well, I guess God loves me more, right?"

"Ma!"

"By the way, what the heck happened to me? All that I remember is that I was sitting on the sofa and a bright light came over me. I must have fallen asleep or something. All that I remember is some horrible nightmare about some cockamamie *(Y.implausible)* little bald creatures with big eyes."

"You must have had a slight stroke or something," Judah offered as an explanation. "You know, Ma, a blood vessel might have burst in your head which could have caused the light sensation, and then you had a bad dream because of the whole thing."

"Are you telling me that I had a stroke like the thing that killed Abba?" Bertha wailed. "Oy vey ist mir *(Y.Oh woe is me)*!"

"No, Ma, not like that one, but maybe it was a milder one. I don't know, I'm not a doctor. Don't say it, Ma!"

"Well, the real Doctor said that I was in some kind of shock?"

"Maybe that nightmare scared you, Ma?"

"I never heard of being that scared by a nightmare!" Bertha said as she shook her head in disbelief. "There have been too many farchadat *(Y. dopey)* things going on here. I want to go home as soon as possible."

"Okay, Ma, Okay"

That very moment the two detectives entered the room.

"Oh, Mrs. Meire," Detective Holmes asked. "Are you awake now?"

"What does it look like?"Bertha countered.

"Can I ask you a couple of questions, please?"

"Go on."

"What happened to you?" Holmes asked as he sat down beside her, looking all over her for signs of abuse.

"I don't remember. The Doctor said that I was in shock, but my son says that I had a bad nightmare. I really don't know."

"Was Judah there when this happened to you?" O'Malley asked.

"No, my dear son was here at the hospital with his wife. Whenever I need him, he is not there. It's all right, I suffered alone. What else is new."

O'Malley looked at Holmes and shook his head. He put up his arms signaling that what Bertha had said confirmed Judah's version.

"What did you dream about, Ma'am,"Holmes decided to ask anyway.

"What business is that of yours?" snapped Bertha.

"We are just trying to find out what happened."

"Happened, schmappened, I am tired now, please leave!"

The two detectives walked out of the room accompanied by Judah.

"Leave my mother alone," Judah asked. "She does not remember what happened."

"She comes in here in total shock and nobody remembers what happened?" Holmes said with a air of frustration. "I cannot believe that. This is the weirdest case that I have ever worked on. I know that something is going on here more than you are telling us, but I cannot figure out what it is exactly. I will figure it out, Colonel. Thank God your mother is all right. Too bad we can't say the same for your wife."

Judah smiled and walked back into the room. O'Malley followed him and tried to ask one more question.

"What is going on here? Is it really a matter of National Security?"

"As I said before, if I told you, I'd have to kill you!" Judah replied, putting his hand on his Uzi revolver.

O'Malley turned around and scampered away like a puppy with his tail between his legs.

"That schvartze *(Y. Black man)* is a nudnik, Judah, a real pest,"Bertha said. "Why doesn't he just leave me alone. What was my nightmare? The nerve of him asking something so personal. Can you imagine? I wouldn't tell him if hell froze over."

53

"He thinks that I did this to you," Judah replied.

"What? He thinks that you put me into shock? Is he meshugge *(Y.crazy)*? That schlemiel *(Y.simpleton)*!" Bertha said, shaking her head.

"Now you see what I meant about Dawn, Ma. He said that I did it to her as well. I did not."

"Oh my poor boy," Bertha suddenly changed her tone. "What you have been through."

The next morning Judah put his mother on a plane for Chicago. He was glad to get her out of the battle. He hugged his Mom and she looked at him funny.

"What's the matter, Ma?"

"You know, tatalleh, during my nightmare I know that I saw you. There were these strange little creatures and this big black thing from drerd *(Y.Hell)*. I was really scared! Suddenly I was rescued by a man in a suit of armor. It was the cockamamiest thing I have ever been through. He looked like Sir Lancelot in one of those old movies. I would have laughed, but I was scared to death of that big black thing. I looked at the man in the armor through his helmet and it was you, Judah. Then I woke up in the hospital. I didn't tell anyone else about this. It was you, wasn't it?"

"Yes, Ma, it was!"

"Oy Gevalt *(Y.Oh No!)*,"she said, holding her heart. "I'm too old for these things. How... oy, I don't want to know."

Judah waved goodbye as his Mom boarded the plane. He was grateful to have her out of harm's way. His mother was difficult to live with sometimes, but he did really love her. Both her and his father had difficult yet noble lives. She had been born Bertha Berkowitz on the Southside of Chicago. After the Jews had achieved statehood in 1948, she had traveled to Israel with her parents to help them build their new country. They had all worked on a kibbutz. Only a few months after they had arrived, her parents had been killed by Arab terrorists who had infiltrated the kibbutz security. Those early days of the country were marked by frequent occurrences such as that. That is also the reason that his mother had reacted so emotionally to his wife Ronit's death at the hand of terrorists.

It was there in Israel that she had met her future husband, Moshe. He was nearly ten years older than she was, but Bertha had fallen in love with this Polish intellectual who had fled Poland in 1938 for Palestine and later fought with the Hagganah. Moshe had been a contemporary of Menachen Begin. They were married in 1951 and shortly afterwards, Professor Meire received an appointment at Hebrew University in Biblical Studies. Although he put aside his gun for his books, he returned to fight in the 1956 Suez Canal conflict and served as an advisor in the 1967 War. When his father had died a few years ago, his mother had returned to Chicago and he had decided to try and attend West Point even though he was too old. As Judah drove back from the airport, he thought of Dawn. She'd been unconscious for weeks, or was it months? He tried to count the weeks, and he thought that it was eight or nine by now. First, he had lost the black haired, blue-eyed athletic woman that he had fallen in love with to MS. Then it was to a life threatening coma. He tried to figure out what she had done to deserve such trials, but then he remembered what the General had told him. "All things work together for good to those who love God, to those who are called according to his purpose."

What good was there in Dawn's condition, thought Judah, but then he recollected his mother's miraculous recovery. God had worked everything together for good for her, but she did not love God? Judah left it all with God. God's ways are not our ways. He trusted and believed that everything would work out for Dawn. In the natural, that did not seem possible, but he knew that he served an awesome God. His malaise suddenly turned to joy and he praised God for everything.

When he got home, Judah just crashed on the sofa. These last few weeks had been exhausting both physically as well as emotionally. He dreamed that AZAZEL was before him once again. It's huge black wings were lifted up and reached nearly to his ceiling. It just stared at him through cold white pupiless slits. Judah could feel heat radiating from it.

"The end is near, Judah. Prepare for the abduction, the Catching Away. You and all your Christian friends that oppose us will be removed from the earth,"AZAZEL bellowed. "We shall rule and reign on this planet for one thousand years. We have been the Princes of the Power of the air, but soon we will come down to earth and cause tribulation to all who oppose us."

Judah stood up from the sofa and reached for his revolver but it was not at his side.

"Aha!" screamed AZAZEL as it flung a flaming arrow at Judah, "be consumed by the fires of Gehanna (H.Hell)!"

Judah recoiled as the ball of fire hit him. The pain was unbearable. It was as if he had been hit by a flamethrower. His skin crackled and he could smell burning flesh. Judah pleaded with the Lord to heal him of this pain.

"Lord, You said by Your stripes we are healed. Lord, I ask that of You in Jesus' name."

Then Judah prayed without ceasing for the Holy Spirit to put upon him the full Armor of God. The Spirit girded his loins with Truth, gave him the Breastplate of Righteousness and covered his feet with the preparation of the Gospel of Peace. He took up the Shield of Faith, the Helmet of Salvation, and the Sword of the Spirit.

AZAZEL recoiled and became increasingly more angry as the flaming bolts now bounced off.

It shrieked an unholy roar that shook the house. It began flapping its wings ever faster.

Judah took up the Sword of the Spirit and screamed "I rebuke you in the name of Jesus Christ. I command you to leave this place, now!"

AZAZEL held its wings over its face and cowered.

"I command you to leave this place in Jesus' Holy Name. I plead the blood of the slain Messiah over myself, AZAZEL, you beast from the pits of Hell!" Judah yelled boldly as he stood right in its face. Judah took the Sword of the Spirit and swiped it across the face of this monstrous dark being. AZAZEL covered its face and continued to shriek. Then it was gone!

Judah woke up and found himself on the sofa. What a nightmare that had been, he thought. He remembered every detail as if it had really just happened. As he got up and walked into the kitchen he found several pieces of china had crashed to the floor and broken. He thought that there must have been a sonic boom from the nearby military facilities, but curiously it had never happened before? When he went back into the living room, he found a burn mark on the carpeting where he dreamed that he was standing. Judah sat down and pulled up his shirt. There was a large circular scar in the middle of his chest where the burning ball of fire had hit him in the dream. He touched it but there was no pain although it felt warm. Judah put his head in his hands and thanked God. Then he began to sob.

"Oh, God why did you choose me for this?" Judah yelled. "I don't want to do it. I am good at killing people, but this spiritual warfare is all new to me. I am not worthy. Please choose someone else. Why me? Why me? There are so many good Bible believing men out there. I did not even want to believe. I went along kicking and screaming. General Desporte witnessed to me, and he is now dead. Dawn witnessed to me and she is in a coma. Oh, God why me! I cannot shoot these things with my revolver. I have to use Spiritual Armor and the Holy Spirit. I do not know what I am doing. One mistake and I am dead. I want to leave the Institute. It is driving me crazy. You want me to be grounded in your word and yet you want me to associate with evil people. That Endora is nuttier than a fruitcake. Her face would make a demon take notice. Stephen thinks he is Krishnamurti reincarnated. The Reverend and Dr.Lazant will smile all the way to hell. The problem is that they will take thousands of unsuspecting souls with them. Why me? Why me? Why can't you just zap the bad guys, Lord. Why do the good guys keep dying off? I am sick of this, Lord. This is a fight that I would handle differently. I cannot just stay there and smile. AZAZEL will tell them about me. He already has once and he will tell them that I am just faking it. What will I do then Lord? Please Lord, choose someone else. Please! I do not want to do this. I cannot do this. I won't do this! Get somebody else!"

Meanwhile, back at the Institute a meeting was just beginning. All the lights were out in the remote viewing room. Around the large wooden table sat Dr. Lazant, Reverend Shea, Stephen and Endora. In the middle of the table was a candle whose flickering wick pasted strange shapes across the walls and ceiling. They all held hands and had their eyes closed. They had meditated earlier and their minds were now empty of the usual distractions of the world. Reverend Shea had led them in prayer.

"Oh, great Universal Spirit, we come to you today in our quest for the truth. We know that you are Lord over all. We four are here for your purpose. We love you

Oh Great One. We have turned our lives over to your will. We know that you want unity among all peoples. You are tired of denominations and tired of religious differences. We are all one and shall have one religion for all. The petty squabbling has got to stop. The judgmental attitude of some has got to stop. We have to love one another without condition as you love us. You are a God of love. Please fill us all with your Christ consciousness so we can become like you. The world needs your godly people to lead it away from the path of destruction on which it is now headed."

The group shook their heads in agreement. There were sighs of Amen and Hallelujah. The candle flickered ever brighter.

"We come to you, oh omniscient and omnipotent Creator as your servants," Dr. Lazant began. "I know that you have instructed and guided me in endowing this Institute. Only a miracle could have provided the funding, but you were there for me. I have always felt that I had a special purpose in life. Ever since I was a small boy, I have felt that I followed the beat of a different drummer. In High School, I studied parapsychology and gnosticism when my friends were reading comic books. I read Blavatsky's *Secret Docrtrine* when they were reading *Playboy*. You have always tugged on my heart, and for that I am forever grateful. We stand now on the threshold of a quantum leap in Human evolution and you are right there with us. Your angels, your Watchers, have always been among us. Now for the first time because of our remote viewing protocol we can communicate directly with them. Thank you Lord for choosing us. Thank you for your faith and trust. We will not let you down."

"Oh great Krishna, Jesus, Buddha, we do love you. We are becoming one with you," Stephen said as he lifted his still closed eyes to the ceiling. "I too believe that you chose me for this special time. I know that my spiritual quest has spanned many lifetimes and thousands of years. I have personally seen you work through special gifted men who have been filled with your Christ consciousness. They have moved not only mountains but the unsuspecting masses as well. As I meditated over the years, and closed my mind to distraction and realized that the world is just maya, an illusion, I have seen your Watchers. Those big black winged beings have visited me before. I never knew what they wanted, but they were there nonetheless. Now I have established direct communication with AZAZEL. I am so excited. In my country, only the Holy men, the avatars, could ever speak to these type of spirits.. I guess I was chosen also for this special time."

"I am a witch, they say," Endora bellowed. "They call me a medium, a sorceress, a practicer of divination, an interpreter of omens, a spiritist. They say that I call up the dead. So what? We all seek the same Universal Spirit. We all want to return to one universal religion. A religion that honors Mother Earth and shuns the Patriarchal judgmental Father God. We want to love all peoples and not call them sinful or evil. The Universal Spirit loves everyone unconditionally. So should we. All the years that I have practiced the so-called Black Arts, I have never found

57

someone from the other world who has gone to the fires of Hell. They have all told me without exception that when they passed on they found a beautiful city of light. They were accepted by loved ones and by a loving, forgiving Universal Consciousness. There is no Hell. There is no sin that cannot be forgiven, that She will not be forgive. Nobody is perfect. We all make mistakes, but we all will be together on the other side."

They all opened their eyes. They all were smiling, and were still holding each other's hands tightly.

"Turn on the lights, Reverend,"Dr. Lazant said to Stephen.

"No wait, Dr.Lazant,"Stephen replied.

"I think that we should contact AZAZEL now. What a perfect time to do it. We are all so spiritually energized right now. I think that it would be great."

"Yeah, and let's try and contact Jesus, okay?" Endora interjected. "He also is a critical part of this project. It is really amusing to me that it was me, the so called witch, that has made contact with Jesus. All those born again Bible believing Christians cannot talk with him, but me the sinner can. I love it. The Great Spirit has a sense of humor."

"Endora, you try first and then you, Stephen," Dr. Lazant said, pointing to Endora.

Endora went through the remote viewing protocol as she had before. The light was off as usual and she concentrated on the flicking flame of the candle as she had done before. The only difference was that there were other people in the room. That had never happened before and she did know if it would work. Everyone became very quiet. The room was perfectly still. As quiet as a tomb.

Endora concentrated on the Jesus entity. She filled her emptied mind with his presence. After nearly an hour, Endora seemed to have maintained contact. Her eyes were closed but she smiled. Although she communicated with this Jesus telepathically, she passed on to the group what the conversation entailed.

"Jesus says that He is pleased that we are all together. He says that we are correct that it was the Christ consciousness within Him that made Him special just as it was in Krishna, Buddha and others. He said that we needed to tap into this Christ consciousness for ourselves. It would make us all avatars, ascended spiritual Masters."

"What does He think of our work with the Watchers?" Dr. Lazant asked Endora.

After a few minutes, Endora answered. "He says that they are angels. They have been sent by the Holy One to watch over mankind, especially as we approach the end of the age."

"What end of the age?" Reverend Shea asked.

"The end of the present age of disunity and judgmental people," Endora quickly responded as she heard from Jesus. "We are preparing to enter a new age. A new world order where we will all love one another and worship the Great Spirit as one. No more separate religions. No more Patriarchal Judgmental Father God. There will be one universal religion for all and it will also honor Mother Earth and Earth-based religions and speak of unconditional love."

"Will this entail the removal of the Christians?" Stephen interjected with a slight snicker.

"What do you think? Of course it will," Endora relayed with a smile. "Mankind cannot enter the new age of universal brotherhood with all those judgmental nitpicking Christians."

"What will happen to them?" Reverend Shea asked with an air of sadness.

"We will find out in due time. Be patient. The battle has only just begun," Endora said as she opened her eyes. She was finished and physically and emotionally exhausted. It was now Stephen's turn.

Stephen went through the same remote viewing protocol as had Endora. It also took him nearly an hour to establish communication with AZAZEL.

"AZAZEL agrees that the battle has just begun. He also says that the Christians will have to go. He says that the Watchers have been trying to figure out what to do with them for centuries. Several scenarios have been discussed."

"What are those?" Reverend Shea wanted to know.

"We will know in all due time. AZAZEL agrees that we will have an important role to play in these plans. We all have been brought together for a purpose. We were all hand picked for this most important mission. All of us except Judah," said Stephen, relaying what AZAZEL had said to him.

"What about Judah?" Dr. Lazant asked concerned. "He came highly recommended by several people. "Is there a problem?"

"No, not a problem," Stephen answered. "Just keep an eye on him. We are not sure who put him here and why."

"He told us that he was now one of us and would support the program even after what happened to his wife," Dr. Lazant said sounding upset.

"That is what concerns me!" said AZAZEL. "I have tried to scare him off but it has not worked."

"Should I get rid of him?" Dr. Lazant queried with the look of concern on his face.

"No! No, don't do that. I need to find out who put him here." AZAZEL continued.

Suddenly AZAZEL appeared before them in all his black demonic horror. He flapped his wings and blew the candle out. Papers went flying all over.

"We shall rule and reign for one thousand years," screeched AZAZEL. "You all shall bow down and serve us. You humans are so weak and pitiful. You think that you shall be like gods, like us. HAAA! HAAA! It did not work for Adamah (H.Adam) or Chavah (H.Eve), and it will not work for you. You humans are no match for us. You never have been and you never will."

# V

Judah got up from the floor completely drained. He had been emotionally and physically exhausted from all that had gone on over the last several weeks, but his rantings against the Lord had been the final straw. He felt totally depleted spiritually as well. He no longer felt in control of the situation. The decisions to be made were no longer his to make. Judah did not like to be in such a situation. The world had always been his to control. And furthermore, to be asked to let go of his will to an unseen supernatural being was something totally alien to this brash Lieutenant Colonel. He really did not want the assignment, and he continued to try and refuse it.

Judah went over to his computer and flipped it on. There was an email message waiting.

*The fool has said in his heart, there is no God. They are corrupt and have committed abominable injustice. There is no one who does good. God has looked down from heaven upon the sons of men to see if there is anyone who understands, who seeks God...Save me O God, by thy name and vindicate me by thy power. Hear my prayer, O God. Give ear to the words of my mouth. For strangers have risen against me and violent men have sought my life. They have not set God before them...Give ear to my prayer, O God and do not hide Thyself from my supplication. Give heed to me and answer me. I am restless in my complaint and am surely distracted, because of the voice of the enemy, because of the pressure of the wicked. For they bring down trouble upon me and in anger they bear a grudge against me. My heart is in anguish within me and the terrors of death have fallen upon me. Fear and trembling come upon me and horror has overwhelmed me. --Maskil.*

Judah sat there in disbelief. The message from Maskil was a direct restatement of his earlier pleading with God. How did Maskil know? How could he know?

Judah cried out, "Oh Lord, answer me. Who is watching me? Who seems to know my every move and thought? Who is Maskil?"

The computer buzzed again that there was an email. Judah looked at the screen in consternation. This couldn't be an answer could it? He was hesitant to open the message but finally he did. He read it and was shaking so badly that he nearly fell off of the chair.

*As for you, Judah, you shall call upon God and the Lord will save you. Evening and morning and at noon, you will complain and murmur and He will hear your voice. He will redeem your soul in peace from the battle which is against you. Cast your burden upon the Lord and He will sustain you. He will never allow the righteous to be shaken. But Thou, O Lord will bring them down to the pit of destruction. Men of bloodshed and deceit will not live out half their days but you, Judah, will trust in Him. --Maskil*

Judah looked all around. Someone must have bugged the house. Who would want to do that and why? His first thought was that it was Dr. Lazant, but obviously it was not him. He was leading Judah away from the Lord, not towards Him. Who else could it be? Judah searched the house looking for listening or monitoring devices. That was his job at the Institute, and he was very good at it. After several hours, Judah found several remote camera devices- one in the living room in the ceiling, one in the study in the wall and one in the hallway in the light. They were state of the art devices, the latest in technology. He removed them and examined them closely to see if he could determine who might have put them there. They were definitely government issue; probably from the CIA or NSA. Judah wondered why they would want to monitor him?

After erasing the two Maskil messages on his computer, he collapsed on the bed and slept for nearly twelve hours.

"What did AZAZEL say again?" Dr. Lazant asked as he blinked his eyes. "Hey what happened here? The place is a mess. All the papers are scattered everywhere."

"He was saying that we all had been brought here for a purpose," Stephen said in a daze. "Gee, I must have lost contact with him. That is strange. I wrote down the time of contact at 9:45pm. It is now 10:30pm. We did not maintain contact for 45 minutes? Does anybody else know what might of happened to thirty minutes or so?"

"Look at the videotape!" Dr. Lazant yelled. "You know we record all our remote viewing sessions for security reasons. Where is the camera? It is not up there on the wall where it should be."

Reverend Shea found it laying battered on the floor. It apparently had been knocked to the ground by the same turbulence that scattered the papers. They all went back to the security room and played back the videotape of their meeting. They saw and heard the initial meditation exercises and the ensuing prayer session as they had sat in the dark holding hands, and a candle flickered in the center of the table. They listened to Endora relaying her communication with Jesus. Then they watched as Stephen began to relay what AZAZEL had said.

"AZAZEL agrees that the battle has just begun. He also says that the Christians will have to go. He says that the Watchers have been trying to figure out what to do with them for centuries. Several scenarios have been discussed."

"What are those?" Reverend Shea had then said.

"We will know in all due time. We will have an important role to play in these plans. We all have been brought together for a purpose. We were all hand picked for this most important mission..."

The tape had then gone mute. They watched as Dr. Lazant was apparently asking

61

AZAZEL some questions through Stephen. Dr. Lazant looked concerned about something. Suddenly the tape was filled by a huge black angelic like being. It was AZAZEL. He began flapping his immense wings and papers went flying as did the video camera. The last image was of AZAZEL apparently laughing or shrieking or both.

"What was I asking him, Stephen?" Dr. Lazant said as he looked over at Stephen.

"I don't remember, Sir."

"Do any of the rest of you?"

Nobody remembered a thing about the conversation. In fact, nobody remembered AZAZEL in the room either. All of them looked at the tape over and over again. They could not figure out what AZAZEL was doing there and why he was roaring or whatever it was that he was doing. They also could not figure out what is was that they had all forgotten and the reason for that mass amnesia.

"I wish that Judah were here," Dr. Lazant said. "This is his domain, security. Don't touch anything else here anyone. I'll have Judah look at it tomorrow. Let's all go home and get some sleep."

Judah woke up after noon. He must have been exhausted. All of a sudden he remembered that he had not called his mother to see if she arrived home all right.

"Ma, how was your flight?"Judah asked, yawning.

"Now you call? I got home last night. The flight was very bumpy. I almost threw up."

"Sorry to hear that, Ma. You have to take care of yourself. Okay?"

"What are you doing home so late? Shouldn't you be at work," Bertha asked. "Have you eaten the stuffed peppers that I left for you?"

"I overslept, Ma," Judah answered with a chuckle. "No, I have not eaten the stuffed peppers yet. You just left yesterday, Ma."

"I know, but I worry about you eating, tatalleh."

"Ma, I'll be fine. You take care of yourself, and I'll be in touch. I've got to get to work now. Love you."

"Okay son. I love you too."

Judah quickly showered and prepared to go to the Institute. He took the surveillance equipment that he had discovered and put it in the truck of his car. He wanted to show it to friends at the CIA. Afterall, he could not, nor would he, show it to Dr. Lazant. He was certain that he and the others at the Institute were his adversaries. As for this Maskil, he wasn't so certain since he had always steered him to the Lord, not away from Him. Again, Judah felt that he was being used. He never volunteered for this assignment. He was drafted without having any knowledge of what he would be asked to do. This Maskil character apparently wanted him to stay at the Institute, but why didn't he at least tell him what he was doing?

As he was leaving the house, he looked one last time at his computer. There was another email.

*You cry aloud with your voice to the Lord. You make supplication with your voice to the Lord. You pour out your complaint before Him. You declare your troubles before Him. When your spirit was overwhelmed within you, then the Lord knew your path. In the way where you walk they have hidden a trap for you. Look to the right and see. For you believe that there is no one who regards you. You believe that there is no escape for you. You need someone to deliver you from your persecutors for they are too strong for you. I need to bring your soul out of prison so that you may give thanks to the Lord. The righteous will surround you for the Lord will deal bountifully with you. --Maskil*

A postscript to that message read, *Meet me at the Watergate Hotel, Room 888 in 60 minutes. This message will automatically delete itself in sixty seconds.*

As Judah was heading out of the door, the phone rang. It was Dr. Lazant. He left a message that surprised Judah.

"Judah, where are you? I need you here. Someone or something has compromised our security surveillance system. We think that it was AZAZEL! Come as soon as you can!" pleaded Dr. Lazant.

Judah was curious about what had happened but decided instead to go and meet Maskil. Things were happening so quickly that his head was spinning. He sped along the beltway all the while wondering who Maskil was and why he had bugged his house. Judah became increasingly angered as he thought about it. When he finally wheeled into the Watergate parking lot, he was fuming. It was thundering and lightning all round. The sky was pitch black, and it was getting ready to storm. As Judah dashed from his car to the lobby door, he glanced up and saw a dark saucer shape. His heart dropped into his stomach, and he let out a loud sigh.

"Oh, No!" Judah wailed. "They are here too. I've been lured into a trap."

Judah entered the Watergate and shook off the few raindrops that had pelted him. He wondered if he should go up to room 888. He paced the floor. He went up to the front desk and had them call up to the room. Someone picked up the phone but then dropped it. There was no further response. Judah felt that he should leave. He went back outside and headed for his car. As he did so, he once again looked up and saw the saucer shape leaving. Judah stood there as the rain began to come down in torrents. After a few seconds, he ran back to the Watergate.

Judah was drenched. He went into the lobby bathroom and attempted to dry himself off. He continued, however, to debate with himself whether he should still go up or not. Finally, he decided to do so. The ride up in the elevator was slow and Judah was freezing. When he got to the door, he knocked firmly. There was no response. He knocked again but still no response. Just as he was turning around to leave, he heard a voice inside moaning.

"Juudahh... Juudaah!" it called out in obvious agony.

Judah tried to open the door but it was locked. He broke it down and entered the room. There before him on the floor was Senator Jordan of the Senate Select Intelligence Committee. He was in obvious shock. Judah ran up to him.

"Son, you are our last best hope," the Senator moaned. "Stay with the program. We picked you for this position. Actually, the Lord picked you."

"Don't talk, Senator," Judah replied as he cradled his head. "I'll call the paramedics. Everything will be all right."

Judah picked up the phone and called the paramedics. He told them that it was a US Senator and to hurry.

"What happened, Senator? Who did this to you?"

"AZAZEL!" Senator Jordan moaned as he gasped his last breath. "He's gotten all of us, including General Desporte. You are the only one left. Remember what my friend Trevor James Constable said, 'the battle with UFOs is not for the planet of man but for the soul of man.' God speed, Jud..."

Judah put his head down on the now deceased Senator. Senator Jordan had been the one who had smoothed over his background with the IDF and the Israeli Mossad so that he could get security clearance to work for the CIA's Remote Viewing program. Judah had never met him before that, but he had come highly recommended by General Desporte. While at West Point, Judah had met the General. He had taken an immediate liking to Judah in spite of their different backgrounds as had the Senator. Both of them had obviously seen something in Judah that even he did not see. When Judah had asked the Senator why he thought that he would like this Remote Viewing project, the Senator had replied that he just had a feeling. At the time, Judah had just shrugged it off since he really needed a job. Since going to work for the CIA's Remote Viewing project, he had not heard from the Senator personally ever again. He did have lunch with the General and Dawn periodically, and the General had known of his Revelation experiences, but he had told the General and Dawn not to tell anyone else. Was the Senator a Christian? Judah did not know. His last words were that AZAZEL had killed the General, not the bloodclot as popularly cited. Why did AZAZEL kill the General? Why did it kill the Senator? Why did it try and kill Dawn? Why did it try and kill his mother? Now Judah was becoming very angry at all that had gone on to people that he loved and cared about. It appeared that AZAZEL was out to destroy all those loved ones around him. But Why?

Judah wondered what they would cite as the cause of death here? He prepared to leave as the paramedics arrived. It was the same two that had assisted Dawn and his mother. He prepared for the understandable comments that would surely ensue.

"Oh, no, not you again!" the woman EMT groaned.

"What happened to him?," shouted the male. "He seems to have been in shock. Looks as though he was frightened to death. Look at his eyes and his hair. Actually the Senator looks very much like your mother did, Colonel!"

"How is she, by the way?" the female barked out.

"She is fine, thank you," Judah answered as he tried to slip out of the door. "She

64

just went home to Chicago."

"Well, that's good," the male EMT replied. "Hey don't go anywhere. I'm sure that the Police will want to know what happened."

"I've got to go. I'm soaking wet."

Just as Judah inched out of the door, he was met by Holmes and O'Malley. He put his head down, shook it back and forth and started laughing.

"What's so funny, Colonel?" Holmes mused. "Once again you are at the heart of a strange predicament, but this time the man is dead! What are you doing here?"

"He told me to meet him here."

"Did you break down the door?" O'Malley piped in.

"Yes."

"You keep breaking down doors and people end up either in a coma, in shock, or in this case dead!"

"The door was locked, and I heard him moaning inside so I broke it down. When I made it inside he was breathing his last few breaths. I called 911, didn't I? I always do, don't I?" Judah said quietly.

"How did you know him?'

"He helped me get my job with the CIA a little over a year ago. He was a friend of a friend of mine, General Desporte."

"Isn't that the guy, Holmes, who died mysteriously not too long ago of a blood clot?" O'Malley asked. "Remember? We covered that many months ago. The wife thought that he had been murdered."

"You knew the General too, Colonel?"Holmes asked with a snicker. "Everybody that you know ends up either dead or in the hospital. Don't you find that awfully coincidental, Colonel?"

"Yeah, wow, Sherlock, far out man!" Judah snapped back sarcastically.

"Hey, wiseguy, did he say what happened to him?"Holmes said as he looked straight at Judah.

"He told me that the same thing that killed him had killed General Desporte!"

"What do you mean the same thing?" O'Malley said as he jumped into the conversation "Do you mean the same person or the same instrument?"

"How am I supposed to know?" Judah said as he sat back down on the sofa. "Look, this guy calls me up and tells me to meet him here. I come to the door, it is locked, and I hear him moaning inside so I break down the door and he dies in my arms. I called the paramedics. I could have just left, you know."

"Yeah, we know, we caught you leaving the room, remember?"

"I did not want to get caught up in the aftermath of this. He is a popular US Senator. I would do an autopsy if I were you and don't tell me that it was a blood clot. It looks to me like he was scared to death by something. Probably his heart gave out. He was in his 70's, you know," softly spoke a tired Judah.

"Let me ask you one question, Judah. Is this a matter of National Security?" O'Malley smiled.

"Actually it is, gentlemen."

"Judah, I think that you had better come to the station with us," Holmes said as he lifted Judah up by the arm.

"For what?"

"There have been too many strange unexplained occurrences going on, and they all have you in common. This time it involves the death of a US senator. I'm sure my bosses, as well as some Federal people, will want to know your role in this. O'Malley, call the FBI and the CIA and tell them to meet us at the station."

"You really do not want to do this, Sherlock," Judah yelled forcefully. "This is too big for you and O'Malley. Why don't you just stick with drug busts and prostitutes?"

Judah was dragged down to the police station in soaking wet clothes. He was put in an interrogation room for hours where he was grilled by the two detectives, their superior Captain Braden and later by a couple of FBI men.

"What was your relationship with the Senator, Colonel Meire," Captain Braden demanded.

"I told you. He recommended me for a security position at the CIA. I have not seen or heard from him in nearly a year."

"Why did you go the Watergate tonight?"

"I told you. He left a message on my computer that I should meet him."

"On your computer? Did he email you before?"

"I don't know."

"What do you mean you don't know?"

Judah did not want to get into the Maskil correspondence. He was not even sure positively that Senator Jordan was Maskil. He decided to be evasive as best he could.

"I never received any other email from Senator Jordan."

"I thought that you said that you did not know?"

"Well, I remembered. No, nothing more."

Judah had to explain all over again and many times over why he had broken down the door and how he had found the Senator. He repeated that his last words were that whatever killed him had also killed General Desporte. He did not mention the other part of the conversation for obvious reasons. He declined to call a lawyer even though he was asked repeatedly.

"Why do I need a lawyer?" Judah yelled. "Are you going to charge me with anything? I think not."

"Judah, you keep saying that all of these cases of accident or death are a matter of National Security," Captain Braden shouted right in Judah's face as his full pockmarked face turned beet red. "What do you mean by that?"

"As I told your two Detectives here, frick and frack, if I told you, Captain, I would have to kill you," Judah laughed as he spoke.

"That isn't funny, Colonel. I'll have your cocky jewboy hide for this."

Judah jumped up in the Captains face and had to be restrained by Holmes and O'Malley.

"I would not mess with this guy, Captain," O'Malley replied. "He has that Post Traumatic Stress Syndrome thing. He can flip out and blow all of us away."

"Maybe that is just what has happened in all these cases," Braden snickered as he loosened his collar.

"Can we have a few minutes alone with him?" the two FBI men asked. The Captain was so mad that he waived them on and rushed everyone else out of the room. He was instructed to shut off the intercom.

"Well Colonel Meire, you are once again in the middle of a nightmare," agent Mallory began. He was a nice looking young man whose boyish looks were offset by a cutting honesty. "We know all about you. We were ordered to watch over you ever since you got security clearance for that CIA job. You being an IDF and Mossad man, we were never certain of where your allegiance lay. You were friends with General Desporte and he died. You were friends with Senator Jordan and he is dead. Are you some kind of mole here to infiltrate the security community and then kill off our top men?"

"Sure, that's it, kid!" Judah snapped back sarcastically once again. "I put my wife in a coma for two months and nearly killed my mother also just to cover my tracks. You idiot!"

"It would be a good cover for your work for Mossad," answered the other FBI agent who introduced himself as Bernstein.

"Thanks Bernstein, you antisemite. The worst kind of a antisemite is a fellow Jew. Sure, I was in the IDF and did some work for the Mossad, but that doesn't make me a spy for the Israeli Government. America is Israel's greatest ally. Why would they want to kill influential people here in the government? It makes no sense. Think about it?"

"Then what do you think is happening?"

"I think that someone killed General Desporte and Senator Jordan. The two deaths are related."

"What kind of work do you do for the Lazant Institute?" Mallory asked with a smile.

"Security."

"What type of work is going on there?" Bernstein followed with an angry tone.

"I cannot discuss it. It is classified," Judah answered with a straight face.

"Classified? What are you talking about? We are the government."

"I cannot talk about the work at the Institute. You will have to ask Dr. Lazant but you will probably get the same answer. He used to work in the CIA and still has many influential friends."

"What do you think that we should do?" Mallory finally said with an air of resignation.

"I would keep an eye on the key intelligence personnel in the government.

Something is out to destroy them," Judah offered up politely.

"Why intelligence people? Do you think that whoever is responsible is a spy or a mole?" Mallory asked curiously.

"I really do not know."

"Then why haven't they come after you, Judah?" Bernstein remarked with a big grin.

"Come here, Jewboy, look at this," Judah said as he lifted up his shirt and showed him his large circular scar.

"How did that happen?" Bernstein asked as he ran his hand over it.

"It was a flamethrower, stupid!" Judah said. "What does it look like? Someone tried to kill me with a flaming arrow."

"What are you talking about? Actually, this looks almost healed."

"You are as deductive as Sherlock out there. The same thing that killed Despote and Jordan tried to kill me and my wife and my mother. You will not be able to catch it though. It only comes out in the dark and will deceive you and fool you."

"What are you talking about? You make the killer seem like a vampire or a ghoul," Mallory asked with a look of confusion on his young face.

"Close... Gentlemen, I have nothing more to say. Let me go or book me," Judah finally demanded.

They had to let him go. They were all the more perplexed now than before. They were not exactly sure that Judah had done the terrible deeds, but they were certain that he was in some unknown way connected to each of them.


The next day the *Washington Post* headline read 'Senator Levi Jordan dies of blood clot at the age of 77'. Judah could not believe what he read. It had ended just as he feared that it would.

He used his many government contacts to get Mrs. Jordan's home phone number. He then called her to offer his condolences and asked if they could meet somewhere.

"Mrs. Jordan, this is Judah Meire," he began respectfully. "I have called to pay my respects at the death of your husband. He was a great American, Ma'am."

"Well, thank you, Colonel Meire," replied Betsy Jordan. "My husband thought a lot of you as well."

"Mrs. Jordan, I do not know how to say this, but your husband did not die of a blood clot," Judah began slowly. "In fact, he died in my arms."

"Oh, my God," Betsy replied with tears in her voice.

"Can we meet somewhere, Ma'am? I have to talk with you."

"Uh, the funeral is going to be in a couple of days, and I have lots to do."

"Did he tell you about AZAZEL, Ma'am?"

"Oh no!" she wailed. "I'll meet you at the First Baptist Church in Reston in two hours."

Judah got off of the phone with Betsy Jordan and then called the Institute. He

68

asked to speak with Dr. Lazant.

"Where have you been, man?" Dr. Lazant asked forcefully. "Did you get my message a couple of days ago? I've been looking all over for you."

"Did you see that Senator Jordan died?" Judah answered.

"Of course I did. It's been all over the news. I hate to say it but good riddance. He is the guy who cut off our government funding last year. He got what he deserved."

"That is a little vindictive, isn't it, Doc?"

"As you always say, Judah, so sue me! I never liked him much at all. He was one of those born again Christians. Well, he is with his Jesus now and out of our hair. Why did you ask, Judah?"

"He died in my arms!" Judah said calmly.

"He did what?" Dr. Lazant shouted.

"I found out that he was the Maskil character who had been sending me those Bible passages. In fact he had bugged my entire house to keep an eye and ear on me. I found the surveillance equipment. It is in my car."

"Wow!" Dr. Lazant burst out again. "But how did he die in your arms?"

"He told me to meet him at the Watergate. When I got there, he was dying of a stroke or something."

"What did he say to you?"

"He said that he had sent me those messages and then he died."

"Do the authorities know about this?"

"Yes, they interrogated me all last night. They wanted to know what we did here at the Institute. I told them that it was classified and could not tell."

"Good, Judah, I appreciate that," Dr. Lazant said with a sigh. "Who talked with you? Police? FBI?"

"Both the Police, a Captain Braden, and two FBI agents, Mallory and Bernstein."

"I'll make a few calls and smooth things out," Dr. Lazant replied. "You did not kill the old man, did you? I've got to know. I really don't care if you did, honestly, he had it coming, but I just need to know."

"I did not kill him, Doc," Judah answered, fighting back his outrage at Lazant's attitude.

"In fact," Judah suddenly began again, "he did say that whoever killed him also killed General Desporte."

"I thought that you said that he died of a stroke? Now you are saying that he was killed? What is going on here, Judah?" Dr. Lazant questioned as his tone turned more accusatory.

"I don't know exactly what happened, but he was dying when I arrived. He looked scared to death. His last words were that General Desporte had not died of a blood clot either. When I saw this morning's paper and it said that the Senator had died of a blood clot also, I became outraged. I did not want to burden you with all this, but I have to get off of my chest."

"Did you tell this to the Police and the Feds as well?"

"Yes!"

"Okay, thanks, Judah. Listen, I need to make some calls," Dr. Lazant said quickly as he prepared to get off the phone. "Come in as soon as you can and we will talk, Okay?"

"Okay boss. I'd appreciate any help you can give me with the authorities. They are trying to pin not only Jordan's death on me but Desporte's as well. They even think that I put Dawn in the hospital."

"Done! See you later."

Judah slammed down the phone and jumped in the shower. He had been up for over 24 hours but was determined to meet with Mrs. Jordan. He wanted to tell her the last few moments of her husband's life. She deserved at least that.

The First Baptist Church in Reston, Virginia was the Church that Dawn had attended. In fact it was also the same Church that the Jordans and the Desportes attended as well. The only time that Judah had ever graced the light of this Church was after he had accepted the Lord. Dawn had brought him along with General Desporte to meet their Pastor and tell of his Revelation experience. Judah was very uncomfortable going into a Church, especially one with a huge Cross in the sanctuary. It wasn't that he denied the Cross but was rather that for Jews there is a lot of historical baggage surrounding Christianity. His ancestors had often been asked to convert or to die; be baptized or be burned at the stake. Hesitantly, Judah had entered the church. Immediately he felt the love and acceptance that he had only recently come to know from a personal God and Savior and His people.

Judah had found himself falling to his knees and sobbing. He had cried out to the Lord for his gratefulness for choosing a poor wretch like him. He held up his hands and wailed his thanks to God for saving the lost. Pastor Calvin was very moved by his show of faith and repentance. He bent down and embraced the uniformed and perfectly neat and clean Lieutenant Colonel who had submitted himself to a Higher Authority. Judah underwent counseling sessions with the Pastor and with Dawn. Judah's decision not to tell anyone else bothered the Pastor. He felt that Judah should not be ashamed of the Lord or of his new found faith, but he reluctantly agreed to keep it quiet for a while until Judah was ready. Then unexpectedly, Dawn was struck down with a particularly rapid moving form of MS. Judah wanted to go ahead with the wedding no matter what the circumstances. He told the Pastor that he really loved Dawn and wanted to spend the rest of this life and the next as well with her. They were married in his study with only General Desporte and his wife Elaine present.

When Judah entered the sanctuary, he found not only Mrs. Jordan but Mrs. Desporte and Pastor Calvin as well. They all came up and embraced him warmly. Judah smiled and kissed the two ladies on the cheek. They all sat under the magnificent Cross hanging from the wall and began to pray.

"Oh Father, thank you for bringing Judah to us today," Pastor Calvin began. He was a man in his early fifties with a grey beard and brown piercing eyes. "We know, Lord, that You have Your hand on this young man and have been using him to do Your will."

Judah listened intently and was speechless.

"Thank you, O Lord, for Judah," Mrs. Jordan continued. "My husband and General Desporte were looking for a person to monitor the CIA's Remote Viewing program. They wanted a Christian man who could replace the man who was killed in that horrible accident. They wanted someone who could and would keep an eye on that Dr. Lazant and his psychic Endora. They were concerned that all kinds of New Age, demonic things were going on there. The two men prayed about it, but they received no peace. Then one day the General told Levi that he found an Israeli soldier at West Point, who actually was too old to be there, but was a man who he really felt good about. But Levi was confused. After all, he was a Jew and not a believer. What good would he be? The General convinced him to trust in his feeling. He felt within his spirit that this was the man. In the natural it was nonsense, but in the spiritual the General knew that he knew. He could not explain why. He prayed about it over and over again and Judah's name kept coming up He finally realized why they had admitted this thirtysomething overaged Israeli. God had a plan all along. Thank You, Lord, for Judah."

"I agree with everyone here," began Mrs. Desporte. "Thank God for your faithful son, Judah. What a glorious name, Judah. Our Lord was the Lion of Judah. Thank You for giving us our own lion, Lord. My husband saw something in this young man which no one else did. Nothing in the natural appeared to make him the ideal candidate for that CIA job, but he went ahead and recommended him anyway to Levi. The Senator trusted in The General and pulled a few strings and got him in. And then lo and behold, a short time later Judah meets Dawn and the rest is history. That ski trip when you saw the man in a suit of armor battling the adversary, Judah, really moved the General. He came home and cried like a baby. He knew that he had chosen the right man. When you accepted the Lord, the angels rejoiced, Judah. It was all in God's plan from the beginning. The General was so grateful that he could play a part in all of this. He died a fulfilled man and was ready to meet his Maker."

"Thank You, Lord, for choosing me!" began Judah. "I am forever grateful to You for the Cross and that You came to seek and save the lost like me. You did not wait for me to call out to You but let me hear Your voice calling me. I am grateful also for my wife Dawn. Please bring her back to me, Lord. I am also grateful to General Desporte and Senator Jordan who saw something in me not yet there. Both of them gave up their lives for this battle with the principalities of evil. I know, Lord, that You welcomed them both home with the words 'good and faithful servants!' I promise, Lord, on the sweetly departed souls of my two brothers, that I will continue to fight the good fight. I will not succumb to the evil and deception of the enemy who roams the earth seeking someone to devour. I promise to these dear ladies and to this man of God that I will seek out the truth and reveal it to the world, so help me God! AZAZEL shall be exposed!"

After the prayers, they all embraced once again.

"Judah, I must tell you something," Mrs. Jordan smiled. "My husband had the NSA bug your home to watch out over you. He regretted it but when he saw that beast AZAZEL flip over your wife he was convinced that he had done the right thing. That is why he kept sending you those Maskil Psalms. We were all praying for you and Dawn, but a little computer email support couldn't hurt, he felt. And when he saw what happened to your mother, and then your fight with AZAZEL, he was convinced that you were our knight in shining armor. How is your burn scar, by the way?"

"It is fine now, Ma'am," Judah replied with a smile.

Everything was beginning to fall into place. At least now he knew where he had come from and where he was at the present. The future, however, still seemed murky.

"I knew that my husband did not die of a blood clot," Mrs. Desporte said with a shake of her head. "They would not let me do an autopsy. They said that he died of a blood clot from his lung that went to his brain. I never believed it for a minute. He was strong as a mule. That old farmer may have been 65 but he could still run circles around those young recruits at West Point. So it was that darned AZAZEL after all. We surely need you, Judah, but please be careful."

"Judah, take care of yourself," Pastor Calvin said as he put his hand on Judah's shoulder. "We are all praying for you. Two good men have already been killed by this beast and your wife is in a coma. I sincerely believe that the Lord has chosen you for this struggle. You need to stay prayed up and to continue to put on the whole armor of the Lord and to plead the blood of Christ for protection. Judah, you are one of God's first born. You are special to Him. He sent the Messiah through your people as well as the Patriarchs, the Prophets and the Apostles. You might not be the *Lion of Judah,* but you are our *Judah the Lion.*"

They all left the Church smiling and hugging each other. It would be the last time that he would ever see Betsy Jordan or Elaine Desporte alive again. They were both killed in a highway accident that dark night on a rural stretch of highway in Virginia.

As soon as Judah got back to his house, the phone was ringing.

"Judah, come to the hospital right away. It is Dawn," Betty, the intensive care nurse, was yelling.

Judah dropped the phone and raced to his car. "Oh, no," he screamed, "not Dawn too?!"

# VI

As Judah got out of the elevator on Dawn's floor, he encountered pandemonium. There were doctors and nurses and support people running up and down the hall. There were even news people and cameras all over the place. Judah pushed his way through all of them and entered Dawn's room. Everyone was smiling.

"Dawn!"Judah yelled as he saw her awake and sitting up on the bed.

"Judah, sweetheart," Dawn answered. "No wait, Judah," she motioned for him to stop. "Do not come any closer!"

"What are you talking about?"

"Just stay there, Judah!"

Dawn swung her legs off of the bed and started to stand up. Judah shouted for her to wait.

"No Judah, it is all right," she replied waving him back.

Dawn stood up and grabbed a hold of a walker and made her way slowly over to Judah. When she got to him, she collapsed into his arms. She embraced Judah and kissed him warmly. Judah scooped up her frail body and carried her back to the bed.

"What happened, Dawn?" Judah asked breathlessly. "Your legs are working again. How is that possible?"

"Judah, our Lord said that all things are possible for God to him that believes. I guess that the Lord must have healed me," Dawn said with a smile. "Have you been praying for me? I know that you have. I felt it! I still feel a little weak because I have not used these legs for months, but I can walk. I have feeling and sensation in my legs. Praise God!"

"She probably went into spontaneous remission, Judah," Dr. Levin spoke up from the back of the room. "There doesn't need to be any supernatural explanation for her recovery."

"Hey Doc," Judah yelled back at him. "I thought that you told me that she had the type of MS that did not show spontaneous remissions but got steadily worse?"

"Well, thank God that I was wrong," Dr. Levin said with a slight smile.

"Thank God? What do you know of God, Doc? You had so much faith that, remember, you wanted me to pull the plug of this so-called vegetable. Don't talk to me of God. You better ask Him for forgiveness. He taught you a mighty lesson about putting to death people in a coma. As Dawn said, all things are possible for God to those that believe!"

73

"Judah, that's enough," Dawn said as she grabbed Judah's hand and kissed it. "We know that it was the Lord who healed me. I feel great, all things considered."

"She is responding unbelievably well to our initial efforts at physical therapy, Colonel Meire," Betty interjected.

Judah waved everybody out of the room and closed the door. He got down on his knees on the floor next to Dawn's bed. He grabbed her hands and began to pray.

"Oh, thank You, Lord, for healing my dear sweet wife Dawn. I love her so much, Lord. You not only have brought her out of her coma, but You have brought her out of her MS as well. What a gracious and awesome God You are. You knew that I needed her so very much, especially at this time. Forgive me, Lord, for doubting you. Oh we of so little faith! Your ways are not our ways, Lord. I cannot fully understand why some things happen the way that they do, but I know that You are in control. Thank You for giving me a helpmate that will keep me on the straight and narrow path. With her at my side, I will be able to accomplish all that You want me to accomplish."

"What is that all about, Judah?" Dawn asked.

"You really don't want to know," Judah answered. "There will be plenty of time for that later. You just be concerned about walking as soon as you can. I want to take you home. I am so excited that you are whole once again. I loved you before, with all of my heart, but I will love you now all the more."

"Yes, Judah, I am whole once again," Dawn said with a smile. "Judah, hand me my Bible over there on the table."

"Why?"

"The Lord just put a scripture on my heart. I know that it is for you."

Dawn shuffled through her Bible which Judah had brought to her room just in case she woke up.

"It says," Dawn began, "have I not commanded you? Be strong and courageous! Do not tremble or be dismayed for the Lord your God is with you wherever you go."

Judah's contemplation of the Scripture from the Book of Joshua was quickly interrupted by a knocking on the door. He looked up to see Detectives Holmes and O'Malley entering the room.

"Oh no, what do you guys want?" Judah spoke as he got to his feet.

"We wanted to come and see your wife," O'Malley answered with a big smile. "We heard that she had regained consciousness."

"Yes, she has. See for yourself!"

"Mrs. Meire, we are Detectives from the Potomac Police Department," Holmes began as he moved closer to Dawn and began to look her over very methodically. "We were called to investigate the circumstances of your injury."

"They think that I flipped you on your head!" Judah blurted out. "Can you imagine that?"

"Oh my God, no, Detectives," Dawn softly spoke. "Judah did not do it. Now why would you think that?"

74

"Then who did it, Ma'am?" Detective Holmes asked as he looked over at O'Malley.

"I don't know. It was some dark intruder. I saw it running down the hall."

"Are you sure that it was not Judah?" O'Malley asked. "And why did you call the intruder 'it'?"

"Judah was outside at the time," Dawn replied. "And what did you say about it?"

"You described the intruder as an it," Holmes said forcefully. "Why would you call a person an it?"

"I don't know what you are talking about."

"Oh just forget it! You are about as cooperative and as difficult to communicate with as is your husband," O'Malley responded.

The two Detectives went over Dawn's account of the accident over and over and over again until they were satisfied that she was telling them all that she remembered. As to whether it was the truth, they were not sure. She remembered no abuse by her husband. She could not recall what the intruder looked like. They decided to let her alone for the time being.

"By the way, Judah, did you know that Mrs. Desporte and Mrs. Jordan died last night in a car accident?" Holmes dropped almost matter of factly. "When was the last time that you saw them?"

"Oh, God no! Not those sweet ladies. I, uh, saw them both yesterday," Judah replied with tears in his eyes.

"You did?! Once again you are nearby when people die!"

"What is he talking about, Judah?"

"Didn't he tell you, Senator Jordan died in his arms a couple of days ago," Detective Holmes said, looking right at Judah.

"Judah?" Dawn called out.

"That's enough, guys," Judah stopped the discussion as he moved the Detectives outside. "My wife has been in a coma for a couple of months, and you are dropping all of this on her now. I don't think so. That is enough. Now beat it!"

"Captain Braden got a call from your boss Dr. Lazant and from some Federal boys. He was told to cool it concerning our investigation of you. You do have some powerful friends, Colonel, but we are not cooling it. What do you know of the deaths of those two women?"

"Look, I met with them at the First Baptist Church in Reston. We met with Pastor Calvin. They left and everything was all right."

"What did you discuss?" Holmes wanted to know.

"We talked about how Senator Jordan's death was blamed on a blood clot even though I was there and disputed that diagnosis. Mrs. Desporte felt that her husband did not die of a blood clot either as was cited as his cause of death. You saw Senator Jordan, guys. Did he die of a blood clot? In fact, you saw General Desporte also. Do you think that he died of a blood clot? I think not. Someone is covering up these murders and it is not me! Why don't you look into that?!"

75

"We are, Colonel," Holmes said with concern. "We are doing just that! We don't know what role you play in these deaths if any, but we do feel confident that you are at the center of them for whatever reason. Those two ladies went off of the road and over an embankment. Their faces were masks of extreme fright. It was as if they saw something that scared them to death."

"You wouldn't know what that was, would you, Colonel?" O'Malley asked with a slight smirk.

"Was it the *it* that Dawn just described?"

"If I told you, Gentlemen, I would have to kill you!" Judah answered once again with a smile.

The two Detectives finally decided to leave. They told Judah that they were pleased for him that his wife had regained consciousness. They again told him that they were baffled by this whole set of occurrences and that they would continue to search them out, even if meant using a more discreet profile. Judah assured them that he would keep them informed as best that he could.

"One last thing, Colonel," O'Malley asked politely. "I thought that your wife had MS. I saw her sitting up on the bed, and I even heard from the nurses that she has begun to walk again?"

"Yeah, that's right. God not only brought her back from unconsciousness, but He brought her back whole again without the MS."

"How is that possible?" Holmes interjected. "It ain't possible. No way! My wife died of cancer and no Preacher done a thing for her."

"Yeah, it's possible," O'Malley said. "Did you pray to the Blessed Mother of God, the Virgin Mary? Hey, wait a minute, you are a Jew aren't you, Colonel?"

"Jesus healed her, guys," Judah responded with a grin. "Nothing is impossible for God to he who believes, even a Jew!"

Judah went back into the room and found Dawn sound asleep. She was exhausted after her most exciting day. Judah just sat next to her and looked her over. Without the tubes and other medical paraphernalia, he recognized the beautiful black haired, blue-eyed woman that he had fallen in love with. They only had each other. Both were only children. Dawn's parents were both deceased from lung cancer. Judah still had his beloved mother, Bertha. He wondered how she would respond to Dawn's recovery?

"Ma, it is Judah, how are you doing?" Judah spoke as he called from the hospital room.

"Is it you, Judah?" Bertha answered sarcastically. "I thought that it was my young boyfriend! Who else would it be? Oy, Judah, you are really something."

"Ma, I have great news. Dawn woke up from her coma!" Judah shouted into the phone hoping that he did not wake up Dawn.

"She what? She woke up? Oh thank God! I bet that you are happy?"

"Yes I am, Ma. You see, all those prayers worked!"

"Worked, shmorked. She probably just woke up. It was time."

"No, ma, her MS is gone also, she can walk again!"

"What are you talking about? That cannot happen?" Bertha wondered aloud. "Things like that just don't go away. That is why we have Doctors. You should have been a Doctor, Judah, not a prayerman!"

"Well it did, Ma. She is up and walking again. I am going to take her home in a couple of weeks."

"That's good, tatalleh. Now she can cook for you. Does she know how to cook, Judah? I mean can she cook real Jewish food like matzo ball soup and kreplach and brisket? Those shiksas *(Y.Gentile women)* can't cook Jewish, I'll bet. Tell her that I'll give her some recipes."

"Ma, stop it!"

"And now maybe I can have a grandson? We could name him Moshe after your late father, God rest his soul."

"Ma, we need to get to know each other first."

"Judah, there are no more Meires. You have to keep up the family name. And I want the baby circumcised by a mohel *(H.man who does traditional circumcisions)*, and I want him brought up Jewish and..."

"Ma, cool it. Relax, slow down"

"I can come out and take care of little Moshe for a few months to help out!"

Judah politely thanked his Mom for her offer, but told her that he had to go. He was calling from the Hospital room and billing it to his home number, and it was getting expensive. She understood and said that she would call him the next evening. Judah went right over to the Institute. As he entered, he was met by two men in dark suits and sunglasses. They escorted him to the conference room where he met Dr. Lazant. They then instructed that the surveillance cameras be shut off.

"Colonel Meire," began one of the men, a man in his late sixties with a scar across his forehead. "We are here to speak to you about what has been going on of late. We have been monitoring your movements over the past year or so."

"Who are you guys? CIA? NSA?" Judah barked out.

"We are from a top secret government project. Very few people know of us or of our very existence or mission. We were created about 50 years ago after Roswell. We monitor UFO activity in the US."

"You what? I thought that the government has denied the existence of UFOs?"

"They have and they will continue to do so. We exist on a need to know basis. You have had numerous encounters with an extraterrestrial by the name of AZAZEL. Is that correct?"

"Yes."

"We know that the work here at the Institute seeks to establish communication with extraterrestrials. We have been watching Dr. Lazant for years. We know that he feels that they are spiritual beings of some sort. We don't care, however, what he wants to call them. We know that their contact with and abduction of American citizens has increased exponentially since 1947. We are convinced that they have been trying to alter our DNA. That has not worked as they had thought that it would, so they are preparing some large scale abduction of human beings here on this planet to prepare for their entrance."

"Who are you guys?"

"We belong to project Ultra. As I said, it is a top secret group that exists on a need to know basis. Anyone, and I mean anyone who breaks the code of silence will be eliminated."

"But then why are you telling me all of this?" Judah asked nervously.

"Because you, Judah, have a direct line of contact of communication that few others have. This AZAZEL has singled you out. If it wants you, then we want you. But nothing leaves this room. Am I clear?"

"Yes, I guess, but what about Dr. Lazant and the people at the Institute?"

"We are fine, Judah. We have worked along with Ultra for years," Dr. Lazant answered quietly. "We personally believe that these UFOs are angels as you know. These guys think that we are nuts. So be it. We will continue to do our research and maybe someday we will be able to convince them."

"That will be a cold day in Hades, Doc!" the other man, a young Oriental, replied. "We are convinced through fifty years of data and observations that these ET'S are bent on taking over our world. You can spiritualize them all that you want, but they will still kill and destroy your father, mother or children. Look at General Desporte and Senator Jordan and their wives. All victims of their insidious plot to rule the earth.They roam all over the earth looking for people to abduct and destroy."

"By the way, gentlemen, did you know that my wife regained consciousness today?" Judah stated. "She was attacked by AZAZEL and not only survived but her MS is gone also."

"Yes, we knew that, Judah. Did you know that her first husband Bob got too close to us and threatened to expose us? We had to take care of him," the old man chuckled.

"You WHAT?! You killed Bob and her daughter Caroline?" Judah shrieked as he jumped up in their faces. He pulled out his Uzi and aimed it right between the eyes of the older one.

"Use it, Colonel, or put it away," he responded without flinching . "Don't try and be the Lone Ranger with us. We have seen too many things and done too many things to be scared by the likes of you. We would just as soon eliminate you as well, but we need you for National Security reasons. If that ever becomes a case of diminishing returns, then you are history! Don't ever forget that, Colonel. We have kept this Project secret for over 50 years by eliminating all of those persons who threaten to expose us. Our Nation's ultimate security is at stake and every person is expendable. Do I make myself clear?"

Judah backed off and put away his weapon. He reluctantly shook his head in approval and went back and sat down. Dr. Lazant assured them that everything would be all right.

"What about the Detectives Holmes and O'Malley?" Judah asked as they prepared to leave the room.

"They're history, my friend, you can count on it!" replied the young man with a sly grin.

The two agents from Ultra left the room and exited the building. Judah sat there in the conference room and looked over at Dr. Lazant.

"They are some eerie dudes, Doc," Judah began. "How long have you known of their activities?"

"I've known of them for a little over a year now," Dr. Lazant responded as he watched on the security camera while they exited the grounds. "As soon as I started using the Remote Viewing protocol to explore the heavens, I got a visit from them. They were prepared to just shut us down or even eliminate us until I pulled in some old markers that I had with CIA and NSA. They think that we are a lunatic fringe group that is searching for the gods in spaceships, but we have established communication with AZAZEL and so they tolerate us to see what we find out. Nobody knows of them except you and I. Not Reverend Shea or Stephen or Endora. I did not want to put their lives at risk. Can you believe, Judah, that the government has had a secret group that has monitored UFOs for over 50 years and while they have managed to keep it from the public, they also are being deceived. They do not realize that these ETs are angels who are here to help mankind achieve a higher state of consciousness!"

"Amazing, isn't it," Judah said with a look of consternation. "Imagine that they killed Dawn's husband Bob and their daughter. He was a magazine editor. He must have threatened to blow the whole thing wide open so they killed him and a little girl. That is our government doing things like that. It makes me sick!"

"There are lots of things that the government does that would make you sick, Judah. Don't think about any more than you have to, or it will make you ill. By the way, why do you think that AZAZEL came into the Institute and messed up the security cameras?"

"Maybe it was trying to block its view from the Ultra boys?" Judah quickly replied trying to divert his attention.

"Do you think that they may have bugged these offices?"

"After what I just heard, I wouldn't hesitate to think otherwise. They will not let anyone or anything get in the way of their attempt to keep this whole thing secret. They as much told us that they are going to eliminate Holmes and O'Malley."

"I guess that you are right, Judah. I never thought of it quite that way before," Dr. Lazant said with a broad smile. "Thank you, Judah, for your insights."

Judah left the conference room and called the Potomac Police Department. He tried to locate Holmes and O'Malley but they were out in the field. He left a message that they should contact him as soon as they called in.

"Is that you, Judah?" Captain Braden suddenly interjected.

"Yes it is, Sir," Judah replied.

"What do you want with Holmes and O'Malley?"

"I just wanted to talk with them. Could you please have them call me at the Institute?"

"O'Malley is dead, Colonel!" Captain Braden screamed into the phone. "You are the kiss of death. Everything that touches you dies!"

"When did this happen? I just saw him a couple of hours ago," Judah questioned with a tone of sadness in his voice.

"He died on the street. Seems that he went into one of those Post Traumatic Stress Syndrome flashbacks to Vietnam. He wounded several people before he was shot."

"Did they kill him?"

"Hey fool, listen to my voice. I told you that he was dead. That means that they killed him, right?"

"Captain, I would do an autopsy if I were you. Someone killed him," Judah pleaded with the Captain. "He hasn't had one of those flashbacks for years. He told me that."

"Was it you, Colonel?"

"No it wasn't me but I... Where is Holmes?"

"I'm not sure. I think that he went to the Dentist."

"Who is his Dentist?" Judah demanded.

"How am I supposed to know?" Captain Braden shouted back. "I am not his mother!"

"Well, ask around!" Judah replied hurriedly. "Go on, Captain, do it. It might be a matter of life and death. Move it!"

"Who do you think that you are talking to, wiseguy?" Captain Braden shouted back at Judah.

"Just ask, Captain! Now!"

Judah held on as he heard the Captain ask around for the name. Finally he came back on the line. He was furious with Judah. Who was he to order him around? What did he know of O'Malley's death and why was he so afraid for Holmes?

"The Dentist's name is Dr. Scott. He is over in Georgetown. What the heck is going on here?"

"Remember, Captain you were told to back off from this investigation by the Feds? You should have listened to that advice! I would cool it if I were you. You are in over your head!" Judah yelled as he slammed down the receiver. He fled the Institute building and went across the street to a pay phone. After finding out the number of Dr. Scott in Georgetown, he dialed it frantically.

"Do you have a patient by the name of Holmes there at the moment?" Judah asked the receptionist.

"Uh, yes we do. He is with the Doctor at the moment, though."

"I need to talk with him right now. It is very important."

"Who is calling please?"

"It is a friend. Tell him it is a matter of life and death."

After a few minutes, Holmes came to the phone. He had novocaine in his mouth and he was not happy.

"Who is this?"

"It is Judah!"

"What do you want? Why are you bothering me here?" Holmes angrily yelled into the receiver.

"Listen to me, Holmes. You need to leave the dentist right now. You need to leave town immediately!"

"I do, says who? You?"

"Your life is in immediate peril. They just killed O'Malley and you are next!"

"What are you talking about? I just saw O'Malley an hour ago." Holmes mumbled through the novocaine.

"He is dead, Holmes. I just spoke to Captain Braden. They said he had another Post Traumatic Stress Syndrome attack and he freaked out and started shooting people. They had to kill him. Don't you see, they did it. They probably doped him up. It was a setup. You are next!"

"Who set him up? What are you talking about?"

"Remember you were told to back off of this investigation by the Feds and you decided not to? Well they have decided that you are expendable. They are a top secret Fed group that answers to nobody."

"Who are they?"

"If I told you, they would kill me! I told you, as I told Captain Braden, that all of you were in over your heads. You better get out before you are murdered like O'Malley was!"

"What am I supposed to do?"

"Do you have any children that you could go visit for a while?"

"Yeah, I have a daughter who just got married in Arizona."

"Leave right now and go see her, Holmes!"

"Right now?"

"Yes right now. They are probably on their way to kill you. Trust me. You'll be dead by the end of the day if you stay here!"

"Will she be safe?" Holmes asked.

"Does anyone know her married name or where she lives?"

"No!" Holmes replied. "She just married this white guy. He is a professor at the University."

"It should be all right, then. Keep a low profile for a while," Judah answered affirmatively.

"Hey, Colonel, thanks!" Holmes reluctantly replied.

Holmes put down the receiver and walked right out of the Dentist's office with the little white bib still round his neck. The receptionist and the dental assistant ran after him but he totally ignored them. He got to his car and opened the trunk. He switched the car's Maryland license with one he had from Virginia in the trunk. He started driving for Arizona and did not stop to sleep anywhere except in rest stops until he arrived there. That was nearly three days without much sleep. He drank enough coffee to stay awake until the next year. When he knocked on the door of his daughter, her white husband answered the door. He collapsed into his arms.

Judah went back to the hospital to be with Dawn. They had so much to talk about. Dawn was dazed by the story that she heard from Judah. So much had happened while she had been in that coma.

"Judah, sweetheart, maybe you are putting too many of these events together when in reality they are just coincidental?" Dawn said with a smile. "I mean, you have put the deaths of General Desporte, Senator Jordan, their wives and Detective O'Malley all together in one grand conspiracy. They cannot be all related."

"Why can't they be, Dawn?" Judah answered. "Actually, there is not just one conspiracy. There are at least two. One is the conspiracy of AZAZEL to keep us blind to his plans for world domination. It is using the misguided efforts of Dr. Lazant, Reverend Shea and the others. It has already eliminated the General, the Senator and their wives because they found out his plan. The other conspiracy is that of the government Ultra project. They want to keep Americans from the truth of extraterrestrials. They have also eliminated Detective O'Malley."

"But Judah," Dawn continued, "If you are correct about AZAZEL, then why did I recover as well as your mother?"

"Good question, honey. I guess you two were in too much prayer."

Dawn continued to argue with Judah. She felt as though his paranoia had gotten the better of him. He saw conspiracies and planned deaths everywhere. She tried to calm him down a bit.

"Judah, the Lord is in control. He would not let all these evil conspiracies to flourish."

"Dawn, what are you saying? That there is no evil in this world? That God is good and therefore nothing bad can happen or will happen? You know as well as I that we live in a fallen, sinful world. Satan knows his time is short and he is out to rob, kill and destroy as much as he can. AZAZEL said that the end of the world is near."

Dawn sat quietly and closed her eyes. She asked the Lord for guidance. She had felt from the beginning that Judah was the soldier that the Lord had chosen to fight this great endtime battle of deception but now she was having second thoughts. Maybe he had come too far too fast. After all, not too long ago, he had been a brash egotistical non believer. He did not know the Bible from the phone book. Now he was quoting her chapter and verse. It was as if she had gone to sleep for many years to awaken to a different man as her husband. Before her coma, he had been a reluctant unsure servant of the Lord. Now he was a self-assured man on fire for the Lord. The student so to speak had become the teacher.

"Dawn," Judah had interjected and broken her line of thought, "I fought AZAZEL two times. He flung his flaming missiles at me but I put on the full armor of God and rebuked him. Here, look at my scar."

Dawn looked at the round scar and began to cry. "Oh, Judah, forgive me for my doubt. It is just that you have grown so much in the Word that I hardly recognized you. Instead of crediting you with your growth, I blamed it on paranoia. It is just that you are a new man, Judah, just as I am now a new woman. I have a new body but you have a new soul and a new heart. Before all of this I could not get you to read your Bible. Now you are quoting it to me. Praise God. Thank you, Lord, for raising up such a mighty man to serve You, Lord. Judah, hand me the Bible. The Lord just gave me a scripture as an answer to a prayer request of mine."

Judah handed her the Bible.

"It is from 2Chronicles 15:7, Judah. It says 'but you, be strong and do not lose courage, for there is reward for your work."

"That is what I have been trying to tell you, Dawn," Judah replied. "There is something very monumental going on here. I have been chosen to reveal this delusion. I did not want the job. I told the Lord that I was not worthy. I asked why He did not choose another Christian brother for the job. Why a poor wretched sinner like me? Remember what General Desporte once told me. That Abraham was too old and David was too young. Many of the figures in the Bible were not perfect men for their circumstances, but they were perfect instruments of the Lord. The Lord knew that I needed you at my side during this battle. I prayed for you, and I battled the demons of hell for you. They will never take you from me again. As for Bertha, I also battled AZAZEL for her. I pray that one day she will see the truth. She is in many ways an embittered little old Jewish lady. She has been through a lot in her lifetime, but I still pray for her. She wants us to have a grandson for her and to name it Moshe after my father. She wants it circumcised and brought up Jewish. She even offered to teach you to cook Jewish. Don't laugh, Dawn, she is serious!"

Dawn smiled and put her arms around Judah. She was so proud of him. He had come so far in so short a time. She had seen something in him right from the beginning that defied outward appearance and actions. He was a brash, agnostic, Jewish man who had no idea what the Lord had in store for him. General Desporte and Senator Jordan had seen Judah with the same spiritual eyes that defied the natural man before them. Now, both they and their wives, had given their lives for this spiritual battle for the souls of mankind. Dawn, however, felt the blessed assurance that they were all now with the Lord. What a comfort that was.

"Dawn, there is one more thing that I have to tell you," Judah began as he held her hand tightly. "Bob and Caroline were killed by those top secret boys from the government."

"What? Oh my God!" Dawn screamed. "It seems as if our lives have been watched and manipulated from the beginning. Why them?"

"I was told that Bob was going to reveal the existence of Ultra in his magazine.

83

They must have sabotaged his car and Caroline happened to be in it at the time. I think that her death was probably an accident."

"Well thanks for that," Dawn said sarcastically. "Who is this Ultra again? I am so confused."

"Ultra is the top secret government group that has investigated UFOs since 1947. Their job is to keep all knowledge of them out of the public eye. They will resort to any means necessary to maintain that veil of secrecy."

"Oh God! But wait a minute. Ultra believes in UFOs but keeps them secret. Lazant and his weirdo cronies believe that AZAZEL is an angel who is about to abduct Christians to enable the planet to evolve-or something like that. Am I warm? What a mess, Judah. If AZAZEL is really a fallen angel, a demonic being as you fear, than these Ultra guys don't really even know the entire truth. They are being deceived by AZAZEL into believing that he is an extraterrestrial while he is in fact a demon or a fallen angel."

"Right, Dawn! And Lazant and Shea and Stephen and Endora are being deceived into believing that they are good angels here to remove those pesky, judgmental Christians."

"Whoa, Judah, we need a scorecard to tell the deceivers from the deceived. Ultra is being deceived by the same deceivers who are deceiving the people at the Lazant Institute. My head is spinning."

"Do you know what you need, sweetheart," Judah said with a smile. "I'm going out and get you a cup of Chai at the cafe. I'll be right back. You know I started drinking it also. I've grown to like it as well. I introduced it to my mother. She went fey *(Y.yuk!)*! So sue me!"

When Judah returned with the hot Chai, Dawn was ecstatic. It was as if he had brought her a pot of gold. She gulped down the sweet flavorful Himalayan spiced tea and tried to relax her mind. After all that Judah had thrown at her at one time, it was racing in all directions out of control. Judah waited until she had calmed down a little and then he dropped another bombshell.

"You know, Dawn, I think that we should discuss going away from the city and hiding out in the country if things begin to deteriorate quickly. I know that Ultra is watching us and AZAZEL has already found out and eliminated my contacts in the government, so I am now probably expendable. Do you know of any Christians that would hide us out for a while?"

"Actually, I do!" Dawn responded with a smile as she finished her Chai.

"Great, Dawn. We need to contact them now as nonchalantly as possible remembering that all conversations are probably being monitored by one or both of the groups."

"As soon as I get home, I will pursue it. Oh Judah, I am so proud of you. What a blessing you have become to all of God's people."

"Remember what you used to tell me. If God spoke through Balaam's ass, He can speak through anyone or anything."

84

That comment triggered an instant response from Dawn. She grabbed a piece of note paper by the side of her bed and scribbled the following.

*Judah, we should have not have spoken so freely here. What if our conversation is being monitored?*

Judah put his head in his hands and fretted. He wrote back to Dawn.

*I cannot believe that I did that. I became too excited. Now they both probably know of our plans. We must keep everything secret from them from now on. I hope that it is not too late.*

# VII

Judah worked feverishly over the next two weeks to get the house ready for Dawn's return. He had new hinges put onto the back door that he had kicked open. He also took Dawn's Chevy Van into the shop not only to replace the parts that had exploded, but he also had them return the car to foot instead of hand controls. The Van had been specially outfitted for Dawn's wheelchair. Judah was so excited for Dawn. While much of the house had been made wheelchair accessible including the bathrooms and the kitchen, there was nothing that he would do about that. It would be a constant reminder to them of God's love.

Judah also went back to the Institute. He wanted to find out as much as he could about AZAZEL's agenda as well as the Institute's part in that plan. When he walked into the office, Reverend Shea was walking into his office holding another framed picture.

"Hey, Rev," Judah yelled, "what have you got there?"

"Oh, Judah, look at this!" Reverend Shea said as he showed it to Judah and smiled broadly. "It is a picture of Pope John Paul II receiving the traditional Shiva mark on his forehead by a Shiva Priestess."

"So what is the big deal about that?"Judah feigned ignorance, knowing full well that the Book of Revelation speaks of the False Prophet, the leader of the New World global religion, who causes all people in the world to take the mark either on the forehead or in the right hand.

"Judah, it shows that the Pope's dream of one universal religion is coming to pass! We are moving ever closer to that dream."

"Judah, Judah," Stephen interjected as he saw Judah and came running down the hall after him. "AZAZEL told us to keep a close eye on you. He said that your life was in danger."

Dr. Lazant walked up and they all decided to go into the conference room to speak.

"Judah," Dr. Lazant began, "we have all been talking about you. We understand that your wife has regained consciousness. Is that true? We all have been praying for her."

"Yes it is. Her MS has disappeared as well. We both are so thrilled by all that has happened. It clearly shows that God's prayers are answered. I know that you all will come to understand where Dawn is coming from."

"What do you mean, Judah?" Dr. Lazant asked with a curious look on his face.

86

"Well, remember you said that Dawn was one of those Evangelical Christians that AZAZEL was talking of removing from the Earth?" Judah said sarcastically without any remorse.

"We were just trying to spare you the heartbreak of possibly losing her again," Stephen said.

"That is mighty loving of you guys!" Judah quipped with a smile.

"What do you know of Detective Holmes?" Dr. Lazant said as he changed the subject abruptly.

"What do you mean?"

"He has disappeared and a Captain Braden was here looking for him."

"Why would he think that I would know where he is?"

"He said that you had tried to locate him at his dentist. He was last seen running out of the dentist's office and has not been seen or heard from since."

"I honestly don't know where he is."

Dr. Lazant did not bring up Ultra in front of his colleagues. He just stared at Judah to let him know that he thought that Judah had alerted the Detective to the danger to his life. The discussion soon turned to the topic of the upcoming world religion.

"AZAZEL told us that it will be necessary soon to abduct people from this planet who stand in the way of world unity," Stephen said excitedly. "Can you believe that some people, those fanatical religious zealots of the fundamentalist persuasion in particular, who are opposed to global unity, will be taken away? What better picture of what will be left than the one that Reverend Shea is holding. A dear Shiva priestess putting the traditional Shiva Hindu mark on the Pope's forehead. We are all one. There is not just one God or just one way to God. There are a multitude of paths to enlightenment. That is why these evangelical Christians need to be removed. Otherwise we cannot move to a higher plane of planetary consciousness and evolution."

"Are you saying that it is AZAZEL's task in this evolutionary process to remove the evangelical Christians like my wife?" Judah asked.

"Yes, Judah, it is," Dr. Lazant replied. "When all of them are removed, than the quest for a global religion and unity will commence in earnest. Reverend Shea and I have contacts at the United Nations who will move for adoption of a world wide religion. AZAZEL and the angels will help and guide us as they always have. They will no longer be the Watchers but will instead become the Helpers."

"What is going to happen to my wife and the others?" Judah asked anxiously

"They will be taken away and reeducated so that they can return to live in our new world order. It will be all right, Judah. She will be gone like she was in the coma," Dr. Lazant said. "I am so glad that you have expressed your desire to work on this project no matter what the sacrifice."

"Does the President know of all of this?" Judah asked as his stomach churned and he desired to be out of this evil place once and for all. Sure, he had told them, actually the voice within him had told them, that he would sacrifice all for them, but he now realized that it was only meant to give him more time to assess their motives and intentions.

"Not at the present time, Judah. We are not sure of the President's religious beliefs. He may be one of those taken. We will have to wait and see."

"Judah, we all need your protection," Endora piped in. "The upcoming times are very precarious to say the least. We do not want to end up crucified like Jesus was. There are many plotters and schemers out there who are bent upon disrupting our work. My Jesus entity told me to be wary of wolves in sheep's clothing. We all need to keep an eye on each other."

The meeting broke up but Dr. Lazant asked to speak with Judah in private. He escorted him into his office and shut the door. Judah felt very uneasy. He felt that he had heard enough now and just wanted to leave, but Dr. Lazant wanted to talk with him.

"Well, Judah, why did you call Holmes at the Dentist?"

"Why do you say that, Doc?" Judah responded with his Jewish ploy of answering every question with a question.

"Because someone tipped him off and Ultra thinks that it was you!"

"Now why would I do that?"

"Did you?"

"What reason would I have to call Holmes, a man who has been bugging me for weeks?"

"Did you, Judah?"

"Why are you so interested in Ultra, Doc? They think that all your talk of a global world religion run by space angels is a little nutty. In fact so do I!"

"Judah, Ultra is a powerful group. I don't want them shutting us down because you warned Holmes to get out of town. Understand? These men would sooner kill you than look at you. They are trying to protect the American populace from contact with the angels, fearful that it will cause world wide panic."

"Then what will they do or say when millions of Christians are suddenly abducted by these angels as you seem to believe? Talk about world wide panic!"

"That is a good question, Judah. I have been trying to explain that to them, but they say that they have everything under control. The world population will not accept abduction by angels but will accept abduction by aliens. They have been conditioned to do so for over fifty years. They point to all the movies and television shows about extraterrestrials. It has been a concerted, conscious effort on their part to promote such ideas. Now, Judah, do you know where Holmes is?"

"Honest to God, I have no idea where he is."

"Judah, why did you say that our belief in a global world religion is nutty?" Dr. Lazant asked Judah with a tone of bewilderment. "I thought that you we were all on the same page now?"

"Sorry, boss," Judah replied with a smile. "It is just that we Jews are always

88

amused by you Christians and your plans for world domination. You have been saying that for 2000 years. One thing has always been certain however-the Catholics distrust the Protestants and the Protestants distrust the Unitarians and the Lutherans distrust the Methodists but they all hate the Jews. I wonder how this global unity will affect my people?"

"Not to worry, Judah," Dr. Lazant reassured. "The Jews will be just fine in the new world order. Trust me! In fact one of the men we have picked out to help lead this new world order is a Jew."

Judah was appalled over what Dr. Lazant had to say. He realized that it was probably time to get out of there for good. He wasn't sure if Dr. Lazant was just humoring him so that Ultra could find out the rest of his contacts; or he was just doing it because he honestly believed that Judah could accept the abduction of his wife for an indefinite period by demonic beings interested in reeducating her? If so, then he had to be a little nuts or just a megalomaniac. In either case, Judah left the Institute, never looking back, and raced to Bethesda Naval Hospital.

When he entered Dawn's room, he motioned to her not to talk. He had brought along a small white board and a marker. He wrote on it that her life was in danger, and he handed her a 38mm Beretta with a silencer which he wrote that she should hide under her mattress. If anyone suspicious or threatening should attempt to accost her, she should blow his head off. Judah had taken Dawn to the pistol range, and she had become an excellent shot. Before her attack of MS, she had even flirted with the idea of trying out for the Olympic Biathlon. Her skiing and marksman skills were well honed. Finally, she had decided that her thirtysomething age was too old for the fierce training. The next week she had been struck down with MS and had been in a wheelchair ever since. She could and would blow away any attacker, however, without a moment's hesitation.

Dawn motioned to Judah for the white board. On it she wrote that one of the Elders from the Church had come over to see her. She had cautioned him not to speak. He thought she was a little paranoid. He told her that Pastor Calvin had taken a sabbatical from his pulpit for a while. He had gone to his sister's house in Georgia. There had just been too many inexplicable deaths in the Congregation of late, and he was concerned that he might be next. Dawn had assured the Elder that he had made the right decision and that they should all continue to pray for the Pastor, his family and of course Judah and her.

Each and every day Dawn felt stronger. Her physical therapy was progressing amazingly well and expeditiously. Her therapists were amazed at her ability to walk on atrophied muscles. She kept assuring them that the Lord was her strength. They could not help but be moved. Of course her hands and feet still tingled a bit and her balance was uncertain, but these were the effects of her battle with MS. Those brain lesions had wrought havoc upon her nervous system and would take time to have their damage healed.

"How do you feel, sweetheart?" Judah asked out loud, changing their conversation from the white board to full blown conversation.

"I'm doing much better, Judah," Dawn responded with a smile. "Every day, I feel that much stronger. I love being able to go the bathroom by myself. What a small thing, but it sure feels great. I still have a little problem with bladder control. When I have to go, I have to go and there had better be a bathroom nearby. Remember the time when I first developed symptoms and we were driving in the country and I had to go. You pulled off the road and I went in the bushes. Not an easy task for a woman. Remember, I thought that I got poison ivy?"

"How could I forget, Dawn. That policeman drove up, and I had to explain your behavior while shielding you from him. He thought that you were drunk or doing drugs. Remember?"

"Ah yes, I do, Judah. You were my knight in shining armor protecting a damsel in urinary distress!"

They both laughed so hard that their sides hurt. Dawn had to go to the bathroom and Judah helped her. Afterwards they just talked of the good times that they had together. It had been so long since they had talked with each other. It was nine or ten weeks.

Dr. Levin entered the room. "How are you doing, Dawn? I hear that your physical therapy is progressing nicely."

"I'm doing great, Dr. Levin," Dawn said with her usual sweet smile. "I hope to be going home soon."

"We'll see about that, Dawn. Squeeze my hand."

Dr. Levin ran through a series of neurological tests with Dawn. He had her stand on one foot and touch her nose with her eyes closed. He smiled and jotted down notes on his clipboard. He looked closely at her legs.

"Your legs are regaining muscle tone at a phenomenal rate. I don't think that I have ever seen anything like this before."

"Well Doc, you can write an article for the *New England Journal of Medicine* or something," Judah interjected. "But don't forget to say that God healed her. You had nothing to do with it. In fact you wanted me to pull the plug, didn't you, Oh great Dr. Kevorkian?"

"Judah, I thought that you were a landsman, a fellow Jew, a member of the tribe? Why do you keep talking of God healing her? You sound like a Christian."

"Are you saying, Doc, that only Christians believe in Divine healing? There are many instances in the Tanakh where God healed people. Do you think that God only heals Christians and not Jews?"

"Personally, I am an agnostic. I do not believe in a God that has caused so much suffering in the world. In fact, I probably am an atheist. I love my lox and bagel, and I give to the United Jewish Appeal and to Hadassah Hospital in Israel, but don't talk to me about God. My grandparents died in the Holocaust. Where was God then, macher *(Y.bigshot)*?"

"Well, so did mine, Doc," Judah answered softly. "But God has given us free will to choose evil or good. He wants us to come to Him by our own free choice. Just because there is evil in this world does not mean that there is no God. Look at Dawn. No matter that she was stricken with MS and thrown into a coma by an intruder, she is now well. He that is in her is greater than he that is in the world."

"What? Listen, I believe that Dawn is in spontaneous remission. It could last a week or a month or forever. Nobody knows. I wouldn't get your hopes up. It could be a fleeting episode."

"Listen to me, Doc. Read my lips. Dawn has been healed by a loving God who exists no matter what you believe..." Judah began to lecture the Doctor.

"Judah, stop!" Dawn broke into the diatribe. "Thank you, Doctor, for all your help."

Dr. Levin turned around and headed out of the room all the while staring at Judah nervously. Judah smiled and held up a finger at him to remind him to think about what he had said.

Judah said goodbye to Dawn. He wrote on the white board that he was going in to the beltway to visit his old friends at the CIA to see what he could find out about Ultra and to see what friends of Senator Jordan or General Desporte that he could find. He asked Dawn if she had any Christian contacts in the Intelligence community that he might contact. She wrote down a couple of names. One was a CIA person and one was a Congressman. Judah quickly erased their names and kissed Dawn goodbye and headed out of the Hospital with all deliberate speed.

On the way, he once again ran into Dr. Levin. Judah put his arm around the Doctor and rubbed his nearly bald head.

"Chill out, Doc, you need to relax," Judah said with a laugh. "You are really uptight."

"Let me alone, Colonel!" Dr. Levin shouted pushing Judah away. "You were in the IDF? I cannot believe it. You married that shiksa, and you are beginning to sound just like her. I'll bet your grandparents are turning over in their graves."

"If they believed like I do, Doctor, they would be in Heaven now, not in their graves!"

"Oy vey. You silly man. You have become like a little child awed by myths and fables. I feel sorry for you."

"I feel sorry for you, Doc. You have no hope of eternal life. All that you can look forward to is the grave. If that is true, than who really is the silly man? I think that it is you, my friend!"

"Judah, I am a Doctor. I know about death," Dr. Levin answered quickly. "When you die you are just dead. It is just like you are asleep, but you never wake up."

"Look, Doc, if you are correct, then I am just a deceived man grasping for eternal life when there really is not any. I am just a fool who will one day die and there will be nothing. But if I am correct, then when you die you will stand before the judgement seat of God and have to explain to him why you did not believe. Unfortunately it will be too late by then, and you will be eternally separated from

God in the fires of Hell. The bottom line is that, if you are right, I face an eternity of nothingness when I die. If I am right, then when you die, you face an eternity of torment, separated from God. Who has more to lose, Herr Docktor?"

"Leave me alone, Judah!" Dr. Levin yelled as he pushed past Judah.

"Gotcha with that one, didn't I, Doc?" Judah yelled back as the Doctor scampered away without looking back.

Judah headed for the CIA building in Langley, Virginia. It was not very far from Bethesda Naval Hospital or the Institute for that matter which was in Potomac, Maryland. Judah had built up some lasting friendships with the people there. One especially, Mike Butrell, was the Deputy Director, and he had taken an immediate liking to Judah. Butrell had friends in the Mossad who had spoken very highly of Judah. Also Senator Jordan had personally vouched for him. That coming from the Chairman of the Senate Select Intelligence Committee was enough for Butrell to ignore his doubts about hiring a former IDF soldier and Mossad operative. General Desporte at West Point also had vouched for Judah.

"Hello, Sir!" Judah said as he was immediately admitted to Deputy Director's Butrell's office. His secretary had recognized Judah right away and had called her boss. Butrell wanted him sent right in.

"Judah, my friend," Director Butrell said as he got up, put down his ever-present box of Cracker Jacks and embraced him. Butrell was a very tall man about six foot eight and had a strong lanky frame. He had always wanted to be a pilot but he was just too tall. He had settled for a lifelong career in the intelligence service now spanning over forty years.

"What is all that stuff that you have with you?" he asked Judah concerning the box of surveillance equipment that he was carrying.

"I found this in my house. It seems that Senator Jordan had the NSA put it there to watch over me. Did you guys know about this?"

Deputy Director Butrell rummaged through the box. He picked up a piece of equipment and looked it over very carefully and then put it back. He then picked up another piece and went through the same process all over again. It appeared to Judah that he was stalling for some reason. Maybe it was just his own imagination or paranoia, although who could blame him, given what had happened recently.

"Well this is definitely company equipment, but I have no knowledge of it being put in your house. Who told you that Senator Jordan had it put there?"

"He did, Sir! In fact, his wife Betsy confirmed it to me also. She told me after he died that he had told her that he was really sorry but that he had felt compelled to do it."

"And now both of them are dead," Butrell responded bewildered. "I heard that he died in your arms? Why were you there, Judah? You didn't have anything to do with his death, did you? Some believe that to be the case - especially the local police."

"The local police?" Judah sneered. "Detective O'Malley has died mysteriously, and Detective Holmes is missing. They were told to back off from this investigation. This whole thing is one big mess, Sir. I think that you know more than you are telling me. Senator Jordan was killed by the same thing that killed General Desporte! These were all friends of yours, Butrell. Have you no compassion for their deaths and the deaths of their wives?"

"I thought that both men died of blood clots and their wives in an automobile accident?" Butrell said as he got up and paced the floor. "What is going on here, Judah? What do you know?"

"What do you know of Ultra, Sir?" Judah asked as he stared directly at Butrell.

"Ultra? I never heard of it," Butrell said with a quizzical look on his face.

"What do know of the work that Lazant is doing at his Institute?"

"I know that he is still doing Remote Viewing. Something about looking into space?"

Judah realized that Butrell either did not know what was going on or was unable or unwilling to share it with him. Judah politely picked up his box of equipment, and said that he had to go.

"No, Judah, don't go," Butrell insisted. "There is so much we have to talk about. I heard that your wife has regained consciousness. That's terrific. What is going on, Judah, with all these deaths? Do you know something that we don't know?"

"Ask Ultra, Sir," Judah replied angrily.

Judah got up and shook the Deputy Director's hand. He told him that they would be in touch. He walked out into the hallway and went up to the receptionist. Judah asked the office number of the man whose name Dawn had given to him. He was told that Major Kole was in room 513. When he got to the room, he took a deep breath and said a prayer before entering. He hoped and prayed that this man would be more cooperative than Butrell. When he told his name to his secretary, and she told the Major who was there, he could hear the man's booming voice over the intercom.

"Oh Judah, God Bless you. I have been waiting for you to come," Major Kole said as he came over and grabbed Judah. He was a short muscular black man with a thick black beard and coal black eyes. He welcomed Judah in and closed the door. He then went over to his desk and turned on a device that Judah recognized. It was a scrambler that would negate any attempt to listen to what they were saying.

"My wife Dawn gave me your name, Major," Judah began with a smile. "I wanted to know who were my Christian allies in the Company. I just spoke to Deputy Director Butrell, and he was cordial but either does not know what is going on or will not tell me. I'll ask you the same question that I asked him, Major. Who is Ultra?"

"Boy, you get right to the meat, don't you, son," Major Kole laughed. "You don't beat around the bushes at all. I like that! You would have made a good marine, son!"

"There isn't time, Major, to play games."

"Right on, bro! Ultra was, as you probably already know, set up as a top secret group in 1947 to investigate UFOs. Very few people know of them. I honestly don't know if the President does or not. This is a group that people do not talk about. It functions in the shadows on a need to know basis. If you talk of them you are eliminated without question or forethought. They will do anything to keep UFOs a secret from the American people. As to if Butrell knows or not, I cannot positively say."

"Then how come you do, Major?" Judah asked with a feeling of concern. "And if you do, then why have they not eliminated you?"

"You really want to know, Judah? I've prayed about it. There is a group of us here in Washington. Some are CIA, some Pentagon, some Congress, some Military. We have been very concerned about the rash of UFO sightings over the past decades. We have not bought the usual line of denial. Senator Jordan fell into Ultra quite by accident one day. We have ever since monitored them. Unfortunately many good men and women have given their lives over the years for this knowledge. Anytime they find out about one of us, they eliminate them."

"They told me that they killed Dawn's first husband."

"They did! The interesting thing is why they have not killed you. They are probably watching you to discover the rest of us, first!"

"But then I led them right to you," Judah said despondently.

"Don't worry about us. They know we are around, but they do not know exactly who we are. They especially loathe all us Christians, probably because we are the only ones that have figured out their agenda."

"How can they function above the law and the Constitution? Who oversees them? Who polices them?"

"Nobody does. Sit down, Judah. I want to tell you something. When this group was set up in 1947, they had the best of intentions. They wanted to examine UFOs and to keep their investigation from generating panic among the population. They kept things very quiet. All of us in the Intelligence Community, believed that these UFOs were real and that they were a threat, but everything was kept on a need to know basis. Then about five years ago or so, the Christians here in Washington who were in the Intelligence Community began to pray about what we should do. We came to the conclusion that these supposed ET's and their UFOs were actually demonic entities not extraterrestrials. General Desporte and Senator Jordan were at the forefront of this revelation. After all, if these were indeed extraterrestrials, than evolution was true and the Bible was false. They would just be more highly evolved creatures from another planet, another galaxy. We did not, nor could we accept that, so we turned to another explanation. And if these beings were indeed demonic beings that what did that tell us about Bible Eschatology. Were we in the end times? Were we about to enter the Tribulation?"

"Major, I can tell you with absolute certainty that you are correct on all counts. I have seen, talked with and fought with these fallen demonic angels. I have seen

94

the people at the Lazant Institute embrace these demons as angels sent to remove the Christians from the Earth and begin a time of spiritual evolution. I have been threatened by Ultra, had a friend killed by them, and another run for his life."

"Oh my God, Judah. Things are happening even faster than we expected. We have watched you carefully. Senator Jordan said that you were our Lion, Judah. God has watched over you and your family. Even though there have been attacks against your wife and your mother, they have survived. That is more than can be said of General Desporte, Senator Jordan, their wives, Bob and Caroline Willis and Detective O'Malley."

"What is the relationship, Major, of Ultra to AZAZEL and the so-called angels?"

"Judah, that is the most intriguing question of all. We believe that Ultra was compromised many years ago. We believe that they are either demons or men controlled by them. Ultra wants to keep the existence of these entities secret until they can overtake our planet."

"Then why doesn't the CIA or the Pentagon just eliminate them?"

"Judah, people do not see things as they really are. Those who know of Ultra are themselves being deceived by them. Satan is after all the great Deceiver and Scripture says that even the elect will be deceived in the endtimes. That is why we have to work behind the scenes. You need to see Congressman Jacobs from Texas. He will fill you in on even more of the work that we are doing."

"That is the other name that Dawn gave me."

"She was a part of our working group. Many of those involved have been killed or have died under questionable circumstances. You are the newest member, Judah, and many of us think the most important. All that we have done has been in preparation for you. You need to find out their plans and expose them."

"I used to ask why me, Major, but now I realize that it is a job that I must do. All of you have sacrificed so much to get me to this point. God Bless you, Sir. I will do what I have to do!"

"Judah, if all else fails I want you to contact this man," Major Kole said quietly. "His name is Captain Peter Knowington. He is commander of a Christian Militia group in the mountains not too very far from here. He is thoroughly briefed on what is going on and will able to hide you out if things get too hot. You can reach him at the following email address. Memorize it and then swallow it."

Judah left the Major after shaking his hand and embracing him. He had memorized Knowington's email address and swallowed the piece of paper that it had been written on. The Major smiled and told Judah that he knew that he would accomplish his mission no matter what the costs. Judah left the building and was startled as he heard a crashing of glass. He turned around to see Major Kole's body falling from the shattered fifth floor window. He started to run towards it as it broke apart upon hitting the cement below, but instead he ran to his car. Ultra had struck again. This time taking the life of Major Kole. It would probably be explained as a suicide. Imagine a man committing suicide by jumping out a closed window.

Judah wondered who would be next. He hesitated to go and visit Congressman Jacobs fearing that he probably would be next.

Judah entered his wife's Chevy Van. He was driving it to see if it were brought back to proper foot controls as he had requested. He put on his seat belt and drove away. Suddenly, he felt a gun at the back of his head.

"Just keep driving," a voice said from the back of the car.

Judah looked in the rear view mirror and saw that it was the older man from Ultra. The one with the scar on his forehead. He was told to drive out into the country. Judah began to perspire. He knew that this man wanted to kill him. He had obviously outlived his usefulness. He had also led them to all the Christian collaborators except Congressman Jacobs. They had probably gotten to him already. Judah swerved the van and the man bounced around behind his seat.

"Stop that!" the man shouted.

"What are you going to do if I don't, kill me?" Judah screamed, "You are going to do that anyway! I might as well take you with me!"

Judah sped up as he left the populated areas. He was going nearly ninety miles an hour now. It reminded him of the time that he was in a similar situation in Israel. A terrorist had sneaked into his jeep and had held a gun to his head. Judah had begun to drive recklessly and the man had become very upset. Judah had smashed the jeep into an abutment at sixty miles an hour and had suffered numerous broken bones but had lived. The terrorist had been thrown right into the bridge and died instantly. Thank God for the steering wheel.

Judah continued to speed out of control. The man from Ultra was very agitated but could do nothing about it. He yelled at Judah to slow down but of course Judah ignored him. They sped past a Highway Patrol car that was stopped giving someone a ticket. Judah honked his horn, and as he sped by her, swerved a few times to get her attention. The Highway Patrol car soon began to chase them. Judah smiled. He could now pull over and be safe from this killer. When the Highway Patrolcar pulled alongside Judah and motioned him to pull over, she could not see the man in the back seat.

Just as Judah started to pull over, the man from Ultra stuck his gun out of Judah's window and fired three shots into the Patrolcar, mortally wounding the officer. She was shot in the head and her car swerved right in front of Judah. They were rounding a corner over a precipice, and Judah slammed onto his brakes. The man in the back seat flew into the front and his head went right into the windshield. Judah fought to regain control of his van but it was too late. It slammed into the patrol car that had swerved directly into its path. The man from Ultra's entire body now flew out of the car into the window of the Patrolcar. Judah had time only to say a quick prayer as he crashed into the Patrolcar and began to spin uncontrollably. His van began to whirl towards the cliff in front of him. Judah could do nothing but pray as his demise approached. The van went over the precipice and bounced off of the side of the cliff breaking into several pieces. When it hit the bottom it burst into flames and sent a plume of smoke high into the early evening sky.

Evening approached and Dawn was worried about Judah. He had not come by to see her, and she was concerned that something had happened to him. After all there were so many people that did not want him to continue poking his nose into their secret business. She reached under her mattress and felt the gun that Judah had left for her. She began to pray for protection for Judah. She kept having the uncomfortable feeling that something had happened to him. She asked the Lord to watch over him and protect him. She remembered how Judah had called her the Church Lady when they first had met. Dawn was an attractive lady and all the men including Judah were attracted to her physically, but she had always quoted the Bible to them. That had made Judah and the other unbelievers feel very uneasy. Several had watched Saturday Night Live and started calling her Church Lady like the character on that show. She was not amused at first, in fact she had never watched the show, but later she had reconciled herself to the fact that it could have been worse. They could have called her crazy lady. From then on, Judah had always called her "Church Lady".

Dawn lay back on her pillow and began to doze off. She thanked God for her new found strength and good health. She had regained almost all of her ability to function normally. She could walk, although slowly, because her balance was still a little off kilter. She was still easily fatigued but what could one expect after being unable to walk for months, nearly a year by now.

Just as she dozed off, she felt a pillow over her face. Someone was trying to suffocate her. She tried to wrestle free, but she was not strong enough. They held the pillow very hard over her face. She began to pass out. She lost consciousness for an instant. She asked the Lord for help and then she remembered the gun under the mattress. She reached down but could not find it. She kept losing consciousness, but the attacker seemed to ease up every once in awhile enabling her to catch a breath. She reached all over the inside of the mattress as she struggled to stay alive long enough to find the gun. Then in an instant she found it. She pulled it out, releasing the safety, as she stuck it against the rotund body of the person over her,. She fired three quick bursts and the pressure of the body and pillow which had been on her suddenly relaxed. She threw off the pillow and saw that it was Betty, her nurse.

There was blood everywhere as she had shot her in the liver and kidneys. Betty fought for life.

"Why you?" Dawn said as she gasped deeply for breath.

"They put me here to watch over you," Betty mumbled through a mouth of blood. "I don't want to die. Oh Mary mother of God please forgive me! They corrupted me. They promised me power, wealth and a high position in their new world order. I succumbed to my own greed and lust for power. I am sorry, Dawn. I am truly glad that it is me, not you, that is dying. I want to be forgiven. I want to go to Heaven with my parents and my daughter, not to hell with my cheating

Catholic husband and those demons! Will you help me, Dawn?"

Dawn looked into her dying eyes and saw what she thought was true repentance. She asked Betty if she wanted to turn her life over to Jesus Christ. It was Him and Him alone that could forgive sin and provide for redemption from Hell by His shed blood. Dawn asked her if she truly wanted to make Him the Lord of her life.

"Betty, do you confess all your sins and ask the Lord, Jesus Christ to forgive you for them? Do you sincerely want Him to be the Lord of your life as short as it appears to be? Do you believe that He is the second part of the triune Godhead and that He took on human flesh? Do you believe that He died for the sins of the world and that He was buried and that He rose again providing the way for eternal life and freedom from death, hell and the grave for all of us? All that believe in Him will have eternal life. Do you acknowledge Him as your Lord and Savior, Betty?" Dawn asked as Betty shook her head in agreement.

"Yes I do, Dawn. Oh Lord, please forgive me for my sins. I know that You are a merciful God who came to save the lost. My mother taught me that. I'm am truly sorry for what I have done. Oh God, I want to be with You for eternity, not with those demonic angels. Oh God, pleeease!" Betty pleaded as she slipped from this world into the next.

Betty died with a smile on her face. She died knowing that a loving, merciful God had accepted the sincere heartfelt repentance of her sins and had welcomed her home to Him.

Dawn collapsed over her and began to sob as the reality of the murder attempt stuck home. She still held the loaded weapon in her hand. The only thought on her mind was Judah. She was very concerned about his welfare. If they had tried to kill her, then she knew that his life was probably in danger as well.

Two men in lab coats suddenly burst into the room.

"Are you all right, Ma'am?" one asked as he quickly surveyed the situation.

Dawn drew her weapon up into his face as she yelled, "Who are you guys? You've got three seconds to identify yourselves or you are history!"

"It's okay, Ma'am, we are from the Joshua Brigade. We have been watching over you ever since you were admitted. We saw the nurse enter your room a while ago, but we became suspicious when she did not leave. Then we saw blood coming out from under the door."

Dawn recognized the name Joshua Brigade. They were the Christian Militia that was set up by General Desporte, Senator Jordan, Major Kole and Congressman Jacob as a last line of defense against Ultra. These men felt that Ultra had been compromised by the extraterrestrials or whatever they were, and the entire government and intelligence community was now suspect. These men had a hideout somewhere in the mountains which was physically and electronically secure from Ultra. These were the men that Dawn was going to tell Judah about when he returned. He had asked about a hiding place.

"We never suspected that Betty was one of them," the other man said. "I guess you can never know! Where did you get the gun, Ma'am?"

"Judah left it for me," Dawn answered as she lowered it and let it fall from her hand. "Thank God that he did!"

"We have to get you out of here ASAP, Ma'am."

Dawn went into the bathroom and got dressed. She thought all of the time about the Joshua Brigade. They were, as Senator Jordan had told her, commissioned like Joshua was by God. They were to be strong and courageous. They were taught that God was with them. He would not fail them nor forsake them. They were commanded to obey the word of God and not to turn from it to the right or to the left so that they would have success wherever they went. They were commanded to not tremble or be dismayed by the things that happened around them for the Lord their God was with them wherever they went. That was put to the test as General Desporte and Senator Jordan were killed. They were required to accept this command with the same words that the people accepted Joshua - 'all that You have commanded us we will do, and wherever You send us we will go. We will obey You and may the Lord Thy God be with us. Anyone who rebels against Your command and does not obey Your words in all that You command him, shall be put to death; only be strong and courageous'.

When Dawn came out of the bathroom dressed, she was put on a cart and covered with a sheet. The two men whisked her down the service elevator to the morgue where a black camouflaged Hummer was waiting for them. Dawn was taken into it and it sped away followed by another identical one. Dawn marveled at all the electronic equipment before her. She was told that they had to blindfold her for security reasons.

"That's all right, guys," Dawn said with a smile, "I've been in a coma for months! Who is in command of the Joshua Brigade at this point?"

"Captain Peter Knowington, Ma'am."

"Ma'am, we have some bad news for you. Major Kole was killed this afternoon. He was thrown out of his window."

"Oh God, not another killing!" Dawn responded obviously very upset. "Ultra strikes again! Judah was going to see him. Have you heard anything about Judah?"

"We know that he was involved in a accident with a police car. Your van went off a cliff and burned. A man's body was found at the scene, but it was a man in his sixties with a scar on his forehead. That was an Ultra operative by the code name of Mad Max. Col. Meire's body must still be in the Van. We will verify that by satellite surveillance as soon as it is feasible to do so."

Dawn put her head down and sobbed for Judah. She became increasingly agitated and soon began to scream out loud. Judah meant everything to her. Life without him was unthinkable. The guys in the back seat with her tried to calm her down but she nearly lost it.

She felt so close to Judah. She had seen him grow from a brash, agnostic Jewish man to a sincere Believer in such a short time. He had tried so hard to do what he was told was expected of him, but he was a new Believer after all. It would have been an awesome burden for a seasoned Believer yet alone a newborn babe, but he had pursued the task at hand without looking back. God had obviously chosen him, he had not chosen God.

"Why, God, did you let this happen to Judah?" Dawn cried out. "You chose him for your purpose and you let him be killed by the agents of the Enemy. Why, Lord? Why, Lord? He wanted so much to do Your will and You let this happen to him? I don't understand, Lord!"

Dawn continued to cry out to God about Judah. The men in the Hummer with her put their hands on her and attempted to comfort her. She shook uncontrollably. She thought about General Desporte and Senator Jordan and their wives and Major Kole and her first husband Bob and her daughter Caroline, all who apparently been killed by the forces of darkness. A spirit of death and persecution had permeated the body of Believers. Satan and his cohorts were on a rampage.

"Do you guys think that we will be able to retrieve his body for burial?" Dawn asked, after she had regained her composure.

"We will do all that we can, Ma'am. Remember that there is Police jurisdiction and a member of Ultra was killed. The place will be crawling with them. They just tried to kill you. I don't see how you can go in and claim the body. I don't know what to say. Pray about it, Ma'am."

# VIII

Dawn cried herself to sleep as the Hummer continued on into the night. They went south on Interstate 495 until they hit Vienna, Virginia and then they turned onto Rural Route 7. They followed that northwest through Hamilton and Round Hill moving quickly and quietly with their blue lights on. They crossed through Winchester with a communications blackout still in effect. They had electronic jamming equipment aboard that also would hamper anyone from tracking them. This stealth technology was state of the art and top secret. At Winchester, they noiselessly switched onto State Route 50 as they entered West Virginia. At Romney, they crossed the South Branch of the Potomac River and went over the Patterson Creek Mountains. Dawn slept through the entire nighttime journey. Finally early in the morning, they entered Maryland again and scaled the highest mountain in the area, Backbone Mountain.

It had taken them nearly four hours to travel 150 miles, but the final ascent took them nearly another two hours. The road was not developed, and it was raining hard. Unbeknownst to Dawn, the entire ascent to the top was monitored by camera equipment in the nearby trees as well as by satellite surveillance . There were also countermeasure boobytraps if anyone unauthorized tried to enter. Dawn began to awaken just as they drove into base camp at the mountain's summit.

"You can remove your blindfold now, Mrs. Meire,"one of the men said. "We are at New Petra."

"New Petra?" Dawn said as she removed her blindfold. "This doesn't look like Jordan to me."

Dawn got out of the Hummer and was immediately greeted by a middle aged man in a Marine's uniform with an eyepatch on his left eye.

"Mrs. Meire, welcome to New Petra," he said as he stuck out his hand in greeting. "I am Captain Peter Knowington, USMC retired, Ma'am. I am in charge of this ragtag militia band."

"Have you heard any more more about my husband's body, Captain?" Dawn asked anxiously.

"No we have not, Ma'am. We are afraid that it perished in the crash of your van."

"Oh God, no!" Dawn screamed. "Why him? He tried so hard to expose the evil intentions of AZAZEL. After all, he was just a babe in the Lord. Why, not that long ago, he was lost and perishing. Now he comes to the understanding of a loving,

101

forgiving Savior and what is his reward, death! I just don't understand it? Why did the Lord groom him for this most difficult task and then let him be killed by the Enemy. It just doesn't make any sense. The Lord healed me and took him. I just cannot understand it!"

"I don't know, Ma'am. Many good men and women have given their lives for this cause and many more probably will. That is why we formed this camp in the mountains. We are the last watchmen on the wall. Everyone here is not only military or retired military with their families, but all are Bible believing Christians. We know that the Enemy is out to deceive the public and to destroy our witness. Your husband died for a noble cause, Mrs. Meire, and he is now probably receiving his blessings from the Lord Himself. It is not for us to reason why, but it is for us to do or die."

"Cute, Captain! I don't need your little homilies right now. I want Judah here! I need him here. We need him here. He is the only one that I know that has waged spiritual warfare with AZAZEL. Has anyone else done that, Captain?"

"No ma'am. He is the only one that has seen AZAZEL face to face," Captain Knowington replied with a pensive look on his face. "We watched him battle AZAZEL at your home also. Only by putting on the full armor of God was he able to ward off AZAZEL's flaming missiles. It was an awesome sight, I must admit. It has not been duplicated as of yet by anyone that I know about."

"That why did God let him be killed? I don't understand! He came so far in such a short time to just end up at the bottom of a ravine burned to ashes."

"God's ways are not our ways, Ma'am. You know that. We cannot question His sovereignty. We just have to believe and have faith. He is in control here. He is the real commander in chief. We must just persevere on, the best that we can. The time is short and AZAZEL is preparing to abduct the Christians. We are preparing a global media message and an Internet program to warn the world about the real meaning of the upcoming mass abduction. Our work must and will continue. We cannot stop because of the death of one man, no matter how valuable that he was. If we did, then we would have stopped at the death of General Desporte or Senator Jordan. We must go on, Mrs. Meire."

Dawn continued to sob. She just could not let go of Judah. They escorted her into the mountain. It was protected by two huge foot thick steel doors. Once that they entered them, they had to pass through a fingerprint and retinal scan. Dawn heard the steel doors closing with a loud clang behind her. This was an old abandoned mining operation that had closed down decades ago. The Military had refurbished it for a base doing CIA operations in the 60's, but it had been closed again the 80's. Senator Jordan, General Desporte and Major Kole had appropriated secret Pentagon and Department of Defense slush money to refurbish the base a couple of years ago.

"New Petra was named for the mountainous Jordanian refuge that many people believe is the place in the mountains that was spoken of in Matthew 24 that the Jews

102

are supposed to flee to when they see the Abomination of Desolation in the Temple," said Captain Knowington to Judah's wife. "Senator Jordan felt that we needed a place in the mountains away from the abominations of Ultra and AZAZEL. This base is full of the most sophisticated electronic equipment that the country has. The top of the mountain is covered with satellite dishes and other electronic communications hardware. The cave also has several levels for living quarters; some for single soldiers and some for families. There are approximately fifty people at New Petra, but that number fluctuates as some soldiers are killed and others take their place."

"How easy is it to become a member of New Petra?" Dawn replied with a quizzical look on her face. "I would think that you would need to be very careful of spies. You also would have to be certain that a person or couple would not choose to leave New Petra. They could compromise your entire operation."

"New candidates and their families are screened very thoroughly and kept on a waiting list. They are told nothing about the location of New Petra until after they have arrived. They have to sever all ties with family and friends who are told that they have died. And, you are absolutely correct, Mrs. Meire, nobody can choose to leave New Petra once that they have decided to come here. We tell them all that right at the outset. There is no turning back once the commitment has been made. It is till death do us part!"

Captain Knowington explained to Dawn that the compound had its own generator and water storage supply. These were guarded 24 hours a day. On one level, crops were grown using hydroponics and artificial lighting. Another level was used to raise some small animals like chickens, rabbits and goats. Pigs and cattle were decided to be just too messy and bulky to be raised underground. Some catfish were raised in large vats also.

Dawn was amazed at what she saw. She was particularly fascinated with the surveillance room. She found out that they had watched both Judah at home and at work, and her in the hospital, with satellites as well as with secretly mounted cameras. They also used, whenever feasible, actual people. Congressman Jacobs of Texas had enabled them to continue to have satellite access after the death of Senator Jordan. He was on the appropriate intelligence committee to enable that to happen. New Petra was budgeted as a black bag operation without any more information given then was needed. Major Kole at the CIA was also most helpful as well.

"Have you heard anything about Congressman Jacobs?" Dawn asked Captain Knowington as she looked over this craggy middle-aged man with white short hair and blue eyes for the first time. "I told Judah to contact him just as I did major Kole. Now that Major Kole is dead, I wonder if Ultra will go after the Congressman as well? How did you lose your eye?"

"I lost it in the bombing of the Marine barracks in Lebanon several years ago. And we have not heard a word from Jacobs. He is traveling on a Congressional visit to the Middle East. We have notified him to be extremely careful of Ultra after what has just happened to Major Kole and to Judah. As you so appropriately observed, they seem to be closing in on our operation... Look, there he is!"

Captain Knowington pointed to one of the monitors. It was a satellite shot of the Congressman and his colleagues at the Kotel, the Western Wall or Wailing Wall in Jerusalem. They were all smiling as they spoke with the Israeli Prime Minister. All of a sudden, there was a burst of gunfire and Congressman Jacobs lay dead on the ground with a fatal wound to the head. There was pandemonium as Secret Service and Israeli security people jumped on the other Representatives. A Palestinian man was shot by the Secret Service and fell no more than fifty yards away.

"Oh my God," Dawn yelled. "It happened again, right before our eyes! Are any of us safe? Ultra seems to be everywhere."

"Yes they do, Ma'am," Captain Knowington said, shaking his head in disbelief. "And this will be explained as just a random killing by a crazed Palestinian gunman, but we know better. It is just too coincidental that Congressman Jacobs is killed right after Major Kole and Judah. You're right, Mrs. Meire, it is the long hand of Ultra!"

It was early morning at the Potomac crime scene. Captain Braden of the Potomac Police Department was accompanied by Mallory and Bernstein, the same two FBI men that had questioned Judah. They examined the Police car which had three bullet holes in the driver side window that had killed the female officer. The car was smashed up after apparently being hit by Judah's van. They could see the skid marks. The body of another man had been found at the scene along with a Glock semiautomatic pistol.

"Gentlemen," Captain Braden asked the FBI agents as he rubbed his pockmarked reddened face, "whatever happened to the body of that shooter? I was told that you had taken it away."

"We never saw it," Mallory responded, shaking his head.

"What are you talking about?!" Braden shouted in response. "I called you guys and you told me that the man found here was the shooter. You did a fingerprint analysis of him and the gun that we found?"

"That was not us, Captain," Bernstein answered. "The FBI never saw the body. Some other agency retrieved it. We got a call from them telling us the results of the fingerprint analysis, but we did not do it."

"Then why did you tell me that you did it? What is going on here? Another Chinese puzzle and Judah is at the center of it. He has given me more gray hairs than anyone that I have ever known. Even more than my kids."

"We were told that the guys that took it are some secret black bag intelligence group, spooks they call them. And we were told that we should back off," Mallory said with a frown.

"What was an intelligence operative doing in the car with Judah? He then shoots a police officer for no apparent reason," Braden shouted. "These are my people and I am not backing off. Already two of my people are dead and another is missing. The only part of the puzzle that seems resolved is Judah. He is dead in that van at the bottom of the ravine. Thank God for small favors!"

"Captain, did you know that a CIA officer, a Major Kole, committed suicide after a visit from Judah last night?" barked Special Agent Bernstein as he grabbed Braden's arm. "He jumped out of his window. The only problem was that the window was closed at the time!"

"That man is a nightmare. I'm glad he is dead already. Now maybe people will stop dying around him. I am getting a little concerned for my own life. Who knows what might happen to anybody associated with that man. I heard that he was a member of the Israeli army. Maybe all of these killings are by fanatical Moslems. You never know, it could be. Anyway, we are supposed to retrieve the van any time now. Look, the truck and the winch have arrived."

Captain Braden smiled nervously as his people had arrived to pull up the van. Two men lowered themselves down the walls of the ravine on the cable. Once that they were at the bottom they hooked it onto the frame of the mangled burnt out van. Immediately the winch began to turn and the van moved up the ravine wall.

When the van reached the street, Captain Braden ran over to the van along with Mallory and Bernstein. He looked into the front seat and found no one. The seat belt was still fastened but there was no sign of Judah's body. Braden looked at the two FBI men and shook his head in disbelief.

"This guy is strange, even in death," Braden said, puzzled. "Nothing with him is ever easy. Nothing is ever as it first appears."

"Do you see any sign of a body down there?" Braden yelled to the two men at the bottom of the ravine.

They shook their heads no. They continued to look around the ravine floor for Judah's body, but they did not find it. Captain Braden rubbed his head and looked at Mallory and Bernstein in bewilderment. Then all of a sudden, out of the corner of his eye, he noticed an Oriental man in a trenchcoat and sunglasses snooping around.

"Who the heck are you?" Captain Braden demanded as he sneaked upon the man and caught him by surprise.

The man looked at Braden and smiled but never said a word. He walked over to his vehicle and opened the door.

Captain Braden pulled out his revolver and aimed it at the man.

"You better not do that," he shouted. "Get out of the vehicle nice and slow."

The man pulled the door shut and started up the engine.

"I'll have to shoot!"

The man put the car in gear and started driving away at high speed. The Captain fired a shot into the rear tire of the car, and it began to spin uncontrollably as it rounded the precipitous turn. The driver lost control and went flying off of the cliff much as Judah must have. His car also burst into flames as it ricocheted off the wall of the ravine.

"I want a full check on his license plate," Braden yelled to his people. "It is Virginia BMT333."

"You did it now, Braden," Bernstein warned. "He was probably one of those secret black bag people. This place is going to be crawling with spooks in a while!"

Captain Braden refused to be alarmed. He was too busy thinking about what this man was doing here and what he had to do with the events of last night. He was not there by coincidence. Maybe he was looking for Judah. Why had he failed to respond to his commands? Was he a spook after all? Captain Braden shook his head and went back to thinking about Judah. How did he get out of the van with his seat belt still fastened? He ordered his people to scour the ravine floor and the walls and trees on the cliff above. That body had to be there somewhere.

Within the hour the area was crawling with guys in black trenchcoats and sunglasses. Captain Braden was blindsided by two of them and forced to enter a black van with a gun stuck into his back. Once inside, he was strapped to a chair and a hood was put over his head. He could feel a needle shooting a hot liquid into his veins. Captain Braden's head began to spin. He was thoroughly questioned about Judah and his whereabouts. When Braden attempted to refuse to answer until he was told who these people were, he was told that this was a matter of National Security, and if he did not cooperate he would be eradicated. In the midst of a narcotic stupor he asked what did Judah have to do with National Security? He was told that if they told him they would have to kill him. When he asked what the man was doing in the van with Judah and why he shot the police officer, he was told to forget about it. They told him that O'Malley had snooped too much and look what happened to him. Finally they told him that they were spooks and they could do whatever they wanted with full impunity.

By this time, the injection had taken full effect and Captain Braden's efforts to remain alert and conscious had failed. They began to question him in earnest about the whereabouts of Judah. Braden truthfully told them that he had no idea. After continuing this for nearly an hour they turned their attention to the whereabouts of Detective Holmes. Once again, he told them that he did not know. When they finally realized that he did not know where Judah or Holmes were, they pulled the bag off of his head and shoved him out of the door. He stood there in a daze as they left, taking with them the smashed up car of the Oriental agent as well as his mangled burnt body.

What Captain Braden did not realize was that they had implanted a surveillance device at the base of his skull so that they could monitor not only his whereabouts but also every word that he said. As he finally regained some lucidity, he looked around and saw the two FBI agents. They were smiling at him. He rubbed the back of his head.

"Hey, guys, what is so funny?" he asked.

"Nothing, Captain, nothing," they both responded in unison and turned around and walked away. They had seen him being forced into the black van, and they saw him reappear from it over an hour later, but they knew what the consequences of asking too many questions would be. They preferred to just look the other way. They got into their car and drove away. Captain Braden just stood there and watched them leave. He knew that he wanted to ask them something but he could not remember what it was, so he just turned around and walked aimlessly towards the precipice still scratching the back of his head.

Dawn continued to grieve for Judah. She spent much of her days in the subterranean mountain cavern known as New Petra just crying. Members of the Joshua Brigade and especially their wives tried to comfort Dawn, but she was not ready yet to let go of Judah.

"Maybe he is still alive?" Dawn said to Captain Knowington's wife, Ann. Ann was a fiftysomething woman who reminded Dawn of her own mother. She had flowing brown hair and deep blue eyes. She probably had been a beautiful woman in her youth but had put on some weight since then. She had a smile, though, that would melt an iceberg.

"Honey, how can that be?" Ann responded. "They found his burnt-out car at the bottom of a ravine. He is in the Lord's hands now. You just have to let go, Dawn."

"But they have not found his body..." Dawn said with a sniffle.

"Maybe it was thrown from the car. They will eventually find it. It could not just disappear into thin air could it, Dawn?"

"I don't know. I just feel that he is still alive somewhere."

"He is alive with the Lord in Paradise, Dawn!" Ann comforted. "That is our blessed assurance, honey. You know that. When we die, we will be with Jesus in Heaven. That kept General Desporte and Senator Jordan going and it certainly kept their wives going after their deaths. Your loss isn't the first that we have experienced here and it won't be the last. We all just need to be strong and remember that we will see Judah and the others someday in Heaven."

"Ann, Judah married me even after I was struck down with MS. I had no sensation from my waist down. We were never one physically. It never seemed to bother Judah but it bothered me. Now I am whole physically once again and the Lord takes him. It just isn't fair!"

"I know, dear, how you must feel," Ann answered with a smile of understanding. "You were one in the Lord and that is all that matters. Maybe the Lord did not want you together physically. I don't know the answer. Nobody does. You just have to remember that the Lord causes all things to work together for good for those who love Him."

The two ladies walked arm and arm though the compound. Dawn was most interested in the surveillance room. She dragged Ann there. They found several men glued to monitors. One of the monitors, Dawn recognized, was showing the inside

107

of the Lazant Institute.

"I didn't realize that you were monitoring Judah's workplace?"

"Yes, Ma'am, we have been monitoring it for quite a while," the soldier at that particular monitor said with a smile. "That is one weird place. Those people are weird."

"What do you mean?",Dawn asked.

"I have seen them do a seance. I have seen them call up all kinds of demonic spirits, especially that woman Endora. She is a witch in my book. They have a Reverend Shea there also. He is unlike any Reverend that I ever knew. Talk about New Age. He is like the False Prophet in the Book of Revelation. All of them believe that the demonic beings in the Heavens above us like AZAZEL are good angels that are here to help us evolve."

"And Dawn, they believe that these so called good angels are here to remove the Christians from the Earth," Captain Knowington interjected as he came upon them. "That was what Judah was doing there. We put him there to monitor their activities."

"But you had surveillance equipment there already. Why did you have to put Judah's life in danger?"

"Surveillance equipment is fine but there is nothing like a man in the field. Senator Jordan and General Desporte felt that we needed a man on the inside. They prayed about it for a long time and finally came up with your husband. We were all a little surprised, to be honest. After all he was a nonbelieving Jew. And to top it off, he had been a member of the Israeli Defense Force and Mossad. Not the ideal CIA candidate from a Christian perspective, but the Senator and the General assured us that he was the man. Well I guess that they were right. Not too long after he took that position with Lazant and the CIA, he came to the Lord. A lot of us here had to eat crow. We would have never guessed. The Lord surely comes to save the lost and your stiffnecked husband was surely lost!"

As Captain Knowington spoke, the monitor showing the Lazant Institute suddenly bustled with activity. The men from Ultra had come to see Dr. Lazant.

"Dr. Lazant, have you seen or heard from Judah, lately?" a man in a black trenchcoat and sunglasses asked.

"No I have not," Dr. Lazant answered cautiously. "I thought that he might be at the hospital with his wife. She awoke from her coma, you know."

"Of course we know, stupid! We know everything about her. She killed one of our operatives and fled the Hospital. Judah went to see a CIA man that she had recommended, but we took care of him. Judah has become too much of a liability. He has led us to many of his collaborators, but enough is enough. We think that he and his wife have fled to that New Petra rebel compound. We are still trying to locate it. We just put a monitoring device in Captain Braden's neck that might help us."

"Wait just a minute," Dr. Lazant said. He buzzed Stephen and called him into his office. He had never told him or Endora about Ultra but that was no longer prudent.

"Stephen, didn't you tell me that AZAZEL had placed a device at the base of the skull of Judah's mother when he had abducted her?"

"Yes, AZAZEL told me that he had placed it there to monitor Judah's whereabouts if possible. Do you want me to contact AZAZEL and see if Judah has contacted his mother?"

"We know all about that, Swami," the man from Ultra responded. "We have been monitoring her to see if Judah tells her something important. We can also get to him through her if need be. You people stick to your new world religion shtik *(Y.nonsense)* and leave the spying to us. By the way, son, if you mention any of what we just talked about to anyone outside this room, I will personally grind you up and feed your flesh to your sacred cows. Comprende?"

"Uh, uhh, yes, Sir!" Stephen said as he visibly shook. "No problem!"

Captain Knowington threw his hands up and roared.

"I just sent some of our people to get Judah's mother and bring her here as soon as I realized that they killed Major Kole and might be after Judah," he shouted. "She will lead them right to us!"

"They seem to believe that Judah is not dead, Captain. What do you make of that?" Dawn burst forth. "I knew it! I knew it!"

"I cannot worry about that now. We have more pressing matters staring us in the face. Someone tell me exactly where the vehicle is that is bringing in Mrs. Meire?"

"Captain Knowington, they are calling in right now! I'll put in on the speaker..."

"Eagle one, This is Eagle two..."

"Eagle two, this is Eagle one. We read you. What is your present status?"

"Eagle one, we are ready to take the turkey out of the oven."

Captain Knowington grabbed the microphone. "Leave the kitchen, Eagle two. I repeat, leave the kitchen and return to the nest."

"Sir, one of us has already entered the kitchen and is taking the turkey out of the oven."

Captain Knowington became very agitated. He knew that if one of his men had entered Judah's mother's home and spoke to her that the Enemy may already be closing in and he did not want any of his people captured. That would mean that the entire operation would be compromised. He asked his man outside her home to describe the area. The young soldier told him that it was dark and raining outside. He could not see much of anything.

"Eagle one, wait a minute, I see a large black disk in the sky moving towards us!"

Captain Knowington 's greatest fears were being realized. AZAZEL was closing in on his people as a result of the device in Mrs. Meire's head.

"Abort mission! Abort mission! Get your buddy and leave the area immediately!'

"What of the turkey, Sir?"

"Leave her!"

The young soldier radioed his buddy in the house. He informed him to abort the mission immediately. When the soldier asked why, he told him to return to the vehicle pronto! He asked what about Mrs. Meire, who was packing a bag? He was told to leave her. The young soldier ran from her house and jumped into the idling Hummer which sped off.

"We are on our way home, Sir. We left the turkey in the oven!"

"Good," Captain Knowington said. "Is anyone following you?"

"I don't think so, Sir."

They quickly drove West on Route 20 which was Lake Zurich Highwood Road. The road was deserted at this time of evening, especially in the rain, but it would take them out of the Highland Park area without having to travel on the main Interstates. The black disk silently moved along with them.

"Sir, our radar indicates that something above us is following us. It could be an airplane but by the size of it, it is probably the disk."

Captain Knowington became very concerned. He did not want them falling into the enemy's hands. These men were brave and loyal but the abilities of AZAZEL to extract information were unknown. Besides that, the Hummer had state of the art surveillance and stealth equipment that he did not want to fall into enemy hands.

"Are there any other birds around you?" he asked the men.

"Yes Sir, there are three black birds approaching," the young soldier replied nervously.

At that moment satellite pictures began coming into New Petra of that stretch of Route 20. It was dark and rainy but they were enhanced and cleaned up. They showed that the Hummer was indeed being surrounded by three black sedans. The black disk interestingly did not show up.

"Can you evade the birds? If they show any hostile intent use countermeasures!" Captain Knowington commanded.

The three black sedans encircled the Hummer and tried to slow it down. The Hummer then rammed the front vehicle. It swerved aside for an instant. Another car on their left attempted to push them off of the road. They caused the Hummer to momentarily lose control but they soon regained their position. The car in back bumped them. Shots rang out as individuals in the cars on the right and the rear opened fire on the Hummer's tires. Fortunately, they were puncture proof. They obviously did not want to kill the occupants, just to disable their vehicle so that they could retrieve the soldiers intact and question them. This went on for nearly ten miles.

Captain Knowington was becoming very upset. If these men fell into the hands of Ultra, his entire operation at New Petra would be compromised. It looked as though it would only be a matter of time until they were stopped. He did not know what to say to them. He could not call in the Highway Patrol because that also

110

would possibly compromise New Petra. He bowed his head and prayed. After a couple of seemingly endless minutes, he opened a covered button on the console. He put his finger on the red button.

"What is that button for, Captain?" Dawn asked as the others at the consoles took a deep breath.

"It will send a signal that will detonate the vehicle if I push it!" Captain Knowington said with a stern yet compassionate expression.

"Oh my God!"

"It is our fail-safe mechanism. We cannot compromise New Petra under any circumstances. Too many good men, including Judah, have given their lives for this mission. All the men here know the risks and they understand the sacrifices that need to be made. What better death can there be than giving up one's life for the Lord's work?"

The young soldiers tried to escape the sedans by dropping some spikes from their Hummer, and they did send the rear car into a tailspin from which it never recovered. They also fired some shots from a special cannon mounted on their front bumper, and they did hit the gas tank of the car in front of them. It burst into flames. The car on their left upon seeing this moved right in and squeezed them against the guardrail over the precipice that they were crossing. They would have to either collide with the burning car in front of them or stop. They decided to ram the guardrail. It did not give. It bent outward but did not break. They were slowing down quickly. Captain Knowington's finger sat ever ready on the red button. The two Army Reserve Corporals, McQueen and McCord, decided to blast the guardrail with their front mounted cannon. As they did so the guardrail disintegrated, and they went flying off of the cliff.

"God Bless you, men," Captain Knowington yelled, "you have been good and faithful servants of the Lord." He eased his finger off of the button of destruction and bowed his head.

Everyone at New Petra was crowded around this one monitor, and they all witnessed this horrifying spectacle. Each and everyone one of them grieved for their fallen comrades. Dawn put her head in her hands and sobbed noticeably. Ann Knowington put her hand on her husbands shoulder to comfort him.

They all watched in horror as the Hummer sailed off of the bridge.

Right in midair, though, it was captured by a tractor beam from the black disk in the sky overhead. The beam stopped the Hummer's downward descent and it began to reel in the vehicle to the UFO above. Corporals McQueen and McCord were dazed. They had closed their eyes and were at peace at their impending demise, but now they opened their eyes in shock. They were not only alive, but they were being taken up to the Enemy.

"Sir, we are being drawn up to the craft," Corporal McQueen said as he fought to regain his composure. "What are we to do?"

The young men had no idea of the failsafe detonation device in their Hummer.

The secret was forever revealed by this mission as all stood around and watched.

"Sorry, son, for what I am about to do. May God forgive me!" Captain Knowington said softly as he pushed the red button, and the Hummer exploded into a thousand pieces.

"I swear by all that is Holy that I will do all that I can to defeat this adversary," Captain Knowington shouted. "We all know that this deception is great and the time is short. Our rewards will be in Heaven. Those two young men are now with the Lord in Paradise. We must not waver from our goal. We must do all that we can to expose this deception."

The entire room was silent. All sat in hushed shock at what had just happened. They looked at each other and held each other in grief. Here were another two young men joining the growing list of people killed by the Enemy. They all realized that it was not what they were doing wrong that had caused all these deaths, but what they were doing right. They obviously were onto the deception of AZAZEL in a mighty way or else this beast from Hell would leave them alone. They assured one another that they would stay strong and resolute about their mission.

"Where is that Jewboy, Judah, when we really need him?" an older man in a Navy SEAL uniform bellowed out. He was a tall man with a still well trimmed body for a man in his sixties. "If you are indeed not dead, Judah, then show yourself!"

"Is that Lieutenant Gregor?" Dawn asked anxiously.

"Yes, it is. How do you know him?"

"He is an old Navy SEAL who did some work with the Israelis once. He and Judah really hit it off. Lieutenant Gregor was one of the guys who prayed Judah into the Kingdom. He cried when he heard that Judah had accepted the Lord," Dawn said as she hugged him.

"Captain, look at this!" one of the soldiers yelled from across the room. "It is a replay of one of our satellite feeds, which was delayed because of the Earth's rotation."

Captain Knowington ran down to the monitor. It was of a satellite that circled the Earth and was unable to send its data until now. Captain Knowington had asked the soldier to search for any data from the area of the Potomac crash scene that looked interesting. What he saw amazed him. He saw Judah riding in the van with a man behind him with a gun at his head. He saw the Police car move alongside and the man from Ultra fire three shots into the Police car, killing the officer. Then her car spun in front of Judah and he slammed into it throwing Mad Max out through the window. Judah's car began to spin uncontrollably and fell off the precipice and burst into flames.

"Dawn, come here quickly!" Captain Knowington shouted.

Dawn raced over to the monitor as it showed Judah caught up in the flaming van as it cascaded down the wall of the ravine. She screamed and held her hands over her mouth in horror. Then amazingly Judah was gone, vanished. Captain Knowington told the soldier to run that sequence again in slow motion. Everyone stared at the monitor intently. The van went off the cliff and burst into flames. Judah was there in the midst of the furnace, but he was not alone. There was another figure there with him although its presence was fleeting. They reran the tape again this time at greater magnification and even slower speed. The figure was a man in long white robes with long hair and a beard. Nail pierced hands.

Everyone knew instantly that it was Jesus. They all began to cry and each fell to his knees. Jesus picked up Judah and they were gone from the flames.

"When you walk through the fire, you will not be scorched, nor will the flame burn you," Lieutenant Gregor recited out loud from the Book of Isaiah, the Forty Third Chapter and Second Verse. "He was protected by the Lord just as were Daniel's friends Shadrach, Meshach and Abednego in the furnace of Nebuchadnezzar. Oh Praise God, Praise God, thank You, Lord, for rescuing Your faithful servant even if he is a Jewboy!"

"He is alive! He is alive," sobbed Dawn. "Oh thank You, Lord, thank You for Your grace and mercy. Oh us of so little faith! Get thee behind us, AZAZEL, for Judah is back!"

# IX

"I just can't stand this place anymore," Rebecca Knowington blurted out. "It wasn't fair for Dad to force us to come here. I hate it here."

"Yeah, that's for sure. I agree. This place sucks! Dad wants to save the world, but we had to lose ours," replied her twin sister Jennifer. "We had to give up our friends and everything for what? I thought that I loved God and could do His will but this is nuts. We aren't Catholic Nuns, for God's sake."

Captain Knowington's twin sixteen year old daughters were definitely a concern in his decision to set up New Petra. He and his wife truly felt empowered by the Lord to do this, but what could they do with their daughters? They could have left them with their grandparents who were good Bible Believing Christians, but they did not want them left behind. They wanted to bring the grandparents along also, but they were old and sickly and would not have been able to receive the proper medical treatment that they needed here on the mountain. The Knowingtons knew that there would probably be problems. They were after all sixteen year olds. They had gone to Christian schools, and they were committed to the Lord, but they were sixteen year old girls. They had to give up not only all the comforts of home but all of their friends and family as well. Both girls had cried for days after arriving at the mountainous cave where they now resided.

Peter Knowington, when setting up New Petra, had decided to enlist mostly young couples with small children. They would be most stable and the children would be young enough to adjust easily. Older children like Jennifer and Rebecca were to be avoided at all costs for the obvious reasons, but he had no choice in his case. He did not like the situation of having his pretty young daughters in a compound with more than a dozen single young soldiers, but he had no choice. He warned the soldiers to not even look at his daughters.

"Maybe we should just leave this place?" Jennifer asked as she pushed back her long red hair and smiled.

"Oh yeah, right," Rebecca answered. "We will just steal one of those Hummers and boogie out of here."

"Maybe we can find someone to help us? Someone who is fed up with this place like we are."

"You know, Jennifer, that we are the oldest kids here. All the rest are either in diapers or on Sesame Street. There aren't any other kids here over six or seven!"

"Maybe we can convince one of the soldiers to do it. You know, one of the young guys who misses girls," said Rebecca as she fidgeted with her blond pigtails that her mother insisted on tying for her. "Let's snoop around a little and see if we can find out who is miserable here."

The two sisters smiled and began to plan out their escape. They did not remember, or actually did not care, that the penalty for leaving New Petra was death. They knew that their Dad would do nothing to them no matter what they did. How could he, since he was the one that dragged them to this mountaintop cave in the first place.

Jennifer and Rebecca were being home schooled by their mother. She would spend hours with them doing their High School work. The girls had very little unsupervised time. They did do some babysitting for the families with small children, but other than that they were not out of their mother's sight for very long. She knew that the men would be attracted to her daughters, and she was not going to give them the opportunity to be tempted. Nobody was allowed to roam outside the cave at all during the day. Occasionally, everyone would go outside at night just to get some fresh air. The Hummer's were stored in a camouflaged motor pool area amidst the trees and bushes and were guarded twenty four hours a day.

"Mom, can we go to the gym to get some exercise?" Rebecca asked sweetly.

"Since when do you girls want to exercise?" their Mom answered with a funny look on her face.

"Mom! We have been just sitting around here for months. We are getting all fat and flabby."

"You girls are beautiful."

"Yeah right! You are our mother. What else can you say?"

"You girls know that I'm always honest with you. You two look great."

"We are all flab. No more swimming lessons and no more Cross Country. We are beginning to look like you and Dad."

"That's not very nice, Jennifer. We are not kids any more, you know."

"I know, but we need to be a little more buff, Mom."

"Okay, but I will come with you," Ann Knowington replied.

"Mom!" both girls yelled simultaneously.

"It's all right, I'll stay back and just watch."

"Great!" Rebecca whispered to Jennifer as they put their arms around one another.

The two girls and their Mom headed for the exercise room on the second level down. They were pretty girls, both around five foot three and a hundred pounds. They had exercised regularly before the mountain, but they were now going to scout out the guys for a possible escape.

"You know, Rebecca, we cannot leave here for good. Where would we go, to Grandma's? We just need to leave for a little vacation and then sneak back up."

"We can't just sneak back here dork! Once we go we have to stay away for a while at least until Dad cools down. He is going to be so mad!" Rebecca answered

115

with a slight chuckle.

Once they entered the gym, they ran into a bunch of the young soldiers. These young guys were all using the equipment to not only stay in shape but to work off the excess energy from there being no young single females at the base except these two girls. They sneaked a peek and saw the young pretty girls, but they knew better than mess around with Captain Knowington's daughters. The base would be too small for them to hide from his rage. The girls said hello to the guys as they walked by them, but the guys hardly looked at them at all. They were fearful that the Captain would see them on a monitor somewhere. Then Ann Knowington walked by them and they all let out a sigh of relief that they hadn't looked very hard at the girls.

Jennifer and Rebecca walked through the exercise area. They pranced about like young fillies on parade, but when they did not get anything more than a quick glance they became agitated.

"These guys are all dweebs," Rebecca said loud enough for everyone to hear. She grabbed Jennifer and they began to giggle nervously.

"What do you expect, Jen," Rebecca whispered as she looked back and saw her mother following behind them. "The mother hen is right behind us!"

The girls waved for their mother to stay back. She would foul up their entire mission if she stayed so close. Ann reluctantly complied and sat down on a piece of equipment. It was close enough for her to keep an eye on the girls.

They spotted that new woman on an exercise bike. She was talking to a couple of the guys. They moved close enough to listen and began to ride their own bikes. They looked back at their Mom and smiled and waved.

"I cannot believe what was said this morning in the prayer meeting," Dawn began, obviously very upset. "They think that my husband is dead. You guys saw the monitor. Didn't you see Jesus carry him out of the flames?"

"We sure did, Mrs. Meire," one of the young soldiers answered shaking his head. "But maybe the Lord was carrying him to Heaven as the others said. He has not come back, has he?"

"How do we know that? We are up here on the mountaintop. They never found his body did they?"

"But we have satellite surveillance all over the area. If he were alive, we would find him. I agree with those at the prayer meeting that he is probably dead. He is in Heaven with Jesus, Ma'am. What a blessed assurance that must be."

"I don't believe that he is dead. I believe that he is down there somewhere," Dawn insisted frustratingly. "Lt. Gregor said that he did not believe that Judah was dead. He said so at the meeting. Why won't anyone listen to him?"

The two guys smiled and left the area. There was no use in arguing with her. Rebecca and Jennifer quickly moved in and mounted the bikes that they had been on.

"Aren't you that new lady that they just brought in here?" Jennifer asked politely.

"Yep, that's me, alright."

"We saw your husband on the monitor too," Rebecca said as she lied with a smile. "We think that he is still alive too. As my mother says, what a bummer!"

"I really think that he is still alive. I need to go and look for him. Maybe I could get Lieutenant Gregor to help me look?" Dawn said before she realized what she had said.

"You can't leave this place, lady. Didn't they tell you that? If you talk to Gregor or anyone else about this, they will lock you up. Don't be stupid!" Rebecca said in a hushed tone as she looked to her mother and smiled.

"Hey wiseguys, just watch me! You kids better not snitch on me, or I'll scratch your pretty little eyes out!" Dawn said with a snarl meant to scare the young girls. They were not scared one iota and in fact reached out and comforted her.

"We want to leave this place as well," Rebecca said as she fidgeted with her pigtails. "Take us with you. We want to go to our grandmothers. This place sucks for teenagers. It is full of old people, kids and dorky soldiers. Help us please!"

"What of your parents? I'm sure that they will be devastated."

"They will be fine. If they want to save the world, that's cool. But we don't. We are going nuts here. We can help you escape," Jennifer said quietly.

The two girls spoke with Dawn for quite a while. They convinced her that they could help her escape if she took them with her. They never let on that they were Captain Knowington's daughters. Heaven forbid! Dawn had her back to Ann and never saw her. When they left they walked all around the room so that Dawn would not see their mother.

They told Dawn that they could get her out of the mountainous cavern at night after the lights went out, and they also could get her the keys for the Hummer if she would disable the guard. They planned to meet at the front iron doors at midnight. When their mother asked what they talked to Dawn about they became agitated.

"Geez, Mom," Jennifer sighed. "Now we can't even talk to a grown woman alone. I mean, seriously! What's the problem now?"

Dawn felt very uneasy about this flight from the camp especially with two teenage girls. She knew that the parents would be after them as soon as they found out, but she needed them to get the keys. She decided that she would let them out of the vehicle at the bottom of the mountain. That would also slow down those people chasing after her. That would not be what the girls wanted, but she knew that she needed them to get away to find Judah. Dawn felt in her heart of hearts that he was still alive and that he needed her. She also knew that she needed him, and she was willing to risk it all to go and find him. Life without Judah was meaningless to her.

Dawn slipped out of her bunk and headed out for the outer metal doors. It was nearly midnight and all was quiet. She saw ahead of her the two teenage girls. Her stomach ached but there was no turning back now. The girls showed her a small crawlspace exit that bypassed the noisy front doors. They knew the code to disarm the security system protecting it. Nobody talked. The girls pointed the way and the three of them crawled through and exited outside into the pitch black night. Rebecca pointed to the motor pool area and they all crawled over there. There was one lone sentry with an M-16 in his hand walking back and forth in front of the vehicles.

Dawn picked up a rock and quietly tried to sneak up on the soldier. Suddenly, he turned around and aimed the gun right at her. Immediately without hesitation, the two girls ran out behind him and started yelling. He turned around to see what the commotion was, and Dawn hit him across the back of the head with the rock. He fell to the ground. She took his gun and his radio and dragged him into the bushes where she bound and gagged him with his belt and shirt.

The girls were already in the vehicle when she returned. She threw open the door of the sleek, black 6.5 liter turbocharged Hummer and the keys were in the ignition. She told everyone to buckle up and started up the vehicle and sped down the mountain. It was pitch black outside. There was no moon and the clouds blocked the stars. The road was windy and treacherous since it had not been maintained for years and was in a state of disintegration. Dawn did her best to keep it on the road. She had not driven in so long and the downhill rush was full of switchbacks. She said a prayer every couple of miles. She turned on all the electronic equipment in the vehicle, but she had no idea what it was or what it did.

"This is Captain Knowington. Who are you? Identify yourself immediately!" a voice abruptly came across the radio after a few minutes. "We know that you stole one of our vehicles. Whoever you are, you know that we cannot let you leave. We have to stop you at all costs," he yelled forcefully. "You can stop willingly or we can blow you off of the road. It's your choice."

Captain Knowington's wife rushed into the control room yelling.

"Wait, Peter, wait!" she screamed. "The girls are gone. Maybe they are on the vehicle? I saw then talking to Mrs. Meire this afternoon. Is she missing also?"

Someone ran to check and quickly reported that Dawn was unaccounted for as well. Lieutenant Gregor accompanied the young man back to the surveillance area. He had been awakened by all the commotion.

"Girls, are you on this vehicle?" Captain Knowington shouted with a loud gasp. "You better answer me!"

Dawn looked at the girls.

"You never told me that you were Captain Knowington's girls! Oy, we've done it now. At least he won't blow us off the road. Will he?"

"I don't know, lady. My Dad goes by the book no matter what. He can be a real pain sometimes with that macho stuff," Rebecca said with a frown.

Dawn realized that she had probably done the stupidest thing in her life. In her zeal to find Judah she had put the commander's girls in harm's way. She stopped the Hummer and told the girls to get out. They refused.

"Get out right now or I'll blow your pretty little heads off," Dawn shouted as she aimed the M-16 at them. The girls scampered out of the Hummer into the cool pitch dark night air. They sat on the side of the road and shivered.

"Captain, I just let out your girls at the curve before the waterfall. They will be waiting for you!

"It is pitch dark out here, and they are on the side of the road, so you'd better go slowly or you will hit them. Sorry for all the commotion but I have to look for Judah. I was planning to let them out anyway at the base of the mountain. I really didn't think that boys were a good enough reason to take them away from their parents."

"Dawn, thanks for letting my daughters out, but you know that we cannot let you go. We can't jeopardize New Petra," Captain Knowington replied as he opened the red covered button on the console and put his finger on it.

"Dawn, I have my finger on the destruct button right now," Captain Knowington said very calmly. "You saw what it did to those boys in the Hummer in Chicago. If I had to sacrifice them for our security, you must realize that I will do the same with you."

Ann put her arm around her husband. She tried to convince him that he should spare Dawn. She had after all let their daughters go. She told him to pursue all avenues before pushing the red button.

"Captain, I must find Judah. You all feel that he is dead and that Jesus was carrying him to Heaven, but I disagree. I believe that he is still alive. Gregor agreed with me. Ask him."

Lieutenant Gregor heard that remark and asked Captain Knowington if he could speak to her.

"Well, what if he is still alive, Mrs. Meire, and you are now dead," Lieutenant Gregor barked into the microphone. "What if he suddenly shows up, and I have to explain to him that we had to blow you up?"

"You would be in a world of hurt, Gregor. You and Knowington both!" Dawn laughed. "He would tear you guys limb from limb, trust me!"

"This is no joke, Ma'am!"

"Who's laughing?"

The first Hummer met up with the girls. They were huddled on the side of the dark winding road and were almost missed by the first group of soldiers. They radioed in that they had the girls and were heading back to the base. The second Hummer sped on after Dawn. She was still a few miles ahead of them. Dawn pulled one of the levers on the dashboard, and she spilled nails all over the road.

The Hummer sped over the nails in the darkened night, but hardly slowed down. The tires were puncture proof, as evidenced by the encounter with Ultra, so a few nails were nothing. Dawn stopped her vehicle and turned it around at a bend in the road. She scanned the lighted panel in front of her. When the pursuing vehicle rounded it, she closed her eyes and pushed several flashing buttons. One of them was the front end cannon. The blast hit the engine of the pursuing Hummer and it exploded. The two soldiers just made it out with their lives. They rolled to the sides of the road and began to fire their weapons at Dawn. She put her Hummer into reverse and fled the scene.

Captain Knowington realized that his options were quickly narrowing. He tried to make use of his countermeasures on the sides of the road, but one of the buttons that Dawn had pressed had activated the jamming equipment in the Hummer which was blocking the signals from the base to the countermeasures. Captain Knowington did not even know if the self destruct button would be able to send its signal to explode the Hummer.

Finally he decided that he would have to push it. Pretty soon Dawn would be at the base of the mountain and blowing it up there would cause even more commotion.

"Captain, can't we wait?" Gregor pleaded. "She is just trying to find her husband after all. She is no threat to New Petra."

"Of course she is, Gregor. Wake up, man! If Ultra or AZAZEL get hold of her, she will lead them willingly or not right back to us. That woman is as pushy as her husband. We have to look out for the good of the entire mission not just one frantic woman."

He pushed the button and waited. They all heard a muffled explosion from down the mountain and all knew that it had worked. Knowington got up from the console and paced the floor shaking his head back and forth. He took several deep breaths and tried to calm down. Ann put her arm around him and tried to comfort him, but he needed to be alone. He walked out into the night air and waited for his daughters to return.

"Happy now, Boss?" Gregor said as he walked by him.

"It's a rotten, stinking job, Lieutenant, but somebody has to do it! May God forgive me!"

Dr. Lazant and Reverend Shea were thrilled to visit with the Vatican Theologian and with their other colleagues at the Watergate Hotel Conference Center. They all sat around a large oval table and feasted on Indian delicacies like Sate Chicken Kambing, Vindaloo Duck, Gram Marsala Trout, Rogan Josh Lamb, and of course Tandoori Chicken. There were also plenty of vegetarians dishes for those so inclined. Steaming plates of Basmati Rice and hot garlic Naan bread were everywhere. A specialty of the chef was a Spiced Potato Dish made with brown mustard seed, sweet curry powder, ginger, cilantro and gram masala. It was heavenly and had all the participants asking for the recipe. There were tall bottles of Taj Mahal Indian beer and steaming mugs of Himalayan spiced Chai tea. The banquet was catered by a man from Goa, a small State nestled in the middle of the Malabar Coast of India. He had come to America a few years ago and had a thriving catering business in the DC area. The food covered the huge table in resplendent beauty. Everyone was very taken with its presentation and was anxious to partake of its undoubtedly delicious eating.

A woman stood up and asked if she could bless the food . She was a Reform Rabbi from Los Angeles. All agreed, since they could not longer resist the fragrant aromas of the food before them.

"Thank you, Heavenly Spirit, for being with us here today. Thank you, Earth Mother Goddess, for this rich bounty that is before us. We all feel your comforting hand on us. You are a wonderful loving presence that welcomes all to you regardless of creed or doctrine, belief or religion. You accept us all to you whether we are male or female, straight or gay or bi. You are non judgmental. You are all loving and accepting unconditionally as the great Mother that you are. Please protect us from the onslaughts of the enemies of unity. Please, Mother, take them away from here as soon as possible. We cannot attain the New Age of Global Unity until these self righteous bigots are removed. Make it soon, Oh Holy Mother, make it soon!"

The meeting was a resounding success. Everyone there planned for the great Millennial Unity Conference for 2001. It was firmly believed by all in attendance that what the world needed was a global outreach to all people in the name of the Higher Spiritual Power. The core of this Millennial "apple" of outreach would be Catholicism with Protestantism around that core and Judaism around that and Islam around that. The outer layers would be Hinduism, Buddhism, Native American Religions and even Earth centered Goddess religions like Gaia and Wicca. The world was entering an Age where it would either unite as one, or it would destroy itself. This movement for global evolution and unity would be spearheaded from Rome but would be greatly enhanced by the United Nations. Reverend Shea had many contacts there, and they reassured him that the United Nations would undertake a global initiative for Religious Unity.

Dr. Lazant told those assembled that he had made contact with the angels in the Heavens and that they had told him that they would assist them in this monumental effort.

"Esteemed colleagues," Dr. Lazant said quietly, "they told me that the so called fundamentalist Christians had to be removed before any global unity could be achieved."

"How was this to be accomplished?" asked the theologian from the Holy See.

"They have not said as of yet, but we are right on top of this. We will let you know as soon as we know something."

"God Bless you, my son."

With Dr. Lazant and Reverend Shea at this meeting were representatives from the World Council of Churches, as well as a Buddhist representative of the Dalai Lama, a Hindu Shiva Priestess, a Moslem Imam from Iran, a Wiccan practitioner of white magic and a Native American Medicine Man. All felt the spiritual tug of the New Age approaching and all wanted to help usher it in. All agreed that there were many guises to the Supreme and many different paths to it.

"Rabbi Ginsberg," Reverend Shea said as he finished his food and gulped some Chai and loosened his belt. "Are you going to be with us at the United Nations meeting next month?"

"I plan to be, Goddess willing!" Rabbi Ginsberg chuckled. "By the way, Reverend, what do these angels look like?"

"Well they are big, black and have huge wings. They don't look like sweet cherubs. They are more like avenging angels! I would not want to cross them. They are fearless and I feel sorry for the Christians in their path. They have no mercy!"

"Wow! Interesting! They sound like the Archangels in the Old Testament. In fact they sound like the angels depicted in the Apocrypha and Pseudopigrapha. Weren't those angels called the Watchers? I love to read the Jewish myths and legends. Lilith, the first wife of Adam in the Garden of Eden, is my favorite," Rabbi Ginsberg said as she smiled broadly. "She would not lie beneath Adam, and she uttered the secret name of God and flew away to the netherworld. She now kills young children at birth. That is why Jewish women wear the amulets to ward off the evil eye of Lilith. She is a powerful woman!"

"You are absolutely correct, Rabbi. We have been so Blessed to have made contact with these Watchers as they call themselves," Dr. Lazant interjected loud enough for all to hear. "Can you believe that these angels have been watching Humanity for millennia and only now do they realize that they need to actively help us achieve this global unity? The entity AZAZEL has communicated with a man at my Institute by telepathic means. He has assured Stephen that the so called fundamentalist fanatical Christians must go and that this most important yet delicate removal would be accomplished by them."

"We obviously must have the Heavenly Avatars on our side," said the representative of the Dalai Lama. "O, Great Krishna and Shiva and Kali! I'll bet these Christians will be most surprised by this removal. Our culture speaks of the coming end of this world cycle. Worlds are created and they die, and then they are recreated again just like people are. All is cyclical. Birth, death, rebirth. This age is dying and we are here to see and participate in the new world which is to come. What a monumental time to be alive."

"Yeah, those Christians think that we are the lost ones," said the Ogala Sioux Medicine Man. "These so called Watchers sound like what the Hopis call Kachinas. They have come and visited our people for centuries. We know what they look like. Our own culture also speaks of worlds being created and then dying. Our elders tell us that this world is also about to die. We look forward to the next world were we all can live together in unity and harmony."

"Let me close us in prayer," continued Lloyd Foot. "O Great Spirit! Be with us as we go from this place. Thank you for your Kachinas who watch over us and protect us. Thank you for your great Mother Earth who nourishes us and sustains us. We all look forward to the day when you shall once again reign Supreme and the white man's Old Father Spirit will be no more."

Everyone bowed his head and were absolutely quiet as the Sioux Medicine Man prayed. You could hear a pin drop. All were totally immersed in his words and began a long meditative state which lasted for an hour. Several people gathered there began to sing. Some chanted mantras, other chanted traditional Native American songs while others just reached their hands up to the ceiling and shook with religious ecstasy. The Wiccan Priestess congered up the spirits of the dead to honor this event. The Representative from the World Council of Churches simply prayed for global unity to Father, Mother, God while the Vatican Theologian Father Saltucci called upon the Blessed Mary, Mother of God to bless this auspicious occasion.

Eventually, everyone came back to their physical bodies which were at the Watergate Hotel Conference Center and slowly the meeting began to break up. There were many hugs and bows and other gestures of true friendship and respect. It had been a wonderful afternoon of good food and good fellowship. All left perfectly content, if not a little too full.

Dr. Lazant was anxious to get back to the Institute. The last that he had heard was that Ultra was looking for Judah. They had tried to kill him, but he had escaped. Dr. Lazant did not tell the group that the angels were traveling in UFOs or that there was a group called Ultra. He knew that Ultra did not want anyone to know of the UFOs or of them. They were very emphatic about that. Somehow he would find a way to tell his colleagues before the removal occurred, but he just could not figure out how to do it at this time.

"Dr. Lazant," Reverend Shea said. "I just heard from Stephen. His communication with AZAZEL has informed him that Judah apparently died in a car crash, but no body was ever found! Ultra was about to apprehend some of the people from a Christian rebel group who were in Chicago to pick up Judah's mother, when the vehicle they were driving in was exploded. Everything is a little sketchy right now but what I cannot figure out is why would they want Judah's mother if he were dead?"

"I guess they were not sure that he was dead," Dr. Lazant answered with a grimace. "They must have heard that no body was found at the crash scene as well. But what bugs me is how did they know that AZAZEL was going to be there also and so they aborted their abduction attempt?"

"Maybe they overheard Stephen telling the man from Ultra that AZAZEL had put a listening device in Mrs. Meire's neck?" Reverend Shea said flippantly.

"If that is true, then that means that they have surveillance equipment at the Institute?" Dr. Lazant suddenly pieced together. "Can you believe that we are being monitored by those stupid Christian zealots. Wait till AZAZEL hears about this!"

"And Ultra as well. They are going to be mighty peeved," Reverend Shea continued.

Before going back to the Institute, Dr. Lazant called his contact number at Ultra and left a message. They met him in front of the Institute.

"Now what were you raving about, Doc?" said the man with sunglasses and an overcoat.

"Those Christian rebel fanatics seem to have bugged the Institute."

"What makes you say that?"

"AZAZEL told Stephen that they were about to capture some of these rebels who had been sent to take Judah's mother to their camp, but suddenly they just left her. I think that they were listening when Stephen told you that AZAZEL had put a listening device into her neck!"

"I told you that Stephen had a big mouth," said the other man from Ultra, a very large man about 6'6" and 250 pounds. He had a pair of small sunglasses that barely covered his large broad nose. He had hands like hams. They were huge.

"Where is Stephen?" this behemoth bellowed.

"Inside," Dr. Lazant said sheepishly.

"Go get him!"

When Dr. Lazant returned with Stephen, the immense blond headed man from Ultra strangled him with his large bare hands right in front of the Institute. Stephen wriggled two feet above the ground and attempted to break free but it was futile. Dr. Lazant and Reverend Shea moved a step forward, but quickly retreated as the man snarled. After a few minutes, Stephen was dead.

"Why did you do that?" Dr. Lazant shrugged as he threw his fists into the air. "Stephen was our contact with AZAZEL"

"We are AZAZEL!" the man said as he wiped off his hands and walked away leaving Dr. Lazant with the body.

Dr. Lazant did not know what to do. He dragged the body into the bushes and stood there deciding what he should do with it. He wondered if it had been Judah that had bugged the Institute? Most confusing was the statement that Ultra was AZAZEL.

The last thing that Judah remembered was going over the cliff in the van. It had burst into flames, and he had made his peace with his Maker. Immediately, he had felt the presence of the Lord. The heat was no longer so blazing. He felt carried away by the Holy Spirit. It was as if Jesus Christ Himself had lifted him up and carried him out of the inferno. He thought that he died and was being carried to Heaven. Then, amazingly, he awakened to find himself in a strange, dark place. His first thought was that he was in Hell, but why would Jesus bring him there? Unless it was Satan in disguise. What a last sinister deception for Satan to carry people to Hell masquerading as Jesus.

It reminded Judah of those so called near death experiences where people die and are greeted by the all accepting 'Light'. Of course, he knew that this Light was Lucifer, the bright morning star, who was deceiving these people into believing that when they die they will go the Light no matter what they have done or not done. It was one of the numerous lies of the Great Deceiver, Satan, that was then spread to the masses upon their sudden reviving. You do not need Jesus or to repent of your sins before you die was the deception. Was this what he was experiencing, Judah wondered? He thought not, because he knew that the only way to the Father and to Heaven was through the Son.

But he had never died before, so he thought that maybe that was the way it happened. It seemed to contradict the word of God, though, so he became increasingly bewildered. Then, suddenly, he heard a loud noise and saw blue eyes approaching, and he became really scared. Maybe it was Satan. He then saw Dawn approaching from behind the blue eyes and loud roar, and he still was not convinced that he was not in Hell. Maybe she had died as well and they would be together at last .

Dawn saw that the man in front of her was Judah. She raced out of her car and threw her arms around him and screamed for joy.

"Oh, Judah, you are alive," Dawn wailed. "I love you so much. I love you. Oh, praise God, you are still alive!"

"Are we in Hell, Dawn?" Judah asked reluctantly as a large explosion shook the area and threw them onto the ground. "I am so scared that we have both died and are in Hell..."

"No, Judah, no, we are together at last here on good old Earth," Dawn answered as she put her arm around him and smothered him in kisses. She was ecstatic. "I don't know how you ended up here, but thank God that you did. Otherwise, I would have been blown to bits!"

Judah just stared at her in a state of shock and bewilderment. The last thing that he remembered was being carried out of the flaming inferno by what appeared to be the Lord.

"Come to think of it, Dawn, the Lord did say to me that my work was not finished yet as he carried me to safety. Oh God, please forgive me. I have doubted Your will and Your rescuing of me from the burning inferno. How could I be so doubting after all that You have done for me?"

Judah began to sob and got down on his knees and pleaded for forgiveness.

"It is all right, sweetheart," Dawn said as she comforted him. "Even Peter denied the Lord three times after he had lived directly with and had seen firsthand His many miracles! We are such weak, sinful creatures after all. It is only by the grace of God that we do not end up in the burning pit forever."

"I cannot believe that I thought that we were in Hell. I guess that I was in a state of shock, but there is no excuse. God, forgive me, please! I am so thankful to be alive and to be with you, Dawn. Our God is so good, isn't He? How did this wretched sinner deserve to be rescued by such a loving God? In fact, how did this wretched sinner deserve such a loving, wonderful spirit-filled woman such as you?"

"As the song says, Judah, it was God's amazing grace, not anything that we did. He picked us out even from our mother's womb for His purpose."

"Where are we, Dawn?"

125

"We are on Backbone Mountain in far West Maryland. On the top of this summit is the Christian Militia group the Joshua Brigade led by Captain Knowington. They call it New Petra. These are the people whom you asked about, remember? They can hide us out."

"Then why did they try and blow you up?"

"It's a long story, honey. There will be time for that later. Now that you are safe and sound we can both return to the camp. Are you up to walking a dozen miles or so?"

"Are you Dawn? Can you walk that far? The MS is really gone?" Judah asked with a loving concern that melted Dawn's heart.

"Yes, I can, Judah," Dawn said with a smile and a hug. "I feel great. You know we never really consummated our marriage, Judah. I think that it is about time that we did!"

Judah smiled and kissed his wife. It had never really bothered him that they had not physically consummated their marriage, but it had bothered Dawn. She wanted to give him pleasure, but he did not want to since she had no feeling from the waist down and thus would not feel any pleasure herself. They stood there in the dark cool mountain air and held each other tight for what seemed like an eternity. Just as they were starting up the mountain, another black, turbocharged Hummer came towards them. It had been sent down to pick up the two soldiers that Dawn had made pedestrians by her cannon blast.

"Captain Knowington is very anxious to see you, Sir," the soldier said to Judah. "He saw you on the surveillance monitors at New Petra once the jamming was ceased by this crazy lady's Hummer. He cannot believe that you are not only alive, but that you found us here at Backbone Mountain. How did you do it?"

"The Lord did it, son. I had nothing to do with it!"

"Is he upset with me?" Dawn asked sheepishly.

"Duh?! Is the Pope Catholic, Ma'am?" he smirked. "You just destroyed two of our vehicles and were sneaking his two daughters out of the base. Other than that, I'm sure that he still loves you!"

"Judah, I also told Knowington and Gregor that, if they killed me in my effort in trying to find you, that you would tear them limb from limb! Captain Knowington blew up my vehicle when he realized that I was really leaving New Petra, which is punishable by death!"

"Dawn... Dawn," Judah moaned, "Lieutenant Gregor is up there as well? As my mother says 'oy vey ist mir'. Oh woe is me!"

126

# PART II

*"Finally, be strong in the Lord, and in the strength of His might. Put on the full armor of God, that you may be able to stand firm against the schemes of the devil."*

*"Therefore take up the full armor of God, that you may be able to resist in the evil day, and having done everything, to stand firm. Stand firm therefore, HAVING GIRDED YOUR LOINS WITH TRUTH, AND HAVING PUT ON THE BREASTPLATE OF RIGHTEOUSNESS, and having shod YOUR FEET WITH THE PREPARATION OF THE GOSPEL OF PEACE; in addition to all, taking up the shield of faith with which you will be able to extinguish the flaming missiles of the evil one. And take THE HELMET OF SALVATION and the sword of the Spirit, which is the word of God."*

Paul's Epistle to the Ephesians 6:10-11,13-17

# X

The Hummer slowly pulled into New Petra with Dawn and Judah aboard. Dawn could see Ann Knowington standing there with her arms around her two daughters. Rebecca and Jennifer looked even younger and more vulnerable to Dawn in the early morning darkness. Everyone was gathered around to see Judah. They all had witnessed his miraculous rescue from the fiery van by what appeared to be the Lord Himself, and it was something that each of them would never ever forget. Captain Knowington and Lieutenant Gregor were standing at the front of the crowd to greet them.

"Judah, we are so glad that you are alive," Captain Knowington said as he embraced Judah. "What a blessing you have been to all of us. We are all looking forward to working directly with you to complete our mission. General Desporte and Senator Jordan thought the world of you, son."

"You stiff-necked Jew," Gregor piped in as he too embraced Judah. "You cannot kill you, boy. You seem to be in the Lord's hand no matter what you do. He is always watching out for you."

Captain Knowington leered at Dawn and his eyepatch curled up. She could tell that he was rightly angry with her actions, especially endangering his daughters. As he moved towards Dawn, his wife yelled out.

"Peter, forget about it. It's all over now. She would be dead now if it weren't for Judah. I think that she has learned her lesson and will not defy you again," Ann said as she moved to restrain him.

"You are a pushy woman, Dawn," Knowington said. "You directly disobeyed my orders and have caused us to lose two priceless vehicles. What do have to say for yourself, young lady?"

Dawn did not know what to say. He was correct after all. She took Judah's hand and pushed right past Captain Knowington into the crowd of the Joshua Brigade.

"My husband and I have some unfinished business, Captain," she yelled back as she pulled Judah by the hand towards her room in the living quarters. "We'll talk later!"

"Nice to meet you, Sir," Judah managed to say as he was whisked away. "Hey, how are you doing, Lieutenant Gregor? Nice to see you here as well. I guess that we will talk later."

Judah was fascinated by what he saw, but did not have the time to really appreciate it because Dawn pulled him into the room and locked the door.

Dr. Lazant and Reverend Shea tried to decide what to do with Stephen's body. Reverend Shea, especially, was in a near state of shock over what had just happened. Stephen was such a nice young man and to see him strangled to death right in front of their eyes was unbearable. They could not just leave his body in the bushes, so they decided to bury it in the earthen escape path of one of the underground bunkers in the basement of the Institute. Judah had convinced Dr. Lazant that they needed just such an escape mechanism in case the Institute was bombed. Dr. Lazant had thought at the time that it was a little impractical but had installed them nonetheless.

"I cannot believe that Ultra did that to Stephen," Reverend Shea sobbed. "He was such a nice young man with such a promising future. He had given up his graduate studies to work full time for us and look what happened to him. It just isn't fair!"

"Life isn't fair - and then you die! But he was the one who we needed to communicate with AZAZEL," Dr. Lazant continued.

"Is that all you can think about at a time like this, Bruce? You are really insensitive, you know."

"Well, excuse me, Rev, but the entire planet is getting ready to jump to a new level of evolutionary consciousness and our link to the Watchers who will perpetrate this move has just been killed. Who cares about one individual life when the entire soul of humanity is at stake!"

"That is cold, Doc, real cold," Reverend Shea said shaking his head and dumping the body into the hole that Dr. Lazant had just dug. "Where is our morality, our compassion? Does the end justify the means?"

"Grow up, Rev!" Dr. Lazant countered. "This is not just some medieval theological enigma. This is the reality of the abduction of millions of evangelical Christians. Do you really think that will be pretty? We have a job to do and we have to do it. Pull yourself together, man. Of course I am shocked by what happened to Stephen. I'm fearful that I might be next. Those guys from Ultra are ruthless. We just need to do our job without wavering from it even one iota. Otherwise, we will end up six feet under as well."

Dr. Lazant and Reverend Shea finished covering up the body and headed back into the Institute, all the while discussing a way to reestablish communication with AZAZEL. The thing that bothered them was the statement by Ultra that they were AZAZEL. What could that mean after all? As soon as they got back into the Institute, they immediately looked for Endora. Surprisingly, they found her still there in the middle of the night. Both pleaded with her to conjure up the deceased spirit of Stephen.

"Endora, Stephen has just been killed," Dr. Lazant feigned anguish.

"By whom?" she asked with tears running down her face.

"By the Christians," he lied.

"The Christians?" she inquired with anger. "What did they fear from him?"

"Well, he established communication with AZAZEL and their group fears the Watchers,"Dr. Lazant began. "We want to tell Stephen how sorry that we are for what happened to him. He was an integral part of our work with AZAZEL. Conjure him up for us, please. Bring up for us whom we have asked of you. Bring up Stephen for us."

Endora sat down and began conjuring the spirits of the dead. She said incantations and moved her hands in strange motions. After a few minutes, Stephen's voice came out of Endora's mouth. Her face and hands took on the mannerisms unquestionably of Stephen.

"Why have you disturbed me by bringing me up?" Stephen said.

"Stephen, we are terribly sorry about what happened to you. We are hopeful that you are doing well in the Light of the All Present Spirit, but we are very confused by Ultra. They say that they are AZAZEL. What does that mean? Therefore we called you that you may make known to us what we should do, now that you are on the other side."

"Ultra is the long arm of AZAZEL. They are one and the same. Ultra does not want anyone to be aware of AZAZEL's plot to abduct the Christians. Oh, Dr. Lazant and Reverend Shea, please rescue me from these flames which I am in. It is pure agony," Stephen moaned. "Please help me. I am in the fires of Hell. The Christians were right after all! Help me! Please! Help meee!"

Dr. Lazant and Reverend Shea ordered Endora to cease her conjuring up of the deceased spirit of Stephen. The information about Ultra was useful, but they just seemed to ignore the plight of Stephen. Abruptly, Dr. Lazant remembered that the Institute had been bugged by the Christian rebels. He could not believe that he had forgotten that fact. It had, after all, been the reason that Stephen had been killed in the first place. He stopped talking altogether and left the Institute motioning for Endora and Reverend Shea to follow him.

"What do you make of Stephen's fate?" Reverend Shea asked Dr. Lazant as they fled the building.

"Forget about it, Rev," he replied nonchalantly. "He disobeyed Ultra, the long arm of AZAZEL, and probably deserves his fate."

"What are you guys talking about?"Endora inquired anxiously. "What did Stephen say?"

"Nothing important, Endora. Don't worry your ugly little head over it," Dr. Lazant said, ending the discussion.

Everyone at New Petra had watched intently as the demonic spectacle unfolded at the Lazant Institute. They all gasped as Endora conjured up the spirit of Stephen.

"That is not possible," one of the soldiers yelled. "You cannot call up the spirits of the dead. That is New Age mystic nonsense!"

"That is not true, son," Lieutenant Gregor responded. "Saul went to the witch of Endor to call up the dead spirit of Samuel. Look, son, in the Book of Samuel. It is not that it is impossible, but rather that it is an abomination to the Lord. According to the Book of Deuteronomy, anyone who practices witchcraft or who interprets omens or is a sorceress, or casts a spell or is a medium or who calls up the dead is detestable to the Lord. This woman appears to be a witch like her namesake in the Scriptures, and thus is under the Lord's judgement."

Some of the younger soldiers cheered when Stephen acknowledged that he was in the fires of Hell not the loving embrace of the so-called Light. Lieutenant Gregor cautioned them to not applaud the fate of poor Stephen. It wasn't something to be made fun of in any manner. It was tragic because God's mercy and grace were not possible for him now, only His Eternal judgment. Lieutenant Gregor led the people assembled in a prayer for Dr. Lazant, Reverend Shea and Endora that their eyes would be opened to the fate of Stephen and what would be theirs as well if they did not repent of their sins and turn their lives over to the Living God.

Judah and Dawn lay in each other's arms perfectly content.

"I was so concerned about you, Judah," Dawn said as she kissed her husband's cheek. "I don't really understand why, but I feel so very close to you. When you are not with me, I feel totally lost. It is as if part of me is missing. No one has ever made me feel like that before."

"Not even Bob?" Judah replied with a smile.

"No, not even Bob, Judah!" Dawn said as she hugged Judah. "Sure, I loved Bob, but nobody has the effect on me that you have. You are my everything, my sunshine. I thank God every day for you."

"I feel the same way about you, sweetheart. It is as if we are two parts of the same whole. Either part by itself is useless. The Lord definitely put us together. In the world's sense we had nothing in common. Me being Jewish, secular and a know it all, and you being a sweet, humble, Christian woman. Remember when you used to witness to me at the Pentagon commissary? I was too busy looking at your beautiful eyes to hear one word that you said."

"I knew that. I could not understand how such a nice man, though, could be so lost. You had no idea of what was really going on, but you were so certain that you did and no one could convince you otherwise. You drove General Desporte crazy. He got so frustrated with you."

"That seems like just yesterday," Judah said with a sigh and a smile. "Sometimes I blink my eyes to make sure that this is all real. That old Judah seems like a different person. I am really born again. I hope that General Desporte can see me now."

"I'm sure that he can, Judah. He is probably telling everyone in heaven about his stiff-necked Jewboy who has come to the Lord!"

"You know, Dawn, I believe that the Lord has a special place in heaven for those people that help bring His lost sheep back to Him. It is a special calling that the Lord should reward for people like General Desporte. The Lord does the calling by

His Holy Spirit, but He uses people like the General to manifest His will. The Lord chose me, I did not choose Him. As it says in the Book Of Isaiah, the Lord permitted Himself to be found by those who did not seek Him, and He used the General to do it. What an honor and a privilege to be so used by the Lord of Lords and King of Kings."

"Where is that Scripture in Isaiah, Judah?" Dawn asked with a big smile on her face.

"It is Isaiah 65:1, Dawn. Sha'ul uses it again in Romans 10:20."

"Judah, you have grown so fast in the Lord and His word. I am so proud of you. The Lord is really using you in a mighty way. I love you so much."

Judah and Dawn continued to reminisce about their time together and their time apart. It really seemed to them that the Lord had brought the two of them together for a critical time such as this. Many people including General Desporte and his wife Elaine, Senator Jordan and his wife Betsy, Major Kole, Congressman Jacobs, Corporals McQueen and McCord as well of course Bob and Caroline had given their lives for the cause of unmasking the deception of AZAZEL.

Judah and Dawn promised each other and the Lord that they would continue the battle no matter what the costs or consequences.

"Dawn, Senator Jordan told me that the struggle with these so-called UFOs was not for the planet of man but for the soul of man. We have been so conditioned over the past fifty years to consider the possibility of extraterrestrial life that we have been oblivious to the reality of the demonic deception. We are such a *Star Trek, ET* and *X-File* generation that we have all been fooled by the real truth. The truth is out there, but it is not extraterrestrial in nature but rather demonic. The deception is far more sinister than anyone could ever imagine."

"I remember, Judah, when you said to me that the struggle was not with flesh and blood but with principalities of wickedness in Heavenly places. At that time, you did even know how you knew that Scripture, but you did know it. Remember?"

"I know, honey. Things have been falling into place really quickly as of late. I tried to fight it, but it is what the Lord wants me to do. I honestly feel that the time is short and this mass abduction of Christians is going to take place soon unless we can stop it!"

"But how are you going to be able to stop it? That is the one thing that I cannot understand," Dawn asked, puzzled.

"I don't know. All I know is that I am supposed to stop this move by the forces of wickedness."

"How?"

"I don't know."

The more that they talked, the more confused that they became. Judah knew that he was supposed to stop AZAZEL but he was uncertain how that would stop the abduction. He felt that he had to stop Dr.Lazant and Reverend Shea as well from their one world religion agenda, but again he was not certain if that would stop the entire movement. Judah and Dawn prayed for answers.

After cleaning up, they went back out into the underground compound. Judah was fascinated by everything that he saw there. He especially liked the communications area, as had Dawn. He was amazed at the surveillance capabilities that New Petra had. One of the young soldiers, Corporal Canon, told him that they had just seen Endora conjure up the dead spirit of Stephen.

"Is Stephen dead?" Judah inquired. "Do you know what happened to him?"

"It appears that Ultra killed him," spoke up Captain Knowington as he entered the surveillance area.

"Captain, it is a pleasure to finally meet you, Sir. My wife has told me such wonderful things about what you have done here."

"I'll bet that she has, Judah. Did she tell you that she knocked out one of my men and stole a vehicle to go look for you? She also endangered the lives of my daughters to accomplish that act of desertion which is punishable by death!"

"Yes, she did, Captain. She also told me that she told you that, if you killed her in the process, you would have to answer to me!" Judah answered firmly with a slight smirk. "And well, you did try and kill her, Sir. Only by the grace of God is she alive today."

"Well, where does that leave us then, Judah?"

"I guess that you got off easy, Sir. Nobody messes with my woman and gets away with it, even if she was being a jackass," Judah replied, slapping the Captain on the back and finally cracking a smile.

"Sir, we need to talk. I have some ideas about military action that we need to take as soon as possible. By the way, could we send some men to retrieve my mother? Her life may be at risk."

"Judah, sure we can talk as soon as I get you some new clothes. Your uniform looks like it went through a furnace," Captain Knowington replied looking at Judah's scorched uniform and all the while glaring at Dawn.

"It did, Sir! It is amazing that my clothes burned, but not my flesh. Praise God!" Judah said. "And please stop glaring at my wife, Sir. She has learned her lesson."

"How about the two Hummers that she destroyed?"

"Well, you got me instead. I am worth two Hummers, aren't I, Sir?"

"Hmmm... As to your mother, Judah, I had already sent some men to retrieve her, but I called off the mission when we discovered from surveillance of the Lazant Institute that AZAZEL put a surveillance device at the base of her skull. In fact that is what got Stephen killed. He blabbed it to Ultra while we were listening and then we called off the retrieval. Those two young soldiers had to be killed before they fell into the hands of AZAZEL. We have to figure out a way to get your Mom without AZAZEL knowing about it. She does need to be here as soon as possible. Otherwise, not only her life, but the survival of New Petra will be at risk."

Judah and Dawn went with Captain Knowington and the others to the mess hall for some breakfast. Judah could not remember the last time that he had eaten. The

133

plates of catfish, eggs and toast were to be washed down with piping hot mugs of coffee and goat's milk.

"Before we eat, can I say the blessing?" Judah asked.

"Sure, brother."

"Father, thank you for all the Blessings that you have given us. Thank you for bringing me safely to this compound of your people. Thank you for the faithful service and leadership of Captain Knowington, Lieutenant Gregor and all the men here. Thank you for my wife, Dawn, and all the other wives that are here backing their husbands and families. I know that it must have been a great sacrifice to leave family and friends. Bless them, Lord. Thank You for the food that we have before us and the hands that prepared it. Know also, Heavenly Father, that we will do what You have authorized us to do without hesitation or even the thought of failure. We are Your army, Lord, and we will do Your will. In Jesus' name, Amen!"

Everyone settled in a time of laughter and fellowship. Judah felt so much better in the new uniform that Captain Knowington had gotten for him. It was the same size as his old uniform with the same stripes, bars and commendations on it as his had. He could not figure out how the Captain had done it, but he never asked. What would be the point? It was a friendly gesture, and he just thanked the Captain for doing it.

Judah thought intently about a way to rescue his mother without the knowledge of AZAZEL.

"How about if I call Mom's Doctor and ask him to call her in for a visit. Once there he can remove the surveillance chip from her neck,"Judah asked Captain Knowington. "And we can meet her there and remove her."

"Think about it, Judah. AZAZEL will therefore know that she will be at the Doctor's office and once the chip is removed, they will know something is wrong and will immediately move in. We will be caught again," Captain Knowington replied. "We need another way to do it."

"Uhh! Good point, Captain. I'll keep thinking about a way. There has got to be a way to do it without alerting AZAZEL," Judah replied frustrated. "We do need to eliminate Dr. Lazant and Reverend Shea in the meantime. I heard that Ultra already killed Stephen, but these two men are part of the move by AZAZEL to institute a one world religion after the abduction of the Christians. They are the like the False Prophet of the Book of Revelation. They will help create the deception that Satan wants. After all, the Christians will be gone and there will be nobody to promote the Truth. All the unbelieving masses will fall for this deception of the Enemy and never find out the real Truth. We probably cannot stop this move for a new world religion, but we can most certainly slow it down. I believe that these men need to be sent to their eternal destiny ASAP."

"Judah, we are preparing a global world media message and an INTERNET website to explain to the unsuspecting world which will be left behind about what has really happened. We are preparing to tell everyone that the sudden

134

disappearance of Christians is not a result of a mass abduction by UFOs but is a plot by the demons of Hell to remove us to prepare the world for their arrival in the guise of a new world religion. We are warning them to reconsider all the false knowledge that they will be hearing about our disappearance, and we will back it up with Scripture. We are waiting to find out exactly when this will happen so we do not release anything before it is absolutely necessary. We don't want to panic the population, especially the Christians. That is why we need to find out exactly when this is to happen, and to stop it if at all possible, but barring that, to educate those left behind as to what really has happened. As to Lazant and Shea, Judah, you are correct. We need to take them and the Institute out as soon as possible."

"Captain, while I agree with you on the need to destroy the Institute and its people, I wholeheartedly disagree with your defeatist attitude concerning AZAZEL. I will not concede to them that they have already won, and that we just need to educate those left behind. Aren't you a soldier, Captain? You would not surrender in the army of the United States, would you? So why are you so interested in surrendering God's army? As Scripture says, the battle belongs to the Lord! We are His army. We will not fail! Is that understood, Sir? I will coordinate the battle directly against AZAZEL and his plot to abduct the Christians. Is that perfectly clear?"

Captain Knowington became enraged but was restrained by Lieutenant Gregor.

"Who do you think that you are, son? I am in charge of this Brigade, not you," Captain Knowington shouted. "I said that I wanted to defeat AZAZEL as my first priority but barring that we need to warn the masses left behind."

"That's not good enough, Sir. If you are really in charge, then act like it," Judah replied pointing his finger directly at the Captain.

They all settled into a hushed time of tense emotions. Captain Knowington glared at Judah as he had previously at Dawn. These two newcomers had challenged his authority and ability to command and lead at New Petra. He anxiously contemplated his next move very cautiously.

Lieutenant Gregor gently changed the subject to ease the tension. He suggested that Judah contact the Lazant Institute to make sure that everyone would be there before they attacked.

"We could have you call and tell them that you will meet them there at a specified time," Lieutenant Gregor suggested.

"I'm sorry, but that will not work either, Sir. If I call, then both AZAZEL and Ultra will be waiting for us when we arrive. In fact, they both may be watching the Institute right now, so in any case they will be there to greet us. We need an alternative plan here also. The jobs concerning both my Mom and these guys need to be fulfilled ASAP. Put on your thinking caps, gentlemen!"

"Colonel know it all, remember, we have surveillance at the Institute. We could have our Hummer ready nearby and verify when those guys are there," Captain Knowington answered. "I will personally lead the mission. We'll see who's in charge here, Judah."

"That is silly, Sir," Gregor shouted. "We need you here. You cannot risk your life on the front line."

"You've got Judah, the lion, remember. He will protect all of you!"

"Captain Knowington, I designed the security for the Institute. You..."

"What do you want, a medal, Judah?"

"No, Sir," Judah shouted, "but I think that we need to talk about it. I put in cameras and motion detectors and even some radar equipment. You will not get within a mile of the Institute without being noticed."

Captain Knowington walked right past Judah and the others. He pointed out the same two men who rescued Dawn to be with him on this mission. They knew the route to Potomac, Maryland better than anyone else. The three of them walked over to one of the remaining Hummers and began loading it with the appropriate gear and supplies. Captain Knowington, himself, loaded the most impressive piece of firepower, a surface to surface shoulder held missile.

"Don't do this, Peter!" Ann Knowington pleaded with her husband. "You needn't try and prove yourself to any of us. We all know that you are doing the best that you can against an unseen enemy. Please stop! You are going to get yourself killed. First our daughters and now you are putting your life in peril. I'm ready to have a nervous breakdown. We aren't kids anymore, you know!"

Captain Knowington continued with his preparations not even looking at his wife or daughters.

"Please, Judah, make him stop!" Ann pleaded.

"Captain, you need not go. We need to plan this out more carefully. One missile will probably not take out the Institute. It is made with reinforced steel and has underground bunkers. Trust me. I helped design it. You're being foolish and impetuous, Sir. I'm truly sorry for questioning your authority in front of your men. Please, Sir, don't do this!"

"He is right, Peter," Lieutenant Gregor said, grabbing him by the arm. "This is crazy. You can't fly off half-cocked and expect to get the mission right. Your emotions are leading you, not your head!"

Captain Knowington ignored everyone. He was determined about completing this mission. All his frustration at not being able to engage the enemy was finally coming to the surface as a result of first Dawn's disobeying of his orders and then Judah's challenge of his tactics. He had enough of all of that now. He would go the Institute and blow it up with Dr. Lazant, Reverend Shea and Endora inside. Then for once he would feel that he was accomplishing something worthwhile for the battle other than making INTERNET websites.

"I want you to feed me the surveillance pictures from the Institute directly into my Hummer," he yelled at Corporal Canon, the soldier in charge of monitoring the Institute. "I want to make sure that those people are in there when I fire my rocket."

"But Sir, as I told you before, that rocket will not bring down the Institute,"

136

Judah said forcefully.

"Oh yes it will, Jewboy," Captain Knowington replied. "It is uranium tipped. Shows you what you know, smart guy You Jews think that you know everything. You guys are pushy, even when you become Believers. No wonder God called you stiffnecked!"

"But, Sir..."

"But nothing. That is what a billygoat does, Colonel! Forget about it!"

"What if you get there and nobody is there?" Ann cried out.

"We will wait for them. I am taking enough supplies to last a week. Don't worry. We'll be fine."

"And what about us here at New Petra?"

"You have the Colonel here and his obedient wife. Actually, Lieutenant Gregor is now in charge. You should be just fine. I would appreciate your prayers, though."

Everyone crowded around as the Hummer prepared to depart. It was almost noon and the vehicles rarely moved in broad daylight especially from the compound, but the Captain was determined to leave as soon as possible. He kissed his wife goodbye and saluted his men. His last act was to look over at Judah and nod his head. Judah smiled and saluted him.

"God Bless you, Sir," Judah said.

"Thank you, Colonel. Watch out for my wife and girls!"

"I will."


Dr. Lazant stood there anxiously as the people from Ultra swept his Institute for surveillance equipment. They went from room to room and managed to locate several pieces of equipment in the remote viewing room, the conference room and even a device in Dr. Lazant's office. Without Judah there to replace them, everyone now felt reasonably secure.

"We saw that you spoke to the dead spirit of Stephen, Doctor," said the same large blond man with the huge hands that had strangled Stephen. "He told you that we were the long arm of AZAZEL, I understand?"

"How did you know that?" Dr. Lazant replied with a look of concern. "Do you have this place bugged as well?"

"In a matter of speaking. We can watch you anytime that we want."

"Are you the long arm of AZAZEL?"

"That is no concern of yours," answered the blond behemoth as took his long arm and stretched it out towards Dr. Lazant's neck. "Do you want me to use my long arm on you like I did on Stephen?"

"No that's all right, thank you," Dr. Lazant said as he backed away.

"By the way , what do make of Stephen's comment that he is now in what the Christians call Hell, not in the Light?" Reverend Shea inquired nervously.

"Well, he disobeyed the angels didn't he? All who disobey AZAZEL will burn in Hell for eternity. That is why you guys need to do what we tell you to do and to not think for yourselves. All that will get you is eternal punishment in the fires of Hell. Understand?"

"Yes, but I thought that there was no such place as Hell?" Reverend Shea anxiously pleaded for an explanation.

"But nothing. Forget about it! You two are to continue to work on the plans for a new one world religion that will take place when the Watchers come down to Earth from their Heavenly places. Once that they remove those vexing evangelical Christians everything will fall into place. For that reason your lives are in danger also."

"Really? What are you doing about that?" Dr. Lazant asked with a slight smile.

"Stop whining, Doc. Everything is under control. We are keeping an eye on you."

"Thank you!" Dr. Lazant said as he tried to put his arm on the blond man's shoulder.

"Don't touch me. Don't ever touch me!" bellowed the man as he grabbed the Doctor's hand and twisted it.

"Ouch!" Dr. Lazant yelled. "What did you do that for?"

The blond man just shook his head and with his other colleagues left the Institute, nearly knocking Dr. Lazant over as they rushed out of the door. With them, they took the surveillance equipment that Judah had installed for Senator Jordan whose pictures had eventually found their way to New Petra. Now Captain Knowington would be arriving without the benefit of this inside surveillance as well as with Ultra/AZAZEL watching the Institute closely for any intruders.

"Eagle one to Eagle two," sounded the call from the base to Captain Knowington.

"Eagle one, this is Eagle two."

"Eagle two, the window into the lair has been closed," spoke Corporal Canon, a twenty something young man with red hair and freckles, and the man in charge of monitoring the Lazant Institute at New Petra. "I repeat, the window into the lion's den has been closed. Return home immediately!"

Captain Knowington shut off the radio and continued to the Institute. There was in his mind no reason to turn around now. If they had removed the surveillance equipment that Judah had installed then they had to be eliminated without delay since their activities could not be monitored any longer. He looked over at his two young soldier comrades and said to them.

"Gentlemen, our cameras have been discovered and removed from the Institute, but I have decided to proceed anyhow. We need to wipe out that den of iniquity once and for all. Do you understand, soldiers? We will be going in blind."

"Yes Sir, we do! Let's proceed to the target!"

The sleek, black camouflaged 6.5 liter turbocharged Hummer sped down Backbone Mountain. Once at the base they traveled the same route in reverse to the

138

one that they had used to bring Dawn to New Petra. They went back into West Virginia and crossed over the Patterson Creek Mountains and the South Branch of the Potomac River. They traveled on a radio silence status as well as a full stealth mode. The men in the Hummer did not speak at all either. Everyone was dead silent. While the Captain was very contemplative, the two young soldiers were scared to death.

They would be confronting evil in its purest form, and they were in constant prayer for strength and courage in the face of it.

The Hummer crossed through Romney without as much as slowing down and entered onto State Route 50. Silently and swiftly they traveled through Winchester and moved back into Virginia. Once that they entered onto Route 7 they sped through Roundhill and then Hamilton, Virginia. They had brought along extra fuel so that they would not have to stop anywhere for refueling. That would draw too much attention. Once they hit Vienna, Virginia they turned North on Interstate 495 and headed for the Lazant Institute in Potomac, Maryland. The entire trip had taken the two young soldiers and Captain Knowington four and a half hours, an hour and half less than the same two soldiers took on their excursion to New Petra with Dawn which was at night. One could move much more quickly down a mountain road in a state of disrepair and along rural routes in daylight than in the dead of night with no highways lights at all.

It was nearly 1800 hours and the sky was full of angry black clouds and an occasional burst of thunder and lightning as they approached the neighborhood of the Institute. It was a largely rural area with a few isolated industrial complexes. Captain Knowington stopped the vehicle about two miles from the Institute. He punched into his vast array of intelligence data streams on his console that he wanted a satellite shot of the Institute. Fortunately for him, since it was not always possible, especially in this dark cloudy environment, a satellite image came onto his console screen. It revealed the cloud shadowed silhouette of the Institute with four cars in the parking lot which would seem to indicate that Dr. Lazant, Reverend Shea, Endora and the receptionist were still all there, but he could not be absolutely certain. The Institute had few windows except for a small skylight in the ceiling. He asked the satellite to zoom in on that window and lo and behold, he could barely make out the silhouettes of Lazant, Shea and Endora all sitting around the conference table talking.

Captain Knowington got back into the Hummer and drove a mile closer and positioned the vehicle in a clump of trees with a clear shot at the Institute. He had a twinge of guilt as he thought about blowing up the receptionist as well but this was war after all. He got out of the Hummer and removed the large shoulder held surface to surface missile launcher. He carefully targeted it using all the necessary data that he had obtained from the satellite. He could just fire it manually directly at the target since he had a clear shot, but he preferred to enter the latitude and longitude fixes from the satellite just to make sure. He armed it and prepared to fire.

All of a sudden from behind the trees, came the whooshing sound of a very large object. It startled the Captain as he looked upward and saw the large black disc. It immediately sent a tractor beam down to capture him. Captain Knowington fell backwards and was slowly pulled skyward. His arms and fingers felt frozen. He knew that he had to fire the missile, but he could not move.

"Oh Lord Jesus, give me the strength to pull this trigger," he moaned. "Please, Lord, give me Your strength to fight this powerful enemy. He that is in me is greater than he that is in the world."

For an instant, his one finger regained some movement. He pulled the trigger and the missile shot upwards. It then began to correct for the targeting data that he had entered. He now knew why the Lord wanted him to do such a seemingly redundant thing when he had visual sighting of the target. The missile shot downwards in the assigned flight path that was entered into its guidance system and crashed into the Institute sending fireworks over the entire area. The sky lit up like a Christmas tree.

The two soldiers in the Hummer, upon seeing the Captain captured by the beam from the black disc, had run out and attempted to pull him back but it was to no avail. They panicked and ran back into the Hummer and sped away from the area without ever looking back. They looked at each other in a state of shock and could not even speak.

"Colonel Meire, look at the screen!" shouted Corporal Canon. "The Institute was just blown up by Captain Knowington. But look here, he is being captured by a beam from that black disk. AZAZEL is getting him. What can we do?"

Judah rushed around in a state of heightened tension. He not only knew that Captain Knowington's life was now in danger but that all of New Petra was in danger as well.

"Gregor, you guys don't happen to have a helicopter here, do you?"

"Yes, we have one Apache on a pad at the side of the motorpool," Lieutenant Gregor replied. "You are not thinking what I think you're thinking, are you? Forget about it!"

"I need it right now. Is it fueled and ready to go?"

"No Judah, don't do this!" Dawn shouted as she grabbed him. "Do you want to kill yourself as Captain Knowington has apparently done? You are not leaving me again. I just got you back!"

"I have to go, Dawn, the Captain needs me," Judah told her as he broke free and shoved her into the arms of Gregor. "Watch out after her, Sir."

"Judah, what can you do now? He is already in the hands of AZAZEL!"

"Spiritual warfare, Sir. Remember? Read Ephesians 6:10. Shalom to all of you," Colonel Meire said as he raced from the mountainous cavern to the Apache Helicopter.

"But Judah, it will take you around 45 minutes to reach the black disk and you cannot climb to that altitude with a helicopter anyway!" Lieutenant Gregor yelled as he restrained Dawn. "They will probably be all gone by then. It will be useless!"

140

"Nothing is impossible for God, you Texas hillbilly," Judah replied as he fastened himself into the seat of the helicopter and revved up the blades. "Oh ye of so little faith! Corporal Canon, come here quick."

Judah whispered something in the Corporal's ear and and he nodded his head affirmatively. Immediately the young man darted away into the mountainous cavern and returned with two large black objects that he flung into the Apache.

"God Bless you, son," Judah said with a smile.

"We'll be praying for you, Sir!"

"Judah, Judah," Dawn yelled as she tried to break free from Lieutenant Gregor. "I love you. You big dumb Jew! You better come back to me in one piece!"

Everyone then rushed back to the monitoring room to watch what was happening to Captain Knowington and the Institute. As soon as Captain Knowington had been brought into the craft another beam shot down into the flaming wreckage of the Institute and had begun to remove the singed but still apparently alive and kicking bodies of Dr. Lazant, Reverend Shea, Endora and the receptionist. All agreed that Judah had been right about underground bunkers. Apparently they had been warned before the missile attack by AZAZEL, because nobody could have survived the blast of that uranium tipped missile. It blew the entire structure to smithereens, scattering radioactive debris over a wide area.

The sound of emergency vehicles soon filled the area. Before long, HAZMAT trucks were everywhere because of the fallout from the uranium warhead. The entire area was cordoned off, but the men from Ultra were allowed to enter the area at their own risk. The two young soldiers in the Hummer turned back on their radio and were told to hide out until dark and then to head back to New Petra as soon as possible. They still shook at the thought of Captain Knowington being captured by that tractor beam from the saucer. Neither soldier said a word but the looks that they gave one another were words enough. They now understood the battle that they were in with the principalities of wickedness in heavenly places

# XI

Judah raced the Apache Helicopter at full throttle towards the Institute. At nearly 220 miles per hour it would only be forty five minutes until he arrived. He did not have to descend the mountain or travel over winding rural roads. In fact he did not even have to travel to Potomac, Maryland where the Institute was, because his target was miles above that point. He just needed to take a direct line of attack from the top of Mount Backbone to the black disk in the skies above the Institute. He knew that the Apache could not travel to the point in the Heavens where the disk was because there was no air to lift his rotor blades, but he went on anyway.

On the way, Judah called upon the Lord to guide and assist him. He was in fervent prayer as the Apache raced along. The Holy Spirit interceded for him according to the will of God. The full Armor of God was upon him. In the distance, he caught sight of the black craft in the midst of angry murky clouds. He was about as high as he could go, so he hovered about four miles beneath it and waited. Just to make sure that they saw him he fired a missile into their underbelly which went right through it. Judah blinked his eyes and tried to figure out how that had happened.

Suddenly, a beam came down and began to reel him in. Judah smiled as he had accomplished the first phase of his mission which was to locate the enemy and to be brought in to him. Judah continued to pray fervently because he knew that not only his life but that of Captain Knowington was at stake. So were the lives of everybody at New Petra including that of Dawn, if AZAZEL could extract the location from Captain Knowington or him also for that matter.

"Lord, give me the strength to battle the forces of darkness and wickedness in these heavenly places. For as You have said, this struggle is not against flesh and blood but against the spiritual forces of wickedness. I have put on Your full Armor and will stand firm against the Enemy."

Judah's entire Apache helicopter was drawn into the gaping mouth of the large black disk. Once inside Judah looked around and saw nothing but the glowing flames of what appeared to be torches way off in the distance. It were as if he were in a massive black cave. Even the walls looked cavernous not high tech like that of an extraterrestrial craft. Off in the distance he spotted Captain Knowington being laid on a table by three grey hairless beings with large black eyes. He looked in a state of shock. His eyes were glazed but stared right ahead open at all times. His limbs shook.

142

After leaving the helicopter, Judah moved towards the Captain as fast as he could. He was carrying a full suit of Armor, but it did not weigh anything at all. When he got to the table, he scared off the entities with a wave of his sword. Captain Knowington stared at him through frightened eyes. He looked at Judah but did not seem to be fully awake.

"Judah, what are you doing here?" the Captain mumbled. "I thought that I was in the middle of a nightmare. Am I awake? Are you really here?"

"Yes Sir, I am," Judah said as he lifted the Captain up and put him over his shoulder to carry him back to the Helicopter.

"STOP!!!" sounded the booming voice of AZAZEL "Don't move another step or I will incinerate both of you!"

Judah turned around and saw the ominous figure of the angel from the heavenlies. Its black wings were raised high into the air, and it began to shriek an ungodly horrifying roar. Captain Knowington began to wail and shake at the sound of it. His body trembled so that Judah could barely keep hold of him.

"You are not going anywhere, Judah!" AZAZEL laughed as it flung a flaming missile at him. It struck the Captain in the back of his leg, and he began to scream in pain. Judah put him down behind him, and he turned to face AZAZEL.

"I have you, Judah, and the leader of your ragtag Christian militia group right here where I want you. Before I roast the two of you alive, you will tell me where your New Petra hideout is, and then I am going to destroy this cell of resistance once and for all. Ha! This is the beginning of the end for all you rebellious Believers."

Judah held up his Shield of Faith and waved his Sword of the Spirit in the face of AZAZEL. Just as he was moving in to confront this angel of the darkness, he noticed far in the distance what appeared to be his mother. Judah squinted his eyes but still saw a small elderly woman with grey hair and glasses. It was his Mom! She was being held in some sort of clear cylinder filled with a gas. She looked alive but was in a state of suspended animation. Her eyes were open but she did not look awake.

"You have my mother, too, again?" Judah yelled. "You beast from the heavenlies. I am going to cut your ugly pointed head off!"

AZAZEL bellowed once again and the entire area shook. Captain Knowington cowered behind Judah and moaned what sounded like a prolonged death rattle. Judah turned around and tried to comfort him.

"It will be all right, Sir. Have faith. Do not despair, but call upon the Lord for strength for you and for me."

Captain Knowington just stared at Judah who held his left arm up as if he were carrying a shield and swung his right arm back and forth as if he were carrying a sword, but the Captain saw nothing. When AZAZEL flung numerous visible flaming missiles at Judah, the Captain shrunk down even lower as he prepared for them to hit Judah. Nothing happened. He looked up as another volley approached, and he witnessed how Judah held his left hand in front of his chest and the flaming missiles bounced off and hit the walls where they exploded like Molotov Cocktails.

AZAZEL turned and sent a flaming missile right at the container that held Judah's mother. It exploded as it was hit and the gas inside was dissipated. Judah's mother fell to the ground in a disheveled heap.

Judah rushed at the beast waving his sword.

"AZAZEL, you will not destroy my mother or my friend. He that is in me is greater than he that is in you. I have all the power of the shed blood of Jesus Christ of Nazareth. His going to the Cross to bear all our sins was your defeat for all time. The battles will continue but we know how the war will end. It is written in the Scriptures. You and all your kind will spend eternity in the Lake of Fire."

AZAZEL shrieked once again and went after Judah's mother. She after all was not a Believer and thus still belonged to him.

"Your mother is mine. She has not accepted your Jesus. She will be my prize and your torment for all of time!"

AZAZEL flew over to Bertha and picked her up in his powerful wings. She had slowly regained consciousness and now gazed at AZAZEL. Her hair stood up on end, her eyes rolled up into her head and she screamed and promptly fainted.

Judah ran over to AZAZEL and sliced his wing with his Sword. AZAZEL cried out in obvious pain. He waved it again and sliced off a piece from the other side as well. AZAZEL could not believe that he was able to do that. It flung another flaming missile at Captain Knowington to distract Judah, but the Captain was flat on the ground and hiding against a wall so that the missile missed him by inches. It did rain red hot embers onto his already burned body and he screamed.

"Let me, Captain Knowington, and my mother leave this place," Judah demanded, "or I will destroy you once and for all."

"You cannot do that, Judah," AZAZEL yelled, "until our time on Earth is finished. You know that! It says it in your Bible."

Judah tried to figure what he could do next. Then out of the corner of his eye he spotted the figures of Dr. Lazant, Reverend Shea and Endora. They suddenly appeared off to his left. The three of them were also on tables, probably to treat them for injuries sustained in the blowing up of the Institute. There was no sign of the Institute receptionist.

Judah darted over to them and grabbed Dr. Lazant by his close cropped crewcut head in one hand and Reverend Shea by his Episcopal collar in the other and dragged them before AZAZEL. The two men awoke from their own unconscious state and began to scream as well.

"Be quiet, you fools!" Judah cautioned them, "Or I will end your misery right here once and for all. Okay, AZAZEL, I'll trade you these two men for the lives of my mother and Captain Knowington. You know that you need them to promote your one world religion delusion. If they are gone, it will set your timetable back quite a while. Isn't that the truth, you big, black angel from Hell?"

AZAZEL became very agitated and flapped his injured wings ferociously spewing bits and pieces of it everywhere.

"You would not kill these innocent men, Judah! You Christians would never resort to murder. Remember, that your Bible says not to kill!" AZAZEL laughed.

"Remember what David did to Goliath?" Judah replied. "Paul told the Church at Ephesus that they should stand firm against the schemes of the devil."

"Judah," Reverend Shea mumbled half awake, "we are just trying to unite the world under one religious system. Why are you evangelical Christians so opposed to our efforts? I don't understand, Judah! There are many paths to God. Why can't we all recognize that and work together instead of hating and condemning each other?"

"Because, Reverend, you are totally mixed up and confused. Did not Jesus himself say that He was the Way and the Truth and the Life and that no one comes to the Father but through Him? There are not many paths to God the Father. There is but one path and that is through Jesus Christ, the Son! Buddha can't do it or Mohammed or Moses or Mary or Joseph Smith or Krishna or the Kachinas or anyone or anything else. Christ is the only path. That is the end of the story. Bottom line. There is no compromise or substitute or other path. One can pray to mother God all that they want but she does not exist. Hey, I did not write the Book, but that is what it says!"

Endora had awakened from her table and heard what Judah had to say. She became enraged as she gazed back and forth between AZAZEL holding Judah's mother, and Judah holding Dr. Lazant and Reverend Shea. Suddenly, she ran over to Judah and kicked him hard in the groin and began to scratch his eyes out in an attempt to free her friends. Judah could not use his spiritual weapons on flesh and blood so he was forced to use his unencumbered foot to kick Endora in the stomach as she accosted him. Endora went tumbling onto the ground. She flashed her black eyes at Judah and they exuded evil. She got up and removed a long hair needle from her salt and pepper bun of hair and stabbed it into Judah's foot, nearly nailing it to the floor. Judah let out a loud yell and kicked her with this wounded foot in the cheek. She once again fell backwards but this time he stepped hard on her windpipe and crushed it, thereby killing her.

"Do you believe me now, AZAZEL?" Judah screamed as he limped forward towards AZAZEL. "The Lord will not let evil triumph over good. Next, I will send the Reverend to his eternal resting place of weeping and gnashing of teeth if you do not let my mother go! Release my mother, and as soon as we are all in the Helicopter, I will let Lazant and Shea go as well."

AZAZEL shook his mother forcefully and threw her onto the ground at Judah's feet. Judah yelled over to Captain Knowington to retrieve her and put her in the Helicopter. Captain Knowington was dazed, covered with small burn wounds, and had a large burn blister on the back of his leg, but he managed to limp over and pick up Bertha and carry her to the Helicopter.

145

"Start it up, Captain," Judah yelled as he dragged Lazant and Shea over to the Helicopter with him limping as well and with a sharp needle still protruding from his foot.

"Open the mouth of this beast, AZAZEL!"

AZAZEL opened the mouth. It knew that they were at 35,000 feet and the Helicopter could not descend at such an altitude. It would fall from the upper reaches of the atmosphere so fast that its rotors would be ripped off, and they would all crash. More importantly, the cabin was not pressurized and the lack of oxygen would also kill them in a matter of minutes.

Judah got into the Apache with Captain Knowington and his mother. She lay unconscious on the floor and Captain Knowington was dazed, wounded, in a great deal of pain and scared out of his mind by this entire bizarre affair.

Judah suddenly remembered that his mother had that implant in her head. AZAZEL could follow them back to New Petra. He needed to prevent AZAZEL from following them. Judah got out of the Helicopter and took his Sword of Truth and flung it at AZAZEL. It struck him full force in the middle of his big black frightening head and pinned him to the wall of the craft. AZAZEL shrieked out a horrifying roar as its body twitched uncontrollably as it was nailed to the wall. The black craft also began to spin uncontrollably.

"Kill those guys, Judah," Captain Knowington demanded as Judah reentered the Helicopter. "They are AZAZEL's pawns for the coming deception!"

"I promised to let them go," Judah replied.

"What is a promise to the devil?" the Captain asked with a quizzical look on his face.

"We cannot take them with us any way. We don't have enough parachutes," Judah said as he pushed the two men out of the craft just as it began to descend out of the whirling black disk.

Reverend Shea looked down at Judah and smiled and shook his head. Judah thought that he saw an twinkling of awareness in his eyes of what was really going on.

Judah put on one of the high altitude parachutes that he had loaded onto the helicopter. He gave the other one to Captain Knowington. The Apache Helicopter left the belly of the beast and began to fall very rapidly. There was not enough air to sustain it and it plunged to the earth from over 35,000 feet. As the rotors ripped off, Judah blew open the side of the craft with a shotgun that he loaded onto the craft as well. Captain Knowington put on his oxygen mask and jumped out of the side of the Apache, followed closely by Judah holding his mother in his arms. He gave his mother the oxygen mask first. All the way down, Judah thought about that implant in his mother's head. Had all of this just been a trap to locate New Petra?

Back at New Petra, everyone was crowded around the monitor that showed the satellite image of the black disk. They had all seen Judah being captured by the beam and brought into the craft.

"Oh my God, No!" Dawn had yelled as she saw her husband disappear into the craft.

"Maybe he will be able to rescue Peter?" Ann Knowington said quietly. "Don't give up on Judah. He is a resourceful man of God. Come on, Dawn, you of all people should not be so pessimistic. You, after all, were one of the only people to think that he was still alive when we all saw him consumed in the van. Remember, you were willing to put my girls' lives in jeopardy to prove it. Judah has survived where others would have been killed. He has fought AZAZEL before and has lived to tell about it. In fact he is the only one to do that! Look at what happened to General Desporte and Senator Jordan!"

"Boy, that sure makes me feel better, thanks for those encouraging words, Ann," Dawn replied sarcastically. "I'm sorry, Ann, for that outburst. Please forgive me! It is just that they are at 35,000 feet. Even by some miracle, if Judah can rescue the Captain, how will they be able to return to Earth? Both were taken to that altitude by beams from the disk. No helicopter can fly that high and there is no oxygen up there anyway."

Ann shook her head and put her hand around Dawn.

"We just have to believe and have faith, Dawn. This battle belongs to the Lord."

"Ladies," shouted Corporal Canon, "Judah took along high altitude parachutes for his escape!"

"Oh, Praise God!" Dawn yelled.

They then all gasped as the Apache Helicopter emerged once again from the belly of the beast which had begun to spin uncontrollably. Magnification showed that both Captain Knowington and Judah were aboard. It also showed the presence of an elderly woman. There was a blast and the side of the plunging helicopter was blown out and first Captain Knowington bailed out and then Judah followed carrying that elderly woman.

"It is his mother," Dawn said frantically. "How did she get there? Can he do a high altitude parachute jump carrying someone else? Will his chute even be able to open with all that added weight?"

The men around her shook their heads dubiously.

Lieutenant Gregor contacted the Hummer in the area to be on alert. They would be used to pick up whomever survived the jump. He then remembered that Judah's mother had that implant from AZAZEL. They could not bring her back to New Petra without AZAZEL knowing about it.

"Eagle Two, this is Eagle One."

"Yes Eagle One, this is Eagle Two."

"Eagle Two, wait for further instructions. We just remembered that the mother hen has a bug in her head. She cannot be brought to the nest."

"We understand Eagle One."

Lieutenant Gregor sat down and watched the men drop down over the District of Columbia. He was anxious to see how Judah and his mother were going to make it, but he was all the while thinking about what to do with her if they did indeed survive the jump. She could not be brought to New Petra with a surveillance device in her head.

Lieutenant Gregor then called Mike Butrell at the CIA. He had his home number which had been provided by Major Kole. It was three o'clock in the morning but he had no choice. He needed to inform him that two of his men were parachuting over the Capitol and that he should inform the necessary Military and aviation personnel.

"Mike, this is Wayne Gregor. I was a friend of Senator Jordan and Major Kole. Sorry to bother you at home in the middle of the night, but it is an emergency."

"Uhh, yes Sir! What can I do for you?" Butrell replied as he got up and flipped on his computer.

"I've got two men parachuting in right now over the Capitol. I would appreciate it if you would notify the proper authorities. We mean no harm. The Apache helicopter that they were in has malfunctioned."

"Just one moment Wayne... Yes, I'm picking them up right now on my monitor. It appears that they jumped from over 30,000 feet. How did they ever get their Apache that high? And one of the men is carrying an old woman. What is going on here, Lieutenant?"

"It's a long story, Sir. We will have our men there to pick them up."

"Aren't you part of that Christian militia group?" said Deputy Director Butrell. "Senator Jordan spoke to me about setting something like that up in the mountains somewhere."

"God Bless you, Sir," Lieutenant Gregor said as he terminated the discussion.


Captain Knowington, and Judah with his mother, sailed over Bethesda and Chevy Chase, Maryland as they finally were at an altitude to release their parachutes. Captain Knowington's opened fine but Judah's jerked back more harshly because of the added weight of his mother. While she weighed only a hundred pounds, it increased the total weight from 225 to 325. The cords on the cute strained to the breaking point but held firm. It was only by the grace of God that it opened at all with all that extra weight.

They crossed over the beautiful Washington National Cathedral, then the beauty of Dumbarton Oaks Park, Oakhill Cemetery, Foggy Bottom, George Washington University, the Department of State, the Vietnam Veterans Memorial and finally landed in the Polo Grounds of West Potomac Park between Alt Route 50 and the Tidal Basin. It was a harrowing ride over the most prized real estate in the world.

Fortunately, it was 300 hours and the Park was deserted. Judah first looked to see how his mother was doing.

"Ma, are you all right?"

"Oy vey," she replied. "What did you do to me? Are you trying to kill your poor old Mother?"

"Ma, what were you doing in the black disc again?"

148

"What was I doing? I went yesterday to the doctor. I was having headaches. Well he examined me and he found something in my neck. It was under the skin. He took it out, thank God."

"And then what happened?"

"Judah, let me finish the story for godsake! He said that I had a computer chip or something in my neck. He could not understand how it got there. I told him that my boy had worked for the CIA and maybe he had put it there."

"Ma!"

"Quiet! Well, the minute that I left the Doctor's office, I found myself being transported up into the sky once again. Oh my heart. I am too old for this meshugge *(Y.crazy)* stuff. You are trying to kill your own mother."

"No, I'm not, Ma."

"Not! Who are you kidding? Then I wake up to find myself in the presence of that big black hellion with wings. I was scared to death. And when he came over and picked me up I lost it. I thought dear Moshe, here I come!"

"Who do you think saved you from that beast, Ma? It was me, just like I did before."

"And then you pick me up and jump out of an airplane. Do you call that love?"

"Ma, we had to get out before it crashed."

"From next to heaven? I could barely breathe way up there."

"Ma, we are safe now back here on solid ground."

"What happened to your foot, tatalleh," Bertha said as she noticed the needle still protruding from the top of his boot.

"It's nothing, Ma."

Judah looked over and saw Captain Knowington about twenty five feet away, and he yelled over to him. Captain Knowington acknowledged him and began to limp rather badly over to him. The scalding wound on the back of his thigh was festering. He needed immediate medical attention. Fortunately, the Hummer from New Petra was fast approaching. The men were instructed to park nearby and proceed to the drop site on foot until the condition of Mrs. Meire could be determined. It was risky to enter the area of the Capitol Mall but it was the middle of the night.

"Look, they all made it safely," Ann Knowington yelled as all the people at New Petra strained to see the monitor showing the satellite surveillance of the drop site. My husband is limping badly, but Praise God, he is still alive!"

They watched as the Hummer came across the Potomac River on the Arlington Memorial Bridge and parked at the Lincoln Memorial. They then radioed back to New Petra.

"Eagle One, this is Eagle Two."

"Eagle Two, this Eagle One. We read you," Lieutenant Gregor replied anxiously.

"We are at the drop. We see the three chickens. The mother hen is there and seems to be all right. What do we do?"

149

Lieutenant Gregor could see the entire scene from his satellite's eye. Knowington, Judah and his Mother all seemed to have made the high altitude jump successfully. Judah's mother was pointing to her head and to the sky, but he could not make out what she had to say. Before he could make a decision another vehicle was fast approaching the scene from the east over the Kutz Bridge on Alt. Route 50. Gregor feared that it was men sent by the CIA's Mike Butrell. He radioed his men to abandon the area as quickly as possible.

"Vacate the henhouse," he yelled. "The fox is fast approaching."

The two men ran back to their Hummer and sped back across the Arlington Memorial Bridge into Virginia where they hid in Arlington National Cemetery and waited for further orders.

Meanwhile, the sleek black sedan had pulled up just to the North of Judah, his mother and Captain Knowington and its passengers had disembarked from their car. There were three men led by a large blond headed man. Lieutenant Gregor quickly realized that it was not Butrell and the CIA, but rather was probably the men from Ultra. If they captured Judah and Captain Knowington not only would New Petra be compromised but so also would be the Christian resistance to AZAZEL. But there was nothing that he could do but watch and pray.

It was out of his hands. For a fleeting moment he did consider sending back the two young soldiers from the Hummer to rescue Judah and the others but he quickly vanquished that idea from his mind as too impractical.

Judah looked up and saw three men fast approaching. He put his mother behind him and he drew his Uzi revolver. Captain Knowington attempted to follow suit but he had lost his revolver in all the commotion.

"Who do you think that it is, Judah?" Captain Knowington asked nervously as he too moved behind Judah.

"Well, I'll bet that it is not the good guys," Judah answered sharply. "They arrive in a black unmarked car and have no uniforms on. What does that tell you? I'll bet that they are from Ultra!"

Judah aimed his Uzi at them and shouted, "Stop right there or I'll shoot!"

"Oh God no," Ann and Dawn said nearly simultaneously as they watched the three men approach Judah and Peter. "What can you do, Lieutenant Gregor? Don't just stand there. Do something!"

"There is nothing that we can do now, ladies. I would suggest that you pray!"

"Relax, Judah," the blond behemoth answered as he motioned for his men to stop. "We are from the government, and we just came to help you."

"Yeah right, and I believe in the tooth fairy. What government agency sends men out in the middle of the night in an unmarked car?" Judah replied as he cocked his revolver.

"We are security personnel for the Capitol Mall. You know that you have landed in a very high profile area. You cannot just parachute into the vicinity of the President without drawing a great deal of attention."

150

"That is true, but you are not FBI or Secret Service people. You look like some sort of covert operation. Identify yourselves immediately or I will shoot!"

"Relax, guys. Put down your weapon and we can talk," the blond behemoth said as he reached into his pocket.

"No way. Throw over your ID and then we will talk"

"Do what the man says, tatalleh" Bertha spoke up. "Don't start anymore trouble. They just want to help us."

Bertha got up and started walking over to the large blond man.

"Ma, come back here!" Judah yelled.

"It's all right, tatalleh" she answered. "See, they are friendly."

As Judah attempted to go after her, she just ran faster. When she got close enough to the blond man he grabbed her and held her tight.

"Give it up, Judah, or I'll have to hurt your mother," he demanded with a sick smile.

"Hey, wait a minute, how do you know my name?" Judah suddenly realized.

"We know all about you and Knowington."

"You are Ultra!" Judah said with a groan. "I knew it!"

They had his mother, and would soon have him and Captain Knowington, unless he did something fast. Judah could not nor would he compromise New Petra or his battle with AZAZEL. Everything and everyone was expendable in the battle for the soul of man. He would not surrender to Ultra even if it meant the life of his mother. It pained him greatly to even consider such a possibility, but he had to do what he had to do.

"Drop your weapon, Judah, or I will harm this sweet old lady," the blond behemoth said as he put his massive hands around her neck.

Judah inched closer and waived his revolver back and forth between the blond man's head and that of his two henchmen who had drawn their service revolvers as well.

"Give it up, Judah!" Dawn yelled at the monitor at New Petra.

"He cannot surrender, Ma'am, or all of us at New Petra are finished," Lieutenant Gregor replied firmly. "He is a soldier and he knows that surrender is not one of the choices even if it costs him his life and the life of his mother."

"The Lord would not let him stand by while his mother is being killed, would He?"

"His ways are not our ways, Ma'am. You know that. We are fighting a war for the soul of mankind. We must keep that in mind. I'm sure that Judah is."

"I can't look."

The two men approached quickly and Judah fired his weapon hitting one of the men right between the eyes killing him instantly. The other man stopped in his tracks and looked back at the blond man. The blond giant began squeezing Bertha's neck and she flailed her arms at the lack of oxygen.

"You want me, you big gorilla. You aren't going to kill my mother," Judah

151

yelled. "Then you will not have any leverage at all."

The blond man became enraged and picked up Bertha and hurled her frail body through the air at Judah. Judah put down his Uzi and caught his mother's frail body which hit him with her feet up in the air and her head against Judah's legs as he fell backwards onto the ground. The other man raced towards them as Judah was distracted by the sight of his mother hurling through the air, but he was cut down by Captain Knowington who had picked up Judah's weapon. That left the blond giant, all six foot six inches and two hundred and forty pounds to deal with Judah.

He raced at Judah at full speed. Captain Knowington pumped three or four shots into his torso, but he kept on coming like a runaway freight train. He bowled over Judah and his mother at full speed and the three of them rolled down the hill with this large man all over them. The blond man tossed Bertha aside and turned Judah over and pinned him to the ground. He began to laugh as he put handcuffs on Judah and lifted him up into the sir with his massive hands.

Lieutenant Gregor watched this entire episode with trepidation. He wanted to prevent Judah from falling into the hands of Ultra, but he was powerless to do anything.

"No, stay put, Peter!" Ann yelled at the monitor as she watched her husband limp down the hill with Judah's revolver. She screamed and nearly fainted when he was knocked over by a hard right cross to his injured thigh from the blond man and the revolver went flying. Captain Knowington writhed in pain and was thereafter useless to Judah .

The blond man picked up Judah and was carrying him back to his black sedan when all of a sudden there was the whirling of the air around them as a helicopter approached. Judah and the blond man looked upward to see who it was. The helicopter was from the Central Intelligence Agency. The blond man took Judah's gun which he had picked up and fired it at the helicopter, but they landed anyway.

Mike Butrell was the first to exit the chopper followed by a half dozen heavily armed men.

"Put the gun down," Butrell demanded. "I mean right now!"

When the blond man hesitated and drew it up to fire, Deputy Director Butrell shot out both of his kneecaps, and he fell to the ground in writhing pain. Judah went tumbling also.

"Thanks, Mike," Judah said as he got to his feet and ran over to his Mom and Captain Knowington. "You are a Godsend, man!"

Lieutenant Gregor jumped for joy at the outcome of this mission. Dawn was ecstatic and even Ann smiled although she was still concerned about her husband's health. Lieutenant Gregor radioed the Hummer and told them to go back to the Polo Grounds and retrieve their passengers.

"Do you have a ride home, Judah?" Butrell asked with a smile as he unlocked the handcuffs.

"I don't know, Sir," Judah answered with a shrug.

152

"We can take you back to New Petra."

"I think not, Sir. But thank you. Wait a minute, I think our ride has arrived," Judah said as he saw the approaching Hummer.

"Okay, Colonel! God Bless you!" Butrell bade farewell as he embraced Judah and Captain Knowington. "See, Judah, you do have friends in high places."

"Thank you, Sir, for everything," Judah said with a big smile. "What of these men?"

"Don't worry, we'll take care of it. You three better be on your way."

"Thank you, Sir, for coming to our defense. I know that it was not easy considering that this enemy is right among the higher echelons of our government," Captain Knowington said as he entered the Hummer.

Judah's mother appeared to have jammed her neck as she had crashed headfirst into her son. She was put into a neckbrace and onto a backboard before being put into the Hummer. She was not conscious. Captain Knowington's leg was treated with the burn treatment supplies on board and he was given a shot of morphine to ease the excruciating pain in his thigh.

"Judah, this is Lieutenant Gregor," sounded a voice on the radio in the Hummer. "God bless you, son! You rescued Captain Knowington just as you said that you would. You are a good soldier, Judah! How are your Mom and Captain Knowington? We witnessed the entire dramatic event from our satellite feed."

"Thank you, Sir. I think that she might have a broken neck. Captain Knowington has a bad burn on the back of his thigh from a flaming missile from AZAZEL!"

"What about the bug in her head? We cannot let her betray New Petra. Maybe you should take her to Bethesda Naval Hospital?"

"I understand, you big dumb Texan, but she is all right. The bug was removed by her Doctor. AZAZEL took her back to the disk so that he could install another one."

"Maybe he did, Judah. Have you checked?"

"Uhh, no!"

Judah looked at his mother and realized that it was impossible to check the back of her neck now since it was enclosed in a brace. He told that to the Lieutenant, and they decided to take her to Bethesda just in case. The problem was that Ultra would probably be waiting for her there, but what choice did they have? Judah stood up and felt something in his pocket. He reached inside and pulled out a small computer chip like device. It must have fallen into his pocket after being jarred loose by all the rough treatment that his mother had undergone at the hands of the blond beast.

"I found the monitoring device. AZAZEL must have put another one in, as you feared, but it apparently was jarred loose in all the commotion here. I've got it, and I am destroying it as we speak."

Everyone at New Petra cheered.

"Come on home, son!"

"We are good to go, Sir!"

Ann Knowington embraced Dawn and they both cried for joy.

"I told you that Judah was a resourceful man, Dawn," Ann Knowington said with a smile.

"Boy, is he resourceful," Dawn lamented. "He not only rescues your husband from the jaws of the enemy, but he also rescues his mother. Talk about jaws of the enemy. Please pray for me, Ann."

# XII

Everyone cheered as the Hummer pulled into New Petra in the early hours of the morning. The sun was above the horizon and it bathed the entire homecoming in a radiant sea of light. Ann Knowington and Dawn were the first two to reach the vehicle. Judah jumped out and embraced Dawn as Ann scrambled into the Hummer to find her husband.

"Oh, Judah," Dawn cried, "thank God that you are still live. I cannot believe your chutzpa *(Y.nerve)*, sweetheart. Do you really think that you are invincible?"

"I don't think that God brought me so far, so fast, to just take me home at this most crucial time," Judah replied as he kissed Dawn on the top of her head. "I really missed you, honey. I thought of you every time that I looked death in the face."

"Wow, that sure makes me feel better," Dawn smirked as she slapped him on the arm. "Why do you do such things?"

"Somebody has to!"

Ann helped her husband out of the Hummer and onto a waiting stretcher.

"Wait a minute, Ann," Captain Knowington said as he looked over at Judah. "Thanks, Colonel. You are all that they said that you were. Sorry, for having to risk your life just to rescue this old Marine. Please forgive me for trying to kill your wife. She obviously knew how much we needed you. Also, please forgive me for calling you a Jewboy. Old habits die slow!"

"That's all right, Captain, Jesus is a Jewboy too. Not bad company I would think," Judah said with a smile and a salute.

"By the way, Gregor," Captain Knowington said as Lieutenant Gregor approached. "Why did you let this man have our only Apache? Now it is gone and we have no air transportation."

"Call it a hunch, Captain," Lieutenant Gregor replied with a smile. "If anyone could have rescued you from the jaws of Satan, I felt that it was this brash Jewboy. Don't ask me why the Lord would pick such a stiff-necked, obstinate man like him. Can you imagine what Paul must have been like? These Jews are a special breed, but they get the job done! And, Sir, your are worth far more than an Apache. As for Judah... uhh, I'm not sure."

Captain Knowington laughed and waved to everyone as he was carried to the infirmary with his wife at his side.

"Thank you, Judah, from the bottom of my heart," Ann Knowington said as she went by him. "I knew that you could do it! I'm so glad that Dawn found you even though it was painful to my entire family. My girls are so grateful also."

Next, they removed the board holding Judah's mother. She had regained consciousness but was still in the neck brace.

"So this is your little hideout?" she spoke softly pointing to the mountain cavern. "I always wanted to go to summer camp in the mountains with the Christian Militia!"

"Well, you can all see that my mother is all right. She may not be able to walk yet but her mouth is working A O.K.," Judah said sarcastically.

"Do you hear how my boy speaks to his mother?" Bertha said more loudly than before as everyone crowded around her, and now she had a captive audience. "First I was manhandled by that black thing, AZAwhatever. Then my dear son jumps out of a helicopter way up the sky holding onto me, and finally as if I haven't had enough excitement, some big blond goy *(H.gentile)* ruffs me up and throws me into Judah's arms from across the park. Wouldn't you be upset? I'm just a little old lady. Oy, what I have to go through because my Judah wants to put on a suit of armor and fight with Hasatan."

"Ma, cool it," Judah replied embarrassed. "These dear people are going to take care of you. Stop kvetching! Remember that it was you who walked right into the arms of that man from Ultra!"

"What is kvetching?" Lieutenant Gregor asked as he came over and patted Judah on the back..

"It means complaining," Dawn answered before Judah could answer.

"Oh so this is my daughter in law, the shiksa," Bertha said as she glared over at Dawn. "You are the one who has taught my son to pray and sound like you Christians."

"No, Mother, God did that!" Dawn replied with a smile. "Your tatalleh has seen the light and heard the Good News right from the Lord Himself."

"What! Are you telling me that he has converted? Judah, are you now a Christian?"

Everyone looked to Judah for his answer. He obviously had not told his mother about his born again experience. They all wondered if he would tell her now considering the circumstances and all that she had just been through. Meanwhile, Judah was asking the Lord if this was the time and place. He got his answer.

"No, Ma, I did not convert to Christianity..."

"Thank God!"

"Let me finish, Ma. I am still a Jew. I always will be a Jew. When a Black becomes a Christian does he give up or lose his blackness? Of course not! I am a Jew and all my ancestors were Jews. Being Jewish is a racial or genetic thing. It is in the blood. But now, I am a completed or fulfilled Jew. I recognize that Yeshua, Jesus, is the Mashiach prophesied in the Tanakh *(H.Torah, Prophets,Writings; the Old Testament)*. He is the Jewish Messiah. I am now more Jewish than ever! I..."

"Oy vey," Bertha interrupted once again. "You are a Jew who believes in yeshu.

Wonderful. Can't you make up your mind what you believe? You are either a Jew who doesn't believe in yeshu or a Christian that does. Figure it out. And you say that Jews are a race. You sound like Hitler! Oy, your father must be turning over his grave right now."

"Well, Ma, if he believed like all of us do he would not be in the grave, but he would be in Heaven with Yeshua!"

"If that is the case, then I'd rather be in the grave with your father than in heaven with your yeshu," Bertha moaned as she put her hands over her ears. "I've heard enough. Take me to the infirmary before I get sick right here."

They carried off Judah's Mom to the infirmary where they put her into traction. It was determined by Xray that her neck vertebrae were not broken, but they were a little compressed and it was hoped that they could be separated again by traction. She complained and whined all the time and everyone got a first hand experience of a Jewish mother at work.

"Judah," Dawn asked as she escorted Judah to the infirmary for a checkup as well, "why did she call Jesus, yeshu?"

"Yeshu is a Jewish name derived to blaspheme the name of Yeshua. It comes from the medieval work *Toledoth Yeshu* where Yeshua was said to be the bastard son of Mary and a certain disreputable Jew, Joseph Pandera," Judah replied, shaking his head. "Many Jewish people have no love for so-called Christians. Can you blame them after the Crusades, Inquisition, pogroms, expulsions, and the Holocaust by these same so-called Christians? With friends like them who needed enemies? These so-called Christians have often stood between the Jews and Yeshua. Isn't it ironic that they have kept millions of Jews from the truth of Yeshua. Satan has been active since the beginning in keeping the Jews from their Messiah."

"Why was that?" Dawn asked as she held her husband tight and a crowd formed around them as they all listened to Judah.

"Satan knew that the Savior would come through the Jewish people. If he could have destroyed them, His ultimate conqueror would never have been born. That is why various peoples from the beginning of time have tried to destroy the Jews, and why God always had his hand upon them. When the Messiah was finally born as prophesied and died for our sins, then Satan tried again to destroy the Jewish people and scatter them across the globe because he knew that the Messiah was to return to the Mount of Olives and that He would rule and reign from Jerusalem in a Jewish nation. If he could try and prevent the Jewish people from existing at all, like in the time of the sacking of the Temple in 70AD and the destruction of Jerusalem in 135AD and the Crusades, and the Inquisition and the Holocaust, then maybe the Messiah would not be able to return. Even now in our battle with AZAZEL and the forces of wickedness in heavenly places, who does the Lord choose to fight this battle? Me, a Jew!"

"Gee, Jewboy," Lieutenant Gregor chimed in, "Don't break your arm patting yourself on the back. You people have a lot of great character traits but humility is

157

certainly not one of them. It says in Proverbs that pride goeth before destruction."

"So sue me, you big Texan!" Judah replied with a laugh "God has chosen to work His will through me."

"Big deal. He also spoke through Balaam's ass. Don't get too cocky, Judah or the Lord will humble you with His mighty outstretched arm," Lieutenant Gregor answered with a scowl as his old Navy SEAL uniform nearly burst as he swelled up in exasperation. "Man, are you people something. I can't imagine what it was like to wander in the desert for forty years with millions of prideful people like you, Judah. You really need to humble yourself before the Lord."

After a cursory examination in the infirmary where it was determined that he had nothing other than bumps and bruises, Judah went back to Dawn's room and slept for nearly twelve hours. He was physically, emotionally and spiritually exhausted. The fact that Dawn had decided to tell his mother about his new found belief without first discussing it with him, was, to say the least, disconcerting. He would have chosen a different time and place. Now in the midst of their battle with wickedness, he also had to deal with his mother. Maybe, just maybe, Judah thought as he drifted off to sleep, that this time and place might be exactly what the Lord wanted to reveal Himself to his mother. Then he mused to himself, yeah right! That was impossible!

Captain Knowington was given emergency burn treatment in the infirmary. The wound on the back of his thigh reached down to the bone and the medics did all that they could to just save the leg. He was heavily sedated but his wife sat at his bedside as did his two daughters.

"How did this happen?" Rebecca asked as she cried and pulled at her pigtails. "I mean, how can you get burned so bad in just one spot. It's unreal!"

"I really don't know, sweetheart," her mother replied. "I guess only your Dad and Colonel Meire know for sure. We will have to ask them when they are awake."

"Is he going to be all right," Jennifer then asked with a tone of concern. "Is he going to lose his leg? Oh God, I hope not."

"Again, girls, I don't know. Keep it in prayer. We don't have the luxury of the best available medical treatment here so we need God's help."

"Why don't we leave this godforsaken place? Daddy's life is more important than all this demonic stuff. Isn't it?" Rebecca said as she became angry and lashed out at her mother. "I knew that we should have gotten out of here."

Ann Knowington explained to her girls that they were in this mountain hideout for a very specific reason. They had all been chosen by Senator Jordan and General Desporte to be a watchman on the wall for the upcoming plan of the enemy. When they countered that both Senator Jordan and General Desporte and even their wives were all dead, Ann replied that for that reason alone they could not quit; otherwise their deaths would be in vain. They had to stay the course no matter what the consequences. She explained that she did not really fully understand what was going on, but she trusted in the wise counsel of not only their father but also

Lieutenant Gregor and Colonel Meire. The Colonel had after all gone after their father and brought him back alive. He had gone into the black disc and returned with their dad as well as his mother.

"That whole saucer thing is really freaky," Jennifer said with a funny look on her face. "I mean, are we talking the *XFiles* or are we talking *Men in Black*?"

"No honey, we are not talking about ET's, but about fallen angels. The Truth is out there, but it is a case of spiritual warfare against the forces of wickedness in Heavenly places. Look at the Book of Ephesians."

"This stuff is way over my head. Fallen angels? Yeah right! The only angels that I have ever seen are on TV and they are all nice."

"Those are not real angels, honey. Only what people want them to be. Fallen angels are those angels thrown out of the first Heaven by God along with Satan."

"What? That's weird, Mom. Its all too freaky for me," Rebecca answered with a shrug.

Nearby to their father in the small infirmary was Judah's mother, Bertha. She was hooked up to a traction apparatus to ease the compression of her spine. There were weights hanging over the bed. The girls looked over at her and giggled. They thought that she looked really silly.

"What is so funny, girls," Bertha said as the giggling woke her up from a much needed rest. "Haven't you ever seen an old lady being tortured before?"

Ann and the girls went over to Bertha's side and tried to make conversation with her. "Mrs. Meire," Ann asked politely, "how are you doing?"

"Doing? What do you think?" Bertha snapped back. "My boy has put me through one thing after another. I've been put into the Hospital by that big black Hellion. Then, I was taken by it another time and pulled into that saucer where it manhandled me again. Only by my son dressing up like a knight was I freed. Then he pushes me out of an airplane holding onto me, only to land and be accosted by a large blond goy. How much can an old woman take? And then I am brought here and told that Judah is a Jew for Jesus. You know that we Jews do not believe in Jesus. He was a nice Jewish boy from Bethlehem whose mother thought that he was god. Big deal. Most Jewish mothers think that of their first born sons. I always thought that of my son  But lately he's become more of a curse than a blessing. Oy!"

Ann and her daughters smiled and left the bedside of this ranting woman.

"What's her problem, Mom?" Jennifer asked as they left the infirmary.

"She is not a Believer, girls. She thinks that her son has gone crazy and abandoned her by accepting Jesus."

"That's not right," Rebecca said. "We all saw him saved from the flames of his burning van by the Holy Spirit or maybe even Jesus himself. He went into the black disc and rescued her and our Dad. She has no right to speak of him like that."

Pastor Calvin awoke startled from the bed in his sister's house. His wife next to him hardly moved, but he had been awakened by the loud blast of a trumpet.

159

Reverend Shea and Dr. Lazant had been thrown around the black disc as it had spun out of control. They tried to move over to AZAZEL but it was very difficult and time consuming. Finally, they crawled over to the wall to which he was pinned by a Sword of Light. Dr. Lazant managed to get to his feet momentarily and he tried to grab onto the sword. All the while, AZAZEL was roaring at a pitch and tone that scared even Dr. Lazant and Reverend Shea. It was not pleased about being pinned to the wall of the craft and thus helpless to do anything. When Dr. Lazant tried to get hold of the Sword it just was not there. He tried again and finally realized that it was non corporeal. AZAZEL yelled even louder and flapped its wings ferociously. Dr. Lazant fell to the floor and he and Reverend Shea put their hands over their ears to block out the terrifying din.

Then suddenly, one of those small grey beings with big black eyes moved out of the shadows. It lumbered over to AZAZEL and put its small hands around the Sword. It tried to pull it out but it could only budge it a small amount. It looked at AZAZEL and then back into the shadows and two more beings appeared. The three of them then pulled on the Sword of light and it slowly came out of AZAZEL. When they had gotten it all the way out it just disappeared. AZAZEL stood there with a big hole in the middle of its black head.

Over the next several days, Judah explored the New Petra compound. He checked out the security precautions since that was his area of expertise. The huge foot thick steel doors and the fingerprint and retinal scans were all right, but what would they do if an enemy came up the mountain and cut off their air supply? What if they kept them trapped in the cave for an indefinite period of time?

"Your precautions seem designed to keep people out of the cave, Lieutenant Gregor," Judah asked. "But what if you cannot get out of the cave. All that they have to do is surround you and keep you from resupplying yourselves?"

Lieutenant Gregor took Judah into the areas where chickens, rabbits, goats and even catfish were raised. He showed him the crops that were grown hydroponically using artificial light. He showed him the generator and their vast water supply. Judah was especially impressed by an air recirculation system that cleaned and reoxgenated their air that they could stay underground indefinitely.

"Well, Lieutenant," Judah said with a smile, "I must admit that I am impressed. You have thought out most of the critical survival needs and prepared accordingly. But what if Ultra decides to attack us with a cruise missile?"

"If pigs had wings, they could fly!" Lieutenant Gregor replied. "We cannot prepare for every contingency. We can just do the best that we can and trust in the Lord. Preparedness is fine, Judah, but it all boils down to faith and trust that the Lord will protect us. We have, I really believe, been set apart as watchmen on the wall to warn the people of the impending invasion. Besides we are several hundred feet down in a solid granite mountain. Even if a missile hit us it would not do much damage!"

Judah put his arm around his tall, muscular, craggy sixtysomething friend in his tattered Navy SEAL uniform. They walked together to see Captain Knowington. He had spent the last week under heavy sedation and had undergone burn treatment. It was not possible to give him the medical treatment that he needed at the New Petra infirmary, and it had been discussed whether he might be better off at a hospital. The problem with that was that Ultra would find him, and that would put all of New Petra at risk. His wife, Ann, argued for hospital treatment but she was outvoiced by the others.

"Dawn," she pleaded, "please help me convince them to let my husband receive the medical treatment that he needs. He is either going to lose his leg or worse, die all together. Please, Dawn!"

Dawn of all people knew what it meant to do anything to save her husband. She had after all tried to escape New Petra herself, putting all of them at risk. She comforted Ann and told her that she would speak to Judah about it. Deep in her heart, however, she realized that she had come to the conclusion that New Petra could not be compromised no matter what the price. They were the only people that clearly understood the spiritual battle that was taking place. A battle over the souls of all mankind. A battle where there could be no retreat, no compromise. Her Judah was at the forefront of this battle, and she finally came to the awareness that first and foremost, the battle had to continue no matter what.

Judah and Lieutenant Gregor entered the infirmary and ran into Ann, her daughters and Dawn.

"How is the Captain doing today?" he asked with a smile.

"Oh, Judah, he is not doing well," Ann cried as she burst into tears. "He needs professional treatment. His burn is so severe that he needs to be in a burn clinic. This infirmary just does not have the necessary facilities. Judah, he is going to lose his leg!"

"Judah, Ann wants him taken to a hospital for treatment," Dawn said shaking her head no behind Ann.

"Hey guys," Rebecca Knowington pleaded, "please let my father out of here. He needs the right kind of treatment."

"I'll tell you what," Judah answered with a thought that just popped into his head. "If the Captain agrees that he should go to the hospital then we will do it. Okay?"

"Whatever," Jennifer replied.

"You know that he will not, Judah," Ann cried out in anguish. "He said that whoever tried to leave here should be shot. He was ready, willing and able to do that even to your own wife!"

"Exactly my point, Ann," Judah said quietly. "The rules apply to everyone. Even my wife and your husband!"

As Ann broke down in tears and was comforted by Dawn, Judah knelt down at the side of Captain Knowington's bed. He put his hands on the man's severely injured thigh and began to cry out to the Lord.

"Oh Father, You said that whatever we asked in Your Son's name would be given to us. Father, in the name of Yeshua Hamashiach *(H.Jesus The Messiah)* of Nazareth, I implore You to heal this man. You said that by Your stripes we are healed. I plead the shed blood of Yeshua all over this man, Father. He is a good man, a man of true character and service to You, Father. He gave up his extended family and friends to come here to this mountaintop to do Your work. Heal him, Father. All things are possible for You, Lord, to those that believe. Heavenly Father, heal him of his burns so he can continue to do Your work and so his dear wife will not worry so about his welfare. Thank You, Father, for Your unending grace and mercy."

Suddenly a loud siren began to blare and the lights flashed on and off. A voice came over the intercom.

"Incoming missile! Incoming cruise missile! Arrival in 13 minutes!"

Judah jumped up and looked around.

"What do we do now?" he asked.

"We need to proceed to the lowest floor of the cave," Lieutenant Gregor said as he moved Judah and Dawn and the infirmary staff along. He told the staff to just roll the beds of Captain Knowington and Mrs. Meire and bring them along. When he looked for the Captain, he was right behind them walking with Ann.

"Praise God! Praise God!" Lieutenant Gregor yelled.

"Look, Judah, Captain Knowington is walking!" Dawn yelled with tears in her eyes. "Look what you did!"

"I did not do anything," Judah countered. "God healed him, not me. "Thank You, Lord, for Your healing mercy. Please save us, Lord, from this incoming missile of the enemy."

"Thank you, Judah," Ann cried as she helped her husband along. "Thank you for interceding for him with the Lord. You are really something, you know. Your mother should be so proud of you."

"Proud?" Bertha interjected. "Why didn't he do that for me? That man is now walking and his own mother is still bedridden. It's a real shonda *(Y.shame)*!"

"What is a shonda, Mother?" Rebecca asked as she hugged her father and helped him along.

"I have no idea, dear, why don't you ask the old woman?"

When Rebecca tried to ask Bertha, she just clammed up and refused to even look at her. "May God have mercy on your soul, Mrs. Meire," Rebecca said angrily. "You are a bitter old biddy. Your son prayed for my father's recovery and look at him walk. Aren't you proud? Don't you see the healing power of Jesus? Helllooo?! Earth to old woman!"

Pastor Calvin was sitting at his sister's kitchen table when he once again heard the loud sound of a trumpet blaring. It was first one loud blast and then three short

162

blasts. He looked at his wife and his sister and his daughter but no one seemed to have heard anything.

"Did you all hear that?" he asked nonchalantly.

"Hear what, Dad ?" his daughter answered.

"Oh nothing."

Deputy Director Butrell of the Central Intelligence Agency was notified that a cruise missile was heading for a remote mountainous location, Backbone Mountain, in far Western Maryland.

"How did that ever take place?" he yelled. "Who authorized such a launch?"

He was told that it was launched from a ship off the Atlantic seaboard by a command that was shrouded in secrecy. Someone with the right credentials and passwords from the DOD had authorized the cruiser commander to launch a Tomahawk cruise missile at the remote site. The Captain of the ship had done what he was ordered to do and knew little else. Butrell figured that it must have been Ultra that ordered the launch and the target was probably New Petra. Frustrated, he smashed down his coffee cup on the table and it burst into shrapnel. He immediately went down to the underground holding cell of Goliath. This was the codename of the six foot six inch blond behemoth from Ultra that Butrell had blown the kneecaps off of at the Capital Mall.

"Okay, big boy, I want you to tell me who authorized the cruise missile attack on New Petra!"

"Yeah, I want to know who killed Kennedy," Goliath smarted right back.

Butrell walked over to the man who was shackled to the bed. His legs were both heavily bandaged as a result of surgery although he would most probably never walk again. Butrell grabbed him by the neck and shook him around.

"No more smarting off, you big oaf!" Butrell said as he motioned for the attending medical technician to administer some sodium pentothal.

Goliath squirmed as the shot was administered. "You will never succeed, Butrell. The aliens are ready and poised to invade the Earth. You cannot stop them. They have been planning this for fifty years."

"Why do they want to abduct the Christians?" Butrell demanded.

"Because the Christians are the only ones who understand their agenda. The rest will be duped into believing that they have come to set up a better world with one religion and one leader," Goliath said as he drifted off into a narcotic stupor. "You cannot win, nor can the toy soldiers at New Petra."

"How deeply have you penetrated the intelligence community here in Washington?" Butrell continued.

"More than you realize. We are everywhere. The beast said that we can rule alongside him if we cooperate."

"How can you trust the Devil? Who authorized the missile attack?"

"It was Admiral... Admiral..." Goliath stammered as he fell off into

163

unconsciousness.

"What is the matter?" Butrell asked.

"He seems to have expired, Sir," said Sergeant Rodriguez, the young Puerto Rican medical officer.

"How could that happen, Sergeant?" Butrell asked in a very agitated state.

"I don't know, Sir."

"Smells like almonds to me, Sergeant. Who prepared the syringe?"

"I did, Sir," the Sergeant answered without a flinch.

"Sergeant, let me see your pistol, please."

The Sergeant removed his semiautomatic pistol from its holster and handed it to Butrell.

"Why did you poison this man with strychnine, Sergeant?" Butrell asked as he pointed the gun directly at his trusted medical assistant who had been with him for five years.

"I did not do it, Sir," Rodriguez answered without a moment's hesitation.

"Then who did, Rodriguez? You were the only one with access to the syringes and chemicals."

"Got me, Sir!"

"Wrong answer, son! I'm sorry to do this but may God forgive me," Butrell said as he blew the young man's head apart with a shot right between the eyes at close range.


Reverend Shea and Dr. Lazant found themselves back on the ground about a half mile from the Institute. Hazmat people were nearby so they scurried away from the radioactive debris.

"All of our work has been destroyed!" Reverend Shea moaned as he looked far down the road at the bombed out Institute. "Stephen and Endora are dead and Judah has joined the other side. Where do we go from here, Doctor ?"

"Reverend Shea, we still have our contact with AZAZEL. He will probably, I guess, communicate directly with us from now on. The time is drawing near for the abduction of the Christians and he needs us to help set up his new world unified religion. Don't forget all the contacts that we have worldwide! These evangelical Christians are a real pain, but we will soon be free of them!"

"But Judah is a Jew, not a Christian," Reverend Shea asked curiously. "Why has he sided with them? I don't understand!"

Everyone crowded into the lowest level of the cave. There were forty-seven people including Judah's mother on her bed. They were all crowded into the level were the water cistern was located. It was very cold almost frigid at this level. Everyone held hands, except Bertha, and prayed.

"Father, please protect us from this incoming missile," Captain Knowington began as he led the prayer. "You are an awesome God who loves His people. Please put Your angels around the mountaintop to defer the blast of the enemy. Thank

You, Lord, for healing me, Your humble unworthy servant. Please protect all the wives and children that are here, Lord. They did not choose to be here but nonetheless are here with their husbands and fathers. Please Lord, protect us with Your outstretched arm!"

The missile crashed into the mountaintop and exploded, ripping off the top of the mountain and all of their surveillance and communications equipment. All of their satellite dishes and antennae were obliterated. Rubble cascaded down the top of the mountain and covered the steel door entrance. The walls of the cavern shook and several of the water pipes ruptured sending water cascading all over. A propane gas pipe broke in the kitchen and was ignited by a spark. Flames shot all over the eating area. The animals were startled and the catfish were thrown out of their tanks onto the floor. Everything was in a state of chaos.

"How did they find us?" Judah asked as he and the others shook from the impact.

"I don't know, Judah," Captain Knowington replied. "Either they followed us back in the Hummer or they put another listening device on one of us."

Judah remembered that he had found the bug that they had planted in his mother when it had fallen out when he had caught her. He frantically ran his hands over his neck and the back of his head looking for a device, but he found nothing. He went over to Captain Knowington and did the same.

"Oh, God," Judah yelled. "They put a bug in your neck as well. Why didn't anyone see this!"

"Cut it out, Judah!"

"What is the use now? They already know where we are!"

"Cut it out! I want no part of AZAZEL on my person!"

Judah took out his knife and carefully removed the device which was just under the skin. He dropped it and stomped on it.

"Actually, they may now feel that we have all been killed since the bug has been silenced," Judah laughed.

"Yeah right!" Jennifer moaned.

"See what all your prayer has done," Bertha piped in. "Nothing! You pray and this whole cave is flooding. I smell gas too. Oy vey ist mir *(Y.Oh woe is me)*! And the Cossacks are at the gates!"

"Ma, we don't know that," Judah replied.

"Trust me, tatalleh! All your praying shmaying isn't worth the effort! Go outside and look. I bet that I am right!"

"Ma! Stop being so negative. Stop kvetching all the time," Judah replied frustrated with his mother's attitude. She had seen Captain Knowington healed but her heart was still as hard as stone.

Upon closer examination, the damage to the New Petra compound had been found to be extensive. There was a blazing fire in the kitchen area and the rest of the floors were flooded. Obviously, the blast had also destroyed all of the satellite dishes and antenna on the mountaintop. They were cut off from any communication

165

with the outside world. While they had survived, their ability to fight AZAZEL had been greatly diminished.

As everyone clamored back to the top level, they stood at the entrance waiting for the huge steel doors to be opened so that they could escape the ravages of flood and fire. Just as the order was about to be given to open the doors, Lieutenant Gregor yelled out.

"Stop, wait a minute. How do we know what is out there? Maybe there are large boulders that will roll into here and injure people. Maybe Mrs. Meire is correct and the Cossacks are right outside waiting for us to open the doors. If Ultra launched that missile, they would know that it would not destroy an entire mountain, and that they would have to mop up the operation!"

"Are you kidding?" Captain Knowington replied. "Do you really believe the words of a nasty old woman!"

"Absolutely! Anyone can be right on an occasion. She has a great deal of experience with persecution, you must remember. Cossacks at the gates is not just an expression to her people. Send someone through the crawlspace to look."

The only ones that had ever used that crawlspace were the girls and Dawn.

"I know where it is," Dawn volunteered. "I'll go and see."

"Dawn, let me go," Judah interjected.

"You won't fit, my dear, sorry!"

Dawn crawled through the same passage that she had used to make her earlier escape from New Petra. When she got to the end of the crawlspace, she peered out and got the shock of her life. There were men and heavy equipment and artillery all around. All of the men were wearing gas masks. The huge steel front doors were partially covered with fallen rock. She quickly crawled back into the cave.

"Judah's mother was right," she said quickly. "There are men and artillery and heavy equipment all around the entrance. It also looks as if they are planning to use poison gas on us since they are all wearing gas masks!"

"How did they make it up the mountain without our countermeasures picking them up?" Corporal Canon asked frustratingly.

"Remember, son, that the missile knocked all of our communications equipment," Lieutenant Gregor replied.

"That's right, duhh," he smiled. "Sorry, Lieutenant!"

"Are they in uniform, Dawn?" Captain Knowington wanted to know.

"They were in combat fatigues but they had no markings," she answered.

"How many are there?"

"I'd say about as many as we are, Sir!"

"What kind of equipment do they have?"

"Well, I saw an armored personnel carrier and a Bradley fighting machine as well as a large howitzer. As I said before, the men were also wearing gas masks so they might be planning to gas us out," Dawn said shaking her head. "If they find that crawlspace it will make for a perfect point for such an operation."

"Block up that crawlspace with something big, hard and impenetrable!"

"I told you boys that the Cossacks were at the door," Bertha chimed in once again. "All your praying didn't do a thing. God listened to all of you like he listened to my family during the Holocaust. There is no God that listens to us. He may be up there, but he has better things to do than answer our prayers. That has been the story of the Jewish people since Moses."

"What are you talking about, Ma," Judah answered sharply. "God has always been there for us, but we have not always been there for Him. He gave us manna in the desert and what did we do? Complain! He gave us his Word and what did we do? Build a golden calf! He promised us a homeland forever. What did we do? Stay in Germany because the living was easier than it was in Palestine! God has always been there for us but we have ignored him and sought other gods whether they be money or comfort or pleasure or a host of other idolatries. God saved me from a burning van. God enabled me to fight AZAZEL. God healed the Captain. Are you blind? As Jennifer said, Helloo! Wake up and smell the coffee, Ma. The truth is right in your face and you refuse to believe. God could stand right in front of you and you would not believe!"

"Judah, you are confusing me. Are you a Jew or a Christian? These goyim have brainwashed you. This whole group sounds like a cult or something. If the enemy is at the doors, then who are these people? They are surely not our friends. Trust me!"

"Ma! Cut it out. These are our friends. I am a Jew who has come to realize that Yeshua Hamashiach is my Lord and Savior."

"Oy vey," Bertha countered. "All of your family perished in the Holocaust at the hands of these loving Goyim. Oh Moshe, I'm so sorry for what has happened to our son. It's my fault. I must have failed him somehow. I'm so sorry!"

"Ma, what will it take for you to believe?" Judah asked, not really expecting an answer.

"Well, for starters if your God will get us out of this terrible predicament," she answered. "It looks hopeless to me!"

The soldiers outside of the crushed mountaintop aimed their Howitzer at the metal doors. They fired a projectile that embedded itself three quarters of the way through the door slicing two men in two in the process. The end of the projectile began to leak nerve gas.

"I told you, Judah," Bertha wailed. "The end is near!"

Everyone inside had been issued gas masks so that any attempt to gas them out would be delayed at least for the foreseeable future.

Suddenly they all heard the muffled sound of Apache helicopters through the mountain walls. Then there was the deafening barrage of rockets and missile launchings which struck the ground and the Earth jumped. They heard the screams of the men outside the door as they frantically ran for cover. Within five minutes all was absolutely still. Then there was a knock on the steel doors.

"Captain Knowington, this is Major Jim Malcolm of the Delta Force, Sir. Please open your doors!"

Captain Knowington opened one of the doors, the other was jammed by the projectile. Everyone inside ripped off their gas masks and ran outside to greet the men from Delta Force.

"Who sent you here, Major?" Captain Knowington asked as he saluted the Major and greeted his counter- terrorism Brigade.

"Deputy Director Butrell told us that a secret military compound was under attack by a group of terrorists. We got here ASAP, Captain."

"That is an understatement, Sir," Judah replied. "You guys were here in a flash. Thank God for that!"

They had brought three Apache helicopters with full missile and rocket armament. After blasting the enemy from above they had repelled out of their choppers and mopped up the operation. Like New Petra, they had also lost two men but had completely destroyed the enemy. Everyone from New Petra had left the flooded and burning cave and had come out to greet the soldiers. Everyone except Bertha.

"Get up, Mom," Judah demanded. "It is time that you walked for yourself again."

Judah helped his mother remove her traction weights and assisted her as she moved to the edge of the bed. She looked at him and at the Delta Force rescuers through her gas mask. "Come on, Ma, get up and walk. Do you believe now? You said that if we were rescued that you would believe? Nu *(Y. so?)*?"

Bertha edged to the end of the bed and began to stand up. She held on to Judah tightly as she continued to stare at Major Malcolm and his men.

"Where did they come from?" she asked bewilderedly.

"The Lord sent them, Ma. See, He was listening!"

She got up took off her gas mask and started walking.

Everyone cheered. She feigned a smile and looked at Major Malcolm again.

"Gentlemen and ladies, we have been given orders to relocate your Joshua Brigade to a new location," Major Malcolm yelled to all assembled. "Please go get whatever supplies and intelligence material that you might need. We are to completely destroy New Petra before we leave."

"Where are we going?" Captain Knowington asked. "Who authorized this move?"

"I was instructed to inform you that Senator Jordan had a fall back site picked out all along if New Petra was compromised."

"Praise God!" Captain Knowington, Colonel Meire and Lieutenant Gregor said, almost simultaneously.


Pastor Calvin was outside in the warm summer air of Macon, Georgia. His sister had a beautiful home which was situated on several acres. As he walked along the thick, lush grass, he looked into the deep blue sky and saw it suddenly covered with UFOs. He blinked his eyes and they disappeared. He then looked into the sky again and sure enough it was covered from one end of the horizon to the other with thousands of black saucer shaped disks. His mouth fell open and he blinked his eyes one more time, and they once again disappeared.

# XIII

Reverend Shea and Dr. Lazant were anxious to attend the Conference on Religious Unity sponsored by the United Nations Global Committee. Co-sponsoring the event were the Gaia Consortium, The Temple of Religious Enlightenment, the Vatican and the World Council of Churches. Even though he had been through a great deal recently with the destruction of his Institute and the killing of his operatives, Dr. Lazant was still very anxious to continue his work. This Conference was a perfect opportunity to re- energize himself in the company of like minded people. It was just what AZAZEL would have ordered.

The Conference began with a prayer by a Wiccan Priestess.

"Oh Mother Goddess. We all honor you today and pray that some day soon you will occupy your rightful place at the head table of Deities. All here recognize that there are many paths to you, O great Mother. We all long for the day, a day that we pray will be soon, that all people can worship as one. There will be no judgmental, condescending attitudes; no more belief that there is only one way to Truth; no more threats of eternal damnation or rejection of any brother or sister. We are all one and we shall all be together for all time so we might as well learn to love each other right here. All Praise and Glory to you, O Great Mother!"

"That was beautiful, Sister Forrest," Dr. Lazant said as she finished and everyone applauded as a sign of their approval. "You know, Reverend Shea and I have been through a living hell because of that exact judgmental attitude that you just expressed. Those Christian zealots that I have mentioned before just blew up our Institute."

"They did what?" Rabbi Ginsberg gasped.

"They used a uranium tipped rocket that not only leveled the building but spewed radioactive debris all over the surrounding neighborhood!" Dr. Lazant lamented. "We cannot even return to salvage any records that might have survived that holocaust!"

"That is so typical of those Patriarchal Christians," Forrest angrily replied. "They trash Gaia, our Mother the Earth, in the name of their Father God. They have desecrated the Earth. They have polluted her, raped her, dishonored her one more time. It will be such a blessing to be finally rid of these fanatical Christians once and for all!"

"One of my own Institute people, a Jew, also killed one of my operatives, Endora," Dr. Lazant wailed. "He stepped on her throat and killed her right in front of me. It was Judah, my man in charge of security. What an irony, that he of all people, would kill one of his own fellow non-Christian colleagues. I think that he went mad when he married that Christian woman. They will get to you, you know?!"

"I knew Endora!" Forrest said. "She was a dear Wiccan sister. Why did he do that?"

"It is a long story," Dr. Lazant replied. Do you all want to hear the entire gristly mess?"

"Of course we do," Forrest and Rabbi Ginsberg answered almost simultaneously.

Dr. Lazant then proceeded to tell all congregated there how apparently the leader of the Christian zealots, a Captain Knowington, had fired that uranium tipped missile into the Institute to try and kill them. They had hid in the underground bunkers after being informed of the attack by AZAZEL. After the Institute was demolished, they were taken aboard his black disk. Soon after they arrived in the craft, they found that Captain Knowington also was brought aboard.

"It was amazing, ladies and gentlemen, to be finally aboard the craft of the Supreme Watcher, the Heavenly Angel, AZAZEL," Dr. Lazant beamed as his tone changed from anguish to pure joy. "All of the struggle and hardship and even the death of friends and colleagues pales in the light of that encounter. We all are participating in a monumental undertaking with the Heavenly Angels, the Watchers, who have watched and influenced Humankind since the beginning. Now they are ready to come to Earth and set up a New World Order; one held together by a unified world religion. That is what you all are working so hard to put into place."

"When are they going to abduct these fanatical Christians?" Rabbi Ginsberg asked intensely.

"Soon, soon, be patient, everything is moving along according to schedule."

"According to whose schedule?" Father Saltucci inquired.

"Their schedule, Father," Dr. Lazant answered with a smile. "They have been planning this for the last fifty years."

"Why only the last fifty years?" Rabbi Ginsberg asked.

"Because fifty years ago Israel was reincorporated as a State. That marked the prophetic time clock for the countdown to the Millennium. This event had been planned and contemplated for 2000 years but it couldn't be put into effect until the Jews were back in their homeland. They will rebuild their Temple and our leader will enter it and declare himself to be God. We will help usher in the 1000 years of peace with our new one world religion. This will be a time of love and respect for all people. There will be no more hate and condemnation and judging and looking down on people who worship different from you. Anyway, we found ourselves in the craft with AZAZEL. While his servants were attending to our burns, we noticed that he had also brought that Christian leader of the zealots into the craft as well. He was the man who destroyed our Institute with the uranium tipped rocket. AZAZEL was preparing to question him about the location of their resistance, when suddenly a helicopter was brought into the craft. In it was our one and only security man, Judah. He went over and took the leader with him and shielded him from AZAZEL's missiles. AZAZEL had also brought Judah's mother onto the craft and he grabbed her, at which point Judah grabbed Reverend Shea and me. It was at this point that Endora came to our rescue, but Judah just kicked her in the face. When she continued to struggle, he stepped on top of her throat and killed her."

"Oh my word!" Forrest cried out. "She died defending the brethren and will be rewarded for that!"

"How can Judah resist AZAZEL?" Rabbi Ginsberg questioned. "He always seems to come out on top."

"He calls upon his God and uses a light sword to ward off AZAZEL."

"Sounds like Star Wars to me," Rabbi Ginsberg quipped.

"It is more like that than you would believe," Dr. Lazant remarked. "He threw this sword at AZAZEL and it pinned him to the wall. We could not even grasp it to pull it out, but his small grey servants managed to do it. Judah is our number one problem right now. He has called on the God of the Christians and has gotten power from Him. It is a battle between good and evil and we are the good guys. We are the people who want true love and unity among all people. It is a battle for the souls of mankind!"

Everyone settled into a day's worth of meetings and discussions. All were made aware of the pending abduction of the Christians, but all swore to keep it quiet until it happened. They realized that their global agenda could not take place until the Christian zealots were removed. In the meantime they would continue to plan for their New World religious order.

"By the way, Dr. Lazant, what happened to my dear brother, Stephen?" the Hindu Holy man asked. "He was a true Avatar, an Ascended Master. He could communicate with spirit beings like no one that I have ever seen. He has reincarnated many times. He is an old soul that is nearing the state of Nirvana or freedom from the karmic wheel of reincarnation."

"Stephen was killed also, before the Institute was blown up," Dr. Lazant answered without telling him that it was by Ultra. "We went to Endora at the time and had her conjure up the dead spirit of Stephen. He provided us with some valuable information about our enemies. I believe that AZAZEL will now communicate directly with us now that Stephen is gone. Maybe I can get him to materialize before all of you someday soon. It would certainly bolster our struggle. He is a beautiful black angel with majestic wings. You cannot believe what power he exudes!"

"Reverend Shea, why are you so quiet?" the Rabbi asked.

"I don't know. I am actually rather perplexed at the present time," Reverend Shea said with a look of trepidation on his face.

"What do you mean?"

"Well, first of all, Stephen told us from his vantage point in the afterworld that

172

he was in what the Christians call Hell. He cried out in pain and torment at the fires that engulfed him but did not consume his flesh. Then, later in the craft, as Dr. Lazant described earlier, Judah was holding the two of us, and AZAZEL was holding Judah's mother. Judah demanded that AZAZEL release his mother and then he would release us."

"Well, did he?" the Rabbi inquired ignoring the earlier revelation about Stephen.

"Yes, AZAZEL released his mother and Judah released us."

"So what is the big deal, Reverend?"

"Well Judah could have just killed us, you know. He remained true to his word with AZAZEL in spite of the fact that we would live and continue to plague him and his people. He did an honorable thing. And if there truly is a Hell like the Bible talks about and Stephen is in it, then what about the rest of us unrepentant sinners? Your unrepentant lesbian lifestyle, Rabbi, is exactly the type of behavior that the Bible says leads one to Hell. And you are not unique to the possibility of that punishment considering all the diverse people that we have in this room, Rabbi. We have Hindus and Buddhists and Pagans and Goddess worshippers and a host of others. Think about what I said carefully and tell me that you are not as baffled and fearful as I am. Endora conjured up the dead spirit of Stephen, and he was in the fires of Hell! He told us so! Thus the Bible is correct about the eternal punishment of those who reject the God of Abraham, Isaac and Jacob and His first begotten Son who came to earth to die for our sins! It says that those people shall perish and not have eternal life. Look at what happened to Stephen! We heard it from his own lips!"

"Oh come on, Reverend," Dr. Lazant said with an air of frustration. "Are you starting that again? If Judah had killed us like you said that he should have, then we would not be here today planning his demise. I think that it was great that he was so weak. It is the survival of the fittest. He gave us the opportunity to ultimately defeat him and his fanatical Christian friends. What a blessing! And as for Stephen, I already explained that to you. He betrayed the cause by telling of the surveillance device that had been implanted in Judah's mother's head by AZAZEL's friends so that they could monitor Judah. Thus, he condemned himself to the fires of hell. Not the Christian Hell that puts people there because they don't accept Jesus Christ as their Lord and Savior, but rather the damnation of the eternal fires of punishment for those who betray AZAZEL and his dominions. We had all be absolutely certain that we do not betray AZAZEL or look what our fate will be! I am more fearful of AZAZEL than I am of an impotent Christian god who was nailed to a cross and couldn't even save himself!"

"Yeah , but..."

"But nothing. Grow up, Reverend. This is the real world and we are all engaged in a spiritual battle for the souls of all of humankind. Don't you ever forget that! You are either part of the solution or you are part of the problem. There is no middle ground. You had better decide fast which side that you are on."

173

"I cannot believe that Stephen would betray our cause," the Hindu yogi argued. "He was, as I said before, a very old soul that had reincarnated many times in his quest for freedom from the wheel of karma. And besides, at death, he would just enter a new body and try again. There is no concept of hell in our religion, just the eternal wheel of karma."

"Yeah, and I don't buy that Christian concept of hell either," the Rabbi said emphatically.

"Those Christians just use the fear of this Hell to try and control my lesbian behavior that they cannot stand. Well too bad! I don't believe that Jews will go to hell by not accepting Jesus Christ any more than will lesbians. I cannot imagine that a loving goddess would treat her children so arbitrarily. She has unconditional love for all of us and accepts us for who and what we are. She made us the way that we are after all. How could she punish us for what she made us? Think about it. It isn't rational."

"Then all of you explain Stephen's fate to me," Reverend Shea yelled out. "You all reject the Christian concept of Hell, yet you will not give me a rational explanation for his testimony that he was in the fires of that place. All except you, Dr. Lazant. You come up with some crazy thesis that Stephen went to a hell destined for those who betray the angelic watchers. Where in Scripture do you find such a bizarre doctrine? Remember, I was a professor at Harvard Divinity School. I might have lapsed a little, or actually a lot, from my training and knowledge of Scripture, but I do know that your thesis is without any sound theological justification. This AZAZEL is, I've decided, a fallen angel who was thrown out of the first Heaven with Satan. He and his dominions are what Paul told the Church at Ephesus was 'the prince of the power of the air', and what Peter called 'your adversary the devil who like a roaring lion walks about seeking whom he may devour'. And Dr. Lazant, Christ was crucified for all our sins but He rose again and now sits at the right hand of the Father in Heaven. Don't ever forget that! Remember what Paul wrote to the Church at Thessalonica, 'For the mystery of lawlessness is already at work; only he who now restrains will do so until he is taken out of the way'. Those are your zealous Christians! 'And then that lawless one will be revealed whom the Lord will slay with the breath of His mouth and bring to an end by the appearance of His coming'. The lawless one is AZAZEL and his fellow fallen angels. But remember what Paul said. He will be defeated by the Lord at His coming! Paul continued, 'that is the one whose coming is in accord with the activity of Satan, with all power and signs and false wonders, and with all the deception of wickedness for those who perish, because they did not receive the love of the truth so as to be saved'. That means that all of you that follow AZAZEL will eternally perish like Stephen did."

Dr. Lazant just smiled and put his arm around Reverend Shea. He joked to all those congregated that he was probably a little frazzled by all that transpired over the last few weeks. He told Reverend Shea that he just needed to relax and get some rest. Everyone nervously laughed as he escorted him out of the Conference Room. When he got him into the hallway, Dr. Lazant accosted Reverend Shea verbally.

"What has happened to you, man? You are undermining our entire operation. You are not following the program. Like Judah you are wavering from our goal, and we cannot tolerate that. You are either with us one hundred percent or you are against us. As I said before there is no middle ground. You will either be a part of the new world religious order or you will suffer the same fate as your fanatical Christian buddies. Well, which will it be?"

"You know, Bruce, it suddenly became crystal clear to me," Reverend Shea lamented. "You and I and AZAZEL and all the rest are actually helping the Devil do his dirty work. But you know what, Boss, I read the Book and I know how the story ends!"

Suddenly, the black angelic figure of AZAZEL appeared before them. It had materialized right in the hallway. Dr. Lazant fell to his knees in awe and submission before the powerful countenance of this being. Reverend Shea just stood there and looked it right in the blackness of its being, and then began to rebuke it in the name of Jesus Christ. Unfortunately he had not yet asked the Lord for forgiveness for his sins and he was not prayed up enough to resist the wiles of the Enemy, so he was picked up and thrown through the door of the conference room. His head suffered a fatal blow of blunt force trauma as he went right through the door upside down. His body went through with his arms outstretched and his feet together which cut out a cross for his body. Out of thin air, nails appeared which bolted him to the cross. Like the Apostle Peter, he found himself crucified upside down right in front of the stunned group. They all witnessed the powerful, intoxicating side of evil, and they all fell to their knees in submission.

"You will continue your mission as you have been instructed or your fate will be like that of this poor pathetic man. He succumbed to the weakness of the folly of the Bible and that of the crucified son of God. It is us that shall rule and reign here on earth for a thousand years. You have been chosen to help us achieve that domination. Either you are with us or you will be destroyed."

AZAZEL bellowed out these words and flapped its wings ferociously as all cowered in abject fear. Before it left, it looked over at Reverend Shea who was trying to say his last words.

"Forgive them, Father, for they know not what they do. Open their eyes to the reality of this Demon from the powers of the air. You defeated it once and for all time on the Cross, Father. We know that it will never succeed in robbing people of their Eternal life with you. Just as you rose from the grave, all of us who believe and trust in you shall also have eternal life. Please, forgive me, Father, for my terrible sins against you. I am truly sorry for all that I have done. I hope that it is not too late, Father. Ohh..."

A voice boomed out, "As long as you still have breath, it is never too late, my son! Today Thou shall be with me in Paradise!"

175

AZAZEL shrieked an ungodly roar and disappeared. All those assembled in the Conference room were left in a hushed, stunned silence. They all stared at the lifeless crucified body of Reverend Shea which stood before them upside down and implanted through the large oak conference table. Before long, the room was filled with United Nations Security Personnel who had heard all the commotion. They also just stared at Reverend Shea and at the conference members and could not imagine what had just transpired at the meeting that had resulted in a man being crucified upside down. Dr. Lazant told them that a disgruntled former employee of his and Reverend Shea by the name of Judah Meire had stormed into the meeting and accosted Reverend Shea.

"Do you mean to tell us that a man came into your meeting and knocked down the door and crucified this poor man upside down while all of you just watched?" asked the blond heavyset middle aged security guard. "I just cannot believe that!"

"That is what happened , Sir," Dr. Lazant replied, shaking his head. "We are a peace loving international group of religious people. We do not believe in violence. I guess we all just froze in shock. This Judah was a member of the IDF and Mossad. He is a fanatical Jewish zealot who became enraged at our attempts to talk about the new Millennium. You know those Jews, they always think that they are being left out. Besides, he suffers from Post Traumatic Stress Syndrome. Ask the Potomac, Maryland Police Department. Call a Captain Braden!"

All of the conference people were taken down to the NYPD station in Manhattan where they once again gave their stories of what happened. They were all put in holding cells until it could be determined if they were to be booked for the crime. Reverend Shea's body was taken off of the makeshift cross and taken to the Coroner's office for examination..

Captain Braden of the Potomac Maryland Police Department was notified of the incident and he was on the next shuttle to New York. When he got to the NYPD station he asked to speak with Dr. Lazant.

"What is the story with this Col.Meire?" Captain Barcellini of the NYPD asked Captain Braden."You have obviously run into him before."

"Oh yes. His wife ended up in the hospital in a coma as did his mother. One of my detectives died mysteriously and the other one just disappeared after associating with this man. In fact, remember the death of Senator Jordan not too long ago? Well, he did not die alone of a blood clot. He died in the arms of this Colonel Meire. He is bad news. I thought that he had died in a car crash but I guess not. In fact, he was also the last person to see that CIA man before he jumped out of his window. I could go on and on."

"I get the point, Captain," Captain Barcellini replied. "Well, I guess that he could have done this heinous crime then after all. He sounds like a loose cannon."

"I'd like to speak with Dr. Lazant," Captain Braden asked as the two of them then went to his holding cell.

"You said that Judah did this?" Captain Braden asked puzzled. "I thought that he was dead?"

"No, he is very much alive," anguished Dr. Lazant, "and he wants to disrupt our efforts. Obviously, he is doing a good job of it too!"

"Looks like he had another Post Traumatic Stress attack. My God, he crucified that poor man upside down. He is more dangerous than even I thought. Why didn't you try and stop him? I cannot believe that you all just sat there and watched?"

"We were in a state of shock, Sir," Dr. Lazant answered softly. "We are peace loving people who abhor violence. We just couldn't believe what we were seeing and I guess we just froze up."

FBI agents Mallory and Bernstein soon found their way to the NYPD as well. They had been trying to locate Judah for quite a while and this was the first hard lead that they had gotten in a long time.

"Why did he do that to Shea?" Special Agent Bernstein asked with a puzzled look on his face.

"You people have a history of crucifying the elect of God," Dr. Lazant smarted off. "I knew that I should not have ever hired a Jew, an Israeli at that, to work with us Christians. Reverend Shea was a Professor at Harvard Divinity School, you know. Judah wanted to make a statement and he sure accomplished that!"

"And what was that, Sir?" Mallory asked with his boyish smile as he saw that Bernstein was fuming about the earlier characterization.

"Well, I guess that he wanted to show not only us, but everyone, that he was not going to be under the authority of Christians. He was sick and tired of us talking of ruling and reigning for a thousand years during the Millennium."

"And just because of this ranting and raving on your part, you want us to believe that he came in here with a hammer and nailed this man to a cross?" Bernstein answered still fuming. "I find it interesting that he left no tools and no fingerprints and even more surprisingly, nobody in security saw or has any surveillance record of Judah entering or leaving the building. I think that you guys did it in some radical cultist ceremony and have decided to blame Judah. We have nothing to tie Judah to this crime except your word."

Captain Braden of the Potomac PD, FBI Special Agents Mallory and Bernstein and Captain Barcellini of the NYPD all sat down to discuss the incident. As Agent Bernstein had said there was nothing to tie Judah to the crime other than the accounts of the conference participants. An APB was issued for Judah, though, to get him in to try and resolve this matter. There was after all a dead man here. They were not prepared to release the conference participants. They decided to question them individually. Each asked for legal representation first and the entire process began to bog down.

"It wasn't Judah, it was..." the man from the World Council of Churches tried to say but he was drowned out by the other people.

"What were you trying to say?" asked Captain Barcellini of the NYPD as

Braden, Mallory and Bernstein looked on anxiously. "My Lieutenant said that you wanted to tell us something about the incident."

All of a sudden a representative of the New York City Police Chief burst into the holding area with two men in trenchcoats and sunglasses.

"Hold everything, people!" Captain Barcellini yelled as he read the order from the Police Chief. "These gentlemen have come for our prisoners. They will be taking them."

"What?" snapped Braden, Bernstein and Mallory in unison. "Who are these people?"

"They are government people and I've got a signed order from the New York City Police Chief to release these people to them. There is nothing that I can do about it. It is a matter of National Security. We will continue to search for Judah!"

"But this guy just said that Judah did not do it," Lieutenant Kowalsky yelled. "Cap..."

"It is out of our hands, Kowalsky. Forget about it!"

"Yeah, please let us out of here," Rabbi Ginsberg burst out. "We have been held long enough without due process. You clowns are lucky if I don't get my lawyer to sue you for false arrest."

"Don't push it, Ma'am," Captain Barcellini replied with a scowl. "You are lucky that we didn't do a strip search of you. We might have discovered that you weren't a woman after all!"

Rabbi Ginsberg protested his snide remark, but the two men in dark glasses escorted Dr. Lazant and the other members of the group out of the Police Station before the discussion could get anymore out of hand. They all went into an unmarked van and sped off

Captain Barcellini and Captain Braden shook their heads at the entire bizarre incident.

"Do you know who those spooks were, Captain?" Barcellini asked Braden.

"Oh yes I do, Sir! Judah was mixed up with the CIA and these are some other intelligence people that keep snooping around wherever he turns up. I was told once that I should back off from investigating them or their relationship to Judah. I was told that it could get me killed. Actually, Judah told me that they killed my Detective O'Malley and forced Detective Holmes to go into hiding because he knew too much."

"Sounds like maybe they are the bad guys, not Judah," Captain Barcellini replied shaking his head. "Hey, somebody get me a latte!"

"You have no idea, Captain," Special Agent Bernstein interjected. "Those are bad dudes. You don't mess with them. You are correct that they are spooks. Black OPs and all that. They only listen to a higher authority, but trust me, they are not Hebrew National!"

"That's pathetic, Bernstein. Don't give up your day job! Well, then it is possible that Judah had no part in this event," Captain Barcellini said as he sat down and folded his hands in his lap and sipped the latte that was brought to him. "I think that we should go and see what the Coroner has found out."

They all headed to the Coroner's office, but to their combined consternation, they found out that Reverend Shea's body had been also released to those same Government Agents as well as all the examination specimens and data and recordings. Only later would they discover that all the names and addresses of the conference suspects were also removed by the men from Ultra as well.

"What did you find out, Doc?" Captain Barcellini asked the short, bearded Coroner.

"Well I determined that he had been severely wounded by a blunt force trauma to the head. He probably was thrown against the door. I found some hair and skin samples embedded in the door. I think that he hit the door with such force that he created the cross by going right through the door with his arms out and his legs together. He was then nailed upside down onto this cross. All of the blood rushed into his cracked head and fractured lungs, and basically he died as a result of suffocation and blood loss from his head wound. The combination of the head wound and the numerous fractures combined with the hanging upside down was too traumatic for anyone to survive," Dr. Kaplan explained in a nervous manner.

"Where is this cross piece and where are the nails?" Special Agent Mallory inquired.

"Oh, those guys took all the evidence with them as well," the Coroner said.

"What did the nails look like?" Captain Braden wanted to know as he suddenly developed a splitting headache. The implant that Ultra had put into his head at the scene of the burning van had begun to throb and he rubbed his big, thick neck.

"It is funny that you ask that," Doctor Kaplan remarked, once again very nervously. "I was just thinking to myself that the nails used looked nothing like anything that I have ever seen before. They were made of a plastic like substance that was light as a feather yet was strong enough to hold a two hundred pound man nailed to a cross upside down. Must have been some secret military issue."

Special Agents Mallory and Bernstein scoured over the Coroner's office for any clues. In the corner of the lab on the floor against the wall, Bernstein found one of those strange nails.

"What did you find?" Captain Barcellini shouted as he saw the man bend down to pick something up.

"Oh it is nothing, Captain," Bernstein said nonchalantly.

"Right!" Captain Barcellini shouted. "Hand it over, son. That belongs to NYPD."

"Sorry, Captain, but this is FBI property!"

"What are you talking about? This is evidence in the death of a man that we are investigating!"

"The man was killed at the UN and thus it is now a Federal crime. We will take care of it!"

179

"Let me see what you found!" Captain Barcellini demanded as he grabbed Bernstein's hand.

Bernstein opened his hand and revealed one of those strange nails that had been used to crucify Reverend Shea. It was long, pointed and covered with blood. But it was as the Coroner had described, light as a feather but was obviously very strong. Captain Barcellini tried to bend it but he could not. He tried to determine what it was but he could not. It was nothing that he recognized, and he had been a Materials Specialist in the Army.

"What the heck is this?" he yelled. "How could this Col. Meire have had access to this type of material?"

"Maybe it came from the Israelis?" Captain Braden offered as an explanation as he rubbed his throbbing head.

"I don't think so!" Captain Barcellini replied as he became so nervous that he burned his mouth with his latte. "They are pretty advanced but this stuff is really unique. I don't really think that even they have capabilities like this."

"Well, what do you think then?" Captain Braden asked as he continued to stare at the long spike.

Special Agents Mallory and Bernstein retrieved the nail and put it into a plastic specimen bag and headed out of the station. They had decided to visit the site of the crime at the UN. Captain Braden and Captain Barcellini accompanied them. When they came to the room where the incident had taken place they found nothing. Everything had been cleaned up and a new door was on the room and there was a new oak table in the room as well. All security camera footage of the hallway and even of the room had been confiscated by the same men in dark sunglasses. When they asked the security guards who had authorized such a confiscation, they just shook their heads and replied that it was some bigshots in the government. They had flashed ID badges and official orders for the entire cleanup operation.

"What do you remember about the incident?" Captain Barcellini asked the security guard as he nursed his burned tongue.

"Well, I don't remember seeing anyone enter this hallway or this room while their meeting was going on," he responded. "They were a strange bunch of people if you ask me. They said that they just sat there in shock while supposedly someone nailed that poor guy to a cross fashioned out of the door. The funny thing was that none of them seemed upset. No one was crying, not even the women. Doesn't that seem strange to you? One of their colleagues is killed in such a brutal way right in front of them and nobody is upset?"

"What kind of meeting was it?" Captain Barcellini asked as he rubbed his square chin.

"I don't know exactly," the security guard answered. "They meet here several times a year and do some kind of religious praying. They have Hindu swamis and medicine men and witches and tree huggers and all kind of weirdos if you ask me. But they are sponsored by the United Nations so I always assumed that it was legit,

180

but after what happened the other day I just am not so sure anymore."

"What do you mean?"

"What do I mean? That Reverend Shea, I knew him. He came to these meetings for years. He ends up crucified upside down right in front of them. I would have certainly tried to stop that, but not these peace loving granolas. They would die to save a spotted owl or a whale, but they let their friend be brutally murdered. As my dear mother used to say, something seems rotten in Denmark!"

Captain Barcellini and Captain Braden just looked at one another. Both were coming to the realization that maybe there was more to the story than they were privy to. Special Agents Mallory and Bernstein also listened to the Security Guard with quiet understanding and frequent smiles and head acknowledgements.

"If those kooks say that someone threw Shea though the door, nailed him to it and drove it into the solid oak conference table, then it must have been Superman. No mere mortal could have done all of that by himself. That is the bottom line," the security guard said. "I was a weightlifter in college. Nearly made the Olympic team by the way. No average Joe could have thrown a man through a solid oak door, nailed him to it upside down, and then picked it up and drove it into a solid oak table! If you are looking for just one man then you better be looking for either Superman or the Incredible Hulk."

Pastor Calvin's dinner was interrupted by the loud blast of a trumpet once again. He looked out the dining room window and saw the sky covered with UFOs. He looked at everyone at the dinner table and nobody saw or heard what he had just experienced. Then the shining face of Judah Meire popped into his head. He knew that he had to find him.

Major Malcolm and his men from Delta Force had loaded all of the Joshua Brigade and their essential supplies onto their Apache helicopters. They had then set extensive charges to blow up the mountainous home of New Petra as instructed. As the Helicopters lifted off and swung around the scarred top of Backbone Mountain, the entire mountainous cavern exploded. They had put all of the men and equipment from the Ultra assault in there as well, so nothing remained of either New Petra or of the mechanized attack by Ultra. The three Apache helicopters had been outfitted with the newest Stealth technology so as to minimize their possible tracking by Ultra or by AZAZEL. The technology prevented look down capabilities by satellite or by flying saucer. It was state of the art technology and still classified as top secret. Also the helicopters were outfitted with electronic jamming equipment so that no one could listen in on their conversations.

"Where have you been instructed to take us, Major Malcolm?" Captain Knowington asked from the cockpit of the lead helicopter where he, his family, Judah and Dawn, Lieutenant Gregor and the other officers from New Petra were situated..

"Our orders are to drop you off at Langley," Major Malcolm said matter of factly.

"Langley?" Captain Knowington replied startled. "What can we possibly do at Langley?"

"Those are my orders!"

"Where are we going, Daddy?" Rebecca asked as she pulled her pigtails nervously.

"We are going to Langley Airforce Base, sweetheart," Captain Knowington replied. "Don't you worry, everything is going to be all right."

"What are we going to do at an airforce base?" Rebecca said suddenly sitting up and smiling. "Will there be more guys there?"

Captain Knowington refused to answer her and just stared out the window as the helicopters flew southeast towards the Airforce Base outside of Newport News, Virginia. They crossed the beautiful yet rugged Allegheny and Shenandoan Mountains and the shockingly green and brown foliage of the Washington National Forest. They picked up US RT 64 and followed it over the urban skylines of Charlottesville and Richmond, Virginia. As they were nearly completing their hour long flight, Judah asked the Major what awaited them at Langley.

"Who are we to report to at Langley, Major," Judah asked with a quizzical look on his face.

"According to my orders, Colonel, there will be transportation waiting for you."

"To transport us where?"

"I don't know, Colonel. My responsibility and knowledge stops at Langley."

"I guess that Butrell is trying to keep our final destination as secret as possible, Judah," Lieutenant Gregor spoke up. "I'll bet that Langley is not our final destination."

"I hope not," Captain Knowington interjected. "What privacy could we possibly have there?"

The three Apache helicopters flew over Newport News, Williamsburg International Airport, over the NASA Visitors Center and approached Langley Airforce Base. Everyone felt a rush of excitement as they prepared to land.

"Langley, this is the Jordan," Major Malcolm radioed. "Do you read me?"

"Yes, Jordan, this is Langley. Do you have Joshua on board?"

"Yes we do."

"Proceed to the landing strip at the Northwest corner of the base. It has been prepared for your arrival."

"Roger, Langley!"

The three Apache helicopters landed at a remote isolated landing area at the Northwest corner of Langley Airforce Base. They quickly unloaded all of their passengers from the Joshua Brigade.

"Thanks, Sir, for all that you have done," Captain Knowington said as he saluted the head of Delta Force.

"That makes two of us, Major," Judah said as he saluted the man as well."And please give our heartfelt thanks to Deputy Director Butrell for all that he has done."

"I don't know what your mission is, Colonel Meire," Major Malcolm replied, "but I have heard some good things about you, Judah. Godspeed!"

Major Malcolm then went back into his Apache and the three helicopters took off leaving all of the Joshua Brigade alone on the landing strip.

"What now, boss?" Judah asked Captain Knowington.

"Look over there," Captain Knowington said as he pointed to an armored personnel carrier off in the distance. "Let's check it out. It is probably for us."

They walked over to the long, black armored personnel carrier and sure enough it had the keys in it. When Captain Knowington tried to start it up it began to ask him personal questions about the Joshua Brigade. All the while a security camera stared him in the face.

"Who is the leader of the Joshua Brigade?" was the first question.

He answered, "I am, Captain Peter Knowington!"

"Where was your last compound?"

"New Petra on Backbone Mountain"

"Who was the Senator who founded this group?"

"Senator Jordan."

"What is the name of the Jew that has joined your group?"

"Lieutenant Colonel Judah Meire."

Finally, the voice from the console asked Captain Knowington, "What is the name of the black fallen angel that is the target of your mission?"

"AZAZEL!" Captain Knowington yelled in and the personnel carrier started up.

"Congratulations, Captain Knowington," the voice from the console cheered. "I am so glad that you have made it to this point safely. This personnel carrier, like the Apache helicopters, has the latest in stealth technology to prevent anyone or anything for monitoring your travel. Also, there is jamming equipment aboard to prevent them from listening to your conversations. You are to proceed down Route 167 to Interstate 64. You are to cross the Hampton Roads Bridge Tunnel and to proceed to the US Naval Station outside Norfolk. When you get there, we will be in further contact. We will maintain radio silence until then. Don't get stopped for speeding!"

Everyone was loaded into the personnel carrier along with the meager supplies that they brought with them.

"Why are we going to a Naval Base?" Judah asked.

"Beats me, Judah," Captain Knowington replied. "You know what? I'll bet that it isn't our last stop either. Butrell is having us cover our tracks which is a good thing. It is difficult to move 45 people around secretly."

"Now where are we going, Daddy?" Jennifer cried out.

"We are headed to Norfolk, Virginia, sweetheart!"

"Wow. Can we go sailing?"

"I doubt it, honey."

"Maybe they are going to put us on a submarine?" Lieutenant Gregor pondered.

"It would give us privacy and keep us away from Ultra and AZAZEL"

"Interesting point, you old SEAL," Judah remarked. "You would be back at home in the sea.

"Hey, Judah," Lieutenant Gregor joked, "don't forget that it is you that has that fifty-foot cabin cruiser. You are the real sailor in this group!"

"Oy vey," Bertha moaned audibly. "First we go on a helicopter ride and now we go on a jeep tour. What's next, Judah? Don't tell me that we are going on a submarine. No, not me. I don't want to go under the water in a sardine can. Judah, I'm too old for all this. Why can't you just let me off somewhere. It's all right, I'll suffer, but I'll be fine. You can't treat your poor old mother like this."

"Relax, Ma," Judah countered. "What are you kvetching about now. You said that if we were rescued from that siege at New Petra that you would believe that God intervened. Well?!"

"Rescued, shmescued. Those soldiers were sent to rescue us. It wasn't God. God would not put us on a helicopter and now on a big jeep and take us to a boat. He would do it all at one time."

"Thank you, Rabbi! How do you know that, Ma? All of a sudden you are an expert on God's ways?"

"Leave me alone!" Bertha yelled as she covered her ears.

"You said, Ma, that you would believe." Judah said as he screamed into her covered ears.

"So sue me!"

The lumbering, black, armored Personnel Carrier went across the Hampton Roads Bridge Tunnel with the beautiful James River on the right and Chesapeake Bay on the left. It was a shame that they could not see the beautiful water scenery after being cooped up on a desolate mountaintop for months, but the transport had no windows.

"Joshua, this is Jordan control. Do you read me?"

"Yes control, this is Joshua, we read you," Captain Knowington replied.

"Proceed to the dock right in front of you. Your ships are moored there. Do you see them?"

Captain Knowington saw a sleek new Sea Shadow. It was the military's answer to the stealth fighters for naval ships. It looked like an inverted V and was dark grey in color.

"Wow, it looks like we are getting one of those new Sea Shadows!" Captain Knowington cheered.

"Didn't they say ships, Sir?" Judah asked.

"Control, this is Joshua."

"Yes Joshua."

"Is that Sea Shadow ours?"

"Negative, Joshua. Nice try! Your ships are right next to it. You have been assigned two Mark V Special Operations Craft. Proceed to board them. Your final

184

destination is in the ship's safe.

As everyone disembarked from the armored Personnel Carrier it was sunset and the view over Chesapeake Bay was magnificent. They had all been cooped up on a desolate mountaintop for so long that the water looked so inviting.

"Can we go for a swim?" Rebecca asked she bounced down to the waterfront.

"No, not right now, honey," Captain Knowington replied. "We have to ship off right away."

"Okay, Gregor," Captain Knowington demanded, "this is your mode of transportation. You are the only Navy man in our group. Take the helm, Lieutenant, of one of the ships. Judah, you take the other!"

"Aye aye, Sir!" Lieutenant Gregor shouted back and ran to the helm of the boat.

"Boy, this is a sleek fast baby," Judah remarked as he looked it over. "These are the boats that they use to drop off Navy SEAL's. These babies can run at 50 knots."

"Judah, these boats are bigger than your cabin cruiser. I'll bet they are eighty feet in length at least. And I see full stealth capabilities as well. Just like the Sea Shadow!"

All boarded the sleek long Mark V's. Captain Knowington had to undergo a fingerprint and retinal scan to open the safe. In it he found sealed orders telling of their final destination which was Spesutie Island at the Northeast end of Aberdeen Proving Ground. It was a snug fit to accommodate all the members of the Joshua Brigade and their families on these two craft but the trip up the Chesapeake Bay to Aberdeen Proving Grounds would only take around four hours. Lieutenant Gregor's safe opened as well and he also found maps and charts of their voyage. Both boats were to use infrared night vision capabilities for guidance. There was also a homing device at Spesutie's Island which only they had the capability to receive. It was night, but the quiet, cool water was very relaxing.

# XIV

Lieutenant Gregor's Mark V led the way up the dark deserted Intracoastal Waterway of the Chesapeake Bay. Crowded into his sleek fast craft were over twenty people. It was a less than desirable traveling accommodation but there were nothing that they could do about it. Everyone just put their heads on each other and went to sleep. Sitting at the helm with Lieutenant Gregor was Corporal Canon.

"Do you think that we will be sighted, Sir?" the Corporal asked nervously. "After all, even if Deputy Director Butrell arranged this, he would have had to utilize the services of others and no one seems to be absolutely trustworthy at this point."

"Stop whining, boy!" Gregor countered as he munched on some sunflower seeds. "Fear is not of the Lord. Is God still on His throne or not?"

"Of course he is, Sir!"

"Then just button it up, son! You are going to scare the passengers."

Their Mark V sped along at 50 knots. All of the guidance equipment on board steered the craft almost effortlessly. Infrared binoculars enabled them to actually see where they were going. They sped past Port Charles and Windmill Point as they neared the toll area at Tangier Island.

"Well, Captain, what do you think about our chances of making this journey without any interference?" Judah also asked as their Mark V closely followed that of Lieutenant Gregor.

"I hope and pray to God that it is uneventful," Captain Knowington replied. "Our families have had enough excitement for the last couple of days to last a lifetime!"

"Excitement?" Judah's mother yelled from amidst the human pile in the holding area. "You wouldn't believe what my boy has put me through. This little old lady has been thrown, dropped, hit, tossed out of an airplane and God knows what else. I can't stand it anymore. You have got to stop this, Judah. Right now!"

Bertha charged at Judah and began choking him. She had lost control of herself and threatened the very well being of the entire craft.

"Stop it, Ma!" Judah yelled as he tried to release himself from her grip.

"Stop it, Mrs. Meire," Dawn also began yelling as she pulled Judah's mother from off of Judah.

Bertha began pummeling Dawn with her little pointed knuckles. She hit Dawn in the eye and Dawn screamed out in pain.

"You shiksas have no respect for your elders," Bertha shouted as Dawn finally

186

sat on her to keep her arms from flaying and causing more damage.

"Respect? Why, it was you, Mrs. Meire, that jabbed me in the eye and nearly caused your son to lose control of the boat. You are really something, lady. No wonder the Bible calls you Jews stiffnecked."

"Well, we needed a stiff neck to put up with the hanging rope of you murderous Christians!"

Dawn was fed up and stuffed a towel into her mouth.

"Don't even try to talk or move, Mother," Dawn scolded her, "or I will tie you up and throw you overboard."

Bertha finally began to calm down just as they entered the area around Tangier Island.

"Do you think that Lieutenant Gregor is going to stop at this hour for the toll?" Captain Knowington asked Judah as he stared at Judah's mother squirming underneath Dawn.

"What did you say, boss," Judah replied. "I'm sorry. I wasn't paying attention with all he commotion caused by my obstinate mother."

"It's okay, Judah. I understand. I was just wondering if you think Gregor will stop for the toll?"

"Yeah, right, Captain," Judah snapped back. "He is going to jeopardize our cover of darkness to stop for a toll? At night? I don't think so!"

Lieutenant Gregor's Mark V sped past the toll area at over 50 knots and never slowed down. Both boats were running at stealth capabilities and their radar geometry was minimal. They did not use lights and thus were nearly invisible to all but the trained eye. Quietly they entered into Maryland waters and past Point Lookout, Lexington Park and Fishing Creek. Just as he passed St. Leonard, he felt the pull of a beam of light from above.

"Lieutenant Gregor!" Corporal Canon shouted. "We are being pulled off course by some sort of tractor beam. Look out the window, the sky is all lit up!"

"Oh no, son," Lieutenant Gregor moaned. "It looks like AZAZEL has found us again. We need to take countermeasures ASAP!"

They fired a surface to air missile into the black craft that hovered above them but it went right through it.

"What else can we do, Sir?" Canon yelled as everyone in the craft began to wake up and sense that something was amiss.

Lieutenant Gregor tried to steer the Mark V out of the way of the tractor beam but it was no use. Slowly the Mark V was being lifted into the air as everyone began to scream and pandemonium broke out.

"Look, Judah," Captain Knowington shouted as he pointed ahead to Lieutenant Gregor's Mark V being lifted into the air by the black craft of AZAZEL looming overhead. "Oh my God, they are all going to be captured by the Beast!"

Judah immediately swerved his Mark V into a nearby cove at Taylor's Island and waited for the inevitable to happen.

"There is nothing that we can do, Captain, but pray," Judah replied. "If they are captured by AZAZEL, then our new hideout at Aberdeen will be compromised!"

"Why don't you go and fight AZAZEL again," Ann Knowington yelled, "like you did for Peter and your mother?"

"Because I have to worry about the rest of you! I am not free to act alone this time. Am I?"

"No you are not, son," Captain Knowington interjected. "This time we need to keep together. The mission is most important at this juncture, not any one person."

"But Oh my God, they all are going to die!" someone yelled.

"Or worse!" someone else yelled from the back of the boat.

As Lieutenant Gregor's boat was being lifted into the air, suddenly people began jumping off of the craft into the dark cold water and swimming for the coastline of nearby James Island.

"Everyone off of this ship!" Lieutenant Gregor had ordered emphatically.

"What about you, Sir?" Corporal Canon asked as he prepared to leave. "Aren't you afraid to die?"

"I'll be all right, son," Lieutenant Gregor said as he smiled and waived the boy out."I know where I am going. No fear for me. Now get out. That's an order!"

Corporal Canon jumped as the craft was now about twenty feet from the surface of the Intracoastal Waterway. Lieutenant Gregor kept firing his forward cannon into the craft to let AZAZEL know that someone was still aboard. He was hoping and praying that they did not see the others abandoning ship. AZAZEL could not stay around for very long any way because this area was heavily guarded and watched because it was so near the Capitol. AZAZEL, he hoped , would only have one shot at this, and he hoped that he had minimized the potential losses.

"Eat this, you beast from the powers of the air!" Lieutenant Gregor had yelled as the Mark V was pulled into the belly of the beast, and he exploded the two hand grenades that he had found on board. "Here I come, Delores!" he also yelled to his dead wife.

The black disc reeled and zigzagged across the dark cloudy night sky and disappeared.

"Oh my God," Dawn cried out. "It looks as though Lieutenant Gregor remained aboard and blew up the ship to ward off AZAZEL!"

"I think that you are right, Dawn," Judah lamented. "God bless him. He died an honorable death serving the Lord and His servants. But darn, he was such a good man too! There goes another righteous man who has given his life for the cause. That is why we must succeed or all of their deaths will have been for naught!"

"Let's go retrieve the survivors before the military arrives!" Captain Knowington ordered.

"Boy, you certainly are a compassionate person, aren't you, Peter?" Ann smirked.

"As Judah says, we have a job to do!" Captain Knowington said as he tried to conceal his deep felt hurt at the death of his friend.

They went out of the Cove at Taylor Island and headed for nearby James Island in the middle of the Intracoastal Waterway to search for survivors. They could only find fifteen survivors of the twenty-two people on board Lieutenant Gregor's boat. A couple of young children and several wives and a couple of soldiers had disappeared into the dark murky waters of the Chesapeake Bay. The survivors were frantic and hysterical about their missing family members. One of the couples who had lost their young children refused to leave James Island without them.

"You have to come with us," Captain Knowington demanded. "Otherwise our destination will be compromised!"

"I don't know or care where you are headed," the young soldier replied. "But Captain, how can I leave without my children? Oh God what have I done? I brought my precious young babies into this situation and now you want me to abandon them?"

"You can't do this!" his wife screamed. "They are our children. We won't leave them. No! We won't!" she yelled as she began to pummel Captain Knowington with her small fists. "You can't make us do this. I won't leave without my children!"

"They are not your children, Ma'am," Captain Knowington said as compassionately as he could. "They belong to the Lord and He has seen fit to take them home. They are now safe in His loving arms."

"No, I can't leave them!" the young soldier cried out frantically as his wife clung to his arm hysterically. "That is easy for you to say. What if your daughters were missing?"

Captain Knowington took out his revolver and pointed it at them.

"Look, I do empathize with your plight, I really do, but we have to go. It is your choice. Either you come with us or you die. You know the rules of the Joshua Brigade!"

Judah ran over and punched the young man in the face and knocked him out. He picked up the man and carried him to the lone Mark V. His wife soon followed reluctantly.

"God will get you for this, Sir!" the young wife screamed directly at the Captain.

"If He does, then He does, Ma'am. I'm just doing what I think that is best! If I am wrong, then may He also forgive me someday!"

Everyone crowded into the remaining Mark V and it quickly sped off. There was weeping and wailing on the ship that was overpowering. Parents grieved for their lost children and husbands grieved for their lost wives and all grieved for a couple of young soldiers who must have drowned as well. The ship was a literal mourning barge for all aboard.

As they approached the Chesapeake Bay Bridge with Annapolis on their left, their radar scanning console equipment picked up something menacing on the bridge nearby and began to sound an alarm. Judah took out his high powered infrared binoculars and went to see what it was. He spotted someone on the bridge

189

with a rocket launcher aimed directly at them.

"Captain, we need to take out the Bridge immediately!" Judah shouted.

"What are you talking about, Colonel? Do you know how many cars travel over that bridge?"

"Sir, someone is about to launch a rocket at us as soon as he gets a visual. They cannot pick us up on radar. Do it now!"

Captain Knowington took a deep breath and said a quick prayer as he fired a surface to surface rocket at the Chesapeake Bay Bridge just as Judah took evasive maneuvers at the same time. The surface to surface missile hit the bridge with a resounding explosion just as the man from Ultra fired his rocket. The missile demolished the part of the bridge that the man was standing on and his rocket shot upwards. Pieces of the bridge sailed skyward and came crashing down into the water of the Chesapeake Bay below. Judah adjusted the course of the Mark V to go under the bridge at the end which was still attached to the land at Kent Island. Military sirens began going off and Coast Guard and US Naval ships and aircraft soon descended on the area. Colonel Meire steered his Mark V and its woeful surviving seafarers to hide at the nearby Eastern Neck Island National Wildlife Refuge until the commotion subsided.

The night had been overcast with huge ominous thunderclouds that had sporadically burst into booming claps of thunder and lightning which had masked the activities of AZAZEL. Even when Lieutenant Gregor had exploded his craft inside the Beast it had registered on the ground as just another burst of lightning and thunder. No one had become particularly alarmed until the Chesapeake Bay Bridge had exploded. From that time on, there was a mass of Military and Coast Guard personnel all over the area.

"Control to Joshua, do you read me?" came a voice over the radio equipment.

"Yes, Control, we read you," Captain Knowington answered.

"Are you all right? I just was informed that the Chesapeake Bay Bridge was blown up."

"Is this a secure line, Control?"

"It should be, son, but one never really knows anymore."

"One fish is safe, the other was taken by the Beast. Gregor is dead and we have lost several others," Captain Knowington replied hesitantly. "We blew up the bridge!"

"Stop talking, Captain," Judah yelled. "How can you be sure that it is not Ultra?"

"It is Butrell, Judah, I recognize his voice!"

"Big deal, they could have faked it. Maybe he is one of them?"

"Joshua, proceed to the nest as directed."

"Where did the bogeyman on the bridge's errant arrow hit?" Judah asked.

"It landed in the marching field at the Naval Academy!"

"Control, who is the Lord of Lords and King of Kings?" Judah asked knowing that the enemy would not say the correct answer directly.

"It is Yeshua Hamashiach *(H.Jesus the Messiah)*, Jewboy!"

Judah nearly fell off his chair at the answer. He gave a thumbs up sign to Captain Knowington. It must be Butrell. He probably heard the Hebrew name of Jesus the Christ from General Desporte and Senator Jordan who had used it to witness to Judah, what seemed like years ago.

"Control, we have encountered both the Beast and the bogeyman on our journey here. How can we be sure that this area is safe and secure?"

"What choice do you have, Joshua?" Control answered. "Just continue to the nest as directed. I will do all that I can. By the way, your Pastor came by this afternoon. He wants to come see you."

"Pastor Calvin?" Judah asked startled.

"Yep, Calvin! God is still on the throne, Judah! Over and out!"

While hiding out at the Wildlife Refuge, Captain Knowington became increasingly concerned about the bedlam of activity that was happening all around them. After listening to the military channels, he wondered if they needed to move on before they were spotted or morning came.

"I think that we had better keep moving," he told Judah. "If we wait too long we will be spotted or morning will overtake us"

"But Captain, if we start moving now we will put ourselves directly in harm's way!"

"Butrell said that he would do what he could to protect us. What do you suggest, Judah?"

"I would say that we should turn ourselves into the authorities," Bertha interrupted once again. She ran up to the front of the Marc V and once again started waving her arms and causing a commotion. When Judah tried to calm her down, she grabbed him and they fell into the console triggering an event which they could not call back. Bertha's actions had set off another surface to surface missile. It left the Marc V and headed due west towards Washington DC. It would reach its target in about fifteen minutes, hardly time for a response. Judah immediately steered his craft back into the Intracoastal Waterway and headed North. When the SSM finally hit, all the assembled Military personnel in the area headed towards that location. By this time, Judah had the craft at Rock Hall heading North while hugging the coastline of the Eastern edge of the Chesapeake Bay along the Maryland shoreline.

"Well Ma, thanks!" Judah said to his mother in a frustrated manner. "Your accidental firing of a surface to surface missile did detract our pursuers, but I only pray that it doesn't hit any populated areas. It looks as though it was heading for the Capitol."

When the missile finally exploded, no one could tell where it had hit.

"So I blew up the White House," Bertha whined. "what have they done for us lately? All that we have been going through and where were they?"

"Maybe they wanted to kill us because I am a Jew, Ma?" Judah asked sarcastically.

191

"You might be right, tatalleh," Bertha answered shaking her head. "Maybe they thought that you had stolen this boat?"

"I thought that I wasn't a Jew anymore, Ma?" Judah laughed. "Gotcha!"

"Gotcha shmatcha!"

"And Mrs. Meire," Dawn chimed in, "how do you explain the capturing of our other ship by that flying saucer."

"I hate that black hellion!" she replied. "I don't know how or why, but I do know that these poor people lost their children and this poor man lost his wife. Where was your God this time? I don't understand how He lets His people just die and does nothing about it. I do believe in Hasatan but this yeshu character, I don't! This is a God that I am supposed to believe in? Big deal! No thanks! Forget it!"

"If you forget Him, He will forget you, Ma!" Judah replied seriously.

"So what? With His help, who needs enemies?"

"What are you talking about, Mrs. Meire," Dawn chimed in. "You have been saved from Hasatan twice."

"That was Judah, not God!"

"Who do you think enabled your son to battle the evil wiles of the enemy? It was God! Not only do you still deny Him but you also reject your son. God will finally get tired of trying to convince you of His existence and will turn you over to a reprobate mind!"

"A repro what?"

"Forget it, Ma! Maybe your are not destined to be one of God's children after all!" Dawn finally shouted as she turned around and walked away frustrated.

"Ma, God causes it to rain on the just and unjust alike," Judah explained painstakingly to his mother. "Sure, bad things happen to good people because we all have free will in a fallen, sinful world, but that doesn't mean that God is not right there with us. He is not there to stop us from suffering but to help us get through it. Sure, these people lost loved ones tonight, but the good news is that they will see them again in Heaven and spend Eternity with them. If you had died tonight I would never see you again. That is what pains me, Ma. I would have liked to have spent eternity with you and Abba."

" What about your Abba?" Bertha asked angrily.

"Well, Ma, only God knows," Judah replied, trying not to provoke her once again. "Look, Ma, at how God has used me to fight against that black beast. Aren't you proud? Can you believe? The God of Abraham, Isaac and Jacob reached down and chose this egotistical, prideful unbelieving Jew for His work!"

"I thought that you converted for that Shiksa?"

"No, Ma. She would not have married me unless I already believed like she did. My religious experience happened before we were married."

"It did? You never told me that!" Bertha replied somewhat shocked.

"Yeah, it did, Ma! God gave me visions and dreams. He chose me, I did not choose Him. As the song goes, 'He did not wait for me to call out to him, but he let me hear His voice calling me!' I fought it just as you are and most of our Jewish people have fought it. I did not become a Gentile, Ma, I became a real Jew. A Jew who believes that Yeshua is the fulfillment of the Tanakh. Did I ever quote you the Bible before?"

"Of course not, tatalleh. You never spoke of God or the Bible. You were a rational well educated Jewish mensh *(Y.admirable man)*. I have always been so proud of you."

"Nu? So, Ma, you should be even more proud of me now," Judah cried, "because I am being used by the God of our forefathers for his purpose. Do you understand that? I am so grateful to the Lord that He came to seek and save the lost like me. His amazing grace for a stiff necked Jew like me is a testament to His unyielding love. None of us deserves His love. We deserve the wrath of Hasatan, but God's loving gift of salvation is free for all those that believe!"

Bertha suddenly fell to her knees as she gazed upwards. Her face was illuminated with a bright radiance even though it was night and they were inside the craft.

"What is it, Ma?" Judah said as he got onto his knees beside her.

Bertha just sat there speechless staring at the source of the light and weeping. Dawn and the others in the boat got to their knees as well and began praying for Bertha. She appeared to be having an encounter with the King of Kings and Lord of Lords. Her weeping turned to wailing and she cried out, "I am so sorry for what I have done. So sorry for my rejection of You. So sorry for what I have called You over the years. Please forgive me, Yeshua, for I have sinned terribly against You. Please forgive me also for my sins against my son, Judah. I rejected him because he accepted You. Oy Gevalt *(Y Oh,help!)* God, please forgive me!"

Everyone in the crowded boat was so overcome by the religious experience of this bitter, hateful woman that they all began to cry and Praise God. He had poured out the Spirit of grace and supplication on this poor, wretched lost woman, and she had looked on Him whom she had pierced with her sins and she had weeped bitterly over Him like the bitter weeping over the death of an only son like her own Judah.

"Ma, you saw the Lord, didn't you?" Judah said as he grabbed her and held her tight.

"I did, tatalleh. I did. I saw His nail pierced hands and knew that it was Him."

"Thank You, Lord, for Your grace and mercy to this unworthy woman," Judah cried out in joy. "Salvation is not by works lest any man boast but only by Your grace and mercy. Bless You, Lord!"

"Wow, Judah," Dawn said in stunned amazement. "She experienced what the prophet Zechariah said in chapter 12, verse 10 would someday happen to all of the House of David. He will pour out the Spirit of grace and of supplication and they will see His nail-pierced hands and cry out as a mother would for her only son."

Judah and Dawn and Bertha all sat in the center of the boat and cried like newborn babies.

"I love you, Judah, and you, Dawn," Bertha said with a newfound smile on her face and glow in her cheeks. "Please forgive me for my annoying attitude and my meshugge actions."

"We love you too, Ma," Judah and Dawn replied hugging the frail white haired elderly woman.

"You know, Judah," Bertha began softly with a sweet smile on her face. "There is something about your father's death that I never told you."

"What was that, Ma?"

"As your father was wasting away from that cancer, the pain had grown unbearable. When the cancer had gone to his hip, he had to be kept on pain medication, but even that did not help all of the time. I sat at his bedside and cried out to God to help him but nothing happened. I cried out to Buddha but nothing happened. I cried out to all the gods that I knew about but nothing happened. Finally in desperation I cried out to Yeshua. If He was, who people said that He was, then let Him ease the pain of my poor Moshe. And you know what happened?"

"Jesus eased his pain?"

"Yes, tatalleh, yes! Your father had a strange look on his face and he smiled. His face was covered with a soft glow that radiated from it. I could tell that the pain was gone, but he just passed from this world soon afterwards, and I just ignored that incident. All I felt at the time was that the Yeshua had let him die"

"Ma, it sounds as though Abba was touched by the Lord before he died. Maybe he will be with us in Paradise for eternity?"

"I believe that he will, son," Bertha said as she began to cry. "You know that I blocked that incident out from my mind for years. I refused to accept the meaning of it until just now. I couldn't accept the fact that Abba had been touched by Yeshua. That is why I kept saying that he would turn over in his grave when he found out that you had accepted Yeshua and all that. I was blind to the truth and acted accordingly. Now that I have seen the Truth, I can accept the fact that your father most probably accepted Yeshua as his Lord and Savior before you or I did!"

"Isn't that just like Pops, Ma?" Judah laughed as he began to cry and hug his mother. "He always had to be the first at everything!"

"Joshua, your own errant arrow struck Patuxent Wildlife Research Center about 22 miles Northeast of Washington," Control suddenly interjected. "All is okay. Proceed immediately to the nest! You are good to go!"

Dr. Lazant and his colleagues had been whisked out of the New York City Police Department by a man from Ultra. He had driven them to John F. Kennedy Airport where they were put on a Military transport .

"Where are we going?" Dr. Lazant asked the man from Ultra as they boarded the transport.

"You are headed for Round Rock, Arizona, Sir," the man with dark glasses responded.

"Round, where?"

"You people need to disappear for a while until things cool down a bit. Besides, some old Navajo woman and her daughter there were visited by the Watchers. You guys need to talk with her."

Their transport headed for Albuquerque, New Mexico. On the way, Dr. Lazant was briefed about the encounter that occurred on the Navajo Reservation. This scenic area near the Four Corners was considered to be spiritual place by the indigenous people who lived there. It was where a Navajo woman and her mother had been visited by what they called traditional Navajo Deities. The daughter, a well respected tribal woman and her 96 year old mother had heard a loud noise outside their Hogan. When they had gone to the door, they found these two ancient male Navajo Deities. These Deities warned them that they were not saying their traditional prayers and they would thus lose their traditional ways.

The flight to Albuquerque was long and monotonous so everyone caught up on some needed sleep. Everyone except Dr. Lazant. He kept thinking about what had happened to Reverend Shea. If there were anybody that he felt understood exactly what was going on spiritually, it was Reverend Shea. Sure, he had been a Professor of Divinity at Harvard, but he had lectured around the world about the coming unity of all religions. How could he of all people, Dr. Lazant wondered, have slipped back into the one and only god of the Christians. He knew better. All in all, however, this strengthened Dr. Lazant's resolve to assist in the removal of these judgmental Christians. Nothing would ever change with them around. Once they were removed from the earth, a new global religious movement could break out which would lead to universal peace and unity. It would be the thousand years of millennial bliss.

When they landed in a private part of the Albuquerque International Airport, they were whisked once again into a waiting helicopter. They headed Northwest towards Arizona. They crossed the Continental Divide and marveled at the beautiful red and brown colors of the Southwest high desert region.. They traveled over the wide, majestic beauty of Canyon De Chelly and approached the Los Gigantes Buttes which rose over 6500 feet into the beautiful blue sky. When they finally landed a little over an hour after takeoff at a small spot on the Navajo Reservation near Round Rock, a couple of Navajo women were there to greet them.

All were taken into one of two eight sided hogans where a piping hot meal of mutton stew and traditional Indian fry bread awaited them.

"Please, everyone sit," Mrs. Begay said as she motioned the conference leaders into her home. She wore the traditional long skirt and squash blossom necklace. "We have been told that you people know of our traditional Navajo Deities."

"Yes, Ma'am, we do. We call them the Watchers," Dr. Lazant remarked politely.

"My mother and I saw them at our door. They told us that we were not praying to our traditional Gods but were instead praying to the God of the Christians and that was not good. We were losing our old ways and were losing our relationship with them."

It was evening by now and a fire roared in the Hogan. Everyone had feasted on the food provided and were thankful for the kind hospitality that they had been shown. Mrs. Begay and her 96 year old mother marveled at how much they looked like the man from Tibet. There were even some words from both of their languages that were the same. When they showed the man a sand painting, he smiled broadly and shook his head. They all felt a spiritual kinship with each other.

"You know, brothers and sisters, that a white buffalo has been found in Wisconsin," Lloyd Foot, the Ogala Sioux Medicine Man, relayed to his friends as they all sat in the Hogan of Mrs. Begay. "The arrival of a white buffalo is like the second coming of Christ. It is like finding Jesus in the manger. It will bring a purity of mind, body and spirit. There will be unity among all nations, black, red, yellow and white!"

"That is amazing, Brother Foot," Dr. Lazant continued. "We all seem to be moving very quickly toward the appearance of this so called Messiah. Most world religions speak of the concept of a Messiah that will usher in world peace. The Christians speak of Jesus, the Jews of the coming Mashiach, the Shiite Muslims speak of Imam Madhi, the Hindus speak of Kalki, the Buddhists speak of Maitreya, the Confucians speak of the True Man and the Zoroastrians speak of Saoshyant. We are to prepare the world for this upcoming time of true peace. What an awesome responsibility we all have. Just imagine! We have been hand selected to help the world leader achieve a world unified religion with which he can reach everyone without the problems of different religions or denominations; without any judgmental or condescending attitudes. What a blessing that time will be! And we are the vanguard of this upcoming world spiritual leader. AZAZEL will remove the Christians and then the real work will begin in earnest for world peace and unity. We must not be detracted by our setbacks. We must remain true to our task at hand. The enemy is all around us. We saw through our own Reverend Shea that he can twist and warp even the most committed resolve. We cannot ever let our guard down and we need to be in constant prayer."

"That's absolutely correct, Dr. Lazant! The Evangelical Christians need to be removed," Rabbi Ginsberg said sternly, "because as God says in Hosea 4:6, 'My people are destroyed for lack of knowledge. Because you have rejected knowledge I will also reject you from being my priest. Since you have forgotten the law of your God, I will also forget your children.' God has rejected these fanatics because of their lack of true knowledge and is ready to do Her thing with all of us. We shall help usher in the time of true peace and harmony when everyone will love and respect everyone else unconditionally. Isn't that what their own prophet Jesus preached? Too bad that they will not be around to see it fulfilled!"

"It is written in our great book the Bhagavad Gita," began the Hindu Priestess, "that whenever the Law declines and the purpose of life is forgotten, I am born to reestablish the law!' This so called Messiah is coming! We are the heralders of the arrival. We shall help the Messiah rule and reign for a thousand years."

"In our tradition," said the Moslem Imam, "it is written that, 'He in the beginning will be a poor stranger, unknown and uncared for. He will, however, defend himself with supreme knowledge'. This supreme knowledge is what the Watchers have. They have watched us for millennia and have seen us kill each other in the name of God. Now they will come and show us how to love each other. Without their help we are all destined to be destroyed by a flaming holocaust."

They all decided to go outside and sit under the beautiful clear sky of the Navajo Reservation. Without all the pollution or even the lights of the big city, the sky was so clear that one could see hundreds, thousands of stars.

"One can really see the beauty of Father Sky and Mother Earth up here!" Mrs. Begay Senior said with a smile. "Look how beautiful everything is. This is how the whole country was before the white man came and ravaged and raped and polluted sacred Mother Earth."

Everyone shook their head in agreement at the wisdom and insight of the old frail 96-year-old woman. Coffee was poured for those who wanted it and everyone took turns using the nearby out house. They then sat back down and resumed their discussion.

"Buddha stated that Maitrya, the bearer of true peace, will appear at the end of this millennium," the Representative of the Dalai Lama said. "And we are fast approaching that time. It is right around the corner."

"Yes, my brother, you are absolutely correct," the Hindu priestess interjected. "In December 1997, the sun, moon and seven planets lined up. That was fulfillment of a Hindu prophesy that says that at the time of this alignment, people will soon be entering the golden age, the age of Kalki. It is found in the Vishnu Purana. See, once again we are told that we are about to enter the golden age of true peace. Isn't it amazing that all of our traditions say the same thing?"

"Who is Kalki?" Dr. Lazant wanted to know.

"Kalki is the final incarnation of Vishnu who will bring righteousness upon the Earth. Buddha was the ninth incarnation of Vishnu about 2500 years ago."

"I know some Hopi medicine men," the younger Mrs. Begay said. "They also say that we are moving into a new Earth cycle. We all will be entering a new world."

"All of our traditions are cyclical," Forrest, the Wiccan woman began. "They entail birth, death and rebirth just like the Earth. Spring, Summer, Fall, Winter and then spring once again. All of your traditions speak of the entire universe being born, living, then dying and finally being reborn again. That is the problem with Christianity. It is linear. Birth, life, death and that's it. They miss the grandeur of cosmic regeneration."

"Once to die and then the judgment is what the Bible says," the man from the World Council of Churches said. "But even Jesus said, before Abraham was I am and John the Baptist said he was Elijah?"

"As the prophet Isaiah said," Rabbi Ginsberg laughed, "'Woe to those who call

197

evil good and good evil. Who substitute darkness for light and light for darkness. Who substitute bitter for sweet and sweet for bitter. Woe to those who are wise in their own eyes and clever in their own sight'. Woe to all those judgmental Christians who are about to suffer for their lack of trust in God!"

"That is why the seer Nostradamus had his body buried upside down," Dr. Lazant said with a chuckle. "He warned people not to call evil good and good evil! As the prophet Isaiah said, 'and the work of righteousness will be peace and the service of righteousness, quietness and confidence forever. Then my people will live in a peaceful habitation and in secure dwellings and in undisturbed resting places.' But this process, this move towards universal peace will not be a easy road. We have already seen the increase of floods, earthquakes, famines and pestilence. But these are but birthpangs of the coming world leader of peace whatever we choose to call him or her."

"These Navajo women saw the deities, the white buffalo has appeared, the Buddhists wait for Maitreya, the Hindu's seek Kalki, the Confucians long for the true man, the Zoroastrians seek Saoshyant and the Jews wait for the Mashiach. The Christians think that it is their Jesus that will return but how is that possible when he died on the cross. If he wasn't powerful enough to rescue himself from that, then how can he be powerful to rise from the dead and come back to Earth and bring about true peace?" the Ogala Sioux Medicine man, Lloyd Foot remarked as Mrs. Begay's husband passed around a pipe filled with the hallucinogenic peyote.

Everyone became very disoriented as an altered state of consciousness took them over. They all began to pray and to chant out loud. The perfectly quiet and still surroundings began to reverberate with their chanting. The coyotes and the wolves began to howl back at them and it created an eerie melody that shook the entire area.

Suddenly a silver Dodge Ram Pickup barrelled into the area. A young man jumped out of the truck and ran to his grandparents and great grandmother.

"What are you doing?" Walter yelled out. "I read in the *Gallup Independent* that you had seen the Holy men. And I could hear you chanting for twenty miles away. No, No! How many times have I told you. Those are demons, not holy people. And Grandpa, are you using that peyote again? It just opens a door for Satan to come in!"

"This is my Christian grandson, Walter," Mrs. Begay responded with a laugh. "Those crazy Christians have warped his mind and he no longer respects his elders or our traditional ways."

"Hey son!" Dr. Lazant said harshly as he grabbed the young man by the arm. "Shouldn't you show respect for your grandparents?"

"Not when they are so deluded by Satan. And who are you all? It looks like the UN here. Are any of you Christians?" Walter replied as he pulled away from Dr. Lazant. Walter was about twenty years old and wore a shirt emblazoned with the letters WWJD.

"We are friends of your grandparents that represent religions from around the world," Rabbi Ginsberg said. "The man right next to you is a friend of the Dalai Lama. He came all the way here just to see your grandparents. Aren't you impressed?"

"Well, next time you see him, Sir, say Hello Dalai for me," the young man said with a laugh. "I am only impressed so to speak by fellow Christians! Are any of you Christians?"

"I am a member of the World Council of Churches!"

"I am a theologian from the Vatican!"

"Let me ask it another way," the bright discerning young man countered. "Has any one of you recognized Jesus Christ as his or her Lord and Savior and turned their life over to Him completely?"

Everyone just chuckled and shook their heads at the young man's arrogance to question them

"Just as I thought. I don't know why you all are here unless it was to see the demons, but I would advise you all to go on home. The freak show is over."

Nobody was really listening anymore because the peyote had begun to take control of their faculties and they began to hallucinate.

"What does the WWJD stand for?" Forrest laughed with a hideous smile on her face.

"What would Jesus do!" Walter yelled. "If He were here, He would cast off all your demons once and for all. You would be free of them!"

"We are all here, Walter," Dr. Lazant began, "to herald the coming of the true Messiah of peace and love. We all call Him by different names but we all agree that He will bring the world a unity of peace and a one world religion."

"You are not talking of the return of Christ but the advent of the Antichrist. According to Scripture, he will fool the world into believing in a seven year period of peace but then in the middle of it all hell will break loose. This will be the great tribulation and it will culminate at the battle of Armageddon when Jesus will return. He will not come as a lamb this time, but as a lion to judge the nations with an iron rod! You people are not part of the solution but you seem to a significant part of the problem."

"Oh shut up, Walter," his Grandfather finally yelled as he grabbed the boy and put him back in his truck. "It was nice seeing you again, but it is time to go!"

"You cannot let him go now, Grandpa," Mrs. Begay shouted. "It is pitch black outside and he has a long drive back to Tuba City. Let him stay the night."

"NO! Ever since he begin going to that Bible College, he has become even more disrespectful. He has become a real apple!"

"What is an apple?" Dr. Lazant asked curiously.

"Red on the outside and white on the inside," Grandpa said as he was becoming a little woozy from the peyote. "And he has become a Bible thumper on top of that!"

"It's all right, Grandma, I'd better be going," Walter said softly. "If I get tired, I'll just pull off the road and use my camper shell. I am going to pray for all of you though. You are greatly deceived. I'll plead the blood of Jesus over you."

As Walter sped off, his Great-grandmother lamented about how those Christians were stealing their children, making them into White people. The Deities were correct, she said, that people were no longer following traditional ways and they needed to be praying to them, not this white Jesus.

"That is why we need to remove these pesky Christians," Dr. Lazant reiterated. "Nothing can happen in a meaningful way until they are removed!"

Grandpa Begay invited the men into the traditional sweatlodge in the Hogan nearby. Rocks had been heated to a high temperature and water was thrown onto them creating a hot mist that would sweat out any impurities. The men removed their outer clothes, put on towels that were provided, and prepared to enter the sweatlodge Hogan.

"What about us females?" Rabbi Ginsberg demanded as did the Wiccan woman Forrest and the Shiva Priestess.

"Traditional Navajo sweatlodges are not coed," Grandpa replied sternly. "There are sweatlodges for women but we do not have one."

"But our sweatlodges are coed, Grandpa," the Ogala Sioux Medicine Man Lloyd Foot spoke up.

"Well this is not Sioux country and neither is it that so called New Age equality garbage," Grandpa said emphatically. "Here, men go into the sweatlodge. You women are free to pray outside if you wish!"

"That is mighty Navajo of you," Rabbi Ginsberg smarted off. "Even you spiritual people are still hung up on sex and gender politics. Imagine only men able to commune with a female deity?"

The men were already flying high due to the peyote and now they were subjected to a sauna of high temperature. Most just entered a wakened dreamstate. Meanwhile the women bayed at the crescent moon with loud chanting and drug induced laughter.

# XV

Judah steered the lone remaining Mark V and its crowded, wet and traumatized passengers towards the homing beacon at Spesutie Island. Just as he passed the Susquehanna National Wildlife Refuge at the southern edge of the Aberdeen Proving Ground, the Mark V was intercepted by a strange looking craft which had not registered on radar. It was just about dawn and they were flagged down by a group of military personnel motioning for them to pull over. Their military insignia read, Aberdeen Military Intelligence. The craft looked like an inverted V.

"That is the Sea Shadow that we saw docked at the Naval Base at Norfolk," Captain Knowington said with a smile. "It is an Advanced Research Project Agency Prototype developed with Lockheed Martin. It is mostly automatic and has a great signature control. That is why we did not pick it up on radar. It also uses electric diesel engines which are very quiet. Wow, what a neat looking ship!"

"Cool your jets, Captain Courageous! You are not trying to sell me the ship! How can we be sure that they are not from Ultra?" Judah warned as he drew his revolver. "You are mighty naive, Captain!"

"Please identify yourselves!" Judah yelled at the men from Aberdeen Military Intelligence. "Why are you following us? Who ordered you to pull us over? We are not going to pull over until we get some answers. And I mean right now!" Judah screamed as he cocked his revolver and aimed it at the head of the leading officer.

The Mark V quickly turned around and headed back into the Intracoastal Waterway. It sped as fast as it could under the still cover of darkness past Spetsikie Island and right between Havre de Grace and Perryville into the Susquehanna River and fast approached the Pennsylvania border. The beautiful yet stealthy angular Sea Shadow turned and headed back south down the Chesapeake Bay's Intracoastal Waterway and under the Chesapeake Bay Bridge Tunnel into the Atlantic Ocean.

As the Mark V crossed into Pennsylvania and headed toward Harrisburg on the narrow Susquehanna, it suddenly picked up a powerboat on its tail. Above it in the cloudy sky appeared the black disc. The Mark V headed Northeast, and as it passed Northumberland at the fork in the river, a light beam from the black disc tried to grab hold of it. The boat shook violently but was, at least for the time being, able to ward off the seizure by its speed and zigzagging course.

The speedboat tried to apprehend the fast moving Mark V. but it was traveling at over 50 knots on the winding river and was not easy to catch. Danville, Espy and Mocanaqua were passed as the sun broke the horizon. The black craft quickly disappeared. The chase went on for hours all through the beautiful Susquehanna River Country of Eastern Pennsylvania. The Mark V kept its lead but it was losing ground to the approaching speedboat. As they neared Tukhannock, a slow barge appeared in the river. The Mark V had to slow down considerably and the speedboat nearly ran into its aft bulkhead. A machine gun mounted on its bow raked the Mark V with high caliber shells and a couple of shattered ,dismembered arms and legs flew out of the craft into the water

Slowly the Mark V maneuvered around the barge with its stern all shot up and taking on water. It limped across the border into New York. The speedboat pulled alongside as it passed Oswego and an incendiary bomb was thrown on board as the speedboat raced away. The Mark V burst into flames and quickly sank, scattering severed heads and torsos all over the murky water. The Mark V had sunk near Endicott, New York carrying all aboard to a watery grave.

Dr. Lazant and his colleagues remained at the hogan of Mr. and Mrs. Begay for several days. When the helicopter had dropped them off, they had also dropped off sleeping bags and food supplies. It was a time of rest and relaxation for the entire group. As Dr. Lazant sipped his morning tea, his phone began to ring.

"How you can you have a phone that rings here in the middle of nowhere?" Rabbi Ginsberg asked befuddled.

"It is a satellite phone," Dr. Lazant answered as he put it to his ear. "It is the latest technology. An iridium hand held satellite phone. Pretty neat, huh?"

"Boys sure love their toys!" Forrest quipped.

"Yes, this is Dr. Lazant!" he said into the phone.

"Dr. Lazant," the voice on the other end began, "all of the members of the Joshua Brigade are dead."

"All of those fanatic Christians? Terrific! Judah was among them? You are certain?"

"Yes Sir, we are. Judah was piloting the craft. We saw his body! All of them are dead. We will pick you guys up at 1500 hours tomorrow."

"Sounds great to me," Dr. Lazant said as he smiled to everyone around him. "Did you actually identify his body?"

"Dr. Lazant," the voice scolded on the other end. "It is not for you to question us. Remember what happened to your buddy, Reverend Shea?"

"I was just told that all of the Christians trying to thwart our plans have been eliminated," Dr. Lazant said to all those now standing around him. "We can proceed to pave the way for a new world religious order now without interference from those zealots."

"Who was that you were talking to?" the man from the World Council of Churches asked.

"Some friends that we have in the government, man! Relax! Everything is going according to plan!"

202

"Did they personally identify Judah's body?" Forrest asked curiously. "I heard you ask them."

"Bug off it, you old witch!" Dr. Lazant snapped back. "Everything is moving along fine. Judah is dead!"

"Cool it, Pops! You needn't use that condescending patriarchal tone when you say the word witch. We have always been around, and we will be a part of the new world order, you know. So watch your mouth!" Forrest replied as she moved right in his face.

"How soon is this abduction going to take place, Doc?" Rabbi Ginsberg asked, trying to defuse the situation.

"AZAZEL said that it will be sometime in September," Dr. Lazant replied.

"Wow, that is only a couple of months away," Rabbi Ginsberg said with a startle. "What a New Year's present to get rid of those zealous Christians! La Shana Tova! Happy New Year! Just imagine! A world without Christians. That hasn't happened for 2000 years!"

"Wait a minute, Rabbi," the theologian from the Vatican interjected, "there will be Christians like us and those from the WCC. It will be just those narrow minded, judgmental evangelical Protestants that will be gone. We peace loving Christians will still be here to bring in the new thousand years of peace and love."

"Well, excuse me!" the Rabbi laughed. "A loving, accepting non judgmental Christian just seems like an oxymoron to me!"

When the men from Aberdeen Military Intelligence had been stymied from boarding the Mark V by Judah, Deputy Director Butrell had appeared in all his six foot eight inch gawkiness.

"Judah, everything is kosher, son!"

"Director Butrell! What a pleasant sight that you are for sore eyes," Judah had replied with a big smile on his face.

"Listen, Judah, we do not have much time. You all need to board the Sea Shadow immediately. Our intelligence reports tell us that Ultra is right on your tail. We will take the Mark V away from here while you can escape."

"God Bless you, Sir!" Judah had once again smiled as he began to hustle everyone into the adjoining craft. "You have been with us all along! Sorry for my doubt, Sir! By the way, where are we headed?"

"You will be taken out into the Atlantic until things cool down, but then you will be brought back to Aberdeen as planned. We have a complete alternative base camp for your operations there as Senator Jordan and General Desporte had planned. Godspeed to us all!"

After the weary inhabitants of the Mark V had been transferred to the Sea Shadow a couple of soldiers had taken their place. One looked very much like Judah with his tall, muscular build and close cropped blond hair and green eyes. He was wearing a uniform identical to Judah. They also had filled the Mark V with a couple dozen very realistic looking crash dummies from the Proving Ground. They had sure looked real enough all crammed together in the hull of the craft.

When Ultra had destroyed the Mark V all those crash dummies had been blown to bits making the event look real enough. Unfortunately the two real soldiers from Aberdeen Military Intelligence had been really killed as well. The body floating on the water looked just like that of Judah.

The Sea Shadow even though it was one hundred and sixty four feet in length was designed to operate with a crew of only ten. It was as automatic as possible. Actually there were only five crew on board plus Director Butrell since they could and did make use of the soldiers that came on board  All of the people received clean dry clothes and a hot meal for which they were very thankful.

"Sir," the young soldier who had lost his children pleaded with Director Butrell, "could you please send out a search and rescue team to look for my lost children? I know that the odds that they are still alive is minimal, but I would sure appreciate it. Maybe they made it to James Island after all?"

"Sure, I will do that immediately, son," Director Butrell replied. "Did anyone else lose a loved one?"

The rest of those who had lost wives raised their hands as well.

"We also lost a couple of soldiers, Sir," Judah began, knowing that hours had passed and the chance for survival was indeed minimal.

Everyone suddenly began to cry for those poor unfortunate people who were lost. They all grabbed a hold of each other and comforted one another. The trauma of the night before suddenly resurfaced in all its horror.

"It's all right. They are all safe now," Bertha said softly as everyone stared at her in wide eyed amazement. "They are with Yeshua now. I know it."

"How can you know that, Mrs. Meire?" the young soldier asked frustratedly. "Not too long ago you were a non believing Jew. You hated all of us. Now you are the expert. That is just like you Jews. You think that you know everything better than everyone else."

"Nu? All I know is what Hashem has told me in my heart. I am not bragging on myself, only on the Father. They all are safe and secure in His arms now. Trust me!" Bertha said as she embraced the young man. "God loves you and your children. They are in a better place. Do you honestly believe that Yeshua would seek and save a poor old, bitter soul like me and let your children perish? No, no, no!"

The young man began to weep, and he fell to his knees right in front of Bertha with his wife. The comforting of the Holy Spirit as evidenced by the old woman really touched their hearts.

Judah watched his mother in wide eyed astonishment. He could not believe what he was seeing and hearing coming from his mother's lips. The hard, bitter edge was off, and a new soft glow emanated from her. He went over and hugged her and began to cry like a newborn child. Dawn came over also and joined in the celebration of the work that the Lord had done.

"Your Mom's unbelievable transformation is proof enough for me as to the concept that we all are reborn as new creatures in Christ," Deputy Director Butrell said with a tear in his eye as well. "I had always heard that she was as stiff necked and as hard hearted as they come. Now look at her. She is born again, a new woman for Christ. Praise God. You know, every time I think that this mission is a little beyond the pale of belief, the Lord reassures me with His actions. For every General Desporte and Senator Jordan and Major Kole that has gone home to Him there arises a Judah and a Bertha. You know, Judah, I will continue to assist you in any way that I can to overcome AZAZEL. We cannot let him complete his mission!"

"Thanks, Sir," Judah replied with a smile. "I can also see that we are doing the right thing for the Lord by His actions towards my mother. What a blessing. I could die today and be assured that I would spend eternity with her and my Dad. What a peace that brings. I agree also that we need to continue to battle AZAZEL. I feel that it will be acting rather soon. The heat on us has been turned on high so the time must be short."

After a day of rest and relaxation the Sea Shadow headed at night back up the Intracoastal Waterway of the Chesapeake Bay and docked at Spesutie Island at around 500 hours. Everyone was taken by a closed military transport to an secret underground fortified bunker complex on the Proving Ground.

"Sir," Judah painstakingly asked Director Butrell as they began the elevator descent to their new subterranean compound, "how can you guarantee security for us when so many men have been involved in this process and transfer? I hate to be so pushy, but you have got to admit that a lot of people have been involved in this. How can we be sure of their allegiances?"

"That is a good question, Judah! I hand picked these men from the waiting list for the Joshua Brigade. All are Bible believing Christians. Although we can never be sure of anything around here nowadays, I feel certain that we picked good men. By the way, all of them have assisted in your escape from New Petra all along the way and all will join you here. A couple of them even gave their lives in the Mark V to a hot pursuit by Ultra when the boat was blown up."

"Oh, my, they did?" Judah replied. "I'm sorry for even asking, Sir!"

"That is all right, son," Butrell responded with a pat on Judah's back. "Just get that no good AZAZEL for all of us!"

The underground bunker was several stories below a corner of the Aberdeen Proving Ground complex. It was equipped with all the same high tech communications and satellite capabilities of New Petra. After everyone got settled and they had some breakfast of frozen bagels and orange juice, the three men sat at in a conference room enclosed by large consoles and computer monitors and drank cups of steaming black coffee.

"Explain to me, Judah, one more time for the record what exactly you are trying to do here," Director Butrell asked as he put his chin on his hand and peered directly at Judah.

"Well, Sir," Judah began with a deep sigh. "It has come to our attention that AZAZEL is going to attempt to abduct the Christians off of the planet in the near future. We have been trying to either thwart that objective if at all possible, or if that is not possible, to prepare a message for the world when we are gone letting them know that their supposed saviors that will appear in our absence are not their rescuers but their enslavers."

"You know, Judah, that we have known of these extraterrestrials and their UFOs for decades. Ever since Roswell, we have monitored their activities on a top secret basis. We created Ultra fifty years ago to do just that, and they have pretty much operated in the shadows unknown to any of us. We created a Frankenstein, I now believe. We wanted to hide the truth from the American public until we could figure out what to do and thus prevent widespread panic. Over the years, I have become increasingly concerned that Ultra has become compromised by the very aliens that they were created to monitor! That is why Senator Jordan and General Desporte came to me several years ago to create a extra governmental group, the Joshua Brigade, to fight this menace. To be honest with you, it took me a long time to even accept the existence of so called extraterrestrials, but to think that they are actually demons of Satan's cohort was a little too much. I respected those men so much that I initially went along without really believing. I am after all just a good old Methodist farm boy from Iowa. I was raised in the Church, but I never really understood spiritual warfare. Funny that it took a Jew to teach this Christian about Satan!"

"Don't feel bad, Sir," Judah laughed. "He had me deceived all of my life. I am the last person who one would ever have thought would be here right now doing this work for the Lord. As the popular television show says,' the truth is out there' but it is more strange than even they could imagine. Just think about it! The government created a top secret group, Ultra, to study the hard reliable data on extraterrestrials that began flowing in around 1947 as a result of the Roswell incident, but even they were fooled by these so-called extraterrestrials, because they were not from another planet or solar system or galaxy but they were actually demonic fallen angels thrown out of the first heaven with Satan by the Lord. These so-called aliens are actually demonic entities bent upon the enslavement of mankind to their wishes. This dwarfs any movie about alien invasion. They do not want only our planet, but they want our souls as well."

"Judah, what is the significance of the work that Dr. Lazant is doing to this picture?" Butrell continued. "We just picked up a satellite phone call that he received in the Arizona mountains telling him that the Joshua Brigade had been eliminated. His group sure seems to be overly interested in you guys!"

"Dr. Lazant is the one, as you know, that first made contact with the angel AZAZEL at his Institute. He and Reverend Shea have contacts with religious people all over the world. They want to create a new world unified religion once the Christians are removed. They have strong ties to the Vatican and to the United

Nations. Captain Knowington shot a rocket into the Institute attempting to kill those men but they were rescued by AZAZEL."

"I sure did!" Captain Knowington interjected. "Then I was captured by AZAZEL and taken into his craft. I was never so frightened in all my life, Sir. I have fought in wartime but this spiritual warfare is a whole different animal. I didn't know what to do. I also never could understand what fallen angels were like. I went along with General Desporte and Senator Jordan because they were good Christian men, but I honestly was a little skeptical too. But when I saw Judah come to my rescue wearing the full Armor of the Lord and carrying the Sword of the Spirit, I believed in a heartbeat!"

"Judah, you are not going to believe this, but Reverend Shea is dead!" Butrell said matter of factly.

"Oh, too bad!" Judah quipped with a chuckle. "Now he is back together again with his boy, Stephen, in the fires of hell!"

"His body was apparently crucified on a door and driven through a table at the United Nations!"

"What?!" Judah replied surprised.

"It happened at a meeting of those religious people. And also, those there, including Dr. Lazant, said that you did it!" Butrell remarked watching for Judah's reaction. "Can you believe that, Judah?"

"How could I do it when I was in transit to here? Praise God, though, about Reverend Shea. I'll bet that it wasn't what he was doing wrong that got him crucified, but obviously it was what he was doing right. Oh my God, someone actually crucified that poor man right in front of them. How horrible! It must have been AZAZEL. If he were martyred in front of those New Agers, then he must have confessed Jesus Christ as Lord. Now why would I crucify a man? It makes no good sense, but evil is like that. AZAZEL didn't crucify Shea, Judah did it. It's nuts! Do the authorities believe them?"

"Captain Braden of the Potomac Police Department and Captain Barcellini of the NYPD did not have any evidence tying you to the crime, and then when Ultra appeared and removed the body and the evidence they were even more skeptical."

"I cannot believe that Reverend Shea died like that," Judah lamented. "I knew that I had seen some spark of life in those dead eyes on the craft. He must have finally seen through the seduction of evil, the seduction of domination that has made those others drunk with power. I just hope that he confessed his sins before he died. Actually, you know what? I feel that he did. I really do, deep down in my gut. Praise God!"

"Gentlemen, you might be aware of this but we have observed large triangular shaped ships in the heavens over the last several years," Director Butrell continued. "In fact they have been evident worldwide. Our colleagues in agencies across the globe have been reporting the increased activity of so called UFOs. If you are correct about the abduction of Christians then that would make sense. But what will happen to the social fabric, the social order, Judah, if suddenly millions of people are removed. There will be panic and fright for those left behind. First of all, every Christian airline pilot or train engineer or automobile driver will suddenly leave a hurtling missile behind. Christian surgeons and firemen and policemen and bus drivers and nuclear power plant managers will all leave their work behind. What a mess."

"That is why and how the fallen angels will take control. I believe that the sky will be filled with UFOs on that day and everyone left behind will be told that the Christians, at least the fanatical evangelical Christians had to be removed before our planet could evolve to a new, higher level of planetary consciousness. A new world unified religion will be initiated." Judah said seriously.

"Does it say anything in the Bible about all of this?" Butrell asked Judah with a look of concern on his face.

"I suppose so," Judah answered, "but I for sure am no expert. What happened to Pastor Calvin? I thought that he was going to meet us here?"

"He was, but because of your delay and change of route, we decided to hold him over at the Company for a couple of days. He wanted to go and visit the Holocaust Museum. I'll go and get him this morning. He was very anxious to see you, Judah," Butrell said quietly.

"You better search him very carefully for implants, Sir!" Judah said angrily. "I cannot believe that you left him free to roam through Ultra territory unguarded. He could come here and compromise the entire mission. Hellooo?!"

"He is being watched, Judah, but I will make sure that he is clean before I bring him here just in case."

"I also think that I need to go and challenge AZAZEL once again," Judah said emphatically. "I need one more attempt to try and thwart his plans. I need to avoid Ultra however. They just want to eliminate me. I've got to figure out a way to attract AZAZEL. Maybe I could use my mother. AZAZEL knows that he can get to me through her. He doesn't know that she is now a believer."

"You cannot use your mother for bait, Judah!" Captain Knowington reprimanded angrily. "She is your mother, for Godsake! What is the matter with you, boy?"

"We have so little time, Sir! We need to use everything at our disposal. Look, she is saved now so the worst that could happen would be that she would go home to be with the Lord."

"You Jews are really something!"

"Let her and I go with you to DC to pick up Pastor Calvin. I'll bet that AZAZEL finds us and tries to abduct my mother."

"But what about Ultra? If they find you, they will kill you!" Captain Knowington interjected. "It seems mighty dangerous and reckless to me, especially with your mother involved!"

"Let's see exactly how Pastor Calvin is doing," Deputy Director Butrell said as he turned around and turned on one of the monitors. He spoke into the microphone

208

and asked to be fed the satellite surveillance data on the Pastor. It was now nearly 1130 hours.

"You can track him through the streets of DC?" Judah asked jubilantly as he swung around in front of the monitor as well. "There is not much that escapes you guys is there, Sir?"

"No Judah, not very much at all! Look, there he is standing in front of the U.S. Holocaust Memorial Museum talking to that elderly woman. See those men around him? They are ours! We not only have him under satellite surveillance, but we are also maintaining a close physical surveillance as well. If Pastor Calvin wants to see you so bad, Judah, then he must be considered to be a target for Ultra or AZAZEL as well. Anybody that associates with you is automatically a target of the enemy in my mind."

"Then why did you let him walk all over DC?" Judah asked again bewildered.

The elderly lady handed the Pastor a camera and seemed to be motioning for him to take her picture in front of the Museum. The traffic light had slowed the oncoming cars so she waved him back into Raoul Wallenberg Place Road. She kept pushing him back with her little frail hand until he was standing on a manhole cover. It suddenly, violently imploded beneath his feet, and he fell into the dark sewer below.

"Oh my God!" Judah yelled, "look what has happened!"

Director Butrell immediately contacted his agents who were already moving to see what could be done.

"Go and help Pastor Calvin," he shouted into the microphone. "One of you get me that old lady!"

The two plainclothes agents looked all around but the elderly lady had vanished. They ran into the street which was now full of speeding traffic. They could not get to the manhole. Just as they were about to dodge the oncoming cars to make it there, one of the cars ran over the hole and got stuck in it. The men ran up to the car and motioned for the driver to back up but his car had blown a tire on the gaping twisted metal shrapnel that had been the manhole. Frantically, the agents tried to move the car. It was a sport utility vehicle and was too heavy to lift out of the hole. Precious time was going by and nothing could be done. The driver of the Suburban had also vanished.

"Look, men, you have got to get to the Pastor before either he dies or they usher him away," Butrell yelled to them. "Ultra probably planned this whole thing. I just saw the driver running away. Watch out, the whole car may be booby trapped!"

Just as he said that, the Suburban exploded, killing the two agents instantly.

"Oh God," Director Butrell shouted into the microphone to his men at the CIA, "I need some men at the Holocaust Museum ASAP! I've got three men down. Bring a medical team also. NOW!"

In a few minutes, a Hummer filled with Company men pulled up. They rammed the still burning wreckage of the Suburban off the manhole. One of them jumped into the jagged hole and found the badly burned body of Pastor Calvin. One of his legs had been blown off and the other was badly mangled.

"Director, Butrell," the agent said as they brought Pastor Calvin out of the hole and were placing him into the Hummer. "This man is badly injured. His legs have been blown to bits and he is in shock. He has lost a lot of blood."

"Transport him immediately to Bethesda!" Butrell commanded. "I will meet you there!"

The scene was being inundated by civilian passersby and the sound of sirens rang out all over. The Hummer left the crime scene, transporting the two dead agents also, as quickly as possible. The medical personnel in the group attempted to stop the rash of bleeding and stabilize the Pastor while transporting him to Bethesda Naval Hospital. The driver put a blue light on the top of the Hummer and used a low level siren to ward off anyone in his path. He went back North on Raoul Wallenberg Place and turned East on Independence Avenue until he got to N.14th St NW and then headed North out of the area.

"Let me come with you, Sir," Judah pleaded. "I need to find out what he wanted to tell me."

"Forget it! Ultra will probably be waiting for you there. They set up this entire scenario. I'm certain of it," Director Butrell lamented. "You were right, Judah, I should never have let him go into DC!"

"Yeah, and they probably put a bug in his neck as well, Judah," Captain Knowington said emphatically. "They want all of us, but they really want you the most, Judah. If AZAZEL cannot defeat you with his spiritual missiles, they want to kill you with real bullets. You are a thorn in their sides."

"But I need to know what the Pastor wanted to tell me," Judah said anxiously. "He came out of hiding and risked his life and limb to tell me something important. I need to know what that is!"

"I'll tell you what, Judah," Butrell said as he headed to the elevator. "I'll wear a mike and you will know everything that I say to him and everything that he says to me. Sit right here and you can also ask any questions that you like. All right?"

"Uh, all right, Boss, thanks!'

Deputy Director Butrell was handed some electronic surveillance equipment as he headed for the elevator, and he quickly put it on.

"I want you to fix it so I can transmit to Judah and he can communicate with me," he yelled to one of the men standing there. "Is that clear?'

"Yes, Sir, it will be done!"

"And I want a chopper waiting for me as soon as I get topside!"

"It will be done, Sir!"

As soon as Deputy Director Butrell stepped out of the elevator shaft onto the ground of the Aberdeen Proving Ground he could see a chopper heading his way. It landed near him and he ran over to it. He instructed the pilot to fly him to Bethesda Naval Hospital. The nearly thirty minute flight time moved very quickly as Director Butrell watched them first skirt past Baltimore and then head directly over Patuxent Wildlife Research Center where the errant missile from Judah's Mark V had caused so much consternation. They crossed over beautiful Silver Springs, Maryland and landed on the Helipad atop of the Hospital.

"Do you want me to wait for you, Sir?" the pilot asked.

"No, you can leave, Lieutenant, but do not go back to Aberdeen. Fly to Stuart field at West Point and wait for future orders. Tell no one where you have been. Tell them at the Point that Director Butrell authorized you to land there!"

"Okay, Sir!"

Butrell headed into the Hospital and was notified by his headset that Pastor Calvin was still in surgery. He waited in the recovery room for him to be brought in.

"You cannot wait here, Sir," the big, black Recovery Room Nurse scolded him and tried to remove him.

"Oh yes I can, Ma'am!"

"Who you think that you are?" the Nurse replied. "I'll call security!"

"I am the Deputy Director of the Central Intelligence Agency, Ma'am. I am the ultimate security and I can go wherever I want!" he replied emphatically. "What do you know of the condition of the Pastor?"

"He is a Pastor?" she replied obviously upset. "I heard that it was very serious. He was just hanging on to life. I thought that you were such a big spyman. Didn't you know that?"

After a couple of hours, Pastor Calvin was wheeled into the recovery room. His attending surgeon was at his side.

"How is he doing, Doc?" Butrell asked as he flashed his CIA ID in the Doctor's face.

"He is stable now but he has suffered extensive trauma to his legs. I could only save one of them at the knee. The other was lost to the hip."

"Will he survive, Dr. Parker?" Butrell asked looking at the Doctor's name tag.

"We will wait and see how his body responds. He is no kid, you know!"

"I need to interrogate him as soon as he regains consciousness, Doc!"

"I wouldn't recommend that, Sir. He needs to relax and let the healing process take its course. He doesn't need any more trauma. He has been through a great deal already!" Dr.Parker shook his head.

"It is a matter of National Security, Doc. I'm sorry but this man may hold the key to saving millions of lives. I must talk to him ASAP."

"Fine, but I will need you to sign a release form. I don't want his family to come back and sue us for negligence," the Doctor replied. "How can a middle-aged Pastor be involved in National Security?"

"If I told you, Doc, I would have to kill you and your nurse, so keep all of this hush, hush. Okay?"

"Sure, Sir, sure!" the Doctor said nervously.

211

Deputy Director Butrell waited another two hours for the Pastor to regain consciousness. When he did, he was right there to interrogate him knowing full well that Ultra was probably listening.

"Pastor, this is Mike Butrell, how are you feeling?" he whispered into the Pastor's ear.

"Haapaso," Pastor Calvin moaned through the tubes in his mouth and throat.

"What did you say?" Butrell asked as he strained to hear what the Pastor was trying to say.

"Harr... pazo, com... ing soon," Pastor Calvin softly whispered.

"What is Harpazo?" Butrell asked shaking his head.

"Setember," he moaned softly again.

"Are you trying to say September?" Butrell repeated confused.

He nodded affirmatively!

"Harpazo September?" Butrell asked bewildered.

"Tumpets"

"Did you say trumpets?"

"Yesss!" he said softly as he nodded his head.

"Harpazo, September, trumpets?"

He shook his head in agreement.

"Butrell!" Judah asked as he listened to the conversation. "September is about the time of the Jewish New Year when the Shofar is blown. Ask him if he is talking about Rosh Hashanah?"

"Are you speaking of the Jewish New Year, Rosh Hashanah?" Butrell whispered into his ear.

Pastor Calvin nodded affirmatively

"Ask him if that is when AZAZEL is planning to abduct the Christians?" Judah asked.

"Is that when you think that AZAZEL will abduct the Christians?" Butrell whispered.

"No! No! Harpazo. Harpazo!" Pastor Calvin moaned as he became very distressed and agitated and slipped from consciousness.

"Nurse, go get me the Doctor, right now!" Butrell demanded sternly as he felt the back of Pastor Calvin's neck.

As Doctor Parker reentered the room, Director Butrell put his finger over his lips to warn the Doctor not to speak. Butrell wrote on a piece of hospital stationary that he had found that there was an electronic implant in the Pastor's neck that needed to be removed as soon as possible. The Doctor shook his head negatively and started to speak but Butrell immediately stopped him from doing so. He brought the Doctor over to the Pastor's bedside and guided his hand to the implant. The Doctor was surprised to find it. Butrell wrote that he should remove it now under a local. It was, he reaffirmed, a matter of National Security. The Doctor left the room and reemerged a few minutes later with a tray of surgical items and he removed the implant as Butrell had desired. Butrell took the implant and smashed it with his foot.

"Thank you, Doc," Director Butrell said with a smile. "I want this man put into a private room , and I want a guard posted inside the room 24 hours a day. Send up one of the Marines from downstairs. Do not tell anyone who or where he is. Is that clear, Doc? I mean anyone including the local Police. Call him a John Doe. Give me his wallet and any identifying materials!"

"They are probably down in the admitting office," the Nurse remarked anxiously.

"What is your name, woman? I see Williams. Nurse Williams, go get them right now, I'll wait!"

"You sure like to give orders, Mr. Whitey," the Nurse said angrily. "This is not your little government world, you know! We are not your personal slaves!"

"This is a matter of utmost security, Doc. I wish that I could tell you what it was, but as I said before, if I did I would have to kill you! You people just have to trust me. I am acting in the very best interests of the American people. This Pastor may hold the key to your survival. By the way, are you a Christian, Doc?"

"I am a member of the Church of Jesus Christ of Latter Day Saints if you must know," the Doctor replied with a strange look on his face.

"Sorry to hear that, Doc!"

"What do you mean by that?"

"Oh, you will be mighty surprised when you find out, Doc," Butrell answered with a smile.

"How about you, Nurse Williams?" Butrell asked staring right at her.

"I am a Pentecostal, Mr. James Bond," Nurse Williams answered tersely. "Do I pass?"

"With flying colors, Ma'am!"

"Are you a Christian, Sir?" Nurse Williams asked Butrell. When he smiled, she said, "Could have fooled me!"

As soon as Director Butrell received Pastor Calvin's ID material and saw him put into a private room under a John Doe name and witnessed a fully armed Marine standing in front of his bed, he prepared to leave.

"Son, watch this man with your life," Butrell said to the young Black Marine "This is a matter of National Security. Don't let any unauthorized personnel into this room. I am the Deputy Director of the Central Intelligence Agency. I will be sending over some of our people to relieve you as soon as I can. Be ever vigilant, Lieutenant, like a good Marine!"

"Yes, Sir!" the Marine responded as he sat inside the room.

"Are you a Christian, son?" Butrell asked as he bade farewell to the fallen yet still alive Pastor.

"Uh, yes Sir, I am. Mt. Zion Missionary Baptist Church in Selma, Alabama is my home Church."

"Great, son," Butrell replied. "Here, read this Gideon's Bible while you guard this Pastor. The enemy is after him. Know what I'm saying, son?"

"I need to get prayed up with God's word to ward off the wiles of Satan?"

"Amen, brother! Little prayers little results, big prayers big results. Pray for his recovery and protection as well as yours. This is spiritual warfare, son. God bless you!"

# XVI

Judah sat at the console in the underground compound at Aberdeen totally bewildered. What was this business with Harpazo? He respected Pastor Calvin tremendously, but he could not fathom what he was talking about. What did the Jewish New Year of Rosh Hashanah and the blowing of the Shofar have to do with AZAZEL?

Dawn had found her way to the conference area that Judah was in. She put her arms around his shoulders and hugged him. "Please don't do that," Judah said shrugging her off. "I am really confused now, Dawn. I need to think."

"Well, excuse me for trying to love you," Dawn replied, moving away. "What is the matter?"

"Director Butrell just spoke with Pastor Calvin," Judah replied shaking his head. "Let me think, Dawn!"

"I think that you need to pray about your attitude, not think!" Dawn said, ignoring Judah's request for silence."How is Pastor Calvin? I haven't heard his name for ages."

"He is in Bethesda Naval Hospital with two blown apart legs!" Judah shouted. "Dawn, please let me think!"

"Oh my God, what happened?" she persisted.

"He got in the way of Ultra. What is disconcerting to me is that he kept talking of Harpazo. Do you know what Harpazo means?"

"Harpazo? Never heard of it. Maybe he was saying harpoon?" Dawn quipped. "How is he doing?" I cannot believe that they got him too!"

"He is in serious condition," Judah said with a frown, "but he is the only one who seems to understand what is going on. He says that the time to watch is Rosh Hashanah and the blowing of the Shofar. When I asked him, through Butrell, if that was when the abduction of the Christians would take place, he said no, Harpazo, Harpazo. I'm really confused."

"Hmm..." Dawn pondered what Judah had said. "He says that Harpazo is coming on Rosh Hashanah, and you say that is why Ultra tried to kill him? It must have something to do with their plans or they would not have messed with him. But what? What does a Jewish holiday have to do with the abduction of Christians?"

"That is the weird thing, honey," Judah answered still baffled. "When Pastor Calvin said that Harpazo was coming on Rosh Hashanah, I asked him if that was the time of the abduction of the Christians and he said no! It was Harpazo!? What does

Harpazo mean? It doesn't sound like English. Sounds Italian or Mediterranean to me."

"You are repeating yourself, Judah. You need to calm down. You are freaking out!" Dawn said as she once again tried to put her arm around Judah.

"Stop it!" Judah lashed out again and pushed her to the floor.

Dawn struggled to get back up. While the previous ravaging decimation of her MS had abated, the weakness in her legs had remained. All of the commotion of the past several days had severely compromised her strength and stamina. Her balance and equilibrium, while always tenuous, were now very vulnerable, so when Judah just pushed her gently away she had gone cascading across the floor.

"I am sorry, Dawn," Judah lamented as he bent down to help his wife off the floor. "I did not realize that I had pushed you so hard."

"Well, Judah, I am not as fit and healthy as I appear sometimes, you big lug!" Dawn said with a pout. "You know that I have only been walking for a relatively short time and that only by the grace of God. I am not that healthy athletic woman that you once knew!"

"I know that, Dawn. Remember, I married you in a wheelchair," Judah answered softly and lovingly. "You are just as beautiful both inside and out as you have ever been. I know that I sometimes act like a real jerk, but this Harpazo thing is driving me crazy. I thought that I had figured out this whole thing but maybe I haven't. I thought that the abduction of the Christians by AZAZEL was for the detriment of mankind, and that was our mission was to prevent it! But now there is this Harpazo thing. I realize that I do not really know what is going to happen, Dawn. Maybe I have been misguided all along."

"Judah, the Lord has shown you all that He wants you to know," Dawn replied. "He not only revealed Himself to you, but His Holy Spirit enabled you to put on the full armor of God to battle AZAZEL. Do you think that this was all for naught? I don't think so. Keep the course, Judah , and the Lord will show you what He wants you to do."

"Dawn, I don't know much about Bible eschatology. I just know that I love God. General Desporte was just beginning to disciple me about endtimes stuff but then he died, or should I say was killed by these guys. From what I thought that I understood, the Christians were to be abducted by the demons, but now I find out that they are to be harpooned instead?"

"The word is Harpazo, Judah, not harpooned," Dawn answered with a smile. "I'm sorry, but I cannot help you in this area either, Judah. Eschatology was never my thing."

"Dawn, that poor Pastor has suffered greatly to tell me something and I cannot get it. I really need to go and talk with him, but I know that Ultra will be all around. Butrell put him in a private room as a John Doe but who knows how long that will last? If Ultra finds him they will kill him and then we will remain in the dark as to this Harpazo thing!"

Judah became very upset. His breathing became labored and he began to toss the furniture around the room. Suddenly, he bolted up from his chair and ran to the elevator. "Where are you going, Judah?" Dawn yelled as she ran after him.

"I have to confront AZAZEL. He will tell me what is going on."

"That is crazy, Judah," Dawn replied as she tried to restrain him. "We need you here to continue the battle. You expect to find out the truth from the Father of lies? It will continue to deceive you as it has all along. Something is getting ready to happen. We all know that, but we need to pray about it, not go and ask Satan about it. What you are doing doesn't make any sense, Judah!"

"What battle? That is my point, Dawn. Pastor Calvin said that he was not concerned about the abduction of Christians but rather the upcoming Harpazo on Rosh Hashanah, whatever that is. I need to know what is going on, and since I cannot find out from my friends, maybe my enemies will tell me."

Judah made his way out of the underground compound with Dawn hanging on to him all of the way. He managed to commandeer a helicopter with the help of one of the men that Director Butrell had just brought into the Joshua Brigade. The young soldier wanted to go with Judah, but he had convinced the young man that he really was not prepared to meet the enemy.

"Here, son, take my wife," Judah commanded. "Make sure that she is all right back in the bunker."

"Judah, this is crazy!" Dawn cried out and fell to her knees. "You are going to confront AZAZEL again. One of these times you are not going to come back. I cannot live without you. Please don't go, Judah!"

"It is a treacherous job, but somebody has to do it, Dawn," Judah yelled and he bent down and kissed her on top of her head. "I need to discover the truth once and for all. Don't worry, I'll be back. The Lord has not brought me this far to let me perish!"

The young soldier escorted a weak, frail looking Dawn back into the underground bunker and Judah started up the helicopter. She appeared to be a brokenhearted dejected woman.

It was nightfall and Judah flew his helicopter out to Sea. He began to pray in the Spirit and seek the Lord in earnest. He was bathed in the light particles of righteousness. He was girded with Truth and was given the Breastplate of Righteousness and his feet were shod with the preparation of the Gospel of Peace. The Helmet of Salvation was on his head and he was given the Shield of Faith and the Sword of the Spirit.

Judah cried out for AZAZEL. He spotted an Unidentified Flying Object above him and went after it. He shouted into the airwaves that he was coming for the beast.

The black disk sent a beam down to capture the helicopter. Military jets were also racing to the scene, drawn not only by the sight of an UFO but also by the ranting that they heard coming over the airwaves apparently from a helicopter. They

217

all watched in stunned silence as the helicopter was captured by the UFO and whisked away from them in blinding speed.

Judah found himself standing before AZAZEL once again. He did not move but stared at the hideous black beast as it flapped its wings ferociously and screamed an ungodly roar.

"What do you want, Judah?" it yelled.

"I understand that the Christians will be taken away on Rosh Hashanah?"

"Yes, that is correct, Jewboy!" AZAZEL shrieked. "Who told you that, the Pastor? Isn't it amazing that it takes a Christian to tell a Jew about the truth of Rosh Hashanah! Then when it finally happens, the Earth will be ours."

"What of the upcoming Harpazo?"

"Harpazo? Ah, Harpazo!" AZAZEL laughed. "You fool! You have been deceived all of this time! You humans are so fickle! You bounce from one explanation to another without ever coming to the truth. Even your own Bible says that in 2Timothy 3:7! You weak creatures deserve all that will happen to those of you left here on Earth when we come!"

"But what of the Harpazo?"

"How could we catch away only the real Christians, Judah?" AZAZEL bellowed. "Baptists and Lutherans and Catholics and Pentecostal and Mormons and Jehovah Witnesses all claim to be Christians. Do you think that we know who the real Believers are? Only Yahweh knows whose names He wrote in the Lamb's Book of Life before the foundation of the world. Some think that they are written in the Book but they are not. We shall have those individuals for ourselves and every one of them will believe that you who are gone have been abducted by UFOs! What a great deception! HAAA! HAAA! You humans are so gullible. You would rather believe a lie than the truth, especially if the truth is painful. That is why we have so long been able to control your emotions. We have been rulers of this Earth ever since we were thrown out of the first Heaven. Even though you may be gone, we'll still continue to deceive your family, friends and neighbors so that they will never join you where you will be. They will be with us for eternity. That is our longest lasting legacy. They will be with us for eternity! HAAA! HAAA!"

AZAZEL flung his flaming missiles at Judah but he was able to fend them off with his Shield of Faith and Sword of the Spirit. Judah charged at it and it just stood there and laughed.

"You cannot defeat me," AZAZEL shrieked. "We have already been judged by your God, but we have a role to play in these approaching times of Jacob's trouble. The birthpangs are about to begin and your Jewish people will be going to the Lake of Fire with me and my cohorts. I will spend Eternity torturing your father and mother and beloved first wife Ronit. All of the Nation of Israel, in their hardheartedness and blindness to recognize Yeshua as their long awaited Mashiach will thus suffer with me forever. Our greatest accomplishment has been to deprive the Jewish people of their Messiah. As much as Yahweh loves them, that is how

218

much we hate them. They were God's first born sons, His chosen people, so we hated them. From them came the Patriarchs and the Torah and the Temple Service, so we hated them. The Shekinah glory followed them as a cloud by day and a pillar of fire by night, so we hated them. From them came the Messiah, Yeshua, who would defeat us, so we hated them. We have deceived the people so that they would kill, maim, and torture the Jews over the millennia. It has been our greatest achievement and it will continue after the Harpazo. You are powerless to do anything about it, Jew-duhh!"

"You are wrong!" Judah shouted. "My mother has accepted Jesus Christ as her Lord and Savior and she told me that my father did also before he died. They now belong to God, not your master. Whatever happens to the Christians, I now see that my efforts belong with those who are to be left behind, namely the Jews and other non believers. I want my Jewish brothers and sisters to spend eternity with the Lord of Lords and King of Kings, not with you and your cohorts in Hell."

"They are blind to see the truth and their hearts are as hard as stone," AZAZEL cackled.

Judah had so many conflicting thoughts racing through his head at this time that he ran back to the helicopter. AZAZEL flung his flaming missiles at it, and it exploded in flame throwing Judah against the wall of the black disc twenty feet away. He lay there in a pile of confusion and self doubt. The helicopter was dropped from the craft. Now he was at the mercy of AZAZEL. Judah fought to continue wearing his full armor of God by praying without ceasing. As long as he wore it he felt that he would be protected from AZAZEL.

"I going to send you to Ultra, Judah," AZAZEL shouted. "They can take care of you where I am powerless!"

"Into Thy hand I command my spirit. You have ransomed me, O Lord, God of truth," Judah cried out as he ran and jumped out of the opening of the craft through which the burning helicopter was dropped. He would rather die than possibly compromise the Joshua Brigade to Ultra.

Meanwhile it was early morning at Pastor Calvin's room in Bethesda Naval Hospital. The young Marine was still sitting in front of the Pastor's bed, ever vigilant. He had not gotten much sleep the night before and occasionally dozed off. The Doctor and Nurse entered the room almost simultaneously.

"Well I see that your prisoner has not disappeared, nor has anyone tried to harm him," Dr. Parker joked as he examined his patient. "Cat got your tongue, son?"

The Marine did not speak but stared straight ahead with his hands on his rifle.

"Leave him alone, Dr. Parker," Nurse Williams spoke softly. "He is just following orders. Would you like some breakfast, Lieutenant White?"

The Marine nodded his head affirmatively.

"How are you feeling, Pastor?" Dr. Parker asked as his patient woke up.

"I'm doing all right, praise God," Pastor Calvin answered. "My legs hurt though, real bad."

"You had a nasty experience, Sir. Your legs were blown off in that explosion. One at the knee and the other at the hip. Your condition has stabilized now, and while I think that you will be all right, you are going to need extensive rehabilitation."

"Thank you, Jesus! What happened to Director Butrell? I seem to remember him being here. I think that I was talking to him. Was I just hallucinating or was he here?"

"Oh, he was here all right," Nurse Williams interjected. "What is a Pastor doing with a CIA bigshot anyway? And who blew up your legs?"

Pastor Calvin just shook his head and dozed off again. Nurse Williams went to get the Lieutenant some breakfast. Just as she left the room she passed two men coming down the hall towards the room.

"You cannot go into that room," she demanded as she ran back and stood in front of the door.

"We are special agents of the FBI," Agent Mallory spoke up and they flashed their ID badges. "We need to see the patient in this room!"

"I was told not to let anyone in that room," Nurse Williams countered with a scowl on her face.

"By whom, Ma'am," Bernstein asked calmly.

"By some CIA bigshot by the name of Butrell! There is an armed Marine in there who has orders to shoot anyone who enters on sight!" Nurse Williams feigned.

Bernstein and Mallory conferred privately and then asked Nurse Williams to go inside and tell the Marine to come out.

"He ain't goin to listen to that nonsense, boys! He won't leave that man. No way."

"Go get him! Right now, Nurse," Mallory yelled. "Or else we will come in shooting and everyone will lose. Got it?"

"The Doctor is in there, too! Don't you go in there shootin!" Nurse Williams bellowed back.

"Go, Williams, NOW!"

Nurse Williams went into the room and told the Marine that two FBI agents were outside and wanted to come in. He shook his head no. He lifted his rifle and aimed it at the door. His orders had been to not let anyone in to see the Pastor. The Doctor quickly scurried out of the door with the Nurse.

"He ain't movin, Jack!" Nurse Williams told them shaking her head. "I told you that he wouldn't. That Butrell guy told him not to let anyone into the room, and he is just following orders."

"Let me speak with Director Butrell," Mallory said into his cellphone as he attempted to contact the Director.

"Butrell here."

"Director, this is Special Agent Mallory of the FBI. I am standing in front of the room where you have placed a man involved in a Capitol bombing under military guard. We need to interrogate him about the incident."

"Forget about it, Mallory," Butrell responded. "He is under my watch now."

"But Sir, we need to talk with him," Mallory replied persistently.

"But is what a billygoat does! Aren't you the agent who was involved in the investigation of Colonel Meire?"

"Yes, Sir, that was me," Mallory answered. "Why? Is Judah involved in this incident as well?"

"That is not for you to know, Agent. Like you were told before, stay out of this. It is a matter of National Security. The Company will take care of it!"

At that instant Judah fell onto the floor right in front of Mallory and Bernstein.

"It's Judah," Bernstein yelled

Director Butrell heard that and immediately disconnected the communication with the FBI agents and contacted Captain Knowington. He told him to scramble the Joshua Brigade and he would have a helicopter topside to take them to Bethesda. While Director Butrell had been informed that Judah had gone out to find AZAZEL, all that had been found of him was his disintegrated helicopter. They had believed that he was dead. How he ended up at the Hospital was open to question but time was of the essence. If the FBI were already there, who knows how long it might be before Ultra arrived.

Bernstein and Mallory moved towards Judah, but he had already gotten up and went into the Hospital room.. A firefight shortly ensued. The Marine saw Judah come staggering into the room. Judah made eye contact with him, and took his two index fingers and made a cross. The Marine hesitated. When Judah hit the floor, the two FBI agents stormed into the room. The Marine began firing as soon as they did. Bernstein was first in and he was killed instantly. Mallory followed behind, and he was hit also but not before he had hit the Marine between the eyes and killed him. Hidden in the bathroom, Mallory took out his cell phone and called Captain Braden of he Potomac Police Department to tell him that he had found Judah.

"Don't move a muscle," Judah yelled at Agent Mallory as he managed to pick up the Marine's rifle and he held it over Mallory. After confiscating his weapon he barricaded the door with furniture from the room. Security personnel were arriving and Judah wanted to keep them out until he could figure out what to do. He tied up Mallory with the telephone cord. He was bleeding from a wound to his leg. Judah tied a tourniquet around it.

"Pastor Calvin?" Judah asked as bent over the man. He had just regained consciousness with all the shooting going on. "What did you mean by the word Harpazo?"

"Harpazo is the Greek word for the Catching Away, the Rapture!" Pastor Calvin moaned, obviously in great pain. He had not received his hourly pain medication with all the commotion.

"Oh my God! Oh my God!" Judah cried out. "How stupid of me. AZAZEL is not going to abduct the Christians, but they are going to meet the Lord in the air. It is the Rapture. That is it! AZAZEL is going to use the deception that they were abducted by UFOs to explain their sudden disappearance. Oh my God, this gets more clear every minute. No wonder AZAZEL said that I could not stop the abduction because it was not the one that was going to do it. It will be the Lord Himself. Pastor, AZAZEL said that they did not know who the real Christians were anyway so how could they abduct them?"

"That is wrong, Judah," Pastor Calvin moaned. "It says in Job 1:6 as well as in Revelation 12:10 and in Zechariah 3:1 that Satan is the accuser of the brethren, who accuses them before our God day and night! Don't listen to the Great Deceiver, Judah. Of course Satan knows who the saints are. He torments them day after day. That is why he is constantly after the Joshua Brigade! That is why he killed General Desporte and Senator Jordan and their wives, as well as Major Kole and Congressman Jacobs and the others."

"Dr. Lazant and all of his cronies want those left behind to believe that the Christians had to be removed so that the planet could evolve to a higher state of consciousness? The truth is that those left behind will suffer through the great tribulation with these fallen angels. That is why AZAZEL said that people would rather believe the lie that the Christians were abducted by UFOs than the truth that the Bible is correct and that they were caught up in the air to be with the Lord in heaven during the upcoming great tribulation. Sorry, Pastor, but I am trying to get all of this but my lack of knowledge of the Word of God is evident. In spite of my ignorance, the Lord has seen fit to use this unworthy sinner. He does have a great sense of humor! As General Desporte once told me, the Lord even spoke through Balaam's ass one time!"

"That is right, Judah," Pastor Calvin groaned. "And by the way, I do not believe that Lazant and his New Agers know the truth about the Rapture. They just believe a lie that it is necessary to remove the Christians to further world unity. They are being deceived by AZAZEL and Satan!"

The security personnel had arrived at the room along with the local police. They evacuated the entire floor for safety reasons.

"I don't want any of you to try and come in here," Judah yelled through the barricaded door. "I want to speak with the Deputy Director of the Central Intelligence Agency, Mike Butrell."

"Who is in there with you? a voice yelled back. "This is Police Chief Reilley."

"I have a dead Marine and a dead FBI agent. Another is wounded."

"How did that happen?" Chief Reilley replied calmly not wanting to upset the man behind the door.

"The FBI agent killed the Marine and the Marine killed one of the FBI agents."

"And you just sat by and watched?"

"Look, get me Butrell."

Meanwhile Doctor Parker and Nurse Williams had returned to the room. They explained that Director Butrell had put a man in the room under armed guard. When the FBI agents had arrived and insisted upon entering the room they told the Chief that they had fled.

"I knew something was goin' to happen," Nurse Williams said, shaking her head. "I knew it, yes I did. Those FBI men were determined to get into that room, and that young Marine was determined not to let them in."

"Then who is the man that has barricaded himself in the room?" the Chief asked.

"There was no other man but the patient and his legs were blown off!"

"Who are you?" Chief Reilly yelled through the door. "Please identify yourself!"

"Lieutenant Colonel Judah Meire."

At that very moment Captain Braden arrived just in time to hear Judah say his name.

"That guy brings trouble wherever he goes, Chief," Captain Braden spoke up. "I have investigated several crimes that all tie him into them. He also suffers from Post Traumatic Stress Syndrome. Maybe he freaked out again!"

"Who are you?" Chief Reilly asked abruptly. "And who called you in?"

"I am Captain Braden of the Potomac Police Department. The wounded agent in that room called me!"

"He says there are a dead FBI agent and a dead Marine in there! He says that they killed each other. Could he have done it?"

"Absolutely," Captain Braden replied. "He was the last person to see Senator Jordan and Major Kole of the CIA alive. People have the tendency to die around him mysteriously. I thought that he had been killed in a car crash, but he also has the uncanny ability to repeatedly cheat death. He was a member of the Israeli military and the Mossad for a while. He is quite a survivor."

"Who is the patient in there?" Braden asked the Doctor.

"Some man that had his legs blown apart," he answered.

"What is his name?"

"Butrell told us that he was a John Doe," Nurse Williams replied keeping the Pastor's identity a secret as requested.

"A John Doe guarded by an armed Marine?" Captain Braden replied sternly. "Something is real fishy here. Did you see Judah arrive?"

"No, he wasn't there a minute ago," Nurse Williams said bewildered.

All of a sudden down the hall came a throng of men wearing trenchcoats and sunglasses. They were heavily armed.

"Okay everyone, we will take over from here," the first man shouted. "This is an intelligence matter."

"Who are you?" Police Chief Reilly asked. "Are you the CIA? He has been asking for Mike Butrell."

"Yes we are government intelligence," the large man responded flashing some ID.

"This man is not Mike Butrell of the CIA," Nurse Williams spoke up firmly. "I spent time with him and this man is not him. Butrell told us not to listen to anyone but him."

"It's all right, Ma'am, he sent us," the large behemoth replied.

"I don't believe you. Let me see your ID," she replied angrily.

"This is a matter of National Security and you best step aside, Ma'am!"

"Hey, whoever you are in the room, there are bunch of men outside here who want to come in," Nurse Williams shouted at the door. "They are wearing long coats and sunglasses. They say they are Government agents. They say that Butrell sent them. Should we let them in?"

"Absolutely not!" Judah yelled back. "They are the enemy that the Marine was guarding this patient from. Wait for Butrell."

"Hear that, Mr.?!" the Nurse said with a smirk.

The man hit the nurse across the head with his M-16 and she went flying into the wall. He and his men quickly disarmed the police and security guards with their superior firepower. They confiscated their weapons and locked them all in the nearby pharmacy. Just as they came back to assault the room that Judah and Pastor Calvin were in, they were met in the hallway by the Joshua Brigade.

"Here they come," Captain Knowington whispered as he caught sight of the men from Ultra coming around the corner. "Lock and load, gentlemen. Take no prisoners. Kill them all!"

Another firefight ensued and automatic gunfire ricocheted across the narrow Hospital hallway and created an eerie reverberating sound of men dying. The men from Ultra were cut to pieces by Captain Knowington and his men. All five men from Ultra, including their large leader, were killed and one of the Joshua Brigade was also killed with another one wounded.

"Judah, this is Captain Knowington, open the door!"

Judah opened the barricaded door and was greeted by Captain Knowington.

"We need to leave the premises ASAP, Judah!"

"I want to bring Pastor Calvin," Judah replied. "He will be as good as dead if we leave him here."

"Then bring him!" Captain Knowington said. "We have to go right now."

Judah wheeled his bed into the hallway where medics put him onto a stretcher along with the killed and injured members of the Joshua Brigade. They went up the roof and quickly boarded their helicopter and headed back to Aberdeen.

"Thanks, Captain, for coming to rescue us!" Judah said with a smile. "Now we are even, Boss. Okay?"

"Sure, Judah, sure. How did you ever survive your helicopter crash and how did you end up at Bethesda unharmed?"Captain Knowington wondered aloud as he played with his eyepatch..

"It is a long story, Sir. The Lord once again saved me like He did from the burning van," Judah said with tears in his eyes. "But this time I found out the real motive of AZAZEL. You are not going to believe it!"

"What are you talking about, Judah?" Captain Knowington replied as he looked back at his wounded soldier and the invalid Preacher.

"AZAZEL is not going to abduct the Christians," Judah said with a big smile. "Yes, they are going to disappear from the Earth, but it will be in the Rapture! Harpazo is Greek for Rapture or Catching Away. When we are all caught up to be with the Lord in the air, AZAZEL will use the deception to explain our disappearance as an abduction by UFOs. Get it? It is not that we are to be removed to further the evolution of the world's consciousness as Dr. Lazant and the other crazies believe, but rather we are to removed before Jacob's Trouble starts."

"Then what is the purpose of the Joshua Brigade?" Captain Knowington wondered. "If we are not to stop AZAZEL from abducting the Christians, and if they are to taken instead by the Lord in the Rapture, then what is our mission? I am really confused now."

"Well, so am I Captain," Judah lamented. "Maybe we were created to protect Pastor Calvin, which we certainly did. After all, he told us of the real meaning of this event. On the other hand, we are still working on a webpage and media information for those left behind. We will have to change it from telling them that we were abducted by demons to the fact that we were Raptured to be with the Lord in the air."

"Shouldn't we warn them now before it happens?"

"I don't think so, Sir," Judah replied. "First of all we do not know when this will actually happen. It could be September of this year or next year or who knows when. If we make a statement that it is going to happen in several weeks, and it doesn't happen, we will lose our credibility."

"You are correct, Judah," Pastor Calvin chimed in, obviously in great pain but determined nonetheless to speak. "Nobody knows the day or hour but the Father. But it will happen on the Feast of Trumpets, Rosh Hashanah."

"How can you be so sure, Pastor?" Captain Knowington asked curiously.

"I have been studying the Jewish roots of Scripture," Pastor Calvin said as he grimaced in pain. "All of the Feasts mentioned in Leviticus 23 are pictures of Yeshua. Passover is a perfect picture of His death as the sacrificial lamb of God who took away the sins of the world. Unleavened bread is a perfect picture of his burial. You know, Judah, how matzah is striped and pierced and unleavened, without sin, just like his body was. That is why the Lord's Supper, the Passover meal, should be done with unleavened bread. The piece of matzah is wrapped in a white linen cloth and buried until the end of the Passover service. It is called the afikoman. The Jews think that afikomen is Greek for dessert but it means He is risen in the aorist tense! First Fruits is a perfect picture of His Resurrection. It is always on the Sunday after the Passover. Shavuot, the Feast of Weeks, is always 50 days after First Fruits and is the day Moses received the Ten Commandments on Sinai. It is the same day that the Holy Spirit was poured out on the early believers at Pentecost. Thus the Spring Feasts are a perfect picture of the First Coming of the

225

Lord and the Holy Spirit while the Fall Feasts of Trumpets, Rosh Hashanah, Day of Atonement, Yom Kippur and Succot, Feast of Tabernacles are a perfect picture of the Rapture of the Church, the Second Coming of the Lord Jesus in Judgement of the Nations and the Marriage Supper of the Lamb."

"Wow! Pastor," Judah said with a big sigh. "I had no idea! And you are saying that Rosh Hashanah is the time of the Rapture of the Church?"

"Yes, Judah. Jewish tradition links Rosh Hashanah with the resurrection of the dead. The Talmud speaks very clearly about this. According to the prayerbook for the Jewish High Holy days, the Machtzur, 'the messianic hope, resurrection and immortality of the soul are intertwined on Rosh Hashanah'. According to the Pirkei D'Rabbi Eliezer, the first Shofar or trumpet blown was the left horn of the ram that Abraham sacrificed instead of Isaac. It was blown at Sinai as depicted in Exodus 19:19; the Last Shofar or Trumpet is the right horn of this ram that will be blown at the Resurrection of the dead on some future Rosh Hashanah. Paul told us in 1 Corinthians 15:52 that 'in the twinkling of an eye, at the last Trumpet; for the Trumpet will sound and the dead will be raised imperishable and we shall be changed.' He clarifies that in 1 Thessalonians 4:16-17 where he wrote that 'for the Lord Himself will descend from heaven with a shout, with the voice of the archangel, and with the trumpet of God; and the dead in Christ shall rise first. Then we who are alive and remain shall be caught up together with them in the clouds to meet the Lord in the air, and thus we shall always be with the Lord.' There is nothing in Scripture that speaks of Christians being abducted by Satan into the Heavens. It does speak of the deception and deluding influence in the days of Satan's coming."

Pastor Calvin began to scream with pain and he was sedated with some morphine until they could get him back to Aberdeen for more complete medical treatment.

Vatican theologian, Father Saltucci, was busy on the web promoting his new book on alien abductions. He had written that all the evidence pointed to the reality of aliens. He stated that while they appeared to be more evolved than we humans, there was nothing in the Bible that precluded them. God was Lord over all of the Universe which included these entities. We could think of them as angels in the Heavenly realm.

His book not only was a runaway Bestseller in Europe and was translated into 70 languages, but Dr. Lazant was so impressed with it that he promoted it exclusively in the United States.

The word began to spread throughout the world that aliens were not incompatible with the Bible, and that they might even be heavenly angels sent here to rescue our planet from its headlong plunge into destruction. The ground was being prepared for the great deception that the disappearance of the Christians was due to their abduction by the angels sent from God, and that their Savior would be coming to liberate them from bondage.

# PART III

*"Who has believed our message? And to whom has the arm of the Lord been revealed?*
*For He grew up before Him like a tender shoot, and like a root out of parched ground.*
*He has no stately form or majesty that we should look upon Him,*
*Nor appearance that we should be attracted to Him.*
*He was despised and forsaken of men, a man of sorrows, and acquainted with grief.*
*And like one from whom men hide their face, he was despised and we did not esteem Him.*
*Surely our griefs He Himself bore, and our sorrows he carried.*
*Yet we ourselves esteemed Him stricken, smitten of God and afflicted.*
*But He was pierced through for our transgressions, He was crushed for our iniquities.*
*The chastening of our well being fell upon Him, and by His scourging we are healed.*
*All of us like sheep have gone astray, each of us has turned to his own way.*
*But the Lord has caused the iniquity of us all to fall on Him."*

Yesha'yahu(ISAIAH) 53:1-6

# XVII

Just as the helicopter lifted off from the roof of Bethesda Naval Hospital into the clear golden sky of sunset, a scrambled coded message came in over the radio.

"You are to proceed to Andrews Air Force Base," the message said after it was unscrambled. "You are not to return to Phillips Army Airfield. I repeat, you are not to return to Aberdeen. Your position has been compromised."

"I knew it," Captain Knowington said with a look of frustration in his face and a note of exasperation in his voice. "First Butrell flew to Bethesda, then you, Judah, flew to AZAZEL and finally we left from Aberdeen to rescue you. Three helicopter flights from a supposedly secret compound was crazy. We should have known better."

"What else could we have done?" Judah answered tersely. "I wonder why we are going to Andrews?"

"And I wonder what happened to our wives?" Captain Knowington replied, scratching his short white hair. "I cannot imagine either of them letting anyone leave them behind. Know what I mean, Judah?"

"I cannot imagine it either, Captain," Judah said with a sigh. "I guess that it is in the Lord's hands though. We have done all that we could do. All that I know is that the Lord put that dear sweet precious woman in my life for a reason and I don't think that reason is over quite yet. Every time that I become too cocky, she is there to bring me back to Earth. We Jews have a tendency to do that more than most people. As that old Yiddish saying goes, 'we are just like everyone else, only more so!' I thank God for her everyday. I really do!"

They changed their heading from northeast to Aberdeen to southeast to Andrews. The helicopter was outfitted with the newest jamming technology so tracking them was next to impossible. Just as they had corrected their course, another scrambled coded message came in.

"Andrews is a no go!" the unscrambled message said. "Proceed to Langley. I repeat, Andrews is a no go. You are good to go to Langley. Your wives and buddies will meet you there. Over and out."

"Who are these guys?" Judah asked the radio officer.

"I don't know, Sir," the young soldier with flaming yellow hair and a big smile answered. "Their communication is one way only. We can only receive from them not talk back to them. Sorry, Sir!"

"Oh great," Captain Knowington said anxiously. "What if it is Ultra luring us into a trap?"

"Then we are dead meat, Sir," Judah replied patting him on the back. "We need to pray about it. We need to ask the Lord if evil men are behind this."

All of the men got on their knees and took their concerns to the Lord in fervent prayer. They changed their heading once again to nearly due south towards Langley Airforce Base which was located between Newport News and Norfolk, Virginia. For nearly the entire 50 minute flight they stayed on their knees in prayer. All of them got a feeling of inner peace from their calling out to the Lord and all felt that it was not a trap set by AZAZEL. They proceeded, however, very cautiously nonetheless.

As they approached Langley, they were told to proceed to a runway at the north end of the base. They then spotted a brown Boeing 707 with Israeli markings on it with its engines running, ready to take off.

"That is an IDF plane!" Judah yelled. "I can't believe it. We are going to Israel?"

The 707 was taxing and preparing to take off. As soon as the helicopter landed, Deputy Director Butrell of the CIA was waiting to greet them.

"Okay, men," he shouted. "Everyone into the 707. It has to take off immediately."

"How did you ever finagle this, Sir?" Judah asked as he embraced the Director. "Do you mean to tell me that the Israelis are aware of our mission? I don't believe that for a minute, Sir. Sorry!"

"Judah, I called in some of my markers with an old friend in the Mossad. The plane is piloted by a Jewish Believer like yourself, believe it or not. Congressman Jacobs met him before he was killed. There is a community of Jewish Believers in Israel that will hide you until your work is done. It is just too dangerous here and Israel is where Biblical prophecy is to be fulfilled anyway. God be with you!"

"God bless you, Sir," Judah beamed. "I just cannot believe this!"

"I think that you had better leave Pastor Calvin here with us. He needs extensive rehabilitation. We will protect him. Now go, Judah! Dawn and the others are waiting for you in the plane!"

Judah ran over to the IDF's 707 and boarded along with all the others. There were the all too familiar cries of great joy and of great sadness as those on board greeted their loved ones and friends and mourned the death of another young soldier. The tall, lanky soldier with an ugly gunshot wound that had torn a hole in his face was also not taken on board, but like Pastor Calvin was taken to the infirmary at Langley. Neither he nor the Pastor was conscious at the time of the transfer and thus it was believed that neither could compromise the mission.

"Judah, oh my dear, sweet Judah," Dawn cried out as she ran up to him and embraced him with a big bear hug. "You have more lives than a cat. I cannot believe that you survived another encounter with AZAZEL. They found your burned-out helicopter. How did you end up at Bethesda? No, on second thought, don't tell me. I probably wouldn't believe you anyway. Praise God, Judah! Praise God!"

"I love you, Dawn," Judah replied as he threw his arms around her and kissed her on the head. "You are right that you wouldn't believe me because I don't believe it myself. I jumped out of the disk to escape AZAZEL and all of a sudden..."

"You jumped out of the disk?" Dawn shouted, backing away and hitting him on the chest. "You tried to kill yourself, knowing that I would be left here alone. That's real nice!"

"The Lord grabbed me as He did in the burning van and deposited me in the hospital," Judah said with a feigned smile. "Then I found myself caught between a Marine guarding the Pastor and those FBI agents Bernstein and Mallory. The Marine killed Bernstein and Mallory killed the Marine. Then Ultra showed up. It was a big mess. Fortunately, Captain Knowington arrived in the nick of time."

Everyone listened as Judah recapped the days events in great detail. They were all tired and disoriented from all their continual relocations, especially Captain Knowington's daughters.

"Now where are we going?" Rebecca wined as she pulled on her red hair. "We have been locked up in a mountain, then flown on a helicopter, put on a truck and taken to a speedboat. From there we went on a weird upside down V whatever, and then we were taken to another underground hole. No sooner had we begun to settle in, than we were forced to leave without any time to get ready and now we are on a plane to Israel. What is going on here? I'm getting sick of all this!"

"Yeah, I didn't join the Army, you know! Did I?" Jennifer replied. "I don't think so!"

All were tired and disheveled and hungry. Dawn and Ann Knowington had managed to bring along some junk food that they had confiscated from the Aberdeen Mess Hall. The Israelis provided some drinks and snack food as well, although they were not equipped for hot meals.

Judah went up to speak with the pilot.

"Shalom, Captain," Judah said with a smile as gazed out into the beautiful black night sky ahead and the moonlit Atlantic ocean far below. "Butrell told me that you are a Believer. How did he ever get use of this aircraft? It belongs to the IDF, doesn't it? I am dumbfounded by all of this."

"Well, relax, Colonel Meire," the Captain answered, "Hashem is in control. Yes, I am a Believer. So is the copilot. My name is Shmuel Labensky. The copilot is Avraham Haralick. We are part of a ever growing number of Messianic Jews residing in Israel. There has been a great outpouring of the Ruach Hakodesh *(H.Holy Spirit)* in Eretz Yisrael over the past several years. Most of us are secret believers, however. We have not told our employers or our families because they would immediately reject us. You know about that, Judah. We know that it isn't Scriptural and Adonai *(H.The Lord)* says that if we are ashamed of Him, He will be ashamed of us, but we just need a little more time, you know?"

"Baruch Hashem *(H.Blessed be the Name[of the Lord])*, Captain," Judah replied as he looked at the pilot with understanding eyes. He was a man with a large head which was almost bald and bullet shaped. He had large kind brown eyes. "God Bless you, Sir. You know, my father was a Professor at Hebrew University, and I was a member of the IDF. I also was afraid to tell my mother of my experience with the Lord. She was already upset enough that I had married a Shiksa who was in a wheelchair. But you know what? Now my wife is up and walking and my mother had a vision of the Lord herself. God is great!"

"We have heard all about you, Yehuda," the copilot Haralick, a younger and smaller man than the Captain and with freckles and red hair, said. "You are quite the talk of the Believers in Yisrael. We all have been updated on your efforts by first General Desporte and Senator Jordan and then by Congressman Jacobs and Director Butrell."

"You know of our mission against AZAZEL?" Judah replied shocked.

"Oh yes, Yehuda," Captain Labensky said while shaking his bald head. "If the Christians were to be taken off of the planet to prepare the world for a new world order, what do you think was going to happen with us Jewish believers? Were we to be left here with the nonbelievers? That's meshugge *(H.crazy)*. We are followers of Yeshua Hamashiach *(Jesus the Messiah)* just as the Christians are. Therefore we would be taken also!"

"Nobody is going to be taken by AZAZEL!" Judah said emphatically with a chuckle. "We are all going to be taken by the Lord. It is the Rapture. AZAZEL is going to deceive everyone by saying that he took us, while in fact the Lord did."

"We knew that," Captain Labensky replied nonchalantly. "Our Rabbis said that is was the Natzal, the Catching Away. We are all to be hidden away while the terrible time of Jacob's Trouble rages here on Earth. It will be the time of the wedding of the Lord and His Messianic Believers. He said that Yeshua was preparing a place for us in His Father's house. We will spend the traditional Biblical honeymoon of seven years there. I know it should be seven days but a day is as a year, right? Most of our Jewish families and friends will remain here to face Armilus, the wicked king of the last generation."

"You knew this and didn't say anything to any of us," Judah said frustrated. "You could have said something. Did Desporte and Jordan know? If they did, then why did they form the Joshua Brigade to thwart AZAZEL?"

"I don't know, Yehuda," Captain Labensky said, "although it seems to me that it was established to protect you, son. You are the only one that has made contact with the Beast and lived to tell about it. Look at what happened to General Desporte and Senator Jordan. Nobody is sure where we go from here but they all seem assured that you will be at the center of whatever happens."

"Oh great. It is all on my shoulders. Why me?"

"Why not you, Yehuda? Hashem *(H.lit. the Name-Name Jews call G-D)* picked you out from your sin and unbelief for His purpose. As one of those American Patriots said, 'it is not for you to question why, but it is just for you to do or die! The Lord has His hand on you, Yehuda. Stop fighting it! Stop kvetching!"

"I know," Judah said with a deep sigh. "I jumped out of AZAZEL's craft and the Lord saved me. I was in a burning van and the Lord saved me."

"And all that you do is question Him!" the Captain said harshly. "Stop questioning everything, Yehuda. Hashem is in control of everything, even AZAZEL. He knows the end from the beginning. He is sovereign. Relax, Yehuda, and get some rest. There will be plenty of time to worry about world events when we get home."

As Judah turned to return to his wife and mother a strange light illuminated the cabin. Judah turned to see the frightening image of AZAZEL hovering outside the window directly in front of them. Captain Labensky stared in frozen horror while co pilot Haralick became so petrified that his red hair turned white.

"Is that AZAZEL, Yehudah?" the Captain questioned while not moving a muscle.

"It is, Captain," Judah replied as he got on his knees and called upon the Holy Spirit to cover him with the full armor of God one more time. He was bathed in the sparkling rain of the righteousness of God and was covered in the full armor. Meanwhile, Co pilot Haralick had left his seat and was cowering under the flight panel.

"Make it go away, Yehudah," he shouted as he trembled in abject fear.

"Yehuda," Captain Labensky asked forebodingly. "What do you think it wants with us?"

"I think that it wants me, Captain," Judah shouted as he went right up to the window and stared at the terrifying image hovering outside."Well, you stupid beast, what do you want with me?"

"You know our plans, Judah," AZAZEL screeched. "You must die along with your cohorts. We cannot let you reveal our coming deception to the whole world."

Suddenly, AZAZEL was inside the cabin. His huge black wings were taller than the cockpit ceiling and folded over. His white eyes had become a crimson blazing red and he screeched like a wild banshee. Captain Labensky put the plane on autopilot and got out of his seat and went behind Judah. Haralick just lay on the floor shaking in uncontrollable fear. Judah's mother and Dawn and the others in the plane heard the terrifying noise and attempted to enter the cockpit in mass but there was not enough room for all of them. Once they saw or heard what was going on most went screaming back to their seats and hid their heads in fear and began to pray.

"AZAZEL!" Dawn yelled. "Oh my God, it is AZAZEL! God help us!"

"Look at my boy, Judah," Bertha yelled. "He has put on that suit of armor once again. With that on, he can battle that beast like he has done before. Get out of here, you creature of the night before my tatalleh slices you to pieces. Go back to the pits of hell where you belong."

"Oh my God, look at that thing!" Jennifer screamed along with her sister. "Is that Satan? Oh my God, I am going to pass out."

232

Jennifer and her sister Rebecca both collapsed from the frightening sight of AZAZEL. Their dad, Captain Knowington, dragged them both to the back of the plane as he also stared in a state of fear at AZAZEL. He remembered all too clearly their last encounter.

"You are going to Israel," AZAZEL bellowed. "That is where the final battle will take place. We have blinded the people there for two thousand years. Their Messiah came and they crucified Him. Your God sent Him and we had Him killed by the very people who had longed for Him. HAA! HAA! What a deception. Then we confused and deluded the early Church in Rome to ignore the Jewishness of that Jesus and His disciples. They slaughtered the Jews, their brothers, in the Crusades and the Inquisition. Then we confused the great Protestant Reformer, Martin Luther, into condemning the Jews and influencing Hitler's Holocaust of the Jews. When this Jesus returns to the Mount of Olives, the Jews will crucify Him again because of how we have deceived them so. HAA! HAA!"

"Shut up, you beast from the heavenlies!" Judah yelled as he walked right up to the black winged demon. "Nobody wants to hear your lies. We are all believers, and we know that what you are saying is truth mixed with lies. The Jews did not kill Messiah. He willingly came to the Earth to die for our sins. He said that He could have called legions of angels to help Him on the Cross, but He did not so that His atoning role could be fulfilled. All mankind put Him on the Cross for their sins. He was the blood sacrifice, the Passover Lamb who took away the sins of the world. Without His atoning death we would have no hope for the remission of our sins. His shed blood on Calvary washed us clean and defeated your kind once and for all. And He is not dead but sits at the right hand of the Father. That horrible lie that the Jews killed Christ has been used by the Church historically as a reason to persecute the Jews. You have deluded good Christian people into denying their own Bible and going after the Jews. And of course you know, Beast, that when Yeshua returns to the Mount of Olives as it says in Zechariah, all the Jews will be covered by a spirit of grace and supplication and realize that Yeshua was their Messiah all of the time. They will cry out as a mother does for a first born son. He will then defeat you and your Master at the battle of Armageddon. I know that you know that, so why do you continue to lie and try and deceive people?"

"Because we want to take as many people with us to the Lake of Fire as we can. Especially all of God's first born children, the Jews! We know our destiny, but we also know that we can continue to deceive and delude people into ignoring the truth and believing a lie right up to the end. Our mission is to deceive the people left behind when you are removed, into believing that the bad people were removed, not the good people. We have been confusing good with evil since the garden. We will continue to do it right up until the end! HAA! HAA!"

Judah charged at AZAZEL and with his Sword of the Spirit he whacked away at AZAZEL's wings. Pieces of black hot feathers spewed all over the cabin. AZAZEL screeched an ungodly roar and flung a flaming missile at Judah. Judah used his Shield of Faith to ricochet it back right into AZAZEL's face. It burst into flame and AZAZEL was gone. Judah fell to his knees and thanked God for the strength and resources He had given him to thwart the enemy one more time. Captain Labensky looked up and uncovered his eyes for the first time in several minutes. He had been shaking so hard that he had feared that he would have a heart attack. Copilot Haralick was discovered under the flight console with his hair as white as snow and sticking out in all directions. His eyes were frozen open in a terrifying stare as he had been scared to death.

"Baruch Hashem, Yehuda!" Captain Labensky cried out as he moved over to embrace Judah. "Thank Hashem for you. I told you that Hashem chose you for a special reason. I had heard about this beast AZAZEL, but I never would have guessed how terrifying it would be. It killed my poor dear friend Avraham. Oy vey ist mir! I will have to tell his family. They are not believers. What can I say? That he was scared to death by a beast from Gehanna *(H.Hell)*?"

Judah went back to be with his wife and mother for the remaining flight to Israel.

"Oh Judah, you did it again," Dawn said as she put her arms around her husband and kissed him. I am so proud of you. You are a mighty soldier of the Lord."

"Yes tattellah," Bertha added. "We are all so proud of you!"

"But a man died in there!" Judah snapped back. "Another good man was scared to death by that beast from Satan! And did you hear what AZAZEL said? They know how this whole thing ends but they still want to take as many people, especially the Jews, with them to the Lake of Fire and eternal separation from God. They are going to try and deceive the entire world into believing that our disappearance was for the good of mankind. The bad people had to be removed, not the good people. Those liars, those deceivers, never stop prowling the earth looking for someone to devour."

"Are you excited to be going home, Judah?" Dawn asked as she put her arms around him affectionately trying to change the subject. "It has been several years since you were in Israel. Does it bring back bad memories of Ronit's death to you?"

"Israel is home, Dawn," Judah replied seriously. "It will always be home to me. It is where I was born and grew up and went to school. Actually it is full of wonderful memories. Memories of my mother cooking matzoball soup and brisket and my Abba coming home from the University and telling me stories. I miss it terribly. America has been very good to me and I am thankful for her, but Israel will always be my home. And sure it brings back memories of Ronit's death, but one cannot live in the past. She is gone now and I will probably never see her again. In fact, I am almost certain that I won't. I am not as sad about her death as I am about her eternal destiny. That is tragic. And I cannot stop thinking about what AZAZEL said. He has blinded the Jews to the reality of their Messiah and he will continue to do so right up to the end. Satan sure hates the Jewish people. All of my family and friends will spend eternity with Him in the Lake of Fire unless something is done!"

"Tatalleh, you remember my matzoball soup?" Bertha said with a smile as she

234

put her hand on Judah's face. "Do you remember the rugelach *(pastries)* that I used to make you? I am so thankful for you, Judah. You are a good man. And you did find such a Godly wife. She is a blessing to all of us. I, too, am so sorry for Ronit and actually for all our relatives and friends who have passed on without knowing the loving grace of our Savior. I would have never guessed what peace I could feel. I'll be forever grateful that He chose me although I rejected Him. I'm telling you that your father had the most sweet smile on his face when he died. He knew! I know that he knew! I am so sad also, Judah, about our family, friends and fellow Israelis. But what can we do? Unless the Ruach Hakodesh *(H. Holy Spirit)* touches them as it did you and me, they will not believe. I sure did not. Hasatan has confused and deceived us Jews into not even thinking about Yeshua. Why, I thought that you were crazy, remember?"

Everyone finally decided to turn off the lights and sleep. The cabin became overcome with an eerie darkness as the IDF 707 streaked across the moonlit night sky over the Atlantic. Judah sat between his mother and his wife. Dawn put her head on Judah's shoulder and his mother put her hand over his. They tried unsuccessfully to sleep the night away. It had been an exhausting week for all of them with all the constant changes of locale and modes of transportation. There had not been a night when they had been able to sleep without a persistent anxiety attack. This frightening night had left them all exhausted yet once again too scared to really sleep. After a supper of dates, figs, nuts and orange juice, they had all closed their eyes and pretended.

The patriarchal, wizened Rabbi Waxman lay on his deathbed in Hadassah Hospital. His pancreatic cancer had grown worse of late and there was nothing more that the doctors could do. He was venerated all over Israel as a sage among his people. His Ultra Orthodox students and followers gathered in his room daily to pray.

"Why do you weep, Rebbe?" one of his students asked as he saw his Master in such sorrow.

"I veep because I do not know vere I am going after I die," the Rabbi replied patting the young man wearing a black coat and a black hat on the arm. "Even de venerable sage Yochanan Ben-Zakkai, convener of de Yavneh Council did not know vere he vas going. According to de Talmud, he is attributed to have said on his deatbed dat he vas being led before de Supreme King of Kings, de Holy One, blessed be He, who lives and endures for ever and ever. Rabbi Zakkai said dat if He vas angry wit him, He vould be angry forever. If He imprisoned him, He vould imprison him forever. If He put him to deat, He vould put him to deat forever. De Rabbi said dat he could not persuade Him vit vords or bribe Him vit money. Moreover, de Rabbi said dat dere vere two vays ahead of him; one led to Gan-Eden or Paradise and one led to Gey-Hinnom *(lit. 'valley of Hinnom', located south of the Old City of Jerusalem where the city's rubbish was burned; hence, metaphorically, because of these fires, known as hell)*, and he did not know vich one vould take him so how could he do anyting but veep!"

"Rebbe, you are a good man," pleaded the young man as he pulled on his fretlocks. "You have lived a frum, righteous life. You have davened *(H.prayed)* three times a day and kept the Sabbath and ate only kosher food. You have done only mitzvot *(H.Divine commandments)* and if anyone has earned his way to Gan-Eden it is you. Your name is surely written in the Book of Life. Why do you despair so? Where is it written about this Rabbi Ben-Zakkai?"

"It is vritten in B'rakhot 28b, Yitzhak. I guess de closer one comes to judgement de more one realizes dat he is a sinner," the Rabbi said reverently. "One realizes dat nobody deserves Hashem's grace. Shlomo wrote in Qoheleth *(H.Ecclesiastes)* dat Hashem shall bring every vork into judgement, vit every secret ting, veter it be good, or veter it be evil. Shlomo also wrote dat dere is not a just man upon eart dat does good and sins not! Yeshayahu *(H.Isaiah)* vrote dat all our righteousness are as filty rags and our iniquities like de vind have taken us avay!"

"But Rebbe, if you aren't going to Hashem, then what about the rest of us?"

"It says in de Torah, in Wayyiqra *(H.Leviticus)*, dat only blood makes atonement for our sins," Rabbi Waxman moaned as he pulled at his long white beard. "Ve need a blood sacrifice to vash our sins as vite as snow. You know dat Yom Kippur is coming soon. Dat is de day de Cohen Hagadol vent into de Holy of Holies and sprinkled de blood of de sacrificial goat on de mercy seat as kapparah or atonement for all Israel's sins. He burnt incense so dat he vould not die. Dat is vat Hashem intended. Blood sacrifice for sin!"

"But without the Temple we cannot do sacrifices, Rebbe," the young man countered with tears in his eyes.

"Dat is vy ve need to rebuild de Temple, Yitzhak," the old, dying patriarch said with a smile.

"But what of the Dome of the Rock, Rebbe?" the young student asked anxiously.

"Hashem vill remove it!"

Yitzhak kissed the Rebbe's hand and went outside with his classmates.

"We need to try and save the Rebbe," he whispered. "We need to destroy the Dome of the Rock."

"Are you crazy, Yitzhak?" one of his classmates countered sternly. "That will surely bring a Holy War against us from the Arabs."

"Well, so be it! Do you want to just wait around and let the Rebbe die? We need to act now."

The brown 707 IDF jetliner entered Israeli airspace and they used their special IDF clearance codeword with the air traffic controller. They then headed right over Tel Aviv with its beautiful white sandy beaches and modern skyline.

"Are we going to land at Ben Gurion Airport at Lod?" Judah asked as he reentered the cockpit for the final descent.

236

"No, Yehuda," Captain Labensky replied with a twinkle in his eye. "We are going to land at Sirkin Field near Petach Tikva."

"Sirkin Field? That is where the Israeli Airforce Academy was originally based," Judah said with a smile as he remembered an important landmark.

"Good, Yehuda!"

"Petach Tikva, the Gate of Hope, is where the first ever agricultural colony was established in 1878 by Jews from the Old City of Jerusalem." Judah gloated as he again remembered something from his school days.

"You sound like a schoolboy who just remembered an important fact, Yehuda. You sound excited about finally coming home," Captain Labensky replied with small painful laugh.

"I know, Sir. It feels so good," Judah replied with a big grin. "What happens to us at Petach Tikvah?"

"Nothing, Yehuda!" Captain Labensky laughed out loud. "That airfield has been closed for years. You have been gone longer than you think. We are going to the airfield at Tel Nof."

"That is the Negev near Rehevot?" Judah asked, wondering if he remembered correctly. "That is just a few kilometers south of here, isn't it?"

"Yes, Yehuda it is! From there you will be taken to meet some Believers in Yerushalyim *(H.Jerusalem)* who will hide you until the Natzal *(H.Catching Away)*!"

Dr. Lazant had come to Rome to visit the short bald cleric, Father Saltucci. It was a blustery, rainy day all shrouded in a dark, dense fog as they talked at a quaint cafe about the theologian's new book, *Heavenly Angels in Flying Saucers.*

"What is this, Father?" Dr. Lazant asked as he devoured the delicious pastry before him that Father Saltucci had ordered.

"It is Cenci alla Fiorentine," the Father replied with a smile. "It is a deep fried sweet pastry sprinkled with confectioner's sugar. You like?"

"Bennisimo!"

They talked of the time that was fast approaching when the troublesome evangelical Christians were to be abducted by the heavenly angels, the Watchers, led by AZAZEL. The time would soon arise when those left behind could pursue a new One World Religion without any hindrances. The next day, they were joined by Rabbi Ginsburg, Forrest the Wiccan, the Hindu Shiva Priestess, the Buddhist Representative of the Dalai Lama, the Islamic Cleric from Iran and Lloyd Foot the Ogala Sioux Medicine man. The man from the World Council of Churches did not show up.

They all met at a beautiful villa overlooking the Seven Hills of Rome. It belonged to a friend of Father Saltucci who was busy traveling in the Orient. The rain continued and put a nasty gloom over the proceedings. The housekeeper of the villa prepared a sumptuous meal for them to dine on. First she brought out a bowl of Caponata, a cold eggplant appetizer with pinenuts, capers and anchovies. They all sat under the covered veranda and watched the August shower clean the dirty monuments of ancient Rome one more time. She then brought out Gnocchi alla Romana with several bottles of Chianti. Everyone drank heartedly except Imam Hadad who restrained himself for religious reasons. Forrest, especially, drank like a fish.

Forrest stood at the railing and raised her hands to the heavens in solemn prayer. She thanked Mother Earth for blessing their gathering with her mist of spirit. Everyone else continued to eat and hardly even paid much attention to her. She threw her long red hair around and around in a dizzying spectacle.

"I am so pleased that all of you could make it to our gathering," Dr. Lazant said as he played with his long sideburns. "The time is short. Soon we will be in control of the minds of the people. Soon we will be free to promote global unity without those pesky, hate filled Christians around. We are to lay the groundwork for AZAZEL and his angels to take over the religious instruction of the world's people. It will be based upon a theocracy centered in Jerusalem!"

"Jerusalem?" Father Saltucci gasped as he nearly choked on his gnocchi. "Why Jerusalem and not Rome?"

"Jerusalem is the Holy City. It is where the Messiah is to return. He is not coming to Rome or New York or Salt Lake City but to Jerusalem. It is where the Temple will be rebuilt and He will rule the world from there. It is all in Biblical prophecy," Dr. Lazant answered reverently.

"Are you referring to the writings of the Prophet Isaiah where it states that 'I will raise my throne above the stars of God and I will sit on the Mount of Assembly'?" Rabbi Ginsberg asked excitedly as she began to laugh in a way that upset even those in attendance. Her perky short cut hair began to fly all around as she rotated her head in wild gyrations much as Forrest had done earlier.

"Yes, my dear," Dr. Lazant replied. "That man, according to the apostle Paul 'opposes and exalts himself above every so-called god or object of worship so that he takes his seat in the Temple of God displaying himself as being God'."

"But the Temple is not there, guys!" Forrest said with a quizzical look on her face. "Helllooo!?"

"It will be rebuilt. It has to be. Scripture says so!" Dr. Lazant said with a soft voice. "Our man has to declare himself to be God from there. No question about its being rebuilt and rebuilt very soon!"

"Wait a minute, people," Imam Ishmael Hadad cautioned as he threw up his arms in obvious outrage. "I never heard this before. I was under the impression that the evangelical Christians were to be removed before the Messiah returns to promote world unity. We Moslems have built a working relationship with the Catholic Church in Rome over the years which has borne much fruit. But now you are talking of Israel and Jerusalem and the rebuilding of the Temple. That city and that site are holy to us Muslims. What is going to happen to the Dome of the Rock and the El Aqsa Mosque? Are you saying that the Jews will remove all of this? We will have a Jihad, a Holy War, if our religious sites are destroyed."

"Relax, Saladin! This man is whom you call Imam Madhi. According to your Holy Koran, He is the Messiah who will defend Himself with supreme knowledge. He will declare himself to be god and take the seat of David in the Temple," Dr. Lazant answered firmly as he stood up and walked right over to Hadad and looked him square in the eye. "But He will be on our side, not that of the Jews. He is described in the Old Testament Book of Daniel. It says that a King will arise, insolent and skilled in intrigue and his power will be mighty, but not by his own power he will destroy mighty men and the Jewish people. He is Daniel's small horn. He is our Savior who will bring world peace."

"How do you know so much about this King? Isn't he whom those crazy Evangelical Christians call the Antichrist?" Rabbi Ginsberg asked, still laughing hysterically.

"Reverend Shea did all the research on this. He was supposed to be the one to explain all of this. Too bad that he got confused by those mad Christians. I will try and do the best that I can from his notes. The king's name is Satan-Armilus according to Rabbi Saadia Gaon's *Midrash Gelullah*, written in 925 AD. He is the King of Tyre, the king of ten nations, the king of the last generation. Rabbi Gaon said that he will be a Jewish king and his name is Satan-Armilus, not, as the Gentiles call him, Antichrist. The Rabbi said that there is no proof of Christian influence on who he really is. He will tell the Jews to bring him their Torah and testify that he is God. All those who will not bow down to him will be killed. Do not worry, Imam Hadad. The religious Jews will bow down to our King or they will die! All will bow down before him, Christian, Jew, Moslem or Pagan. Every knee will bend and every tongue will confess that He is God or they will be killed."

"But he will be Jewish, you say?" Hadad wondered as he played with his headdress and his black piercing eyes tore holes in Dr. Lazant.

"Of course, He has to be of the Jewish line. Otherwise how will He take David's throne in the Temple? But Jesus was Jewish also, so what does it really mean after all? All that matters is that He will rule the world from that seat on the Mount of Assembly, and we will be there with Him. We will help determine the one world religious doctrine that He will promulgate. You descendants of Ishmael were promised to multiply and become a great nation by the Lord Himself. You and the Jews are both of the line of Abraham. You shall both share the center stage during these upcoming years!"

"He is Kalki, the final incarnation of Vishnu," the Shiva Priestess cried out as she stood up and whirled around leaving a trail of color from her sari. Her brown complexion and dark eyes glowed as the dot between her eyes jumped around her face. "It is written in the Bhagavad Gita that whenever the law declines and the purpose of life is forgotten, then Kalki will be born to reestablish the law and usher in the golden age of peace!"

"Our Holy books call him Maitreya," the Buddhist monk interjected as he stood

239

up and bowed to Dr. Lazant with his hands in prayer. "He will be the bearer of true peace who is scheduled to appear at the end of the millennium. The time is fast approaching."

"Our white buffalo has been born," Lloyd Foot bellowed. "The time of the great peacemaker is soon to be upon us."

All of them stood up and formed a circle and held hands. They prayed for unity and wisdom in the crucial days that were to follow. They realized that they were to be the ones to carry the banner for spiritual discernment once the Christians were removed. Father Saltucci embraced Rabbi Ginsberg and they in turn grabbed Ishmael Hadad. There in one unified three headed six armed and six legged body was Catholicism, Judaism, and Islam. They moved as one across the floor slowly picking up the Hindu, the Buddhist, the Wiccan, and the Medicine Man until they were a six headed beast. Dr. Lazant joined in as the whole bizarre multiheaded entity slowly moved across the floor in apparent reverie.

"Let us all go on to Jerusalem to see how that unprecedented undertaking is progressing," Dr. Lazant finally said after what seemed like hours of ecstatic comradarie. "Jerusalem is the navel of the entire planet. It is where the action has always been and where the new world order will first begin and from where it will be ruled. After we enjoy our zabaione with marsala wine, I want you all to go pack up your things. I have use of a private jet that will take us to the Holy Land!"

There was a loud cracking noise and the Dome of the Rock began to shake violently. It was a Friday and it was packed with hundreds of worshippers who began to scream in panic and run for the doors. Scores of people were crushed in the pandemonium. The same thing happened in the El Aqsa Mosque nearby. The entire Temple Mount area shook dramatically and the Dome of the Rock and the El Aqsa Mosque came crashing down in a pile of hundreds of huge broken stones crushing all those inside.

# XVIII

As they made their descent into the Tel Nof Airstrip, Judah gazed reflectively at the beautiful campus of the Weizman Institute in Rehovot. He remembered his studies there among the carefully tended gardens, green lawns, flower beds, trees and shrubs. It was a beautiful campus with some of the best scientists in Israel. It was at Weizman that he had first met Ronit. Their first date had taken them to visit the tombs of Chaim and Vera Weizman carefully secluded in a grove of trees on campus. Ronit had ironically yet prophetically joked that she hoped that their relationship would not forever be doomed because of that initial visit to these tombs.

As Judah was reflecting on his past from his seat in the co-pilot's seat, Captain Labensky stared unbelieving at the site of the Dome of the Rock in the distance shaking violently and collapsing into a pile of rubble with a huge cloud of dust rising into the air.

"Look, Yehuda!" he pointed. "Someone just blew up the Dome. Now all hell will break loose."

"Oh my God," Judah replied shaking his head. "I cannot believe that I lived to see that destroyed. It does set the stage for the rebuilding of the Temple. Can you imagine what excitement must be going on right now with the Temple Mount Faithful people?"

"The Temple Mount Faithful people?" Captain Labensky yelled, "what about the Palestinian Authority and Hamas? They must be enraged. What a time to return to Eretz Yisrael *(H.The land of Israel)*. Maybe we should abort our landing and take the women and children somewhere else?"

"We are low on fuel, Captain, we have to land right here," Judah answered matter of factly. "And besides, the Believers are waiting for us, aren't they? Look, poor Avraham is dead. We have all sacrificed for this mission, Sir. We cannot turn back now. Everything is happening just as Bible prophecy said that it would anyway. We all knew that this day would come."

"I know, Yehuda, but..." Captain Labensky said, patting him on the back. "I understand that we must pursue our goal. It's just that I'd hate to see anymore innocent friends perish, but I do know that Hashem is in control. If He wanted to take Avraham home, then I shouldn't complain. At least I know where he is going. That is more than I can say about his parents or my other Israeli friends!"

The plane taxied on the runway after a smooth landing. The Israeli sky was

241

bright and blue and the desert air was hot. Judah ran down the stairs and kissed the ground as soon as the plane had stopped.

Dawn ran down the stairs right behind him and gave him a big hug. Captain Knowington soon followed with his wife and daughters. Everyone else followed suit. Last to disembark was Judah's mother Bertha.

"Ma, aren't you glad to be home?" Judah asked as he ran up the stairs to give her a hug and a kiss.

"It is good to be home, Judah," she replied. "But these are perilous times, son. Look at that poor copilot, Avraham. He died bringing us here. When will this all end?"

"I don't know, Ma. I hope soon. Rosh Hashanah is right around the corner and there is so much work to do. I wonder where our friends are?"

At that very moment a black bus with its windows darkened pulled up to the airplane and several bearded men disembarked. They were wearing black hats and coats and they had beards. They looked like the Ultra Orthodox.

"Shalom, Yehuda," the first man said. He was about seventy with a grey beard and wild sparkling blue eyes. "My name is Rabbi Yacov Bernstein. It is so nice to finally meet you, mishpoche (Y.family)! Baruch Hashem. Come, you all need to get into de bus. Ve need to leave as soon as possible. De military people only promised to look de oter vay for a few minutes."

"What happened to the Temple Mount area, Rabbi?" Judah asked as he led everyone into the bus. "We saw it blow up from the air. Who claimed responsibility? Have there been any threats of reprisals yet? I bet hundreds perished in the rubble?"

"Come on people, move it," the Rabbi said as he waved them into the bus. "Director Butrell told us dat his friend in de Mossad could only promise us a short vindow of opportunity to retrieve you before de military responded. You vant to know who destroyed de Temple Mount area, Yehuda? De devastation included not only de Dome of de Rock and de El Aqsa Mosque but de Dome of de Spirits, El Kas Fountain, Dome of Solomon and Dome of de Chains. But you know vat, the Vestern Vall of de Temple vas not destroyed at all. Isn't dat a miracle?"

"Well, who did it, Rabbi?" Judah again asked as the bus was filled, and it sped away from the airplane.

"Hashem did it, Yehuda!" the Rabbi said as he smiled, revealing a mouth full of gold.

"What are you talking about? We saw it explode in a column of dust?"

"It vas an eartquake, Yehuda! It measured 8 on de Richter scale at de Technion. But it only destroyed de buildings on de Temple Mount. Baruch Hashem! De Arabs cannot blame us. Ve did not do it! It is a mechya! A miracle! Baruch Hashem!" the Rabbi said triumphantly.

"Rabbi Yacov," Bertha interjected. "Are you a real Rabbi? Are you Orthodox? You sure look frum to me."

242

"You must be Yehuda's mother," the Rabbi said as he reached over and kissed her hand. "Ve have all heard of you here in Yisrael. About how you had a direct confrontation vit Yeshua. Vat a B'rakhah. Vat a blessing. Yes I am a real Rabbi, an Orthodox Rabbi. Who do I look like some Santa Claus schlemiel *(Y.simpleton)*?"

"Well I don't know Rabbi," Bertha replied pensively. "I just never met a Rabbi before that believed in Yeshua?"

"Vell, Mrs. Meire, it is a miraculous story. I kept asking Hashem about dis Yeshua. I vanted to know who this imposter vas dat vas leading so many of my Jews avay from Him. The only place that I had seen his name vas in an old manuscript called *Toledoth Yeshu.* It is an old blasphemy that claims that yeshu was the bastard son of Miriam *(H.Mary)* and a disreptuable Jew, Joseph Pandera. I had also found an old Munich manuscript of the Talmud *(collection of Jewish Law and tradition)*. It said in Sanhedrin 68a dat 'on de eve of Passover, dey hanged Yeshua de Nazarene, and an announcement vent out in front of Him for 40 days saying, Yeshua de Nazarene is going to be stoned because he practiced sorcery and enticed and led Israelites astray. Anyvon who knows anyting in His favor let him come and plead on His behalf. No one did, and He vas hanged'."

"I don't remember that in that Sanhedrin 68," Bertha replied as she smiled affectionately at the Rabbi.

"Like I said, Mrs. Meire, this was from a Manuscript found in Munich that vas dated from the 14th century. Most copies of the Babylonian Talmud had anything referring to Yeshua expunged during the Middle Ages because of fear of the wrath of the Christian inquisitors. I vas fascinated how this Nazarene Jew could lead so many of our people astray. Vas He a bastard, a sorcerer or vas He who He said dat He vas? All of my life I had spent my time trying to undermine the work of Yeshua. But the more I tried to expunge Him for our Jewish people, the more He touched my heart. The scriptures about the Mashiach, Yesha'yahu *(H.Isaiah)* 53 or Sepher Tehillim *(H.Psalms)* 22 or Michayahu *(H.Micah)* 5:2 always left me looking back to Yeshua. I hated myself for it but it would not go away. Then all of a sudden one day as I vas reading Yesha'yahu 9 that 'for a child vill be born to us, a Son vill be given to us and the government vill rest on His shoulders; and His name vill be called Wonderful Counselor, Mighty God, Eternal Father, Prince of Peace', I vas confronted vit the awesome presence of de Holy One Hallowed be His Name. He spoke to my heart trough de Ruach Hakodesh. I vas slain in de spirit and fell to my knees. He gave me a new heart and filled me vit His Spirit. He had obviously picked me out before the creation of de world for His purpose. Now I have joined a group of several other Rabbis who have also seen de light of Hashem in all its glory. Ve are of course still Jews but ve realize dat Yeshua Hamashiach is our Lord and Savior. Once you are born a Jew from Jewish parents you are always a Jew. Nothing can change dat fact anymore dan a schvartze *(Y.Black man)* can change who and vat he is. It is in de blood. And furtermore, ve know dat He is coming back soon for all of us in the Natzal, the Harpazo, the Rapture! Dat is vy Hasatan is so angry because

243

he knows dat his time is short. He also has to deceive dose left behind to believe dat ve vere not taken by the Lord but vere taken instead by UFOs."

"Oh Rabbi," Judah and Bertha and Dawn all said simultaneously. "What a beautiful testimony!"

"Rabbi, are you married?" Bertha asked pointedly as she stared at him with a big smile on her face.

"I am a vidower. But my stance with Yeshua has cost me my family and my congregation. All dat vas important to me, but I had to do it. Many of the oders in our group have not told deir families or congregations yet."

"Isn't he cute," Bertha whispered to Judah.

"Ma, stop it," Judah answered embarrassed. "Act your age, Ma!"

The bus streaked through the Judean hills towards Jerusalem. Since nobody could see out the darkened windows, everyone chose to sing songs to the Lord. Dawn led the boisterous rendition. She was accompanied by one of the Orthodox Believers who sang in Hebrew.

"Where are we going, Rabbi?" Judah asked.

"Ve are going to our compound in Jerusalem. It is near Independence Park. Do you know vere Keren Kayemet Road is, Yehuda? Ve are right between it and Ben Yehuda Street. Ve have a large house ready for all of you."

"And what kind of equipment do you have for our mission?" Judah wondered. "Do you have computers?"

"Computers, shmuters, you ask, Yehuda?" the Rabbi laughed. "Ve have a regular Technion in our basement. Your friends in America provided so much equipment dat ve had to expand de building. Ve have some of the best computer literate Believers in Yisrael at our disposal. Ve are linked to satellites and all dat mishegoss *(Y.absurd stuff)*. I don't know anyting about any of dis stuff, but I have been told dat it is state of de art and even some of it is still top secret. Our security has to be first rate. Vile you had Ultra to worry about in America, ve have Arab terrorist factions dat are really linked to AZAZEL. Dey vant to kill us all before ve expose deir plans for vorld domination."

"Did they know that we were arriving?" Judah asked apprehensively

"Probably! But dis bus is armor plated and de vindows are bulletproof," Rabbi Bernstein said as he knocked on the walls. "Ve all are at de mercy of de Ruach Hakodesh however. Vitout it ve are powerless."

The private jet carrying Dr. Lazant and his followers began its descent into Ben Gurion International Airport at Lod. Most were sleeping when Ishmael Hadad began to scream.

"Look! Look! the Mosque of Omar and the El Aqsa mosque have been bombed. There will be Jihad for this. Every Zionist will die for this. They have destroyed our Holiest sites. Death to the infidels!"

"Relax, Ishmael!" Dr. Lazant yelled as he was awakened from a sound sleep. "I told you that this had to happen. In order for the Temple to be rebuilt for our man to enter and declare himself to be God, those structures had to be removed."

"Dr. Lazant," the pilot's voice came over the intercom, "the Israelis are reporting that the destruction on the Temple Mount was done by a magnitude 8 earthquake centered on a previously undiscovered fault line under the Temple Mount."

"See, Ishmael. I told you that the Holy One had this all under control. It was not the Israelis but the powers of our people in Heavenly places."

"I still cannot sit idly by as our Holy places are destroyed. The Jews will rebuild their Temple and make Jerusalem their city."

"So what, Ishmael? The end justifies the means, doesn't it?" Father Saltucci answered quietly.

"In the end, our man will rule from the rebuilt Temple and all the Jews will bow down to him," Dr. Lazant countered as he went right up to Ishmael and attempted to calm him down.

"Relax, Ishy!" Rabbi Ginsberg smirked as she looked at the ruins of the Temple Mount out of her window. "Those fanatical Orthodox Jews will rebuild the Temple and we will occupy it. Don't you see that? They hate my kind as much as they hate you! Let go of your anger."

Imam Hadad did not let go of his anger. Instead it grew inside him to the boiling point until he grabbed his AK47 and began waving it in the faces of everyone on board.

"Don't tell me that everything is all right," he shouted as everyone moved back in fear. "Those Jews are a crafty people. How do I know that they did not blow up the Dome and the Mosque and say that it was an earthquake? They are as deceitful as Satan himself. They are his children after all. I will not let them deceive me into believing that I need to sanction their rebuilding of the Temple on this Holy Site of Islam. This is where Mohammed ascended to heaven on his horse. And you want to desecrate this Holy site by rebuilding the Jewish Temple there. No way. Death to the infidels."

Imam Hadad was approached by Dr. Lazant, who held out his hand in friendship but was met only by the barrel of the AK47 in his chest.

"Come on, Ishmael," Dr. Lazant pleaded, "you need to put down the rifle. We can discuss this rationally when we land. If you fire that weapon in here, the plane will do down."

"Relax, brother," the Shiva Priestess said as she stared at him with her hypnotic black eyes. "You must leave this to the powers that be that are greater than any of us. Put down the rifle. Please, put down the rifle."

Her soothing, hypnotic voice eased the Imam's anxiety and he slowly lowered the AK 47 assault rifle. Then Forrest made a wild rush for him, and he responded by raising his rifle and firing. Forrest did manage to hit the end of the rifle with her pudgy fingers and knock it to the side. The rifle blast blew a hole in the fuselage of the plane and it began to immediately lose air pressure and dive. The pressure differential sucked Ishmael and Forrest out of the plane's cabin in a mass of confusion, terror and screaming. The rest of the passengers grabbed for dear life onto the seats to prevent their following the two of them to their deaths.

The jet made a quick descent and shortly stabilized itself in spite of the loss of air pressure in the cabin. The pilot came back to see what had happened and found a gaping hole in the wall of the passenger cabin. He was informed that two passengers had been sucked out including the one who had perpetrated the deed. He informed Father Saltucci that the man must have been wearing a parachute under his coat because he was spotted gliding down towards Lod on his own.

"That fanatic almost cost all of us our lives," Father Saltucci moaned. "Oh Mary Mother of God! Poor Forrest is now in Heaven with our blessed Virgin. Bless her soul!"


The bus carrying the Joshua Brigade raced along deserted hilly dusty roads between Tel Nof Airstrip and Jerusalem. Just as they came around a deserted mountain pass, they were attacked on all sides. A mine went off under the front of the bus and blew up the engine. There was the sound of automatic gunfire all around them. The women began to scream and fell on the floor covering their children. Captain Knowington and Judah immediately stood up and assembled the men.

"Let's go, men!" Captain Knowington shouted. "We must disembark this bus to engage the enemy. Have your weapons ready. Let's go before they storm the bus and kill the women and children!"

"Yeah, he is right!" Judah countered. "These windows are bulletproof and the bus is armor plated. The women and the Rabbinic students will be safe in here, but we must engage the enemy before the try to enter the bus."

Captain Knowington gave an automatic weapon to Captain Labensky and told him to sit right in front and guard the women and children. He was not to open the door for anyone unless he could verify their identity.

"Do you understand, Captain?" Captain Knowington barked.

"Sir, I was in the IDF for 8 years. I want to come with you."

"Don't worry, none of them will enter this bus if I can help it," Dawn said as she picked up a rifle and sat at the front of the bus. "Captain Labensky can go with you men! Be careful, Judah."

"Now you go and kill those momzers *(Y.untrustworthy persons)*!" Bertha said with a scowl on her face.

As Captain Knowington opened the door of the bus and disembarked with his men, they were hit with a hail of gunfire and many died on the steps of the bus. Before they had all disembarked, a dozen men lay dead. Judah and Captain Knowington miraculously escaped serious injury. They hid under the bus and returned fire with high powered automatic gunfire and grenade and rocket launchers. The enemy pulled back from both sides of the bus.

"We need to make them retreat even farther away from the bus," Judah said to Captain Knowington as he shot two more terrorists dead with pinpoint accuracy.

"Judah, you take some men and move northward, and I will take the rest and attack those south of us. On my mark. Ready? Go!"

Judah's men raced forward blasting their weapons and rocket launchers until their attackers began to turn and run. As soon as Judah and his men rounded a hillside in pursuit, however, another group of these Palestinian terrorists jumped up and tore Judah's men to pieces. Seven men were cut to ribbons. Judah screamed and mowed the terrorists down with his automatic weapon. They tried mercilessly to kill him, but he would not be hit. Finally as he stood over the last terrorist he looked into his eyes and they were glowing red.

"Our time is fast approaching, Judah," it laughed as Judah stood on its chest. "Soon we will dominate the earth and rule from right here in Jerusalem! Our leader is coming!"

Judah screamed and blew its head off. He then ran to see how many of his men were still alive. He only found a handful and they were all wounded. Captain Labensky had a shoulder wound but he still managed to gather up the men.

"Men, let's go and see how Captain Knowington is doing," Judah yelled. "I know that some of you are wounded, but this is no time for commiseration. Our women's and spiritual leaders' lives are at stake!"

Judah raced back to the bus with his ragtag soldiers tailing closely behind him. He found Captain Knowington and all of his men dead on the side of the road. Nearby was an empty box of Cracker Jacks. All of the terrorists had been killed as well.

"Oh God no!" Judah wailed as he mulled over the empty box of Cracker Jacks. Had Mike Butrell been there? Was he one of the enemy after all? Did he kill Captain Knowington?

Judah headed back to the bus distraught. When he knocked on the bus, Dawn asked, "Who is it?"

"It is Judah, please open the door."

When the door was opened and everyone realized the scope of the massacre, the wives and mothers began to weep and cry out to the Lord. Dawn ran up to Judah.

"Oh thank God that you are safe, Judah," Dawn screamed as she through her arms around him. "All of the men died, except this handful?" Dawn asked stunned. "Oh my God! Oh Ann, I'm so sorry."

"Oh my God, why did we come so far to have him die on this deserted mountain road?" Ann wailed. "Oh Jennifer and Rebecca, I am so sorry. Your father was a good man who gave his life for the Lord."

"But why him," Rebecca shrieked out. "Why not Judah or someone else? It isn't fair!"

"Oh God, this is why we came all these miles?" Jennifer screamed. "To see our father killed? I want to see him," she said as she raced out of the bus.

"No Jennifer, wait!" Judah yelled as he raced after her.

"Oh, look at him," Jennifer cried out as she found him with a bullet through his right eye which had entered his brain. She began to gag and vomit all over him. "Now look what I have done. I have desecrated his body with my throw up. Oh God, I am so angry!"

Jennifer stood up and began pounding Judah in the chest with her fists. He let her continue until she broke down and cried.

"I know that it is painful, dear," Judah said reassuringly. "Your father was a brave man who died along with all these other men protecting not only you and your mother but in protecting all of us from the approaching demonic horde. Many good men have died to get us to this point and I will not be deterred now lest they all died in vain."

"I cannot believe it," shrieked the woman who had lost her children off of the Mark V. "Oh no! Oh no! Now my husband too! We have lost dozens of men from this group. They all died in protecting you, Judah. Everyone dies but you continue to live. How can you live with yourself?"

The small pudgy lady with short blond hair and now wild yellow eyes picked up a rifle and stuck it in Judah's face. She knew how to use it. That was painfully obvious in a second.

"It is your time to die now too, Judah!" she cackled.

Dawn and Bertha made their way toward the distraught lady, but Judah waved them off.

"Go ahead, shoot!" Judah yelled at her. "I agree with you that it is not fair that all these good men have died for me to live. I never wanted this assignment. I never thought that I was worthy enough. Go on, kill me and then I can be with these good men again."

"No, don't do it!" Dawn replied. "Judah, I can't believe that you would leave me here all alone. You would rather be with your soldier buddies than with me?"

"Come on, lady, make my day!" Judah yelled at her without flinching.

"Go on, lady, end his misery!" Bertha said emphatically. "He is so miserable here alone with us women that he probably would be better off in heaven if that is where Hashem wants him to be!"

"Bertha, stop it!" Dawn said as she inched ever closer to the lady.

Suddenly Mike Butrell jumped into the bus with his tall lanky frame. Judah glanced over and caught sight of him and quickly grabbed the rifle out of the woman's hands and aimed it at Butrell.

"Funny meeting you here!" Judah shouted at him. "I found your Cracker Jacks box at Captain Knowington's head. Did you kill him and his men? Are you working with Ultra and AZAZEL after all?"

"Judah, oh ye of so little faith!" Butrell replied. "We came as soon as we heard."

"What are you talking about? How did you come thousands of miles in a few minutes? I may be dumb, Butrell, but I am not that stupid."

"I followed you here from the U S of A!" Butrell said. "I wasn't sure what kind of reception that you would receive, and I knew that the IDF would probably not come to your rescue. We arrived and killed off the terrorists after they had killed your men. I've got a helicopter from the Mossad ready to take all of you to Jerusalem."

"I don't know," Judah questioned. "Why should I trust you? Why didn't you save Captain Knowington or his men? Seems mighty coincidental that you arrived after they have been killed and want to take the rest of us with you!"

"You just have to trust me, Judah!" Butrell answered. "Come here with me, Judah."

Deputy Director Butrell took Judah over to Captain Knowington's body. He reached down and pulled aside the eyepatch over his left eye. Under it was a radio transmitter.

"We knew exactly where you were going all of the time," Butrell said. "Peter encouraged us to put this in so that we could monitor the Joshua Brigade."

"Did you know about this, Ann?" Judah asked nervously.

"No, I did not, Judah!" Ann replied still sobbing uncontrollably.

"How do we know that Ultra did not put it there?" Judah questioned. "What do you think, Rabbi?"

"I just know dat he helped get de plane dat brought you here and got us permission to go and pick you up. If he vanted to kill you, he could have done it earlier. If he is part of de Adversary's legions den God vill judge him harshly for his deception."

They all settled into an uneasy truce. Everyone gathered up all of the bodies and Rabbi Bernstein said a prayer over them.

"Dey are all now in Heaven wit Hashem de Fadder and Yeshua. You can be assured of dat fact. Dey are out of dis vorld now and are at peace," Rabbi Bernstein said. "Ve vill all be vit dem soon in de Natzal, de Harpazo, de Rapture. Dey died so dat ve could live and continue to finish our vork. I don't believe dat de Lord is finished wit Judah or me just yet. Dese dear men died so dat ve could continue on. I am sure dat Hashem velcomed dem vit de greeting, vell done good and faitful servant. I know dat ve vill miss dem dearly. Of course dat ve vill. But dey are still in our hearts and our prayers and ve vill see dem all very soon! Dat is de real encouragement! Dey are separated from us for a short vile, but ve vill be vit dem for eternity. Dat is far better dan our oter unbelieving family and friends who ve spend our time here on Eart vit, but who ve vill not see during all of eternity. Tink about dat!"

Those wives who had lost husbands all held hands and cried and sang praises to the Lord. They were terribly devastated by their losses but they were also elated by what their husbands had done for them and the Joshua Brigade's mission. Ann and her girls fell to their knees sobbing and Dawn comforted them as best that she could. Bertha comforted the short blond headed woman and as many others as she

249

could reach. After burying their dead and seeing to the wounded few survivors, they boarded Deputy Director Butrell's waiting unmarked Mossad helicopter for the flight to the safe house in Jerusalem.

Yitzchak hastily returned to Rabbi Waxman's hospital room to tell him that the Dome of the Rock and El Aqsa Mosque had been destroyed by Hashem in an earthquake and that the Temple could now be rebuilt. But when he arrived at the Rebbe's room he was not there. He ran up to a nurse and asked where he was.

"I am looking for Rabbi Waxman," he asked nervously."He has not passed on, has he?"

"Not yet," Nurse Goldman answered, "But it won't be very long now. His condition worsened and we had to put him into Intensive Care. He has slipped into a coma. His organs have shut down. Why don't you pray for him? That is what you religious people do all the time, isn't it? Funny, isn't it, that in spite of all your prayers, he still is dying like the rest of us mortals."

"How one lives determines where one goes when he dies," Yitzchak cried out. "He was a good man who did many mitzvot and if anyone deserves to go to Gan Eden, it is the Rabbi."

"Well, he told me that he did not know where he was going and he was worried," the Nurse smirked as her enormous belly rippled with laughter.

"Well, the Temple Mount has been leveled and the Temple can be rebuilt. We can start blood sacrifices again for our sins."

"Blood sacrifices? You Orthodox are meshugge, crazy! It will be too late for this old Rabbi no matter what. He has only hours to live!"

Yitzchak knelt down outside the Intensive Care Unit with his classmates and began to pray earnestly for the Rabbi. The Nurse just shuffled around them shaking her head and huffing and puffing all the while.

As the helicopter flew over Jerusalem towards its destination, which was a large stucco and stone house between Ben Yehuda and Keren Kayemeth streets, they were monitored by the Israelis but Butrell had previously told them that they were a CIA covert training operation, and they were allowed to continue unobstructed. When they approached the house it suddenly exploded in a crushing blast, throwing billows of dark chemical clouds into the air.

"Oy, vey ist mir!" Rabbi Bernstein moaned. "More good people, Hashem's people, have perished for His cause. Dis battle is really heating up. Ve must be close to de end!"

"Oy! Oy! Oy Gevalt!"*(Y. Oh No!)*, one of Rabbi Bernstein's students cried out. "My wife and children were in that house!"

Now the cries and lamentations had spread from the widows of the Joshua Brigade to the Orthodox Jews who had families in the house. Everyone in the helicopter was brokenhearted. They all cried out to the Lord for peace and for Him to ease their terrible pain. Butrell began munching on another box of Cracker Jacks.

"Do you have to do that now?" Bertha yelled at him. "Have you no respect for the dead?"

"Sorry, ma'am. I meant no disrespect. I was only dealing with the stress in my usual fashion by munching on Cracker Jacks. I have been doing this for over thirty years since I quit smoking and drinking. It has worked real well. Sorry!"

"Where do we go now, Rabbi?" Butrell asked solemnly.

"Head up to Sfat," the Rabbi replied. "I know some believers in de Galil *(H.Galilee)!*"

"Wait a minute," Mike Butrell interrupted. "We just got a message that you are supposed to go immediately to Hadassah Hospital on Mt. Scopus. You, Rabbi, and Judah. Your friends in the safe house got a message out right before they were killed that there is a famous Rabbi that is dying that you have to meet."

"Vat is his name?" Rabbi Bernstein asked curiously.

"Rabbi Waxman!" they said.

"Rabbi Vaxman!" Rabbi Bernstein replied shocked. "He is one of de most respected Orthodox Rabbis in Israel. He is a sage, a prophet among his tousands of followers. Vat can ve do for him? He honestly believes dat he is a righteous man but unfortunately he is really lost and going to hell. Vat are ve supposed to do on his deatbed? Show him de light in a few verses dat he has read and reread for 50 years and still doesn't see de trut."

"Rabbi Bernstein, calm down," Judah said as he attempted to reassure the Rabbi. "Maybe we are to lead him to Yeshua?"

"Dat vould be nice, but..."

"All things are possible for those who believe and trust in Yeshua Hamashiach," Judah said with a smile.

"This was the last communication from your people, Rabbi," Butrell said emphatically. "I would honor their wishes if I were you. It will be a blessing to their memory!"

"But how did dey contact you? Dey did not know dat you vere here, and dey certainly did not have any radio transmission equipment," Rabbi Bernstein said suspiciously.

"They did not?" Butrell asked matter of factly.

"No dey did not!" the Rabbi replied nervously.

"Maybe it is another trap by the Adversary to get Rabbi Bernstein and me?" Judah responded angrily. "I don't trust you, Butrell. Isn't it ironic that you receive a message from a group that has no transmitter which tells you to drop me and the Rabbi off at Hadassah Hospital? I don't know about all this, Sir. You better come up with a better story or I am going to take over this helicopter."

Judah brought up his automatic rifle and aimed it right at Butrell. Butrell shook his head and picked up his box of Cracker Jacks and began munching from it again.

"Take us to Hadassah Hospital on Mt. Scopus!" he said to his CIA pilot.

"Maybe you should get off at the Hospital, Butrell?" Judah shouted as he cocked his rifle.

"No, you and the Rabbi are getting off," Butrell said with a smile.

"I want to go too!" Dawn yelled. "I don't want to be separated from Judah again. If he dies, then I will die also!"

"Dawn, you are crazy," Judah countered.

"Yeah, crazy in love with you. You big dumb Jew."

"I want to go too," Bertha yelled as she ran up to Rabbi Bernstein and put her arm inside his.

"Forget it, Ma!" Judah replied as he went up and separated her from the Rabbi and sat her down.

"Judah, we have learned that there is a concerted effort here in Israel to kill off the Jewish believers before they can witness to their family and friends throughout Israel. You and I both know that the end is near and once we are gone the Israelis here and the Jews all over the world will be deceived by the Anti Christ, Satan Armilus, into believing the lie that we were abducted by UFOs. Who is going to be left behind to tell them the truth? Maybe it will be Rabbi Waxman's students? All of our other avenues have as you said been closed. God is still in control though. Do you honestly believe that all of the men of the Joshua Brigade as well as Senator Jordan and Congressman Jacobs and Major Kole and General Desporte have all died in vain? No, they have all given their lives so that you and Rabbi Bernstein could make it to this point at this time! I really don't understand exactly what is going on. I'll admit that. But it appears that the Joshua Brigade was created to get you here to Hadassah Hospital to speak with Rabbi Waxman. What will happen? Only God knows. But I am telling you from the bottom of my heart, so help me God, that I am on your side, Judah. You just have to trust me!" Butrell pleaded.

"But who told you about Rabbi Waxman and Hadassah Hospital, Butrell?" Judah shook his head and put down his rifle. "I need to know before I can believe in you."

"You wouldn't believe me if I told you, son," Butrell answered shaking his head. "Just let it go!"

"No, tell me or we are not going anywhere!"

"It was me, Judah!" his mother finally piped in. "The Lord laid it on my heart and I just shared it with Director Butrell."

"What?" Judah said with a look of bewilderment on his face.

"That is correct, Judah," Butrell answered with a smile.

"And you believe what she said as gospel? Hellooo!? This woman just accepted the Lord a heartbeat ago and all of a sudden she is the maven *(Y.expert)*?"

"Stop it, Judah," Bertha cautioned sternly. "Stop making a jackass of yourself. Yes, the Lord told me that you and Rabbi Bernstein were supposed to go and see Rabbi Waxman. What do you think, God only uses stiff necked soldiers for His work? He uses little old ladies as well!"

When the helicopter landed on the roof of Hadassah Hospital, Judah, Rabbi Bernstein and Dawn disembarked. Director Butrell gave Judah a satellite phone to contact him when they wanted to come home. Rabbi Bernstein instructed his student Yossi to guide them to his house in the Galilee near Safed.

"Do you want me to send any men with you, Judah?"

"No, we are fine," Judah said as he left his rifle but kept his Uzi pistol tucked into his pants. Dawn took a revolver with her as well. Judah glanced at the phone and thought that now Butrell could track his movements if he were indeed the enemy.

"Take care of Rabbi Bernstein!" Bertha shouted. "The Lord has plans for the two of us!"

"Ma! Stop it!" Judah yelled, thinking all the while that maybe his mother was not hearing from God but from her own lonely heart.

Judah and Dawn went cautiously down into the Hospital with Rabbi Bernstein trailing after them. They asked the first person that they saw where Rabbi Waxman's room was located.

"You are looking for the great Rebbe Waxman?" the orderly said reverently. "They put him into the Intensive Care wing on the Fifth floor. He is not supposed to live out the day."

They raced down to the fifth floor and found Rabbi Waxman's students outside the unit all covered with their tallit *(H. prayer shawls)*, and praying for their Master. Rabbi Bernstein went up to them and spoke in Hebrew and Yiddish. He asked them how the Rebbe was doing and if it were possible to see him.

"He is dying, Rabbi." Yitzchak said. "He is preparing himself to meet Hashem. They will not let any of us in. Sorry, Rabbi. You are welcome to come and pray with us. Who are your friends? Of course the woman is not welcome to pray with us, but she can sit over there. Do they know the Rebbe?"

"Hashem sent dem here. Dat is vat they say." Rabbi Bernstein rattled off his tongue before he had really thought about what he said.

"Are they mishpoche *(H.family)*?" Yitzchak said. "The woman looks like a shiksa."

Rabbi Bernstein just shook his head and waived his hand in a downward movement indicating that Yitzchak should forget about it. He then walked over to Judah and Dawn and put his arms around them and whispered.

"Dey said dat no vone is allowed in de room. Dey are especially suspicious of you guys, especially you, Dawn. I look and talk enough like dem dat I am kosher but you two are vorrisome to dem. I tink dat you two need to distract dem so dat I can sneak into de room vit Rabbi Vaxman."

Judah and Dawn immediately walked up to the Ultra Orthodox men and began to harangue them in Hebrew and in Yiddish.

"You think that your Rebbe is going to Gan-Eden when he dies?" Judah barked out at them. "He does not really know Hashem. He is just a gonif *(Y.thief)* who wants to take all your money. When he dies, he will go to Gehanna like the rest of us and you will all be left with nothing. You are a bunch of shmendricks. Losers!"

The Ultra Orthodox began to follow after Judah and Dawn as they walked away.

"Yeah, and I am a goy *(H.Gentile)* who knows that your Rebbe needs Yeshua or he is going to hell," Dawn screamed right in their faces and ran down the hall.

The Ultra Orthodox men chased Judah and Dawn down the hall and Rabbi Bernstein slipped into the Intensive Care Unit and barricaded the door and pulled the blinds. He would not have much time until the nurses returned. He got down on his knees at the side of Rabbi Waxman's bed and cried out to the Lord to heal this wizened old patriarch.

"Oh mighty Adonai," Rabbi Bernstein pleaded. "Baruch Hashem Adonai. Bless the Name of de Lord. Please, heal dis man in bot body and spirit. Give him a new body and a new heart so dat You can vork trough him to reach the masses after we are gone. Only You, Avinu, Father, can do dis at dis late date. He already has one foot in de grave. I don't know vy You brought me to dis man oter dan You plan to use him in a mighty vay. By Your stripes ve are healed!"

All of a sudden the room was filled with light. Rabbi Bernstein fell onto the ground face down. The presence of the Ruach Hakodesh was too powerful for even him to look upon. When he sat up, he heard pounding on the door. Before he could get up to open it, they had broken it down.

"What was going on in here?" the heavyset nurse bellowed out as security personnel stood at the broken door. "There was a bright light coming out from under the door?"

"It vas the Shekinah Glory of Hashem," Rabbi Waxman spoke up from the bed. He was now sitting up and smiling.

"What happened to you?" Nurse Goldman shrieked and promptly fainted.

"Look Yitzchak," Judah said with a smile as he stepped over Nurse Goldman. "Your Rebbe was healed by Rabbi Bernstein. By the way, I'm sorry for what I said about your Rebbe. It isn't true but I needed to distract you so that Rabbi Bernstein could heal him."

"I did not heal him, Judah," Rabbi Bernstein said. "Hashem healed him."

"Are you into Kabbalah, Rabbi?" Yitzchak replied, looking at all of them. "I once knew a Rebbe who could heal by doing magical incantations."

"No son, I am not," Rabbi Bernstein answered. "It vas as your Master said, the Shekinah Glory, the Ruach Hakodesh *(H.Holy Spirit)* healed him. I merely vas a conduit for it."

The students crowded around both Rabbis. They praised the work of Rabbi Bernstein and greeted Rabbi Waxman with all deference and respect.

"Baruch Hashem, Praise His Name," Rabbi Waxman said as continued to praise Hashem over and over again. "Who are you my friend?"

"I am Rabbi Bernstein from Yerushalyim! Hashem sent me here to bring you back to healt."

"Bless His Holy Name forever and ever! I don't understand vy He vould vant to do dat for dis unworthy servant, but His ways are not our ways," Rabbi Waxman replied. "Aren't you dat Rabbi dat became an apostate not too long ago? I heard about you. You accepted Yeshua as de Mashiach and you were trown out of your synagogue."

"Yes, dat is me, Rebbe," Rabbi Bernstein smiled. "Hashem spoke trough Balaam's ass, remember! He can even use a so called apostate to assist in the healing of a great Rebbe like you."

"Rebbe, is he a meshumed *(H.traitor, a jew who accepts Yeshua)*?" Yitzchak yelled as he approached Rabbi Bernstein. "This woman looks like a goy to me. I knew all along that they were up to something!"

"Yeah, we were up to healing your Rebbe!" Judah shouted as the doctors arrived. "He is back to health by the prayers and efforts of Rabbi Bernstein. I would be angry at him also if I were you. Forget about it! Look at your Rebbe!"

The doctors were astonished at his recovery. They took his vital signs and they were all normal. They did extensive blood tests and then wheeled him over to the MRI and other equipment and found him totally in remission. The pancreatic tumor had disappeared and all his organs were working fine. They finally wheeled Rabbi Waxman back to his original hospital room and went away shaking their heads in disbelief.

"Those Ultra Orthodox are scary," the Internist said with a shrug. "They seem to have a pipeline to heaven that bypasses even us Doctors!"

"Yeah, you are correct, Shmuel," the oncologist replied, "But those other people in there were Jews for Jesus people. Didn't you hear them being called apostates and meshumed?"

"Do you mean to tell me that the other old Rabbi was one of those Messianic Jews or whatever they call themselves nowadays? Do you mean to tell me that they believe that Yeshua healed him? I don't want to hear this. It is enough to deal with those Ultra Orthodox, but to deal with Jesus freaks on top of it is too much. Do you know that my daughter Ariel got involved in one of those cults? It has broken my dear wife Rivka's heart."

# XIX

It was nearing the beginning of Shabbat and the Ultra Orthodox followers of Rabbi Waxman prepared to go home.

"Is it all right to leave you, Rebbe, with these people?" Yitzchak asked with a air of concern.

"Sure, son, it vill be fine," Rabbi Waxman smiled. "Vat can dey to me? Go be vit your families on Shabbat. Tank Hashem for healing me!"

Judah parked himself outside of Rabbi Waxman's hospital room. He closely scrutinized, however, everyone who attempted to enter the room. He told them that he was an Mossad operative and when he drew his Uzi pistol nobody questioned him further. Meanwhile inside the room, Rabbi Bernstein was in deep discussion with Rabbi Waxman.

"Rebbe, can't you see dat Yeshua healed you?" Rabbi Bernstein said as he looked into the sage's soulful brown eyes.

"Hashem healed me, Rabbi," Rabbi Waxman countered. "I don't know dis yeshu. I don't vant to know him. You know how many of our people have been killed in his name. He vas a sorcerer according to de Talmud. You know all dis. You studied de same Yeshiva material in Poland as I did. Didn't you read Rabbi Izaak of Troki's polemic against the Christian claims of yeshu? How can you say dat he healed me? By da vay, vat is your first name, Rabbi?"

"It is Yacov, Rebbe. Of course I read Rabbi Izzak's sixteenth century *Faith Strengthened.* Ve all had to. But, I prayed to dis Yeshua Hamashiach to heal you. Dat is how I know. I didn't pray to Buddha or to de Wirgin Mary or to Mohammed. I prayed to Yeshua and look vat happened!"

"Yacov, my friend, you are confused. Yitzchak and all my students also prayed to Hashem to heal me if it vas His vill to do so. How do ve know dat it vasn't deir prayers dat vere answered, not yours?"

"Because it happened just as I entreated the Lord on my knees at your bedside! I don't believe in coincidences, Rebbe. Do you?"

"Of course not. You know, ven I vas a young man in Poland, I remember my parents coming home one day and telling me about a children's book dat dey had seen. I vill never forget de look on deir faces. It vas vone of abject fear and horror. I shall never forget vat it said. It has haunted me ever since and vit de killing of my parents at Aushvitz it has been burned into my soul. It said 'Jesus Christ says de Jew is a murderer trough and trough. And ven Christ had to die, de Lord didn't

256

know any oter people who vould have tortured him to deat, so dat he chose de Jews. Dat is vy de Jews pride demselves on being de chosen people'. And you, Yacov, vant me to believe dat dis same yeshu healed me. I cannot!"

"I know of dat book also, Rebbe. It vas vritten by a German voman named Bauer and vas called *Don't Trust de Fox in de Green Meadow Nor de Jew on His Oat.* Remember, Rebbe, I come from de same ghetto experiences as you do. My family for the most part also died in the Holocaust. But Yeshua healed you. Look at you. And yes, Mashiach had to die for all our sins. He came to die and villingly gave up his life so dat all dat believe in Him vill not perish but vill have eternal life. So de Jews did not kill him anymore dan anyvon else. Ve all put him on de cross. And yes, de Jews vere chosen by Hashem to be de people who brought Him into dis world. Ve vere chosen for dat."

"I am an old man, Yacov," Rabbi Waxman smiled. "I am too old to change. If I accept vat you have said, den I would lose not only my tousands of followers but my Jewishness as well. I vould become a goy *(H.Gentile)* and everyting dat I have been taught and believed in for eighty years vould be gone. Poof!"

"Dat is vat I tought, Rebbe," Rabbi Bernstein replied. "But you know vat? I am more Jewish now because I recognize our Mashiach. He is de fulfillment of our Torah."

"Our Mashiach is supposed to come as a King and bring in de millennium time of peace. De lion is supposed to lie down vit the lamb and swords are beaten into ploughshares as described in Michayahu *(H.Micah).* Dat surely did not happen ven your yoshke came. He vas hanged as reported in the Talmud. Ve Jews vere looking for a powerful deliverer to free us from Roman oppression and all ve got vas a sorcerer who did miracles and den vas killed and left us stranded."

Judah and Dawn sat outside the door and listened to the two Rabbis argue for hours. Dawn finally put her head on Judah's shoulder and fell fast asleep. It had, after all, been an exhausting couple of days. Judah prayed that the Lord would reveal Himself to Rabbi Waxman. All of the Scripture in the world, while it was the word of God and as the Prophet Yesha'yahu *(H.Isaiah)* said would thus not return to Him void, was still no substitute for the Ruach Hakodesh in bringing a non believing Jew to the Truth. It had happened to him and to his Mom and even to Rabbi Bernstein. The Holy Spirit often has to personally confront a Jew to break down the walls of prejudice and the negative historical baggage of so called christians that block the Jews from seeing the truth even more than most other people.

"Rebbe, vat of Mica'yahu 5 :2 vere Mashiach is said to be from Beit Lechem *(H.Bethlehem)* Ephrathah?"

"Mica'yahu vas speaking of King David!"

"Sure, David vas also born in Beit Lechem, but Rabbi Vaxman, David lived two hundred years before Mica'yahu!" Rabbi Bernstein countered. "And it says that this future leader goings forth are from long ago from the days of eternity. It cannot be

David! And, Rebbe, you know the Tanakh speaks of de Mashiach coming as a servant as vell. Yesha'yahu *(H. Isaiah)* speaks of de Redeemer coming to Zion. De Talmud says dat if de people are vordy, He vill come vit de clouds of heaven, but if dey are unvordy He vill come poor and riding a donkey. Zekaryah *(H.Zechariah)* speaks of de Mashiach riding in on a donkey and dat is exactly vat Yeshua did."

"Enough already, my friend," Rabbi Waxman shouted as he covered his ears. "Please leave dis old man alone. I don't vant to hear anymore."

"You don't vant to hear?! You remember vat Hashem told Moshe *(H.Moses)* in D'varim *(H.Deuteronomy)*? He said 'yet to dis day de Lord has not given you a heart to know, nor eyes to see, nor ears to hear.' You, Rebbe, are also in a state of stupor or sleep and even ven de Lord heals you from certain deat, you still don't believe!"

"Vell, how can you blame me ven it says dat Hashem Himself made us dis vay?"

"Because it is now time for Him to give you a new heart. Remember, Rebbe, vat it says in Yirmeyahu *(H.Jeremiah)* 31 and Yehezke'l *(H.Ezekiel)* 36 that Hashem vill sprinkle clean water on you and give you a new heart and put a new spirit vithin you and make a new covenant vit you? Dat is exactly vat He did for me and I know dat He vants to do it for you as vell."

"Oy vey ist mir *(Y.Oh woe is me!)*! You sound like one of dose Evangelical Christians dat I hear from all of de time. Dey are praying for me and love me. If dey love us so much then vy did dey slaughter our people from time immemorial?"

"Dose people dat slaughtered our people are not real Christians. Dey vere mostly Catolics who used de Crusades and de Inquisition and even de pogroms to try and show de world dat de Jews vere no longer Hashem's people and dat dey had replaced us as His chosen. Nobody can believe in de Bible and hate de Jews. It is impossible. The Patriarchs vere Jewish, de Torah vas given to de Jews, de Temple vas given to de Jews, de covenants vere made vit de Jews as vere de promises. The Mashiach came trough us as vell. Dose so called christians vere impostors of Hasatan!"

"How are ve Jews supposed to tell de real Christians from de impostors? It vas not only de Catolics. Look at Martin Luter. He advocated burning de synagogues and he called de Jews devils. His ideas had a great influence on Hitler's Holocaust! Here in Israel ve have Catolics, Protestants, Jehovah Vitnesses, Mormons, Evangelicals and who knows how many oter groups. Dey cannot even agree among demselves so how are ve supposed to figure out de trut?"

"You shall know dem by deir fruits, Rebbe. De bottom line is dat de Mashiach is ours. He is not a Christian Messiah vit blond hair and blue eyes."

"Speaking of dat, Yacov, vere did you get your blue eyes?" Rabbi Waxman asked smiling. "Have you some goyishe blood in you?"

"My modder said it probably vas from some Cossack in our past dat raped one of our ancestors! So I guess dat I must have some goyish blood in me. Isn't dat vy ve now trace our bloodline through our modders, instead of trough our fadders as vas Biblically. If our modder is Jewish, den ve are considered Jewish."

The two of them settled into an uneasy truce. They just sat next to one another and did not say a word for an hour. When the two doctors and the nurse came in to check on Rabbi Waxman, they just shook their heads.

"You seem to be doing fine, Rabbi," Dr. Katz, the short, bearded Internist, said with a slight air of disdain. "All of your organs are functioning normally now."

"Baruch Hashem!" Rabbi Waxman answered with a big smile.

"Vat do you make of his miraculous recovery, Doctor?" Rabbi Bernstein interjected.

"Well, it appears to be a spontaneous remission," the self assured, tall, bald oncologist Dr. Freidman, said with a piercing stare at Rabbi Bernstein.

"You really believe dat his pancreatic tumor suddenly and completely disappeared just like dat? It takes more fait to believe dat, Doctor, dan to believe dat de Lord healed him. Have you ever tought of dat?"

"Look, Rabbi or Reverend or whatever you are, don't give me that cockamamie (Y.farfetched) yeshua stuff. I am sick and tired of hearing about him."

"How do you know of Yeshua, Doctor?" Rabbi Bernstein asked curiously.

"My daughter Ariel got caught up in one of those cults and it is breaking my wife's heart," Dr.Freidman said waving his hand in a negative gesture. "Don't tell me about Yeshua, I don't want to hear it."

"You bot are velcome to sit and listen to me explain Him to Rabbi Waxman if you desire," Rabbi Bernstein replied with a straight face.

"Please, Doctors, tell dis man to leave me alone," Rabbi Waxman said emphatically. "He is not letting me rest!"

"Okay, Holy Man, it's time to leave!" Dr. Katz said as he put his arm under Rabbi Bernstein.

"I don't think so, Doc," Judah shouted as he had overheard the discussion and had entered the room. "This is a matter of National Security. If you try and interfere I will have to kill you. Rabbi Bernstein has to continue to speak with Rabbi Waxman. The eternal lives of every Israeli are at stake. You better leave and do not say a word about this to anyone or I will track you down and terminate you. Trust me, this is a matter of utmost secrecy and importance. Did you see how the Lord destroyed the Temple Mount area yesterday? Rabbi Waxman is an integral part of what the Lord plans to do."

"What are you talking about?" Dr. Freidman said incredulously. "You people have tsedrayter kops (Y.deranged heads)! Gay in Drerd (Y.Go to hell)! I'm out of here."

"Rabbi, you can be discharged in a couple of days," Nurse Goldman said as she left and closed the door. Judah and the doctors had already left.

"Rebbe, de Babylonian Talmud in Yoma 39b says dat for de last 40 years of de Temple de red crimson sash tied on de kapparah (H.atonement) goat did not turn vite, indicating dat de sins of Israel had not been forgiven by Hashem. Dat is in our own Rabbinic writings, Rebbe. From de time dat Yeshua died as our one and for all time sin offering, de Lord no longer accepted de sacrifices of de Cohen Hagadol on Yom Kippur as He had always done. Ve no longer need to have our High Priest do a sacrifice on Yom Kippur and go into de Holy of Holies and sprinkle its blood over the mercy seat to cleanse us as He did during Temple days. He no longer needs to place his hands on de other goat and place on it therefore all de sins of Israel and den to drive it out of town to die. Yeshua vas our sacrifice once and for all time. All our sins vent on dis lamb of God. He died once for all time so dat ve do not need to do Temple sacrifices for our sins any longer. He vas sacrificed once for all who vould accept Him. You don't have to earn dis atonement. It is a free gift to all dat believe in Him."

"The crimson sash no longer turning vite vas not because of yeshu. It vas because of our unrepentant hearts," Rebbe Waman countered. "And let me ask you a question, Yacov. Yesterday Hashem destroyed de Arab structures on de Temple Mount. Do you believe dat de Temple should be rebuilt?"

"I believe dat it vill be rebuilt, Rabbi," Rabbi Bernstein replied. "Daniye'l speaks of de setting up of de abomination of desolation in de Third Temple. Saadia Gaon describes dat in his *Midrash Gellulah.* His description of de great king Armilus of de end of days is similar to dat described in the Testament to de Patriarchs. Armilus vill go into the rebuilt Temple and declare himself to be Hashem. He is whom de Christians call de Antichrist. De Temple has to be rebuilt to fulfill prophecy! Yeshua Hamashiach vill come and defeat him at the battle at de plains of Meggido."

"Not yeshu again?" Rabbi Waxman lamented.

"Rebbe, vat of Yesha'yahu's statement about a virgin birth? Who vas dat, besides Yeshua?"

"Dat vas King Hezekiah!" Rabbi Waxman countered deftly.

"Rebbe, even Rashi *(Rabbi Shlomo Yitzhaki who lived in France in the 11th century and who is considered to the foremost commentator on the Tanakh)* said dat de Immanuel prophecy could not refer to Hezekiah because he vas born nine years before de prophecy vas given."

"You are now quoting Rashi? Vat of the statement by him dat de suffering servant in Yesha'yahu 42 and 53 is indeed Israel, not yeshu?"

"He had to do dat because it vas a time of persecution of Jews by so called christians and to refer to their Messiah as suffering vould just have brought even more persecution. Have you heard of Rabbi Moshe Alshekh? He vas a Rabbinic scholar who lived in de 16th century in Sfat. He said of Yesha'yahu 53 dat our Rabbis vit one voice accept and affirm de opinion dat de prophet is speaking of King Messiah!"

"Yeah, yeah!" Rabbi Waxman replied. "The Talmud has many differing opinions as to dat."

Judah and Dawn sat quietly and listened to the two Rabbis arguing vociferously.

Suddenly a tall skinny black man came strolling down the corridor. He was accompanied by a young black woman who appeared to be his daughter and a young white man with a goatee beard and glasses.

"I don't believe this," Judah said to Dawn. "Look who is coming down the corridor! It is Detective Holmes of the Potomac Police Department. Quick, hide your face!"

"Hey man," Holmes shouted as he walked by them and recognized Judah, "Isn't that you Colonel Meire? I'll be a son of a gun! Loisha, this is the crazy Jew that I told you about. I cannot believe that after all this time I would run into you again here in Israel."

"How are you doing, Sherlock?" Judah said as he was caught and had to acknowledge Holmes. "How has hiding been treating you and your daughter?"

"I read the papers and every time I hear of some bizarre thing going on in the DC area, I know that you must be involved! Were you involved in the rocketing of the Chesapeake Bay Bridge?"

"You don't want to know, man!" Judah smiled as he shook the hands of Holmes daughter and son in law. "Why are you here in Israel? Did your daughter marry a Jew?"

"You got it, Colonel. He is an astronomer at Kitt Peak in Tucson. His name is Dr. Freddie Silverman."

"Nice to meet you, Sir," Judah introduced himself. "And this is my wife Dawn."

"I thought that you had MS?" Holmes asked bewildered.

"Well, I did, but the Lord healed me. Isn't it amazing? Thank you, Jesus!" Dawn beamed.

"She probably is in remission," Dr. Silverman whispered to Loisha.

The five of them stood around and chatted for an hour. They had come to Israel because Freddie had received a grant to give a paper at the Weizman Institute and they all had decided to come. Holmes had maintained his low profile and had not contacted the Potomac Police Department in all these months. He had heard through the grapevine that Ultra was still looking for him as a way to locate Judah. Judah did not bother to fill him in on what had transpired since they had last met. He would probably not believe any of it.

"What are you guys doing here?" Holmes asked with a sly grin.

"We have a friend that is recuperating from an illness," Dawn remarked with a smile.

"You came all this way for that?" Holmes asked. "Yeah right!"

"Stop playing detective," Judah replied. "You are retired now!"

They finished talking about nothing and went on their way. Holmes was intrigued to know what Judah and Dawn were really doing there at the hospital. He knew that it probably would result in an explosion of some sort.

"Well, take care, guys!" Holmes said as they prepared to leave. "Wish I knew what you were up to! You sly fox you!"

"Nice seeing you again, Holmes," Judah replied and he shook his hand. "Stay out of trouble, will you?"

"Do you really believe that Rabbi Waxman will believe, Judah?" Dawn resumed their discussion while grabbing his arm. "I just don't see it happening that quickly. It took months to get through your hard stiff necked self. And imagine how much more anti Jesus Rabbinic learning that Rabbi Waxman has to surmount!"

"All that I know is that we don't have much time left," Judah answered shaking his head. "All of our avenues for leaving the truth behind when we leave have been eradicated. Satan is very busy in these last days because he knows that his time is short."

The nurse brought Rabbi Waxman's dinner tray. Judah said that he would give it to him. He also asked her for another kosher tray for Rabbi Bernstein and a plain one for each of them.

"You sure are pushy!" Nurse Goldman replied.

"You don't ask, you don't get! As I told you, it is a matter of National Security. Do you want me to have to kill you?" Judah said as he put his hand on his pistol.

"No problem, Moshe Dayan!" she said as she sped away from the door.

Rabbi Bernstein continued. "In the Talmud's Tractate Sanhedrin it is said dat de Rabbis say de Messiah's name is Suffering Scholar of the Rabbi's House. It continues dat surely he has born our grief and carried our sorrows yet ve did esteem him stricken, smitten of God and afflicted."

"You know, Yacov, dat de Talmud speaks of two Mashiachs," Rabbi Waxman said as his heart softened all so slightly. "The first Mashiach Ben Joseph is to be pierced by Satan and killed. Den Mashiach Ben David is to come as de conquering King!"

"Well, Rebbe, maybe dat is the same Mashiach coming tvice? Once as a suffering servant to die for our sins and de second time as de conquering king? Dat is all dat I am saying dat you should consider. The *Pesikta Rabbati* also portrays de Mashiach as de one who before creation consented to suffer for de sins of de souls of men in order to redeem dem. Dat is exactly vat it says in de Brit Chadasha *(H.New Covenant)* about Yeshua. And it says dat He is coming back soon!"

"Yacov, you also know dat de Talmud varns us not to try and figure out de end. It says dat 'may dey drop who try and figure out de end for dey say since de time of Mashaich's coming has already arrived yet He did not come, derefore He vill not come at all."

"But Rebbe, you know dat according to Daniye'l *(H.Daniel)* 9, the Mashiach vas supposed to come in 69 weeks of years, 173,880 days, after de decree to restore and rebuild Yerushalyim vas issued. Nearly a century later two declarations vere issued by King Artaxerxes I of Persia as described in Ezer *(H.Ezra)* 7 and Nehemyah *(H.Nehemiah)* 2. The first in 458BCE enabled a contingent of exiles to return under de leadership of Ezer in order to reestablish de law in Yerushalyim. De second came in de year 445. Ven he made it official in de spring of dat year dat de walls of

262

Yerushalyim could stand once again, the Messianic countdown began. The prophetic clock vould tick off de days until de Mashiach arrived. De Mashiach had to come in de first century CE not at any oter time in history. Vat happened 173,880 days after Artaxerxes said rebuild Yerushalyim? A Galilean named Yeshua entered the city on a donkey just as Zekaryah had said dat Mashiach vould do. De crowds cried out Hosanna to de Son of David as dey laid palm branches before him. Exactly as Daniye'l had predicted, on dat spring day just before Pesach in 33CE Yeshua vas first publicly heralded as Mashiach."

"Daniye'l vas speaking of King Agrippa. Dat is vat the sages have told us!" Rabbi Waxman said, frustrated. "Please leave, Rabbi. I have heard enough. I just do not believe. Maybe I am blind to de trut as you say. Maybe if I saw de burning bush I vould believe, but so far all I see and hear is you and it isn't vorking!"

Judah was still holding Rabbi Waxman's food tray when Nurse Goldman returned with the three other trays.

"Thank you, Ma'am," Judah said as he smiled for her.

"You all are a little farchadat *(Y.dopey)*," she whispered. "You scared those poor, young two doctors to death with your threats. They are afraid to even come back here."

"That is okay, because Rabbi Waxman is fine and will be going home soon."

Suddenly down the hall approached an Iranian man who looked really out of place. How he got through security at the front desk was a mystery. It was Imam Hadad. He had been told that Rabbi Waxman and Rabbi Bernstein were part of the enemy plot to destroy the Temple Mount. He was told that they wanted to rebuild the Temple on that very spot. He was assigned to kill them at all costs. He was also warned that Judah might be there to try and stop him.

"Dawn, look out!" Judah yelled as he dove on top of her, knocking her to the ground as soon as he spotted Hadad. Hadad began firing his automatic rifle and he cut poor Nurse Goldman to pieces. He fired at Judah and Dawn but they had crawled behind the corner of the hallway. They returned fire and he also took shelter. The two Doctors had decided to come back to the room against their better judgment and they were nearly caught in the crossfire and escaped by the skin of their teeth. They called security as they saw Nurse Goldman lying in front of the door in a pool of blood and spilled food and drink.

Rabbi Bernstein barricaded the door and made Rabbi Waxman get under the bed. He instead got onto the bed and pretended that he was Rabbi Waxman.

"Vat is going on here?" Rabbi Waxman yelled as he was forced under the bed.

"Hasatan is after de two of us but he especially vants you!'

"Vy me?"

"Because he knows dat Hashem is going to use you in a mighty way, Rebbe," Rabbi Bernstein said as he lay on the bed and pushed the Rebbe's head back under it.

"You will not succeed, Judah," Imam Hadad shouted. "The Temple will not be rebuilt. Not on our Holy land, no matter what Lazant says!"

"Lazant?" Judah questioned. "Are you one of those New World Order people that Lazant has rounded up?"

"I was one of them, but they kept saying that the Temple had to rebuilt so that their god could sit in there and rule the world!"

"That is absolutely correct!" Judah replied. "Don't you understand that? You big dumb camel jockey!"

Hadad suddenly rushed Judah and Dawn in a hail of automatic gunfire. He managed to get to the door of the room which he had cut to ribbons when Dawn fired a volley that hit him in the neck and nearly severed his head from close range. He went head over heels through the door of the hospital room and ended up in a pile in the middle of the floor. Although he ended up dead, he had however managed to release a hand grenade as he flew into the room. It exploded as he expired and blew much of the small room to pieces.

The entire area was inundated by security personnel. Rabbi Waxman came out from under the bed and sat on it with Rabbi Bernstein. They both watched as the body of Hadad was removed as was the body of Nurse Goldman. They were both in a state of shock. Rabbi Waxman could barely speak. He just looked at the dead Iranian and the dead Nurse and then over at Rabbi Bernstein and finally at Judah.

"I, I, just don't understand?" Rabbi Waxman said. "Vy me? Are you all right, Yacov? Vy did you protect me at de risk of your own life?"

"Dere is a battle going on, Rabbi, over your soul," Rabbi Bernstein said slowly as he regained his composure. "Yeah, I'm fine," he said as he clutched the pillow to his abdomen.

"Over my soul?"

"Yep! Let me ask you a question, Rebbe. How can ve know the lineage of de Mashiach ven He comes since de Temple and all its records have been destroyed? The Mashiach had to come before de destruction of de Temple, didn't He?"

"Dere are oter ways of knowing!'" Rabbi Waxman said begrudgingly. "Look, dat is enough already. People have died and you are still proselytizing. Stop already for the sake of de dead nurse!"

"Dat is precisely vy ve cannot stop because de time is short," Rabbi Bernstein continued. "Dozens of people have died for me and you to talk right now and right here. Hashem vants us together but Hasatan does not and he vill stop at noting to destroy you and me."

"Oy vey!"

Holmes came running around the door when he heard the gunfire. He knew that it had to be Judah. He was not surprised to find another scene of death and carnage.

"You sure attract trouble, don't you, boy?" Holmes shouted as he stepped through blood.

"Did your mother have any kids that lived, Holmes? Listen, this was perpetrated by Lazant or Ultra. You better beat it before they spot you!"

264

"What about you, Colonel?"

"I can fend for myself. Now go!"

"Rabbi Akiva tought dat Bar Kochba vas de Mashiach in 135 CE and dat he had come to save his people," Rabbi Bernstein continued, still clutching the pillow. "Ven he vas killed, dat is ven de writings about not trying to predict de time of de Mashiach vere developed. It vas because according to Daniye'l de Mashiach vas supposed to come in de First Century, and since our people rejected Him ven He came, den He vas obviously not coming after all. Rabbi Akivah tried to fudge de Daniye'l prophecy vit Bar Kochba but it failed."

Rabbi Waxman was placed in another room. Rabbi Bernstein asked Judah to help him into the new room.

"What is wrong Rabbi?" Judah asked concerned.

"It is noting, son," Rabbi Bernstein grimaced. "Just get me into de new room."

Judah could see that the Rabbi had a wound in his abdomen which was bleeding quite a bit.

"You need to have that looked at, Rabbi."

"Don't you dare say a vord! Dere is no time to vaste on me. Ve need to reach Rabbi Waxman before all hell breaks out even more dan it already has! De time for de Catching Away is drawing near and ve don't have any time to vaste. Be quiet, Yehuda, I am begging you!"

Rabbi Waxman was very happy with his new room. It was on another newer wing of the hospital. Dawn accompanied Judah as he carried Rabbi Bernstein down to the new floor. When they arrived at the room, Rabbi Waxman was beaming.

"Look at my new room, Yacov!" he shouted. "And dey aren't charging me a penny extra."

"I'm glad that you like your new surroundings, Rebbe," Rabbi Bernstein said as Judah put him down on the chair and pushed it up to the bed. "Rebbe, ve have much more to talk about. I know dat you are tired but as you can see from our last encounter, people vant us dead. Ve must be doing something right. Nu *(Y.right?)*?"

"I cannot understand vy anyvone vould vant to kill me. I am just an old Orthodox Rebbe who doesn't have many more years left. I didn't steal someone's vife or deir money. Vy vould dey vant to kill me?"

"Rebbe, it vas an Islamic terrorist who tried to kill you," Rabbi Bernstein said painfully. "He vas sent here by Hasatan to prevent us from speaking."

"You are meshugge, Yacov," Rabbi Waxman laughed. "How could you possibly know dat? Oh I guess you tink dat since you know Hashem's son yeshu you can know Hasatan. Maybe they are the same person. Did you ever figure on dat?"

"Rebbe, I vas sent here to you to tell you de good news of Yeshua Hamashiach so dat you can be of the greatest service to Hashem after ve all are caught avay by de catching avay."

"Vat are you talking about? Dat is the Natzal and refers to de resurrection of de dead, not de living. You have once again mixed in Christian bubbe-mayse

*(Y.lit.grandma's stories-absurd explanations)* with the Tanakh."

"Rebbe, listen to me carefully," Rabbi Bernstein said seriously, but obviously in a great deal of pain. "De Believers in Yeshua Hamashiach, de Christians and de Jewish Believers, are going to be removed from de Eart on Rosh Hashanah. Dey vill be caught up in de air vith Yeshua. Hasatan is going to explain dis to de world as de fact dat ve vere abducted by flying saucers. Ven ve are all gone dere need to be people here to tell dose left behind de trut. It vas felt dat your tousands of followers vere a likely candidate if dey saw you as one of dose taken!"

"Oy vey! You are crazy, Yacov!" Rabbi Waxman again laughed out loud. "You talk of people flying into de air, abductions, Hasatan and flying saucers and de whole megillah *(H.long rigmarole)*. Do you tink dat I am dat stupid? I vasn't born yesterday. Alright already! Vat do you really vant from me?"

"I vant you to see the burning bush of Yeshua! I vant you to see the trut, Rebbe. Hashem has a special place for you in de end of days. Greater dan even you could ever have imagined!"

Surprisingly, Drs. Katz and Friedman approached the Rebbe's room. They sneaked up quietly as Judah and Dawn appeared asleep in front of the door. As the Doctors attempted to inch past them Judah with his eyes still closed reached for his revolver and the men stopped in their tracks.

"Nice try, Docs!" Judah smirked as he opened his eyes. "You need to leave them alone. They are discussing the fate of the world and that includes you two sorry excuses for men."

"Judah, you cannot keep us from seeing Rabbi Waxman," Dr. Friedman said without much force. "He is our patient, after all."

"Well, excuse me!" Judah smarted back as he stood up. "Remember what happened to Nurse Goldman? Remember what happened to that Iranian terrorist who tried to disrupt their discussion? I'm telling you one more time that you better beat it right now before you get killed. I'm telling you this because I honestly don't want anything to happen to you poor, pitiful guys!"

As Rabbi Bernstein was still trying to convince Rebbe Waxman of his beliefs, AZAZEL suddenly appeared in the room in all its resplendent horror. It lifted up his wings and shrieked, "Death to all who would disrupt the plan of my Master!"

Rebbe Waxman's feisty good nature quickly turned to fear and loathing at the sight of the beast. He ran and cowered in the corner of the room.

"Is dat de Abracadabra *(Aramaic. Devil)*, Yacov?" he cried out. "Oy gevalt! My wife used to pray a kineahora *(Y.saying to ward off the evil eye)* to vard of such evil spirits!"

"It is His angel, AZAZEL!" Rabbi Bernstein answered, trying to remain calm. "It has been after Yehudah and us all along. I told you dat all dis vas true. I'm not crazy now am I, Rebbe?"

"You called it AZAZEL?" Rabbi Waxman asked as he shook in fear and trembling. "In the *Apocalypse of Abraham* AZAZEL is accused of having scattered

266

over de earth de secrets of heaven and having rebelled against the mighty one! AZAZEL is also the demon who inhabited the Judean wilderness and it vas de place vere de Yom Kippur goat vas driven. Oy vey ist mir!"

Judah heard a commotion in the room and he burst in, quickly followed by Dawn and the Doctors.

"Oh my God, it is AZAZEL!" Dawn shouted as she quickly retreated from the room. "Take care of him, Judah!"

"What the hell is that," Dr. Katz screamed as he turned white as snow and collapsed on the floor.

Dr. Friedman began yelling in abject fear and horror as he gazed into the face of the beast. He pulled Shmuel's body from the room and slammed the door. He then fell down and began sobbing at the experience.

"What the hell was that?" he asked Dawn.

"You are right, Doctor, it is from Hell," Dawn shouted at the Doctor. "It is a fallen angel of Hasatan who has been after us. Judah told you that it was a matter of National Security. Actually, it is a matter of Eternal Security. The forces of Satan, the forces of evil are battling the forces of Hashem and Yeshua. You have witnessed something that few people have lived to tell about. Judah will fight the beast and rescue the Rabbis. You better talk to your Believing daughter about what all of this means. Otherwise you will find yourself with these same beasts for all eternity when you die!"

Dr. Katz slowly regained consciousness and Dr. Friedman grabbed him and ran down the hall. They both slipped and fell several times, but they were so scared that they wanted to get as far away as possible as soon as possible. Neither of them dared to look back even for an instant.

Judah immediately prayed for the Holy Spirit to clothe him in the Holy Armor of God, which It did almost instantaneously.

"Judah, HA! You never give up, do you?" AZAZEL bellowed. "You will never recruit this poor old Rabbi Waxman. He is ours forever as are his thousands of followers. He will never accept the truth of Yeshua because we have so confused the Jews with our lies and deceptions. We have misled so called Christians to persecute and hate and even to murder the very people that gave them their Messiah. We have gotten them to kill the very people who brought our nemesis into this world and then first spread His message of Salvation. Rabbi Waxman is one of our greatest triumphs. A good man who loves his God, but a man who is still blind to the truth that only those who trust and believe in Yeshua will not perish like us, but will have eternal life with Him!"

Judah took his sword and ran it into the face of the beast without a moment's hesitation. AZAZEL shrieked an ungodly roar and attempted to hurl one of his flaming missiles at Rabbi Bernstein but he appeared already dead. It shrieked and shrieked and found Rebbe Waxman cowering in the corner of the room. It flung a missile at him which barely missed but hit on the wall above him and started an incendiary conflagration. Judah smacked AZAZEL across the head with his shield and knocked him across the room. AZAZEL struggled to get up and moved again towards Rebbe Waxman. Judah charged after it and continued swinging his sword and using his shield to ward off the beast's flaming missiles. The room was now ablaze and the fire alarm had gone off and the sprinklers had gone off to no avail with so much heat and redhot fire. Dawn came into the room reluctantly as she smelled the smoke and felt the heat. She grabbed Rabbi Waxman and dragged him out of the room. He was dazed and in shock. Judah continued to battle AZAZEL.

"You will not succeed, Judah, because Rabbi Bernstein is already dead," AZAZEL shrieked. "There will be no one left to tell the people what really happened to you. They will bow down and worship us as their emancipators from your fanatical Evangelical Christians! HA! HA!"

Judah looked over at Rabbi Bernstein and he did appear to be gone. He ran over to him and found his abdomen had been ripped open by the shrapnel from Hadad's hand grenade. Judah felt his neck and there was a slight pulse but the good Rabbi was slipping fast. Judah knelt beside him and prayed. He begged the Lord to not take him home yet because he was not finished with Rabbi Waxman.

AZAZEL saw what was going on and immediately began hurling his flaming missiles at Judah and Rabbi Bernstein. He began to scream a blood curdling cry that sent shivers up the spine of Dawn and Rabbi Waxman who were cowering outside the room.

"I never tought dat I vould meet Hasatan or one of his angels, Dawn," Rabbi Waxman whispered as he shook uncontrollably. "I still cannot understand vy it vants me?"

"Because you are to be used by Yeshua in a mighty way, Rebbe," Dawn replied as she held him tight. "Yeshua is coming to take his followers away from this beast. Those left behind will be told that extraterrestrials abducted us but as you can see it is a demonic being, not an ET."

Detective Holmes came cautiously down the corridor. He just could not leave until he had figured out what was going on. When he came to the room and saw the flames and heard the shrieking, he turned as pale as a black man could. He felt faint and sat down next to Dawn and the Rebbe.

"What the hell is going on in there?" he asked, not really expecting an answer.

"Look for yourself, Holmes," Dawn answered pointing to the door. "You never believed Judah or me about our encounters with a fallen angel from the powers of the air, now did you? Well, see for yourself, Sherlock!"

Holmes slowly opened the door to the burning room and gazed into the face of AZAZEL in all its resplendent horror. AZAZEL looked upon him and shrieked even louder and flung a flaming missile right at him. Judah threw his shield out to knock it off course which it did and it hit the opposite wall and burst into flame. Holmes looked over at Judah and nodded his head in thanks and quickly closed the door and ran down the hall yelling like a wild man.

Judah needed to get back his shield, because without it he was defenseless. AZAZEL turned towards him and Rabbi Bernstein and prepared for the final kill. Judah took his sword and said a prayer to the Lord and flung it as hard as he could at AZAZEL and it caught him right at the apex of its wings and pinned them both to the wall above its horrifying head so it could not fire any more missiles. He then ran over and picked up his shield. As he approached AZAZEL it disappeared.

He ran back over to Rabbi Bernstein only to discover that one of AZAZEL's flaming missiles must have hit him in the abdomen after all. The flame had cauterized the wound and stopped the bleeding.

"Are you all right, Rabbi?" Judah asked knowing that he was still dying.

"Bring Rabbi Waxman to me!" Rabbi Bernstein replied. "My time is short and I have to show him de trut. Dere is not much time left. Go get him, Yehuda, please!"

"The room is burning, Rabbi, we have to leave here!"

"Dere is no time!"

"But Rabbi..."

"But noting," Rabbi Bernstein grimaced as a strong wind blew through the room and put the fire out.

Judah raced outside and brought in Rebbe Waxman. He left the two men alone and went back to his former job of keeping all personnel out of the room. When firefighters arrived and hospital risk management people attempted to enter the room, Judah scared them off with his Uzi and his chutzpa (Y. unmitigated gall). They were all afraid of him. He told them that it was a matter of utmost security and that everything was under control. If they did not leave, he would have to shoot all of them. He blasted away the nursing cart down the hall to further make his point.

"Rebbe Waxman, can you not see dat all of dis has transpired because Hasatan vants you killed," Rabbi Bernstein pleaded in obvious pain.

"It is you dat is mortally vounded, Yacov," Rabbi Waxman replied. "You need to seek medical help. Forget about dis poor old Jew. Take care of yourself."

"No, I must die in order for you to live, Rebbe. I don't vant to die but it is necessary so dat you can live and spread the good news of Yeshua to all your followers."

"Dat is crazy, Yacov! I hardly even know you. Vy should you lay down your life for me?"

"Dat is vat Yeshua did," Rabbi Bernstein replied as he doubled over in pain. "He died for all our sins because de Fadder loved us so much in spite of our sins dat He sent His Only Begotten Son to die for us."

"Don't start dat again, Yacov!" Rebbe Waxman countered as the room suddenly filled up with light.

In front of them an image of Yeshua standing on the Mount of Olives appeared with his nail pierced hands.

"Vat are dese wounds between your arms?" Rebbe Waxman asked as he had fallen to his knees.

"Those with which I was wounded in the house of My friends!" Yeshua answered.

Rebbe Waxman began to mourn for Him as one mourns for an only son, and to weep bitterly over Him like the bitter weeping over a first born. Rabbi Bernstein sat in utter amazement as the prophecies of the Prophet Zekaryah 12-14 were being played out in advance for Rebbe Waxman. The spirit of grace and supplication was poured out on Him and he suddenly knew that Yeshua was his Lord and Savior. It was not head knowledge but heart knowledge. He continued to wail and mourn for what seemed like an hour. Judah heard the commotion but kept Dawn and him outside even though he wanted to see what was going on.

Long after the image has gone, Rebbe Waxman was still prostrate on the floor.

"Baruch Hashem, Baruch Hashem, Baruch Yeshua Hamashiach," he said over and over again.

When he finally sat up, he was a new man. He looked at Rabbi Bernstein with the biggest smile on his face and he put his arms around him and continued to cry like a newborn baby.

"I am free at last, Yacov," he shouted. "I now know vere I am going and de answers to all my prayers for 80 years. Baruch Hashem forever and ever, Amen! Amen. He died for all my sins. He vas my Passover Lamb, my kapparah, my sin offering. Oy yoy yoy!"

"Rabbi Waxman, repeat after me," Rabbi Bernstein mandated as he was slipping quickly from this world. "Avinu Malkeinu *(Our Father, Our King)*, have mercy on me as a sinner."

"Avinu Malkeinu, have mercy on me as a sinner," Rebbe Waxman repeated.

"I believe vit perfect fait in de prophet Yesha'yahu's *(H.Isaiah)* vords Musar Shalomeinu Alav *(H.the punishment, the chastisement, dat brought peace vas upon Him)*!"

"I believe vit perfect fait Yeshayahu's words, dat de Musar Shalomeinu Alav vas upon de Mashaich," Rabbi Waxman said firmly.

"I admit dat I need dis kapparah *(H.atonement, forgiveness of sin)* and I tank Hashem for de Shalom *(H.Peace)* of Mashiach's kapparah."

"I admit dat I need dis kapparah and I tank Hashem for de Shalom of Mashaich's kapparah."

"Because of dis I believe dat I am cleansed from my sin which I now freely confess, believing dat Hashem is faitful and just and vill forgive my sin and set me free from all unrighteousness," Rabbi Bernstein said slowly and deliberately.

Rebbe Waxman once again repeated the words exactly and with great emotion.

"I confess vitout shame Mashaich Yeshua is Lord and I believe in my heart dat Avinu the Fadder raised Him from de dead as prophesied in de Hebrew Bible."

Rebbe Waxman once again repeated the words exactly.

"Since Avinu, the Fadder, sent his Devar *(H.word)* as the Ben Haelohim *(H.Son of God)* to be our Mashiach, I for my part vill obey Mashiach and his words in de complete Holy Jewish Scriptures as dese are opened to me by de guidance of de Ruach Hakodesh *(H.Holy Spirit)*," Rabbi Bernstein now only could whisper.

Rabbi Waxman struggled to understand what he was saying and repeated after him.

"I promise to fellowship vit oter Holy Believers in Mashiach and to vork and pray vit dem in one accord to share my vitness and dus help to fulfill the Mashiach's Great Commission to Israel and de nations of de whole world, B'shem Mashiach *(H.Bless the name of Messiah)*, Amen."

Rebbe Waxman repeated the words and gave Rabbi Bernstein a big hug. His body was ice cold. He obviously had been dead for quite a while! Rabbi Waxman wondered who had been speaking to him.

"Yehuda, Yehuda!" Rabbi Waxman began to yell.

When Judah and Dawn reentered the room, they saw the most beautiful glow around Rabbi Waxman's face.

"Free at last, free at last, Baruch Hashem, I am free at last," the Rabbi shouted. "I saw Yeshua Hamashiach. I saw his nail pierced hands and I knew dat I knew," the Rabbi said and began to wail once again. "But you know vat is cockamamie? Rabbi Bernstein vas having me say dis prayer, but feel, he has been dead for a long time!"

"The Lord works in strange ways, my friend," Judah replied as he hugged the old Patriarch. "We must leave here as soon as possible and plan for the upcoming Catching Away. There is not much time left. I need to call Butrell to come and pick us up."

"Beam us up, Scottie!" Judah said into the satellite phone. "He has seen the light!"

# XX

Judah and Dawn put Rabbi Waxman onto a cart and covered him with a sheet. They then proceeded up to the roof to wait for Butrell. It was sunset on Saturday night and Shabbat was ending. The sky was illuminated with the beautiful colors of sunset. There were reds and yellows and even some glorious oranges and pinks. It was as if the heavens were celebrating the rebirth of Rabbi Waxman.

"Judah, I am so proud of you," Dawn said as they waited on the rooftop. "It looks like you have accomplished what Hashem wanted you to accomplish. You not only got Rabbi Bernstein and Rabbi Waxman together but you fought AZAZEL one more time. Bertha will be devastated that Rabbi Bernstein is dead. You can assure her, though, that he did the Lord's work in a mighty fashion, and that we will see him again real soon. You truly are a soldier for the Lord, Judah. I am so proud of you!"

"I did not do anything, Dawn," Judah replied with a look of concern on his face. "It was Rabbi Bernstein who did the Lord's work. And it isn't over yet! We still have to protect Rabbi Waxman from the forces of evil. They now will be after him with a vengeance because they know that their time is short. We need to watch over him until Rosh Hashanah. You have been such a supportive, loving partner, Dawn, through it all, for this, how did you say, big, dumb Jew. I know that the Lord will thank you but I just want to thank you as well. I couldn't have asked for a more endearing wife than you. I love you, Dawn. I truly do!"

"You two stop dat schmaltzy *(Y.overly emotional)* talk," Rabbi Waxman whispered out from under the sheet. "Vat a marriage made in heaven you two have. Vat a blessing! Oy!"

When they reached the roof, Judah barricaded the door with the cart. After a while the Hospital personnel came pounding on the door.

"Open this door!" a voice shouted. "We know that you have Rabbi Waxman, and we want him back. You cannot take him with you."

Judah did not answer but stood against the door to prevent its opening. Thankfully after nearly an hour or so, he could see the approaching helicopter. It looked so beautiful against the twilight sky. It was their salvation from the hands of the enemy. As soon as it landed, Butrell and Yossi jumped out of the craft.

"Where is Rabbi Bernstein?" Yossi asked as his smile became a frown.

"He did not make it, Yossi," Judah answered as he patted Yossi on the back in reassurance. "He helped lead Rabbi Waxman to the Lord but he was killed by a

272

terrorist working with AZAZEL. I'm so sorry, Yossi."

"Don't be sorry, Yehuda," Yossi replied, forcing a smile. "Hashem used the Rabbi in a mighty way. We all need to be grateful for that. Rabbi Bernstein gave his life so Rabbi Waxman could regain his. Baruch Hashem."

"You are correct, Yossi," Judah said. "And we shall see him again very soon in the Catching Away."

Yossi helped Rabbi Waxman into the helicopter.

"I thought that you had pancreatic cancer, Rebbe?"

"I did, but Yeshua healed me," Rabbi Waxman boasted. "Baruch Hashem. First He healed my body, den He gave me a new heart and a new spirit. I have begun life all over again! And it vas your Rabbi Bernstein dat vas right dere to guide me!"

"Rebbe, I have heard about you since I was a small child. You are a venerable sage of our people and now you are even more so because you know Yeshua Hamashiach. I cannot believe it. When Rabbi Bernstein accepted Yeshua, we all were greatly humbled. He was a Rabbinical scholar who everyone admired. Now you, Rebbe, the Rebbe of the Rabbis, has accepted Yeshua. What a miracle! Hashem is surely pouring out His spirit of grace and supplication on Yerushalyim in these last days. We need to witness to our people before Armilus arrives with all power and signs and lying wonders."

"Ve vill, Yossi, be patient. It's okay! Ve vill do vat the Lord vants us to do."

"What happened to Rabbi Bernstein?" Deputy Director Butrell asked Judah.

"We were attacked by an Islamic terrorist," Judah answered shaking his head. "He killed a nurse and tried to get the Rabbis. While my dear sweet wife blew his head off, he managed to throw a grenade into the hospital room where they were talking. Rabbi Bernstein was hit by shrapnel which tore open his stomach. The Lord kept him alive until Rabbi Waxman could have a Born Again experience, however. Then Rabbi Bernstein led him in the sinner's prayer. In the middle of all this AZAZEL appeared also and tried to kill the men. It was a real mess but the end was amazing. Rabbi Waxman accepted Yeshua as his Lord and Savior; imagine this stiff necked old Orthodox Rabbi with thousands upon thousands of followers all over the world. Maybe, just maybe, his people will be those left behind as the evangelists to the world described by John in the Book of the Revelation."

They all climbed into the helicopter just as the rooftop door was bridged and they sped away to another Messianic safehouse near Sfat in the Upper Galilee. The moonlit trees were a vibrant brown and moved in the wind like a giant ocean wave. The smell of the pine trees permeated the helicopter. As they finally approached to land, Bertha came running out to greet Rabbi Bernstein.

"Oh, Yacov, I am so glad to see you," Bertha shouted as she ran up to Rabbi Waxman. "Hey, you are not Rabbi Bernstein!" she suddenly realized, because this Rabbi had brown eyes, not those sparkling blue eyes of Rabbi Bernstein. Besides, he was wearing a hospital smock.

"Yacov has gone home to be vit de Lord," Rabbi Waxman consoled her. "De

Lord vanted him to be vit Him, but ve shall see him again."

"Oy vey ist mir!" Bertha shrieked. "Another good man dead. I'll bet that he was killed. Who killed him, Judah. One of those terrorists?"

"Yeah, Ma," Judah replied. "He died protecting Rabbi Waxman and in leading him to Yeshua."

"Why must all our good men die?" Bertha said weeping. "All these women have lost their husbands and these poor men have lost their wives and children. When will the killing stop?"

"This is a battle between the forces of good and those of evil. They may win some battles but we know how the war ends. It ends with victory for the children of Hashem. Yeshua will reign from Jerusalem for a 1000 years as King and Judge over all. Every knee will bow and every tongue will confess that Yeshua Hamashiach is Lord. They know all this, but they want to deceive as many people as they can for as long as they can. The more people that refuse to accept Yeshua, the more people that will eventually spend their eternity in the Lake of Fire with Hasatan and his demons. They want the people left behind to believe that we were abducted by flying saucers rather than that we are with the Lord in the air."

"I know all that, tatalleh, but why..."

"Because the fate of the soul of humanity is at stake," Judah answered deliberately. "We Believers should not fear death. We know where we are going. We know that we will be with Yeshua upon leaving our physical body. Sure, we miss Rabbi Bernstein as we miss Captain Knowington and the others, but they gave their lives so that the plan of Hashem could be fulfilled. What a glorious martyrdom that is. They were all good and faithful servants of the Lord and will be rewarded in Heaven as Scripture says that they will be. As Sha'ul wrote to Timothy, 'For if we died with Him, we shall also live with Him; If we endure, we shall also reign with Him'. Now we must get to work. There is not much time left."

Yitzchak and his friends returned to Hadassah Hospital on Sunday morning to see their beloved Rebbe. When they arrived, they found that the Rebbe was not there.

"What do you mean, he is not here?" Yitzchak yelled as he waived his arms in the air.

"He was taken out of the hospital," the Hospital administrator, a large, heavyset, bearded man, replied coyly.

"By whom?" Yitzchak shouted angrily.

"We are not sure," the administrator replied throwing up his arms in a futile gesture of pretending not to know.

"What are you talking about? Rabbi Waxman was a very important Rabbi who has thousands of followers. If I don't get a satisfactory answer right now, we will all come here and strangle your operations. Am I making myself perfectly clear?"

"He was taken by that Mossad operative, Yehuda, we think."

"Him?! The one with the Shiksa wife?"

274

"Yes, we think so"

"What about that meshumed *(H.traitor-a Jew who accepts Yeshua)* Rabbi Bernstein?" Yitzchak asked irately. "He said that sorcerer yeshu healed the Rebbe. He was trying to tell him about yeshu against his will."

"He was killed by an Arab suicide bomber!" the Hospital administrator answered quickly.

"What? There was a suicide bombing here?" Yitzchak said as he became so enraged that he jumped at the administrator. "Do you know how well known this Rebbe is? First you let a meshumed apostate Rabbi bother my Rebbe with another so called Jew and his Christian wife, and then you let a terrorist nearly kill him? We are going to sue you for putting our Rebbe in life threatening situations. And then, to top it off, you let this Yehuda whatshisname take the Rebbe out of the Hospital! You're lucky if you have bedpans left when our lawyers get through with you!"

"There was nothing that we could do! Here, look for yourself," the administrator said as he showed Yitzchak the bombed out room. "Then we moved Rabbi Waxman to another room and there was a fire there too. Here, look!"

"Oy vey," Yitzchak answered as he surveyed both rooms. "Where was your security during all of this? And what does Yehuda want with Rabbi Waxman? Did they leave out the front door?"

"No, they went up to the roof and left by helicopter."

"Hey, I saw the whole thing," Detective Holmes interrupted. He had not left the hospital, and he was anxious to get his two cents in. "Judah saved your Rabbi from that Islamic terrorist and then he battled Satan to save him again. I kid you not. I looked into the room and that demon was flinging firebolts around and Judah was batting them away with his shield!"

"What are you talking about?" Yitzchak replied shaking his head. "You meshuggeneh shvartzah *(Y.crazy black man)*! What do you know of our religion? Hasatan and firebolts and shields? You are crazy!"

"Hey, Jewboy, I don't know what you just called me but I have the feeling that it wasn't nice. I saw what I saw. Do you people believe in Demons? Well, if you don't, then you better start right now. I'm telling you that they were after the Rabbis. And it was Judah that saved them. So don't worry your little beanied self that your Rabbi is in danger. If Judah wanted to harm him, he had plenty of opportunity to do so! He probably took him to a safe location to protect him. I've known this Colonel for quite a long time now, and I know that he saved my life once. I don't know exactly what he is involved in, but I do know that your Rabbi is safe. Dig it?"

Rabbi Bernstein spent the next couple of days reading the Brit Chadasha *(H.New Covenant)* through in Hebrew. As he did so, he kept shaking his head and saying ummhuh, ummhuh, over and over again.

"Look, Yehuda, vat it says here in Mattityahu *(H.Matthew)* 26," Rabbi Waxman eagerly pointed out. "It says dat Yeshua said dat his talmudim *(H.disciples)* should put avay deir swords ven He vas arrested because He could ask his Fadder and He vould instantly provide more dan a dozen armies of angels to help Yeshua. But He did not ask because He said dat, how den could de passages in de Tanakh be fulfilled dat say it has to happen dis vay? So how can the goyim blame us for killing Him?"

"Keep reading, Rebbe," Judah replied. "The word of Hashem is full of light for this dark world."

"Yehuda, I vant to call my people," Rabbi Waxman suddenly jumped up. "Dey vill be vorrying about me. I should let dem know dat I am all right. Don't you tink?"

"Definitely, Rebbe,"Judah answered with a smile. "And listen, could you tell them to email us here your list of followers and supporters. They must have it on computer disc."

"Yes, of course dey do, Yehuda," Rebbe Waxman replied with a smile. "Dat list has tousands upon tousands of names. It is as waluable as gold. I don't know if dey vill send it to you?"

"They are not sending to me, Rebbe, they are sending it to you!"

"But vy vould I need it in hiding? Dey vill be suspicious. I know my people!"

"Tell them that you are in protective custody from Islamic terrorists who want to kill you. That is true, you know. Tell them that you want to get an urgent message out to all your followers and supporters."

"Dey vill ask me vhy I cannot have dem send it out?" Rabbi Waxman asked perplexed.

"Who is the macher *(Y.bigshot)* here, Rebbe? You or your followers? You are the leader, aren't you?"

"Okay already," Rebbe Waxman finally said frustrated. "I'll try, but my people are tough."

"Then pray about it, Rebbe," Judah said with a smile. "You now have a personal relationship with the Ben Haelohim *(H.Son of God)*. Remember?!"

Rabbi Waxman put down his Brit Chadasha and picked up Deputy Director Butrell's satellite phone. He closed his eyes and said a small prayer and then dialed his headquarters He got Yitzchak.

"Yitzchak, dis is Rabbi Vaxman!" he said quietly.

"Rebbe, Rebbe, oh thank Hashem you are all right," Yitzchak shouted. "Baruch Hashem, Baruch Hashem! Where are you, Rebbe?"

"I am in a safe place, Yitzchak. Dose Islamic terrorists have a price on my head and I must maintain a low profile."

"Why would they want to kill you, Rebbe? It doesn't make any sense. Who is protecting you? I heard that guy Yehuda took you. Who is this guy? Is he the one holding you?"

"That is right, Yitzchak, Yehuda took me away from the danger. He is a former Mossad operative and an IDF officer. He is treating me fine."

"But isn't Yehuda a crazy meshumed? Aren't he and his shiksa wife trying to fill

276

you with that yeshu mishegoss *(Y.nonsense)*?"

"Everyting is fine, Yitzchak," Rabbi Waxman tried to reassure him. "Listen, I need a big favor from you. I need you to email me my entire mailing list. I'll give you de address. I need to contact all of my followers and supporters immediately."

"What are you talking about, Rebbe? You told us never to release that to anyone. It is our lifeline and the names are confidential."

"Who is de Rebbe here, Yitzchak?" Rabbi Waxman replied sternly. "Do as I say!"

"I don't know, Rebbe. How can I be certain that it really is you speaking? Maybe this is a conspiracy to destroy our group? There is a rumor circulating around Yerushalyim that Rabbi Klingfeldt has put a Kabbalistic curse on your head. You know what happened to Rabin when such a curse was put on him."

"Vy did he put a curse on me?" Rabbi Waxman asked with his eyes crossed.

"They say it is because you were bewitched by that Rabbi Bernstein. They say that you have come under the power of the sorcerer yeshu and that you must be stopped!"

"Dat is meshugge, Yitzhack," Rabbi Waxman countered immediately. "Dose Kabbalists are an evil bunch. Dey can afflict people vit der demonic curses! You know vat it says in D'varim 18 about people who use divination, or who practice witchcraft or who cast a spell. The Lord says dat dey are detestable to Him and He vill drive them out!"

"What are you talking about, Rebbe? You never criticized Rabbi Klingfeldt or Kabbalah *(H.tradition-Jewish mysticism)* before?"

"Forget it, Yitzchak. Just email me de list!"

"I have to discuss it with the board!"

"Yitzchak, I am de Board! I am whom I say dat I am. Do I have to remind you how during your Brit Milah *(H.circumcision)* the mohel *(H.Traditional Orthodox circumciser)* cut off too much by accident and you almost bled to death?"

"No Rebbe, I remember, I remember. I'm so sorry. I'm so sorry. I know that it is you. Give me the email address!" Yitzchak said because the Rebbe had been at his circumcision.

"Bless you, Yitzchak," Rebbe Waxman said as he read off the email address. "I vill see you all on Rosh Hashanah at de Kotel. Dat vill be a glorious night as de Shofar blows and ve prepare to rebuild de Temple. Shalom, Yitzchak!"

They all sat around a large wooden table and enjoyed some fresh fruit, dates and figs. Ann Knowington was still very remorseful as was Bertha to a smaller degree. The other widows and widowers tried to maintain an air of calmness and normalcy but it was next to impossible. They had all suffered so much over the last few days that they could only try and feign that everything was all right.

"If you get that mailing list," Butrell said, suddenly breaking the gloom of silence, give it to me and I will make sure that all of them are notified. How many names are on the list, Rabbi?"

"Nearly fifty tousand!" Rabbi Waxman said gleefully. "I have followers and supporters all over Israel as vell as all over de vorld. Dat number probably has grown because many of my followers have had children since den. Ve encourage our people to have as many children as possible."

"Then we will need at least 50,000 Brit Chadashas in Hebrew. At least one for each family," Judah replied. "Where can we get 50,000 New Covenants printed in a few weeks?"

"I will take care of it," Mike Butrell said. "Just get me one New Testament in Hebrew and I will make your copies."

"How can de CIA do dat?" Rabbi Waxman replied.

"Don't ask, Rabbi!"

"Rabbi, what you need to do is sit down and write up a letter explaining that you disappeared on Rosh Hashanah not because you were abducted by aliens but because you were caught up in the air with Yeshua. Spell out the Scriptural passages explaining not only that, but also how Yeshua is the Mashiach after all. Make references to the Tanakh that they can look up," Judah said as he patted the Rabbi on the back. "If you need any help, I'm sure that Yossi or I or Captain Labensky will be glad to assist you."

"But ve cannot send dese out until ve are gone, can ve? Vat if ve are not caught avay in de air until next year?" Rabbi Waxman said bewildered. "And if ve are dis year, how can ve be sure dat dey vill be sent?"

"Don't worry about it, Rabbi," Mike Butrell said with a smile. "My people will take care of it. I've got some good loyal people who are not Believers who work for me. If and when I disappear, they will realize that what I have been telling them for years was true. Some are Mormons. They are good, loyal, hard-working people, but unfortunately we do not get into heaven by good works, lest a man boast, but only by the grace of God. Their Jesus is not our Jesus. When I am gone and they are left behind, they will send out the Bibles as I will tell them to do. Hopefully they will also seek the God of Abraham, Isaac and Jacob for the first time and turn their life over to Him, not to the delusions of Joseph Smith. I know that I can trust them to do what I ask of them."

"But how can we know whom the Lord will ransom from the Great Tribulation, whom He will seal on their forehead as John described in the Book of Revelation?" Captain Labensky asked concerned. "We should not try and play being God, should we? If God wants to raise up an army of Jewish Evangelists as John described, then maybe we should let Him do it. He doesn't need our help, does He?"

"Of course He does not, Shmuel," Judah answered with a smile. "Only He knows which Jews He will seal for His work when we are gone, but both Rabbi Bernstein and I and even Director Butrell, have I think, been led in the spirit to do this preparation. Thousands of young Jewish undefiled men will have access to the Brit Chadasha as well as Rabbi Waxman's testimony and thus will be prepared for their monumental work if they are chosen by God. We do not choose the harvest.

278

We only help to cultivate it."

"Yehuda," Yossi suddenly spoke up, "I don't know if our system can handle a file of 50,000 names and addresses?"

"What can we do, Director Butrell?" Judah asked impatiently.

"That will be a huge file," Butrell replied as he realized that their small computer network was not that of the CIA. "Yossi, you need to dump everything that you have in your email files right away. Hopefully there will be enough memory. But you know what, just in case, I am going to forward all of your emails to my computer. Show me what you have, Yossi!" Butrell said as they ran to the computer room.

When they arrived, Director Butrell began typing furiously the code information for Yossi's computer to forward the incoming emails to his computer at the Central Intelligence Agency in Langely, Virginia. The room began to fill with light and AZAZEL reared its hideous image once again.

"Stop that," it screeched at Butrell and flung a flaming missile at him that struck him in the shoulder.

Butrell let out a terrifying scream of intense pain but he continued to type in his code. Judah called out to the Lord for His armor. Yossi sank to the ground in unmitigated fear and terror.

"Oh my Lord, is that the dreaded angel AZAZEL?" Yossi shouted. "It is a beast from the pits of Gehanna *(H.Hell)*. Kill it, Yehuda!"

"I cannot kill it, Yossi, but I can try and battle it into submission and retreat," Judah answered as he was clothed in the full armor of God once again.

"Go away from here, AZAZEL!" he shouted. "Your time is short and we will not let you prevent the enlightening of those Jews left behind. No way!"

"Judah, you will not succeed. The followers of Rabbi Waxman will not go around the world evangelizing. They will never believe the rantings of a Rabbi who has disappeared and cannot be vouched for face to face. They will not believe your futile ravings about Yeshua. They have been conditioned over the millennia by us to ignore such nonsense."

Rabbi Waxman appeared in the room and he began shaking his fist at the beast.

"Be gone from here, you beast from Satan. You stalk about like a roaring lion looking for somevone to dewour. I just read dat in first Kefa *(H.Peter)*!"

"Get out of here, Rabbi," Judah yelled as he ran between the Rabbi and the Beast. "He wants to destroy you and your future testimony. Get out of here!"

AZAZEL flung his flaming missiles at the Rabbi but Judah managed to ward them off with his shield. In the meantime, Director Butrell had managed to finish his forwarding of the supporters list to his computer back home. He had then looked up at Judah and given him a thumbs up sign as the material began to arrive and was forwarded elsewhere. He then collapsed onto the floor in shock.

Judah moved closer to AZAZEL. He could not decide whom he should protect, the Rabbi or Butrell. Both were essential for this post Rapture undertaking to succeed. The Rabbi had to be present in front of his supporters when the Catching Away took place and Butrell needed to send Brit Chadashas, as well as the Rabbis testimony, to all his supporters. With the list now at the CIA, Butrell could not be lost.

"Go back to your home in the Second Heaven, AZAZEL!" Judah shouted as he approached the Beast. "Go back to your Flying Saucer. Go prepare for the Catching Away of all the Believers. You cannot stop the will of God. You know that. You know how the Book ends. You and all your kind will burn forever in the Lake of Fire!"

"Yes, but we will take a lot of your Jews with us!" AZAZEL laughed an ungodly high pitched cackle. "They will believe that you all have been abducted by UFOs with all the Christians. They will say good riddance. They will help us set up a world without your influence. They will come to the new rebuilt Temple and bow down to our leader and proclaim him to the God that he says that he is. You people are so weak and fickle. You just love to believe a lie."

"They will not believe that Rabbi Waxman was abducted with the Christians," Judah sneered. "Why should he have been?"

"You are correct, Judah," AZAZEL screamed, "That is why he must die and be hidden before the removal of all you Christians!"

"I will not let you succeed," Judah yelled as he rushed fearlessly headlong at the beast swinging his sword.

AZAZEL found itself being cut into ribbons and it disappeared. Judah bent down to catch his breath and lose the suit of armor. He ran over to Butrell and found him severely burned and in shock.

"We need to get Mike some medical treatment right away," Judah yelled as he looked for Mike's helicopter pilot. "Where is the CIA pilot that brought Mike here?"

Ann Knowington and her daughters stood there in stunned disbelief. They had gotten a peek at AZAZEL before it had disappeared and they were frozen in their tracks. The sight of the beast had once again shaken them to the core of their being and left them standing there in a state of confusion. Captain Labensky also was confronted with the terrifying image of the beast once again and he also stood there in frozen horror. Judah ran past them as he looked for the helicopter pilot.

"It's all right, people," Judah said as he whisked past them. "You have seen the evil that we have been fighting against and what killed your Peter and Avraham. But our God is above all other gods. He will defeat this beast and his demonic hordes on the plains of Meggido as Scripture says. Take solace in the fact that you will see Peter and Avraham again real soon!"

"I am right here," the pilot finally answered as he was found taking a nap and aroused. "I'll take him to the Mossad base where we got this helicopter. They will fix him up. Do you guys have any blankets or morphine?"

Yossi was a medic in the IDF reserves so he had some bandages and morphine to tide Director Butrell over until they arrived at the Mossad base. Everyone said a quick goodbye and they prayed for Butrell's recovery. Judah took Rabbi Waxman's Hebrew Brit Chadasha and gave it to the pilot to give to Director Butrell when he regained consciousness. It was after all an important piece in this ultimate endgame. As the helicopter took off and sped south, everyone watched as the early morning sky was suddenly filled with SAM missiles. The helicopter had the best of jamming and electronic countermeasures technology that the Israelis had but it was still in serious danger.

There was a knock at the door of the safehouse in the Galilee. Everyone had retreated there as Mike Butrell's helicopter had disappeared over the horizon chased by surface to air missiles.

"Who are you?" Yossi asked the elderly looking Orthodox man through the intercom system in the large steel protective door.

"I am Rabbi Klingfeldt, and I am here to see Rabbi Waxman," the old man with wild red hair and spinning eyes replied. "Please, get him for me!"

"Rabbi Waxman," Yossi yelled, "there is a Rabbi Klingfeldt here to see you."

"Rabbi Klingfeldt!" Rabbi Waxman whispered to Judah, "he is de man who has put a curse on me."

"For what, Rabbi?" Judah answered as he grabbed the Rabbis arm.

"Yitzchak told me dat it vas for my relationship vit Rabbi Bernstein. He tinks dat I have been bevitched by Yeshua."

"Well, as the Scripture says, Rabbi, He who is in you is greater than he that is in the world. It is time for you to confront this evil head on. I will be right at your side, so don't fret. Be strong and don't deny Yeshua and He will not deny you."

"Vat do you vant, Rabbi Klingfeldt?" Rabbi Waxman asked the man who stared at him with icy, piercing eyes.

"Open the door so I can see your face!" Rabbi Klingfeldt shouted. "What are you afraid of?"

Rabbi Waxman opened the door and stood right in the face of Rabbi Klingfeldt.

"You have been cursed by the sorcerer yeshu, Rabbi," Rabbi Klingfeldt shouted as he gave Rabbi Waxman the evil eye. "I have been given the powers of Kabbalah to turn you to bone as Simon bar Yochai did to evil people as recorded in the Zohar *(H.Book of Brilliance-Book of Jewish Mysticism)*. You are encased in the husk of evil and must be liberated from it!"

"Vell, I guess my Yeshua is more poverful dan your demons!" Rabbi Waxman countered directly staring the Rabbi down. "Hashem himself said in D'varim *(H.Deuteronomy)* 18 dat dis behavior vas detestable to Him. It is you dat is caught up in de sorcery of Hasatan. I know de Trut , de Vay and de Light and it is Yeshua Hamashiach. And no von comes to de Fadder but trough Him! Now get behind me, Hasatan! Be gone vit you!"

Rabbi Klingfeldt cowered in the doorway and reeled as if he had been hit by a brick. He tried to speak but no words came out of his mouth. His legs lifted up until they were perpendicular to his torso and he flew away down the pathway from the house in fear and trembling.

Dr. Lazant and his colleagues settled in to their place of residence overlooking the city of Jerusalem. They all looked down on the Temple Mount area now covered with rubble. There were still special Israeli units all around searching for buried survivors. Hundreds of persons had lost their lives in the earthquake.

"You see, I told all of you that the Temple would be rebuilt," Dr. Lazant said as he laughed and gulped his third glass of Israeli wine. "Now all obstacles to that have been removed and the building can commence unhindered!"

"But what of the Islamic fundamentalists like Hadad?" Rabbi Ginsberg replied as she too swallowed her third glass of wine. "They seem determined to prevent that from happening."

"After the abduction and disappearance of the Christian fanatics in a short while, all of that will be forgotten," Father Saltucci said with a smile. "When the sky is filled with UFOs and the new world leader takes center stage, all signs of dissension will also disappear. He will unite us all for one common goal!"

"I feel that He will be a great avatar, a great spiritual being," the Shiva Priestess said as she began to dance and twirl effortlessly on the veranda. Her eyes rolled back into her head and she began singing a haunting eerie melody.

Everyone got caught up in it and began to enter an altered state of consciousness. They all began to sway and move like one giant multiheaded beast.

"Wow, this is better than peyote!" Lloyd Foot the Ogala Medicine man moaned out loud. "This is powerful medicine."

Rabbi Waxman spent the next couple of days preparing his testimony to those left behind. He had obtained another Hebrew Brit Chadasha which he used to mark down the appropriate passages like 1Corinthians 15:52, 'in a moment, in the twinkling of an eye, at the last Shofar; for the Shofar will sound and the dead will be raised imperishable and we shall all be changed.' In 1Thessalonians 4:16-17 it stated that 'for the Lord Himself will descend from heaven with a shout, with the voice of the archangel and with the Shofar of God and the dead in Mashiach will rise first. Then we who are alive and remain shall be caught up together with them in the clouds to meet the Lord in the air and thus we shall always be with the Lord'. Orthodox Jews, Rabbi Waxman knew, believed that the resurrection of the dead would take place on some future Rosh Hashanah as told in the Talmud in Tractate Rosh Hashanah. That is why many ancient headstones in the local cemetery in Jerusalem had Shofars on them. But what Rabbi Waxman now knew from the Ruach Hakodesh was that it was also the time of the Harpazo, the Natzal, the Catching Away of the living Believers as well. He also came to see deep within himself and by no action of his own that this was going to be the time of the great delusion of Satan mentioned by Sha'ul in 2Thessalonians that was to happen in the end of days. Those left behind were to be deceived into believing that those that who were gone had been abducted by aliens in UFOs. Rabbi Waxman knew that there are no real extraterrestrials or UFOs. To believe that other creatures had evolved into beings more advanced than man would deny the Bible. Humans are created in the image of God. We are special and unique in this Universe and there cannot be other more advanced or evolved life out there or the Bible is false. The so called aliens are in reality demons from another spiritual dimension. AZAZEL is as real as any man or woman but he is a fallen angel that is interdimensional rather than extraterrestrial.

Rabbi Waxman's letter explained that he had gone to be with Yeshua while the terrible time of Jacob's trouble would rage here on Earth for seven years. He told them to read Yesha'yahu 53 and Tehillim *(H.Psalms)* 22 and Danyi'el 9, but he also knew that Hashem would have to seal them first and ransom them from the world. His material would be of use to them after they were sealed on the forehead by the Lord, not before. He then sent the letter to Butrell's email address in Langely Virginia which he got from the code that Butrell had used to forward the mailing list to the CIA.

The setting sun on the beautiful landscape of the Upper Galilee brought the resounding blasts of incoming katyusha rockets which exploded all round the house.

"The enemy is hell bent on destroying us before Rosh Hashanah," Judah yelled. "We need to get out of here."

"We have an old bus," Yossi replied. "Let us head for Yerushalyim tonight. It is our only alternative. I know a safehouse of Rabbi Bernstein's people".

They all piled into the old Volvo Bus as quickly as possible. The rockets were exploding all around the house and it was only a matter of time before they hit it directly. Jennifer and Rebecca were fighting their anguished mother all of the way. They did not want to go to even one more place. They were completely distraught.

"Come on, girls, we have to go," Ann yelled as she dragged them along. "Do you want to die here?"

"Why not?" Rebecca replied as she pulled back on her mother's arms. "I am sick of running. Let's end it right here already!"

Judah saw what was going on and ran over and picked up a girl in each arm and carried them forcefully into the bus and threw them down in a seat.

"Don't give me any grief or I'll make you wish that you were dead!" Judah told them.

"Hurry, everyone," Captain Labensky shouted as his shiny bald head turned beet red. "I'll drive this bus. Let's go!"

The bus started up and hurled down the mountain trails in the dead of night with breakneck speed. There was a sudden explosion and fireball and everyone gazed at the house that they had been in, burning from the katyusha rocket that had just annihilated it.

"Baruch Hashem," Yossi said. "We got out just in time!"

283

They continued down the road towards Jerusalem. Suddenly a rocket crashed through the roof of the bus but did not explode. It landed right between Rebecca and Jennifer.

"Oh my God, Oh my God!" Jennifer screamed and fainted as she felt the rocket crash through the roof and land right at her feet.

"What is this? What is this?" Rebecca said in absolute fear shaking all over. "Is this one of those rockets? Oh my God, it is!"

Rebecca fainted along with her sister. Ann and Bertha began to scream hysterically. Shmuel turned around to see what had happened.

"Don't worry about it, Captain," Judah told him, trying to make light of the grave situation. "A rocket hit us but did not explode."

"But it might explode from all the jarring of this bumpy mountain road, Yehuda!"

"I'll take care of it," Judah said as he turned and told everyone to stop screaming. "I'll try and defuse this rocket, but you all must be absolutely quiet. Is that clear?"

"Maybe we should leave the bus?" Dawn asked.

"It is the middle of the night in the mountains?" Judah answered. "Also, someone is obviously after us. I don't think so!"

"Well, it is better than dying in this rickety old bus," Bertha said shaking. "Are you sure that you can disarm this thing, tatalleh?"

"Why don't all of you stop kvetching *(Y.complaining)* and pray for me, for us!"

Judah had spent a tour of duty in the IDF doing bomb disposal but that was many years ago. He had no choice however. He spent the next hour carefully removing the warhead as the other members of the group whimpered and moaned to themselves. All that he had to work with was an old toolbox full of rusty tools that he found in the bus. Judah prayed before he made each move. Slowly and methodically he disarmed the warhead. He was covered in perspiration and his hands were shaking when he finally finished his task.

"It is done, thank God!" Judah finally shouted, waking up the members of the group. He then fell over in complete exhaustion and was out like a light.

Early the next morning they arrived at a house of Rabbi Bernstein's fellow Messianic Believers in the Old City. Several other Rabbis were there who had accepted the Lord but had remained silent. When they saw the great Rabbi Waxman they fell to their knees in front of him and praised Hashem. Rabbi Waxman told them to get up. God is no respecter of persons he told them. He was just a man like them.

"You all say dat you vere looking for a sign from Hashem before you told your people of your belief in Yeshua Hamashiach," Rabbi Waxman berated them lovingly as he sipped the glass of hot tea that they had given to him. "Vell, now vat is your excuse? If my salvation is not enough of a sign for you, den noting vill be. You all need to vrite a letter to your mishpoche *(H.family)* explaining your disappearance in de upcoming Natzal. Ven ve all go to de Kotel *(H.Wailing Wall)* for Rosh Hashanah and de bloving of de last Shofar, ve vill disappear right in front of dem. Dere vill be dose cockamamie flying things all over de sky. Dey need to know dat you vere taken by Yeshua not by de demons in dose flying tings."

"But Rebbe," an old, wizened Rabbi like him asked seriously, "Why would we be taken with the Christians, they will ask? All over the world the Christians will be gone. If we say that we went with them without any more explanation, our followers will be confused!"

"Confused, conshused!" Rabbi Waxman answered enraged. "How much vorse could it be for dem? Better confused dan damned! I am leaving all of my followers a copy of de Brit Chadasha in Hebrew as vell as a letter from me explaining my catching avay to be wit Yeshua Hamashiach my bridegroom. I am also giving dem de passages in de Tanakh dat point to Him as de Mashiach."

"But Rebbe, Hashem will have to seal them first as it says in the Book of the Revelation."

"But, But. Stop kvetching and get to vork. Prepare something for your mishpoche."

"We all need to be extra careful for the next couple of days," Judah interjected. "The enemy wants to kill us Messianic Believers and remove us from Jerusalem so that we cannot disappear at the Harpazo or Natzal. If we are not at the Kotel when it happens and nobody actually sees it happen, then it will all be nothing but hearsay. It won't fly. No pun intended, sorry!"

# XXI

They all sat around a large round wooden table for their Erev *(H. night before)* Rosh Hashanah dinner. The friends of Rabbi Bernstein and Yossi had prepared a huge festive meal. After all, this might be their last meal on Earth for quite a while. There were the traditional round Challahs for a well rounded and wholesome year. They were higher in the center to show that one's prayers ascend to heaven. There were the usual apples and honey to show the sweetness of the New Year. This New Year would be especially sweet for all those Jews that were to be caught away to be with the Lord. It would be especially bitter for those left behind to deal with the Antichrist, Armilus.

There were platters of gefilte fish with red horseradish, and pickled herring. As soon as these were devoured, out came steaming hot bowls of matzoball soup.

Rabbi Waxman had begun this festive food celebration with a prayer.

"Baruch Atah Adonai Eloheynu Melech Ha'olam, hamotzi lechem min ha'aretz," he had sung. "Blessed art Dou, our Lord, our G-d, King of de Universe, who gives us bread from de eart."

"Baruch Atah Adonai Eloheynu Melech Ha'olam, boray pri hagafen."

"Blessed art Dou, our Lord, our G-d, King of de Universe who gives us de fruit of de vine, Amen! Ve also tank Avinu Malkeinu *(H.Our Father, Our King)*, for sending His Ben Haelohim *(H.Son of G-d)* to die on de cross for our sins as our kapparah *(H.Atonement)*. Ve also tank Him for giving us a new heart and a new spirit. And on dis night especially, ve tank Him for coming again soon for us, His children, His bride, in de resurrection of not only de dead but of de living as vell. Baruch Hashem(H.Bless His Name)! La' Chayim! To life everlasting!"

"Rabbi, our mishpoche say La'shana Tova Tiketavu on Rosh Hashanah," Yossi said as he slurped his matzoball soup, "But that means may you be inscribed in the Book of Life for the coming year. We know that we all are inscribed in the Lamb's Book of Life for all time because we belong to the Lamb, Yeshua. So what do we say to them?"

"Say La' shana Tova, Tiketavu!" he answered laughing with a bib under his chin and gefilte fish in his beard. "You vant dem to be inscribed in dat Book, don't you? Vell, say it den!"

Next the ladies brought out platters of tzimmes, a sweet roast stew with beef, sweet potatoes, squash, prunes and apricots and a Moroccan spicy chicken dish with sesame seeds, tomatoes, cinnamon and garlic.

Bertha carried the tzimmes over to her son and held it under his nose. "I made this just for you, tatalleh," she kvelled *(Y.burst with pride)*. "Remember when I used to make this for you when you were a little boy and you loved it so?"

"Sure I do, Ma," Judah answered, "But I am not a little boy anymore."

"You will always be my little boy, tatalleh!"

Dawn and Ann and the girls came in and sat down and enjoyed the meal.

"Rebbe, why is Rosh Hashanah associated with the resurrection of the dead?" Shmuel asked as he gulped a big forkful of tzimmes.

"Because it is written in de Talmud in Tractate Rosh Hashanah dat dis vill be de time ven de dead vill arise. Moses Maimonides' tirteent article of de Jewish faith vas dat he believed vit perfect faith dat dere vould be a resurrection of de dead. Ve tend to believe dat dis is a Christian concept but it is Jewish. Daniy'el 12:2 states dat 'many of dose who sleep in de dust of de ground vill awake, dese to everlasting life, but de oters to disgrace and everlasting contempt'. Yesha'yahu *(H.Isaiah)* 26:19 states dat 'your dead vill live, deir corpses vill rise. You who lie in de dust awake and shout for joy, for your dew is as de dew of de dawn and de eart vill give birt to de departed spirits'. Ven Yeshua comes, de dead in Mashiach vill rise to be vit him. De oders vill rise on de day of de Great Vite Trone judgment at de end of time mentioned by Yochanan *(H.John)* in his Revelation."

"Rebbe, that is what Sha'ul *(H.Paul)* wrote to the Church at Ephesus," Judah interjected as he munched a big piece of Challah. "He wrote 'Awake, sleeper and arise from the dead and Mashiach will shine on you'. And if you continue with Yesha'yahu into verses 20 and 21 he says that 'come my people, enter into your rooms and close the doors behind you. Hide for a little while until indignation runs its course. For behold, the Lord is about to come out from His place to punish the inhabitants of the earth for their iniquity and the earth will reveal her bloodshed and will no longer cover her slain'. That is a perfect picture of the Harpazo(GR.), the Natzal(H.), the Rapture that is, God willing, going to take place tonight. We will be taken to the Father's house to be hidden with our bridegroom for the seven years of the Tribulation. The seven years when the Antichrist Armilus, the great King of the endtimes will rule and reign on Earth as prepared by AZAZEL and his demonic hordes."

The orange honeycake was finally brought out and everyone sighed that they were too full to eat it but it disappeared nevertheless in a matter of minutes. Then everyone prepared themselves to go out to the Kotel *(H.Western wailing Wall)* for the evening service. It was a cool blustery evening and the women put scarfs over their heads. The men wore their Tallit *(H.prayershawls)* and hats. When they walked over to the Kotel they were all surprised that there were thousands upon thousands of people gathering there.

"I have never seen so many people here in all of my years," Rabbi Waxman said with a big smile. "It must be because de Dome on de Rock and de El Aqsa Mosque have been destroyed by Hashem. Dis may be de last year dat de Temple vill be not

287

here. Next year it vill hopefully be rebuilt. Dis truly vill be a monumental service. De last one at de Kotel! Baruch Hashem!"

Rabbi Waxman was escorted by Judah, Shmuel, Yossi and the other men. Dawn, Bertha, Ann and her girls, as well as the other women went separately and stayed in the background. Women were not allowed into the area of the Kotel. While in the outer limits of the Temple area they too were still flush with the excitement of what was about to happen. Ann cried as she anxiously awaited the reunion with Peter.

"Why are you crying, Mom?" Jennifer asked as she shook her red hair in the wind

"Because tonight we will be reunited with your father in the Rapture," Ann smiled through her tears.

"Get real, Mom!" Rebecca answered shaking her head and grimacing. "You don't really believe that, do you? It would be great but I'll believe it when I see Daddy and not a minute before."

"Rabbi Waxman, Rabbi Waxman!" Yitzchak yelled as he caught sight of his esteemed Rebbe and ran up to him.

"Shalom, Yitzchak," Rabbi Waxman answered as he they embraced and the Rabbi patted him on the back affectionately.

"I really thought that we had lost you, Rebbe," Yitzchak said as he motioned to the thousands of Rabbi Waxman's followers that had found the Rebbe. "You are well and here to celebrate the New Year with all of us at the site of the soon to be rebuilt Temple. La'shana Tovah Tiketavu."

"La'shana Tovah Tiketavu to you also, Yitzchak!"

The Rabbi was then inundated by a huge throng of his followers. They were so excited to see him alive and well with all the rumors that they had heard, that they began to chant and sing praises to Hashem. They nearly crushed Judah, Yossi and Shmuel with their advances. Dawn and the other ladies watched this reunion from afar with a pair of binoculars that Dawn had surreptitiously taken out of her purse and used without drawing too much attention to herself from a far off vantage point.

"Rabbi Waxman's followers have found him," Dawn told the other women. "They are so excited to see him. They aren't stoning him. Praise God!"

"Come, Rebbe, we must go up to the Kotel, the Maariv *(H.Evening)* services are about to begin," Yitzchak said as he grabbed the Rebbe by the arm and dragged him away from Judah and the others towards the Wall.

"La'shana Tovah Tiketavu, Yitzchak!" Judah said smiling as he ran after the Rabbi and Yitzchak. "May you be inscribed in the Book of Life for a good year! See, I took good care of your Rebbe, Yitzchak. Now we are all here to welcome in the New Year with the blowing of the last Shofar!"

Yitzchak gave Judah a funny look but did not say a word. When they reached the Kotel, They lifted Rabbi Waxman up gently for all the huge throng to see. He waived his arms to them and they let out a tremendous roar.

"Okay, Okay , dat is enough already," Rabbi Waxman said motioning for them to put him down. "Dis night belongs to Hashem, not me."

Off in the teeming masses, Drs. Katz and Friedman spotted the upraised Rabbi Waxman. They just shook their heads and looked bewildered at each other.

"Can you believe that Rabbi had such a spontaneous remission?" Dr. Katz asked his colleague. "What a blessing for this New Year celebration."

"I don't want to talk about it, Shmuel," Dr. Friedman replied. "I told my wife about the entire affair and she told our meshugge daughter. She then started on me about that Yeshua and how He must have healed him. It has ruined my entire holiday. Those people just never stop proselytizing. It drives me crazy. They want so bad to save your soul. No thank you! I know that I need to ask Hashem for forgiveness about my feelings of anger and rage towards her. That is why I am here for the first time in many, many years."

"I see that the crazy army guy, Yehuda, is right here also," Dr. Katz said nervously. "He really gives me the creeps. Wherever he goes, trouble seems to follow. I hope that he didn't bring that black angel thing with him. I have had nightmares for days."

Off to the other side were Detective Holmes and his son in law Dr. Silverman. Dr. Silverman had brought him here to the Kotel to show him how Orthodox Jews celebrate the outset of Rosh Hashanah. Holmes had been reluctant to come especially since he had to leave his daughter off in the distance. He was amazed at the size of the crowd which he estimated to be around 100,000 people.

"Look, there is your friend," Dr. Silverman said to his father in law and pointed to Judah. He caught sight of him when Rabbi Waxman was lifted up above the huge crowd.

"Well, I'll be a son of a gun!" Holmes replied as he caught sight of Rabbi Waxman and Judah. He smiled as he saw that the man who was so upset about Judah stealing his Rabbi was now lifting him up into the air and rejoicing.

"That Judah is really something. I hope that trouble does not find him here as it always does. Especially when my daughter is off somewhere by herself!"

Dr. Lazant and Father Saltucci were also there in the midst of the huge teeming throng of people. Never before had either of them seen such an outpouring in the Old City. They knew that this might be the night when the abduction of the fanatical Christians would take place and inauguration of the New World Order would commence right here at the future sight of the rebuilt Temple.

"It is not too long now," Dr. Lazant smiled. "There are Judah and Rabbi Waxman. We must remove them as soon as possible or they will be abducted with the Christians and we know what that will initiate!"

"Our people have arranged to remove them as soon as they get the chance," Father Saltucci replied. "Look, they are moving in right now!"

Slowly yet deliberately, several men were approaching Judah and Rabbi Waxman. They did not want them to be abducted by AZAZEL in front of their followers. Not that it would cause a panic. It could be just explained that they did become Believers and thus had to be removed, but what was most troubling was the possibility that they might leave behind some telling information about what had just happened. There orders came down from none other than AZAZEL himself. "Get Judah and Rabbi Waxman out of there as quickly and quietly as possible," was his order. But it was next to impossible to get close to them. Rabbi Waxman's followers pressed around him tightly in all directions.

The service began and the Shofar was blown. Judah, Rabbi Waxman, Yossi, and Shmuel began to shake and their eyes looked upwards but nothing happened. Dawn, Bertha, Ann and the girls anticipating the Catching Away began to scream but nothing happened.

"I told you nothing would happen," Rebecca said as she ripped away her mothers arms from her shoulder. "Talk, talk, that is all that I hear. I'm sick of it. We are going to see our dead father, yeah right!"

Judah looked over at Rabbi Waxman who was surrounded by his followers and put his hands up and shook his head indicating that obviously nothing had happened. His gesture gave the impression that he was disappointed and frustrated. Rabbi Waxman gestured back that everything was all right by pointing his finger upwards and smiling. Yitzchak caught sight of their communication and looked back and forth at the two of them. "What is going on, Rebbe?" he asked. "You and that Yehuda seem to have your own lines of communication? Who is he to you?"

"Quiet, Yitzchak, listen to de service," Rabbi Waxman answered sternly. "He is just a good friend who has kept me alive to be at dis place at dis important time."

"What is so important about this Rosh Hashanah?"

"Shah (Y.Quiet)!" Rabbi Waxman said. "You vill find out soon enough. Look, dere is Rabbi Klingfeldt! Do you know dat he came by and gave me de evil eye?"

"Yes, of course I have heard rumors to that effect," Yitzchak replied with a smile. "So, what did you do, Rebbe?"

"I told him dat D'varim (H.Deuteronomy) 18 varned us not to do vitchcraft or cast spells. I told him dat Hashem vould not be happy vit him for doing it and he just left!"

The evening Maariv service continued without incident. The Shofar was blown on several more occasions but nothing happened. There was no Catching Away and no UFOs filled the sky. The men after Rabbi Waxman still pressed in towards him but it was a slow deliberate process. Dawn, Bertha and Ann all wept over the lack of fulfillment of their dreams of the Rapture.

Rabbi Waxman and Judah davened (H.prayed) with the others using the Machtzur (H.High Holy Day prayerbook). While all the others prayed to Hashem for forgiveness of their sins and that they might be written in the Book of Life for the coming year, Judah and the Rabbi knew that Yeshua had already died once and for all for all their sins, past, present and future. He was their sacrifice on the cross one time for all time and by accepting Him they were written in the Lamb's Book of Life for all time and could not be erased from it. They had a peace of mind and an understanding of the Lord that these Orthodox men sought so deeply. The Orthodox truly loved Hashem and tried to do everything that they could to be righteous in His eyes, but of course they failed as all men do. Nothing that any of us tries to do can earn us our salvation. It is all done by the grace and mercy of a loving, forgiving God lest any man boast. He does it all not us. God chooses us, we do not choose Him. It happened that way to Judah and Rabbi Bernstein and Rabbi Waxman.

As the evening Maariv service drew to a close, everyone prepared to go home.

"Come with us, Rabbi," Yitzchak said boisterously. "We have so much to talk about. All of your people are anxious to visit with you."

"I don't tink so, Yitzhack," Rabbi Waxman replied sleepily. "I just underwent a long hospital stay and my feet are tired. I am still veak. Go on vithout me and I vill see you all again at de Shachrit service in de morning."

"Are you going with Yehuda again? I am really confused about that whole relationship. Who is he anyway? Is he the one that wanted your member list? I think, Rebbe, that he is just using you for his own ends!"

"Yitzhack, here you are at Maariv services vere you are supposed to be asking Hashem for forgiveness for your sins as vell to ask any person dat you have wronged for forgiveness and vat do you do? You bad mouth Yehuda. Oy vey, Yitzhack, you vill need to come back tomorrow and start all over again. Do you vant to be written in de Book of life? Badmouthing Yehuda vill not help! Trust me!"

Judah made his way over to Rabbi Waxman and grabbed him by the arm. Yitzhack gave him a dirty look and moved on. Judah was determined to lead the Rabbi back to the safehouse in the Old City without incident. His best laid plans were quickly broken as two men approached them. They motioned that they had automatic weapons under their trenchcoats and that they should follow them.

"Judah, you old son of a gun," Detective Holmes yelled from nearby as he tried to move towards Judah. When he finally arrived Judah ran up to him and embraced him.

"These two men have rifles under their coats and are trying to abduct us," Judah whispered to Holmes. "Help me get rid of them!"

"Arab terrorists!" Holmes yelled. "These two men are suicide bombers, run for your lives!"

The crowd began to panic and scattered in all directions. Several soldiers jumped on the men and knocked them out. Judah and Rabbi Waxman ran for cover as the bedlam increased. Before they knew what happened, they were back at the safehouse where they rejoined Yossi, Shmuel, Dawn, Bertha, Ann, the girls and the others. They all embraced.

"I thought that something had happened to you," Dawn emotionally said to Judah. "I heard someone yell bomb and the whole place panicked."

"Two men tried to abduct the Rabbi and me," Judah replied shaking. "I told you that it would happen. The powers that be do not want us there at the Kotel when the Catching Away takes place. Holmes was there again and it was him that yelled bomb!"

"Well, Judah, the Shofar sounded and no Rapture?" Ann said disquietingly. "Maybe you are all wrong and it won't happen. Maybe it will happen next year or five years from now. Maybe I will not see my husband again. maybe..."

"Maybe, shmaybe! Ve are not talking maybe here! Yeshua himself said dat no one knows de day or de hour but de Fadder in Heaven," Rabbi Waxman said forcefully. "Rosh Hashanah is not over yet. Ve still have a couple of days. De Shofar is blown 100 times during Rosh Hashanah. It could be the ninety nint or one hundredt blast dat vill free us from dis world. Stop kvetching. You all sound like the murmurers in the desert who complained to Moshe for forty years."

There was a knock at the door.

"Who could that be?" Yossi asked. "Should I get it?"

"I would not," Judah answered. "It can only be one of our adversaries since all our allies are right here in this room."

The knocking turned to banging and everyone became frightened.

"It is Rabbi Klingfeldt," a voice shouted. "Open this door right now or I will break it down!"

"What do you want?" Judah yelled back as he stood in front of the door.

"I want Rabbi Waxman!"

"Why?"

"Because he is confusing the brethren!"

"What makes you say that?"

"Because they want to see him and he is hiding here with all you meshumedim! Now open this door!"

"Why should I open this door when you want to do God knows what to the poor Rabbi? Do you think that I am crazy? Now be gone before I put a bullet in your kishkas *(H.guts)*!"

Rabbi Klingfeldt knocked down the door with his mind. It just fell open right off of the hinges. Judah stood there in stunned disbelief. The Rabbi walked in with his red hair flying and his eyes spinning even though the night air was perfectly calm. He gave Judah the curse of the evil eye and then moved on to Rabbi Waxman. Judah could not move. Yossi and Shmuel ran up to the crazed Kabbalist but suddenly went flying backwards into the wall. Dawn picked up a kitchen knife and tried to stab it into the Rabbis back but she could not bring it down and it suddenly turned and stabbed her in the shoulder.

"Judah, do something," Dawn yelled as she fell over with the knife sticking out of her shoulder.

Judah began to pray and called upon the Ruach Hakodesh to cover him with the armor of God. It had worked to battle AZAZEL and he hoped that it would work with the likewise evil Rabbi Klingfeldt. After all, Sha'ul said to the people at

Ephesus that they should put on the full armor of God to help them stand firm against the schemes of the devil, to battle the spiritual forces of wickedness in heavenly places. This was not a battle with flesh and blood but was again spiritual warfare with the forces of the Adversary. Judah was now clothed in the full armor of God and first went over to assist his stricken wife. He pulled out the knife from her shoulder and placed the tip of his sword against the wound. The wound stopped bleeding. He then went after Rabbi Klingfeldt.

"Be gone from here, you demonic presence!" Judah yelled at him.

"My powers are greater than yours, Yehuda," The Rabbi replied as he stared at Judah with his evil eye. "Turn into bone!" he cursed.

Judah smiled and went right up to the Rabbi and removed his evil eyes with his Sword of the Spirit and handed them to him. The Rabbi became hysterical and ran from the house screaming obscenities in Yiddish and Hebrew.

"I guess that He that is in me is greater than he that is in the world, Rabbi Klingfeldt," Judah shouted as he opened the door for the charging Rabbi and guided him out of the house and pushed him into the street. Rabbi Klingfeldt ran down the dark street holding his eyeballs and screaming uncontrollably.

"Maybe now you will be able to really see the Truth, Rabbi!" Judah yelled after him and closed the door.

Rabbi Klingfeldt darted aimlessly down the street unable to see where he was going. He finally tripped and tumbled hard onto the cobblestones. He still held his eyes in his hands however, fearful that to lose then would forever trap him in this present darkness. Suddenly there was a bright light inside his head. Everything became illuminated and the deep despair that he had felt melted away. Standing in front of him in his mind's eye was Yeshua. The Rabbi recognized him by his nail pierced hands and he began to sob. The Lord poured out His spirit of grace and supplication on the sorcerer.

"Adonai *(H.Lord)*, I am not worthy to be in Your presence," Rabbi Klingfeldt sobbed as he got to his knees. "Why do You come to this poor, pathetic, unworthy sinner?"

"It is not those who are healthy who need a physician, but those who are sick; I did not come to call the righteous but sinners," Yeshua said. "Go, My son, and sin no more!"

The next morning Judah and Rabbi Waxman and the others had a breakfast of fruit and eggs. They all talked anxiously about the possibility of the Rapture happening sometime today at the blast of the Shofar.

"Do you think that it will happen during this morning's Shakarit service, Yehuda?" Yossi asked as he slurped on a sweet juicy Jaffa orange.

"I don't really know, Yossi," Judah answered. "Remember, nobody knows but the Father! I do know that we need to be extra careful of those people who do not want us at the Kotel when and if it happens. They want to prevent our testimony at all costs. There were those two men at the Kotel, and Rabbi Klingfeldt even had the chutzpa to come here. Evil has no bounds or no fear so we must be prayed up."

Dawn and Ann and the other ladies cleaned up the breakfast table and prepared to go with the men to the Kotel for the morning services. Amazingly, they spent as much time as they normally did fixing their faces even though on this day they would hopefully lose their perishable earthly bodies and put on imperishable bodies cloaked in immortality. Old habits die hard!

As they all walked out to the Kotel there was a spirit of anticipation so thick that you could cut it with a knife. They were all so joyous that they bounced as they walked. Quietly and unceasingly they prayed to the Lord for strength and protection and the fulfillment of their mission. As they neared the Kotel, the crowds became so thick that one could not see anything but a sea of men in prayershawls and black hats. Then off to one side they heard a man calling out.

"Repent, repent, the Lord Yeshua Hamashiach is coming for His flock! Repent!" the voice bellowed.

They could not see who was yelling this but there was pandemonium as the crowd suddenly turned towards him.

"Can you believe that someone is yelling that here at the Kotel on Rosh Hashanah?" Judah asked. "What a blessing. I wonder who it is? They will surely shut him up as quickly as possible or these Orthodox will stone him.

Judah and Rabbi Waxman and Yossi and Shmuel pushed though the crowds to see who it was that was yelling. The man was being jeered by all around him but he persisted nonetheless. The women stayed behind as required by Jewish Law, but they could still hear him and his detractors as clearly as a bell.

"Look, it is Rabbi Klingfeldt!" Rabbi Waxman shouted. "Oy, Baruch Hashem, Baruch Hashem! He is telling everyvone about Yeshua. I cannot believe vat I am seeing and hearing. It is a miracle!"

There was Rabbi Klingfeldt dragging a huge wooden cross. He caught sight of them and smiled and waved his hand. The crowd would have torn him to pieces but they hesitated because he was such a well known Kabbalistic Rabbi. His many followers just stood there in stunned silence. A couple of them finally ventured forth and bowed before the Rabbi and turned their life over to Yeshua.

"Rabbi Klingfeldt," Judah finally got close enough to ask, "what happened to you? You can see! But I cut your eyes out?"

"I can see not only because Yeshua healed my blindness by putting my eyes back in, but He enabled me to see that He was the Way, the Truth, and the Life and that no man comes to the Father but by Him. Baruch Hashem. I now walk in the light instead of the darkness and only by His amazing grace. It was nothing that I did. I was playing with the ways of Satan. You can attest to that, Yehuda! He obviously chose me, I did not choose him!"

"Bless you, Rabbi Klingfeldt," Rabbi Waxman said with tears in his eyes as he embraced the Rabbi. Rabbi Waxman's followers were all round and they watched in total bewilderment. Here was their beloved Rabbi embracing a meshumed, cockamamie Yeshua preaching apostate. Rabbi Klingfeldt's followers likewise were stunned to see their beloved Kabbalistic Rabbi dragging a cross and preaching that Yeshua was the Way, the Truth and the Life. Everyone was raised to a fevered pitch of anxiety, and when the Shofar finally was blown to begin the service, everyone left Rabbi Klingfeldt to the security police who removed him as he continued to preach to them as well. Dawn watched the entire event through her binoculars and she wept as she told the other women what she had seen. She then put her hand onto her shoulder wound and felt no pain even though there was a huge gash there. They all praised God and fell to their knees.

"This is a sign," Ann said. "I know that it is. The Lord is coming today. Praise God!"

"You said that yesterday, Mom," Rebecca said with a tone that broke the beauty of the moment. "I'll believe it when I see it!"

Dr. Friedman was there again with Dr. Katz. Neither had been particularly religious and had not come to the Kotel for Rosh Hashanah in many years, but they were both drawn there this year for unexplainable reasons. Maybe it was the miraculous recovery of Rabbi Waxman or maybe it was their confrontation with AZAZEL? Maybe it was as Dr. Friedman thought, that he just needed to ask forgiveness for his rage at his daughter for her belief in Yeshua? It was, however, something deep in their inner being that brought them to this place at this time and they were not conscious of what it really was. They were soon going to find out.

"Isn't that the Kabbalistic Rabbi that put a curse on Rabin?" Dr.Katz said as he had seen Rabbi Klingfeldt dragging the wooden cross and praising Yeshua.

"I think that you are right, Shmuel," Dr. Friedman had responded squinting his eyes. "He is now preaching that yeshu. Oh God they are everywhere! Even a Kabbalistic magician is caught up in this yeshu hysteria. What is the world coming to? I cannot believe what I am seeing. Up is down and in is out. The world is turning upside down. I've fallen into the rabbit hole. This is like Alice in Wonderland."

"Calm down, Friedman," Shmuel said as he grabbed a hold of his friend and colleague. "You have got to take it easy and not let this stuff get to you so easily."

Yitzchak glared at Rabbi Waxman all through the morning service. He could not believe what he had seen Rabbi Klingfeldt doing and then to top it off he had witnessed Rabbi Waxman embrace and praise him. Yitzchak's fears about Rabbi Waxman going over to the other side were finally realized. They obviously had gotten him ensnared in their sorcery.

As Rabbi Klingfeldt was being dragged out of the Kotel, he went right past Rabbi Ginsberg and the Shiva Priestess.

"Look, there is Rabbi Klingfeldt," Rabbi Ginsberg told her friend. "He is one of the most famous Kabbalistic Rabbis in Israel. I have read all of his books and he truly is a tzaddik, a higher spiritual being. But why is he dragging a cross?"

"Repent, repent," Rabbi Klingfeldt shouted at the two women. "Yeshua is coming for his people. Repent, the end is near! You, Rabbi, must repent for your homosexuality. Hashem loves you but not your sin. You must repent for your abominations!"

"Oh my God," Rabbi Ginsberg screamed. "He too is now one of them! I can't imagine a Kabbalistic Rabbi is now a Jew for Jesus!"

"Well that means that he will now be abducted along with the crazy Christians, doesn't it?" the Shiva Priestess asked as she looked on the Rabbi and grimaced.

"Yes, I would think so. He is no longer part of the solution but he is now part of the problem and needs to be removed! I cannot believe what I am seeing. I have studied Kabbalah for years. Lilith is one of my heroes, my role models!"

All throughout the morning service the Shofar sounded but nothing happened. The girls became very agitated and Ann became despondent.

"Relax, relax," Bertha told them. "It is not over until it's over as my son says. Rosh Hashanah is a two-day celebration. It could happen tomorrow! Look at what happened to that meshuginah Rabbi Klingfeldt. If the Lord could touch him, then He can do anything, right? I mean, that old man came to us and tried to use his evil eye to destroy Rabbi Waxman and now today he is dragging around a wooden cross and praising Yeshua. Wake up, kinder, and smell the gefilte fish! The Lord is coming for all of us at any minute!"

"Yeah right, Grandma, who made you the expert?" Jennifer replied as she fidgeted with her red hair.

The morning service ended but nothing had happened. They all headed back to their house for some lunch before the afternoon, Mincha service began. As Rabbi Waxman and Judah prepared to leave they were accosted by Yitzchak.

"So Rebbe, I was right all along," he yelled. "You have been won over by these people. I saw the way that you embraced Rabbi Klingfeldt. I never thought that I would see him of all people praising yeshu and then, to add insult to injury, you embraced him. First Rabbi Bernstein, then Rabbi Klingfeldt and now you, Rabbi Waxman. I cannot believe it. What is going on here? And during the Days of Awe nonetheless. Have you no shame? Oy vey ist mir! Get away from me."

"I'm sorry dat you feel dat vay, Yitzchak," Rabbi Waxman said with a smile of regret. "Dis Rosh Hashanah vill be one dat you vill never forget, my son. Trust me! Remember vat you have seen here. It is not by accident. Look here, I have oter Rabbinic friends who have also realized dat Yeshua is deir Lord and Savior. One day it vill, God villing, happen to you also, Yitzchak."

Mike Butrell had lost his left arm in the encounter with AZAZEL. When he had been flown back to Bethesda Naval Hospital, the Doctors had taken one look at the smoldering mess and removed it without hesitation. Butrell had informed them the next day that he had to be released as soon as possible.

"Are you nuts, Sir," the surgeon had remarked with a slight laugh. "You just lost your left arm to what I do not know and you will probably never tell me, right? But nonetheless you need to stay and recover here for a week or so. Sir, you are not a

296

kid anymore. How old are you, sixtysomething?"

"Look, Doc, I need to be released tomorrow," Deputy Director Butrell insisted. "It is a matter of National Security. In fact it is a matter of Global Security! Do you know who I am?"

"Is the Pope Catholic? Of course I do, Sir!" the surgeon quipped.

"Then listen to me. Do exactly as I say. Fix me up so that I can leave here for a couple of days. If I am still here then, I will return to the hospital. Okay?" Director Butrell replied dead serious.

"What do you mean if you are still here?"

"Just forget about it. Get me ready to leave tomorrow! And get me a box of Cracker Jacks!"

"What about your daughter who is flying in tomorrow from Iowa?" the surgeon asked concerned.

"Tell her that I went back to work and she can meet me there! Any more questions?"

"No, I don't think so."

"Then get cracking on what you have to do to get me released tomorrow. That is an order!"

Butrell was released the next day which was the first day of Rosh Hashanah. He suddenly realized that the Rapture had not taken place the night before or the following morning. Maybe Judah and the others were wrong about the date. Maybe it would happen next year or in five years. Scripture said that nobody knows the day or hour but the Father in heaven. Butrell had his driver take him directly to his CIA office anyway just in case it would happen later in the day. He was carrying the Hebrew copy of the Brit Chadasha that Judah had given him.

When he arrived at Langely, he was surrounded by his friends and colleagues who were concerned about his well being.

"I'm fine. I'm fine," he said with a smile as his left arm sleeve waived in the breeze. "I never used this arm anyway!"

He pushed through the crowd and went up to his office and immediately called for his two trusted aides.

"Jack! I want you to get this book duplicated ASAP," Butrell said to Jack Warren, his young, clean cut Mormon aide as he reached into his desk drawer for a box of Cracker Jacks.

"Boss, how are you doing?" Jack asked. "What happened to you over there in Israel? How did you lose your arm?"

"I'm fine, Jack. Don't ask. Listen, I need fifty thousand copies right away!"

"Fifty thousand copies, right away?"Jack gulped. "How..."

"Just do it, Jack, it is a matter of the utmost importance!"

"Hebrew Bibles?"

"Yeah, Hebrew Bibles! And by the way did I receive a roster of addresses on my email?"

297

"You sure did, Boss," Alex, his other Mormon aide replied. "In fact, it was 50,000 names. Nearly overloaded your system."

"Great. When those Bibles are finished, they need to be sent to those addresses. And did I receive a letter from a Rabbi Waxman also?"

"Yes, you sure did, Boss," Jack said, now totally curious about what was going on. "It was in Hebrew so I could not understand it."

"Listen carefully to what I am about to say, boys," Butrell said seriously as he stared right at them munching his Cracker Jacks. "What I am about to tell you is of the utmost security and confidentiality. I do not want it to leave this room until I am gone..."

"What you mean gone, Boss?" Alex asked.

"Shut up, son, just listen!"

"The time is short. I believe that sometime today or maybe even tomorrow all the true Believers will be Raptured to be with the Lord Jesus in the air..."

"But, Boss!"

"Be quiet and listen!"

"I frankly believe this will include me, but not you guys. Even your current leader, Gordon Hinkley, has said that the traditional Christ of Christians is not the same Christ of the Mormons. Anyway, it breaks my heart to say this but I believe that I am right. You will be in good company, however. The President calls himself a Christian but I don't think that he will be Raptured either, but only God knows. When this happens and millions of people disappear it will be explained as abduction by aliens in UFOs. The sky will be full of them."

But..."

"Quiet and listen. I need you two to accomplish a mission that is unparalleled in the history of man. It will be your responsibility to see that those fifty thousand Bibles are sent to the names on the list with the Hebrew cover letter. It cannot be done until I leave. If by some reason I am not taken until next year, then obviously do not send them out. Is that clear?"

"Yeah, Boss but why the Jews?" Jack asked curiously. "And why are we Mormons not to be taken? We are the Church of Jesus Christ of Latter day Saints after all, aren't we?"

"The Scripture says in the Book of Revelation that 144,000 Jews will be chosen by the Lord to go out and evangelize the world. That's why! And it really breaks my heart that you two and your dear families will probably not be taken. Only God knows, so I cannot say, but your adherence to the Book Of Mormon is error incarnate. If and when I disappear, remember that I was not abducted by the UFOs outside the window which is what the world will tell you, but that I was caught away to be with the Lord in the air. Read 1Corinthians 15:52 and 1Thessalonians 4:16-17. In fact, if it happens, throw out your Book Of Mormon and read the Bible through. But please see to it that the Jews get their Bibles. Promise me?"

"Sure, we will do what you ask, Boss," Jack and Alex answered simultaneously.

"But where did you come up with this crazy abduction idea? I know that you have had us monitor the alien presence though AZAZEL and you have had us work with Senator Jordan to support Judah and the Joshua Brigade, but now you have combined the two and it all seems crazy!"

"Remember what Senator Jordan used to say?" Butrell asked still munching on his favorite food.

"He said that the battle with UFOs is not for the planet of man but for the soul of man!"

"Vell de cat is out of de bag now," Rabbi Waxman laughed as he ate some gefilte fish and very hot horseradish. "Yitzchak knows vere I stand now."

"That is all right, Rabbi," Judah replied. "He will keep an eye on you and when the Natzal happens and poof, you are gone, he will wonder if it was Yeshua or AZAZEL. Everything is falling into place for the Lord to act."

"Well, what if He doesn't want to act?" Rebecca said sarcastically. "I'm sick and tired of you guys trying to play God. You don't know any more than we do. Stop acting as if you do."

"That is enough, Rebecca," her mother answered. "All of these people just believe that the time is here. They may be wrong as you said, but remember, they may be right. And if they are right, then you will see your father real soon. Won't that be worth all these prognostications?"

"Prog... nosta... what?" Jennifer said bewildered. "Talk English, Mom! Hello?"

"It is time to go back for the afternoon service," Yossi motioned.. "Leave the women here to clean up and they can meet us later."

The men prepared to head back to the Kotel. It was a another blustery cloudy day and they put on their coats and hats. Judah did not know why but he put his Uzi semiautomatic pistol into his trousers in the back under his belt. That was obviously not something that someone would take to the Kotel but he was concerned for Rabbi Waxman's safety. As they walked down the cobblestone road to the Kotel two men suddenly appeared from an alleyway and grabbed Rabbi Waxman. They looked Arab even though they dressed like Orthodox Jews. The giveaway was their red eyes. There were part of AZAZEL's demonic horde!

"Let him go, you workers of Hasatan!" Judah yelled

The two men pulled out semiautomatic weapons from under their coats and aimed them at Judah and the others.

"Just back off and no one will get hurt," one of them said in a thick Arabic accent.

Other people were coming down the road headed for the Kotel. The two men took Rabbi Waxman and headed into the alley. Judah ran after them. He found them in a secluded yard and one had a gun to Rabbi Waxman's head. Judah retrieved his Uzi from behind his belt and drew it up immediately. He fired at the man holding the gun on Rabbi Waxman and blew his entire head off with three dead center shots.

Rabbi Waxman fell to the ground shaking. The other man fired his weapon at Judah hitting him in the chest. Judah fell backwards violently but still managed to fire at the man on his way down. The man was hit in the neck and died instantly. Judah hit the ground and began to bleed profusely. Yossi, Shmuel and the other men came running and found Rabbi Waxman and Judah.

"He saved my life again," Rabbi Waxman cried out. "But he looks real bad to me dis time!"

"He is very severely hurt," Yossi answered. "We need to get him to a hospital right away."

"On Rosh Hashanah," Shmuel moaned. "Good Luck!"

"No, take me to the Kotel," Judah moaned obviously in great pain.

"But you will die if we do that," Yossi answered shaking.

"So?" Judah replied softly. "Take me to the Kotel!"

Yossi bandaged up his wound as best that he could to stop the bleeding. He realized that Judah had a collapsed lung and it appeared that his aorta had been severed. Yossi could not believe that he was not dead yet. Rabbi Waxman and Yossi and Shmuel carried Judah to the Kotel as the afternoon Minchah service was beginning. Dawn looked for them as she and the other women finally entered the general area of the Kotel but they were far off in the distance. She scanned the sea of men in prayer shawls and hats until she finally found Judah.

"Oh my God!" Dawn screamed, "Judah has been shot. Oh my God! Oh My God!"

"My Judah, my tatalleh, has been shot?" Bertha wailed. "Oh God no, not him, not now!"

Dawn dropped her binoculars and ran towards Judah with Bertha at her side through an unwilling male-only crowd who impeded them at every step.

"Oh Judah, don't die!" Dawn yelled hysterically with fear and trembling over the plight of her husband.

"Get out of my way, you black hats, my son has been shot!" Bertha herself yelled as she knocked down men right and left who attempted to impede her movement towards Judah.

Detective Holmes saw Judah being carried into the area and pressed through the crowd with his son in law to see what had happened.

"What happened to him?" Holmes asked as he arrived at the Kotel.

"He was shot in the chest by a terrorist attacking Rabbi Waxman," Yossi answered nervously.

"Again? Well, why didn't you take him to the hospital! He is going to die here and it looks like it might happen real soon!"

"He wanted to be brought here!"

"Well, I want a beautiful, rich, young wife but it is stupid to grant me my wishes so why did you honor his? You idiots!"

"What happened to him?" Dr. Katz asked as he and Dr. Friedman also saw the commotion and came over.

"He was shot in the chest and these idiots brought him he rather than to the hospital," Holmes said flippantly. "Can you believe that? Here we are at the Holiest place in Judaism at the Holiest time of the year and they acted like idiots!"

"This man is near death," Dr. Friedman said as he checked him over. "Oh my God, he just passed away. Bless his soul."

"Judah, Judah," Dawn yelled as she finally made it to him.

"I'm sorry, Miss, but he is dead," Dr. Katz said and pulled her away from him. "There is nothing that you can do now. At least he died in this Holy place on this Holy day. You can be thankful for that!"

"What kind of stupid statement is that, Doc," Bertha answered as Dawn threw off his embrace. They both began to scream and wail and beat their fists on Dr. Katz.

Yitzhack watched the entire affair from a distance but he did not dare enter the area. Rabbi Waxman was all right but Yehuda was dead. Well, that was one less meshumed *(H.traitor)* apostate that he had to reckon with. He continued to stare at the group. He did not remove his eyes from the spectacle. He just could not.

Suddenly, Rabbi Klingfeldt appeared on top of the Kotel. He had escaped from his Israeli captors, but they were hesitant to walk out on the Kotel after him. Rabbi Klingfeldt sang and danced, yelling "repent, repent, the Lord is coming soon. As it says in Yesha'yahu *(H.Isaiah)* 45:23 'every knee shall bow and every tongue will swear allegiance to the Lord.' It says in Yo'el *(H.Joel)* that all who call upon the name of the Lord will be saved! Repent! Repent! The Lord of Lords and King of Kings is coming!"

Everyone began to throw stones up at him. They jeered him and cursed him for desecrating the Kotel. Yitzhack and the thousands of followers of Rabbi Waxman were outraged at what this well know Kabbalistic Rabbi was doing. They wondered if all his mystical studies had driven him crazy as it did to many, or was he under the sorcerer yeshu's diabolical power?"

The Shofar blew one more time as it had for dozens of times since last night but this time a chill ran through the spines of all Believers. It quickened their inner spirit for an instant. Then Yeshua Himself descended from Heaven as Scripture had prophesied. Judah's imperishable spirit body began to rise slowly into the sky. His clothes and his wedding ring and watch remained, but his body rose. Dawn saw this and fell to her knees crying with joy. She looked up and the sky was suddenly full of UFOs.

"It is here, the Rapture is here," she screamed. "Praise God!"

Rabbi Klingfeldt, Yossi, Rabbi Waxman, Shmuel and the other Believers began to scream and praise God. Holmes became dizzy and sat down next too his son in law who was in shock. Drs. Katz and Friedman also looked bewildered at Judah's clothing and jewelry left behind. Dr. Friedman began to throw up from the shock of it all. Yitzchak raced over and looked at the clothing.

301

"He must have been taken by someone in those flying saucers," Yitzchak yelled as he looked up at the UFOs. "Oy vey ist mir! What is happening here?"

Then in the next instant, as the Bible predicted, those Believers who were alive and remained were caught up together with the risen dead believers in the clouds to meet the Lord in the air. Rabbi Waxman and Yossi and Shmuel and the other Believers as well as Dawn, Bertha, Ann and Jennifer were gone in an instant, leaving behind only their clothes and jewelry and Bibles. Rebecca began to scream as her mother and sister suddenly disappeared and she was left behind. Rabbi Klingfeldt was gone in an instant and all the thousands of people at the Kotel saw him disappear right in front of their eyes, leaving only his clothing on the top of the Kotel.

There was a glorious spiritual reunion in the clouds between Dawn and Judah, Ann, Jennifer and Peter, Bertha and Moshe, the men and women of the Joshua Brigade and their deceased mates and children, the men of Rabbi Bernstein's group and their wives and children, and the meeting of Rabbi Bernstein, General Desporte, Senator Jordan, Major Kole, Lieutenant Gregor and all the others who had given their lives to the Lord and now had their bodies resurrected. They then went off to the Father's house which has many mansions to sit out the seven years of the Tribulation that was to rage on earth.

"Now really, Boss," Jack asked with a smile. "Do you really believe that you are going to be Raptured into the sky to be with Jesus? I don't remember our Mormon religion teaching us anything about that?"

"Well, you know what? When I am out of here and you are left behind, then dump your Mormonism and search the only word of God, the Bible, for the Truth," Butrell replied. "Okay ? Have we got a deal?"

"Sure, Boss, sure, whatever you say," Jack laughed as left the room and went into the adjoining office to get something. "I agree too," Alex added.

Jack finished what he was doing in the other room when he heard a loud trumpet blast.

"Hey, did you hear that, Boss?"

"Boss, did you hear that?"

"Boss," Jack asked again and entered Director Butrell's office. He found Alex sitting there in front of the Deputy Director's desk but he was not there.

"What happened, Alex?"

"Iiii, Iii," Alex moaned as he shook uncontrollably. "He disappeared right in front of me just as he said. Look, his clothes and jewelry and weapon and beeper are all here but his body is gone. Oh my God. Oh my God!"

"We better make sure that those Bibles get out to the Jews as he requested," Jack yelled. "It was his last request of us before he died or whatever!"

"Look, Jack, the sky is covered with UFOs as he said would happen. I am really confused now."

AZAZEL's image was there for all to see as well as being on every TV and

302

computer screen.

"All the fanatic narrow minded, judgmental so-called Believers have been removed from the Earth. They have been abducted by us to prepare the way for the new millennium of peace, love and unity. The planet is now ready to enter a new stage of evolutionary development- a raising of your planetary consciousness. Our man will rule the Earth's New World Order from the soon to be rebuilt Temple in Jerusalem. Our time has begun!" AZAZEL bellowed.

Yitzchak ran over to where Rabbi Waxman was standing and found only his clothing, hat, Tallit and his Machtzur. Stuck inside of it was a piece of paper which Yitzchak removed. While he was terrified by the sound of AZAZEl's voice and the presence of all the saucers in the sky, he tried to concentrate on what the paper said.

"Yitzchak, I hope and pray that it is you that finds this note. As you can see I have disappeared into the clouds along with Yehuda and the other Believers. We were not abducted by that AZAZEL as it would like you to believe. We have been taken into the clouds to be with Yeshua as it says in Yesha'yahu 26:20-21. Rosh Hashanah is, according to the Talmud, the day of the resurrection of the dead. According to our own High Holy Day Prayerbook, the Machtzur, the Messianic Hope, Resurrection and Immortality of the Soul are all intertwined with the Shofar on Rosh Hashanah! I am sending all my followers a copy of the Brit Chadasha and a letter similar to this one. It will also show them why Yeshua is our Mashiach. The man who will go into the soon to be rebuilt Temple and who will call himself Hashem is Armilus and he is of Hasatan. Heed my warnings. Turn your lives over to Yeshua Hamashiach and you will be delivered. Baruch Hashem!"

"Look, the people were abducted by AZAZEL just as we expected," Dr.Lazant said jubilantly. "Even here among the Jews there were obviously some Believers. Good riddance!"

"AZAZEL is obviously correct! Our man will soon take his rightful place in the soon to rebuilt Temple and declare Himself to be God!" Rabbi Ginsberg shouted. "No more judgmental people like Rabbi Klingfeldt telling me that my lifestyle is of my own choosing. Our time has begun!"

"It certainly has," Vatican Theologian Father Saltucci responded with a song in his voice. "Look at the skies. Our friends are here at last to guide us into a new glorious millennium."


**The battle with UFOs *was* not for the planet of man but for the soul of man!**
**The Great Harpazo Deception had begun in earnest!**
**THE END?**
**THE END OF THE BEGINNING?**
**THE BEGINNING OF THE END?**

# Epilogue

*"And the man of lawlessness is revealed, the son of destruction, who opposes and exalts himself above every so called god or object of worship, so that he takes his seat in the temple of God, displaying himself as being God...that is, the one whose coming is in accord with the activity of Satan, with all power and signs and false wonders, and with all the deception of wickedness for those who perish, because they did not receive the love of the truth so as to be saved. And for this reason God will send upon them a deluding influence so that they might believe what is false, in order that they all may be judged who did not believe the truth, but took pleasure in wickedness."*

Paul's Epistle to the Thessalonians (2Thessalonians 2:3-4, 9-12)

*"And I looked, and behold, the Lamb was standing on Mount Zion, and with him one hundred and forty four thousand, (sealed from every tribe of the sons of Israel) having His name and the name of his Father written on their foreheads...*
*and they sang a new song before the throne... and no one could learn the song except the 144,000 who had been purchased from the earth.*
*These are the ones who have not been defiled with women for they have kept themselves chaste. These are the ones who follow the Lamb wherever He goes. These have been purchased from among men as first fruits to God and to the lamb. And no lie was found in their mouth; they are blameless."*

The Revelation to John (Revelation14:1-5, Revelation7:4-8)

*"About the time of the End, a body of men will be raised up who will turn their attention to the prophecies, and insist on their literal interpretation in the midst of much clamor and opposition."*

Sir Isaac Newton, Observations Upon the Prophecies of Daniel and the Apocalypse of St. John (1733; published six years after his death)

# Hebrew/Yiddish Glossary

Abracadabra(Aramaic)-Devil
Abba(H)-Father
Adamah(H)-Adam
Adonai(H)-Lord
Aliyah(H)-return to Israel
Apocalypse of Abraham-Jewish Pseudopigraphal Work
Armilus-Great evil King of last days(Antichrist)
Avinu Malkeinu(H)-Our Father our King
AZAZEL(H)-demon
Baruch Hashem(H)-Blessed be the Name(of the Lord).
Bar Kochba-Jewish leader of an unsuccessful revolt in 132 CE who was Proclaimed to be the Messiah by Rabbi Akiva.
Beit Lechem(H) Bethlehem
Ben Haelohim(H)-Son of God
Brit Chadasha(H)- New Covenant Scriptures
Brit Milah(H)-circumcision
B'shem Mashiach(H)-Blessed be the Name of Messiah
Bubbe(Y)-grandmother
Bubbe-mayse(Y)-lit.grandma's stories-an absurd explanation
Challah(H)-Sabbath bread
Chavah(H)-Eve
Chutzpa(Y)-unmitigated, brazen gall
Cockamamie(Y)-implausible, farfetched
Cohen Hagadol(H)-High Priest
D'varim(H)-Book of Deuteronomy
Daniye'l(H)-Book of Daniel
Davened(H)-prayed
Devar(H) word
Drerd(Y)-Hell
Eretz Yisrael(H)-the land of Israel
Erev(H)-night before
Ezer(H)-Book of Ezra
Farchadat(Y)-confused, dopey
Feh!(Y)-exclamation of disgust; yuck!

305

Gan-Eden(H)-Paradise-Heaven
Gay in drerd(Y)-go to hell
Gefilte fish-Jewish fish loaf-Jewish soul food!
Gey-Hinnom(H)-literally 'valley of Hinnom', located south of the Old City of Yerushalyim, where the city's rubbish was burned; hence metaphorically it is Hell
Gehanna(H) Hell
Gevalt(Y)-help!
Gonif(Y)-thief
Goy(H)-Gentile
Harpazo(G)-the Catching Away -Rapture
Hashem(H)-the Name(of the Lord).
IDF-Israel Defense Force-Army
Kabbalah(H)- Tradition-Jewish Mysticism
Kapparah(H)-atonement;forgiveness of sin
Kefa(H)-Peter
Kinder(Y)-children
Kineahora(Y)-saying to ward off the evil eye
Kotel(H)-remaining western restraining wall of Temple -wailing wall
Kvelled(Y)-bursting with pride
Kvetching(Y)-complaining
Lilith(H)-Lilith according to Kabbalists was the first wife of Adam-his equal-demon
Maariv(H)-Evening Service
Macher(Y)-bigshot
Machtzur(H)-High Holy Day Prayerbook
Mashiach(H)-Messiah;Annointed One
Mattityahu(H)-Book of Matthew
Maven(Y)-expert
Mazel tov(H)-congratulations
Megillah(H)-long rigmarole
Meshugge(H)-crazy
Meshumed(H)-traitor;a Jew who accepts Yeshua
Mica'yahu(H)-Book of Micah
Mincha(H)-Afternoon Service
Mishegoss(Y)-absurd, boring belief
Mishpoche(H)-family
Mohel(H)-circumcizer
Mitzvot(H)-Divine commandments
Momzer(H)- untrustworthy person
Moshe(H)-Moses
Musar Shalomeinu Alav(H)-the punishment, the chastisement, that brought peace was upon him
Natzal(H)-Catching Away

Nehemyah(H)-Book of Nememiah
Nu(Y)-so? Right?...
Oy(Y)-Exclamation.Oh!
Oy gevalt(Y)-oh no!
Oy vey ist mir!(Y)-oh woe is me!
Payess(H)-fretlocks
Pesikta Rabbati-Book of Homolies on the Torah readings
Pirkei d' Rabbi Eliezer(H)-Rabbinic work
Qoheleth(H)-Book of Ecclesiastes
Rashi-Rabbi Shlomo Yitzhaki who lived in France in the 11 century and who is considered to be foremost commentator on the Tanakh
Rebbe(Y) teacher
Rosh Hashanah(H)-Jewish New Year- time of blowing of Shofar
Ruach Hakodesh(H) Holy Spirit
Rugelach(?)-sweet filled cookie
Saadia Gaon-famous Rabbi of the Ninth Century CE
Schlemiel(Y)-simpleton
Schmaltzy(Y)-overly emotional
Sepher Tehillim(H)-Book of Psalms
Seventh Vision of Daniel-Testament of the Patriarchs-Jewish Pseudopigraphal work
Shachrit(H)-Morning Service
Sha(Y)-quiet!
Sha'ul(H)-Paul
Shekinah(H)-Divine Presence
Shalom(H)-goodbye, hello, peace
Shiksa(Y)-non Jewish woman
Shtik(Y)-nonsense
Shtiklech(Y)-little things; pieces
Shofar(H)-Ram's horn- trumpet
Shonda(Y)-shame
Shvartzeh(Y)-Black person
Tallit(H)-prayershawls
Talmud(H)-collection of Jewish law and tradition
Tanakh(H)-acronym for Hebrew Scriptures consisting of Torah, Prophets and Writings
Tatalleh(Y)-little boy
Toledoth Yeshu(H)- Medieval blasphemy of Yeshua as son of Miriam and Joseph Pandera
Tsedrayt(Y)-mixed up, confused wacky
Tsedrayter kop(Y)-deranged head
Tzaddik(H)-Holy man-spiritual-mystical?

Wayyiqra(H)-Book of Leviticus
Yehezke'l(H)-Book of Ezekiel
Yehuda(H)-Judah
Yerushalyim(H)-Jerusalem
Yesha'yahu(H)-Book of Isaiah
Yeshiva(h)-Rabbinical college
Yeshua Hamashiach(H)-Jesus the Messiah, Jesus the Christ
Yeshu(H)-derogatory expression for Jesus
Yeshua(H)-Jesus
Yirme'yahu(H)-Book of Jeremiah
Yisrael(H)-Israel
Yochanan(H)-John
Yoel(H)-Book of Joel
Yom Kippur(H)- Day of Atonement in Judaism;the Holiest day of the year
Zekaryah(H)-Book of Zechariah
Zohar(H)-Book of Jewish Mysticism attributed to Moses de Leon

Printed in the United States
24184LVS00003B/261